Imogen Parker is the author of *More Innocent Times*, *These Foolish Things*, *The Men in Her Life*, *What Became of Us* and *Perfect Day*. She lives on the south coast with her husband and son.

THESE FOOLISH THINGS

Imogen Parker

BLACK SWAN

For Nick and Connor

Acknowledgements

I am grateful to the Family Resource Centre at Great Ormond Street Hospital for Children NHS Trust, and to Barnardo's.

Chapter 1

JULY

It was the hottest summer for almost twenty years.

The tinted windows of her sixth-floor office made the sky a deep, cool blue. Alison gazed out, watching an invisible aeroplane's vapour trail cut a white gash through the pure, even colour. The air inside the building was thin and chill, almost alpine. It was difficult to believe that outside the pavements burned like coals. There was no let-up from the heat, even when dusk fell. The concrete city was a giant storage heater, absorbing the sun and radiating it out again. Alison tried to imagine the wall of hot, thick air that would hit her the moment the revolving door downstairs twirled her from fridge to oven, but she could not. It was safe up here, sealed in a cold, glass-sided box, protected from the noise of traffic, the smog of exhaust, the elemental ferocity of the sun. The office was like a calm haven, where she knew what she was doing, and the world outside suddenly seemed a terrifying realm of uncertainty. For a moment, she wished she could stay for ever just as she was, sitting at her desk, in the cool air, suspended in the sky, insulated from real life.

Alison looked back at her screen. All she needed to do was give the article a title and then her work would be over for four whole months. She was going to come in the next day, but only to tidy up and leave some instructions for her replacement.

' "All Things Nice", how does that sound, Ramona?' She spoke across her desk to the fashion editor. 'It's an article about spices . . . all right, I know it's weak, come on, my brain's scrambled, help me out.'

' "The Wages of Cinnamon"?' Ramona offered, demonstrating her origins as a sub: ' "Cumin Feel the Noise"?'

Alison laughed. 'That's worse than my worst effort, "Amazing Mace".'

' "Fennel Old World"?'

'Fennel's not a spice, is it?' Alison said with a worried look, 'because if it is, this comprehensive guide is going to be slightly less than comprehensive . . .'

'How about "Spices: Aniseed to Zafferano"?'

'Perfect.'

As Alison struck the key that sent the copy to the subs with a determined flourish, her phone buzzed.

'There's a man waiting down here for you,' the receptionist announced wearily.

'OK, I'll see him on my way out,' Alison said and replaced the receiver with a long sigh.

'What's up?' asked Ramona.

'Someone in reception for me. It's probably this photographer who's been plaguing me to look at his portfolio. The last time he rang he said his work makes food look like sex – as if *that* was going to turn me on . . .'

'Oh, not that food and sex thing again.' Ramona raised her eyes to the ceiling. 'Where's he been? Doesn't he know it's almost impossible to find a food page that *doesn't* look like sex these days?'

'I'm not sure I could face food photos that look like food at the moment,' Alison commented drily.

'Sneak out the back way,' Ramona suggested.

'No, I might as well get it over with. I don't want him turning up again tomorrow.' She looked at her watch. 'Anyway, I can only give him five minutes. I've got the excuse of my class.'

'You don't actually need a real excuse you know,' Ramona said, 'you could always invent one.'

'Yes, but I'm never very convincing when I lie. I'll see you tomorrow.'

'Good luck at the class,' said Ramona, adding, 'they'll tell you that all you need to do is breathe, but a word of advice – Pethidine. Mmm, the thought of it almost makes me want to have another baby!'

Alison blew Ramona a kiss across the desk and heaved her soft leather bag on to her shoulder.

In the lift, she prepared a short getaway speech for the photographer, and, as the doors opened, composed her face into a business-like frown, which dissolved instantly as she saw who her visitor actually was. 'Stephen!' she laughed with relief.

Her husband spun round and smiled at her. Even after five years of knowing him, his smile still had the capacity to surprise her. It transformed his serious, almost severe, expression into one that promised spontaneity, intimacy, and lifted her with an exhilarating buzz of pride and desire.

'Anything interesting?' she asked wryly, walking towards him and nodding at the staff noticeboard he was reading. Stephen was simply incapable of doing nothing. He preferred to study a memo from the personnel department about her company's new policy on luncheon vouchers than to sit in one of the low armchairs, as anyone else would, making small talk with the receptionist.

'A cost-cutting exercise neatly disguised as a bonus,' he pronounced as they wandered towards the revolving door.

'Unheard of in your workplace, of course,' Alison teased.

'Oh, for us, it's closure of another emergency bed dressed up as an efficiency measure, rather than a reduction in the general sandwich levels . . .'

11

There was always an edge to Stephen's humour. She admired his intelligence, and yet sometimes she wished he would just lighten up.

'What a nice surprise, you coming to meet me,' she said, trying to hold on to the feeling of delight she had experienced at seeing him a moment earlier.

He smiled at her and took her hand. It was a public gesture of love that only someone who was genuinely unselfconscious could make, and it set off another surge of affection in her body. In their single days, she thought, slightly wistfully, he had often come to meet her from work, or even in the lunch-hour, grabbing her hand, whisking her into a cab, racing to one or other of their flats to make love. Since they had been married, they didn't do that any more. It wasn't marriage, Alison reminded herself quickly, it was the fact that they now lived in the suburbs. You couldn't just pop back to Kew for a quick fuck, and since she had been pregnant, the mere thought of sex made her feel sick anyway.

'Tube or taxi?' she asked him brightly as they stepped into the busy street. A wet film of sweat broke instantly all over her skin, and her clothes felt suddenly grimy.

'Oh, I think the tube, don't you, at this time? A taxi would take hours,' Stephen replied.

'Yes, but at least we could talk. It's impossible to talk on the tube when it's crowded, and I just can't stand up all the way,' she said, regretting offering him the choice.

'Surely people give up their seat for you,' Stephen said, looking at her belly.

'Well, sometimes, but that's not the point,' she said, impatiently. She didn't want to have a logical discussion about it, she wanted him to stretch his arm in the air and hail down a black cab.

'OK, we'll get a cab, of course it's the sensible thing to do,' Stephen agreed, acknowledging her rising distress.

12

I don't give a damn about the sense of it, she suddenly wanted to scream at him, I'm eight months' pregnant. I want to sit down.

The taxi was an old one, with no air-conditioning. The interior smelt of years of cigarette smoke. Alison pulled down a window. The traffic was moving slowly, as if the hot air were glue. She could feel the underwire of her bra cutting into her ribcage and the backs of her legs sticking to the seat.

'So, what's going to happen at this class of yours?' Stephen asked her, wafting his copy of the *Evening Standard* backwards and forwards like a fan beside her face. She smiled, grateful for the movement of air. That evening they were attending the first of a series of ante-natal classes she had read about on a notice in the doctor's surgery.

'I don't really know,' she said, 'they'll probably explain about the stages of labour, or something.'

'But we know all about that,' he said, since they had both read just about every book on conception, pregnancy and birth available.

'Yes, but we're not going in order to learn, we're going in order to meet people,' she told him, adding, gently amused, 'it's what you do when you have a child.'

'Oh, is it?' Stephen sounded vaguely reassured by this information.

She smiled to herself. Stephen liked rules, even when it came to something as unpredictable as the process of making friends. They knew virtually no-one with children and they were each so busy at work, there hadn't been any opportunity to meet people who lived in the area. Sometimes she wondered why they had ever bothered to move there. It had been much more convenient living right near to her newspaper's offices and Stephen's hospital, but it had all been part of the plan:

Stage one: find a property in a leafy suburb with a garden for future children to play in. They had finally settled on an Edwardian house in one of the avenues that led away from the Royal Botanic Gardens at Kew. It needed redecorating throughout, and Alison had enjoyed that bit, even featuring her new kitchen on the Interiors pages of the lifestyle section she edited in the newspaper.

Stage two: conceive. That hadn't gone according to schedule at all, and even after she had finally become pregnant, she had somehow always associated the house with failure. Recently, there had been odd occasions when she had found herself filled with nostalgia for her little garden flat in Islington, now rented out to another single career woman in her early thirties, for the cheap pine furniture she had once saved so hard to buy, the shabby kitchen where she had hosted dozens of informal dinner parties, serving her friends pasta and salad from every shape and size of plate.

The taxi crawled along in the rush-hour traffic. Alison glanced at her watch. She had been hoping to have a cool bath and change out of the black linen suit into a clean, loose dress before the class, but at this rate they were going to be late. Stephen had been right. It would have been better to take the tube. A lot of men she knew would have pointed this out, but Stephen wasn't like that. He didn't harbour unspoken resentment. It was one of the things she most liked about him.

'I booked a table at the River Café for afterwards,' he remarked casually, as they approached the Hammersmith roundabout.

'Really?' she said, delighted by the reminder that, amid his generally methodical approach to life, Stephen was capable of conjuring up treats when she least expected them.

'Yes, I thought it would be pleasant to have dinner together by the river before I go . . .'

'Oh!' she said, her mood sinking.

There had been so much to do at work, she had

14

momentarily forgotten he was flying to a medical convention in America the next day. The dates coincided almost exactly with the first week of her maternity leave. When the invitation had arrived a couple of months before and they had discussed whether he should go, she had imagined it would be fun to have a little time on her own before the birth. It would give her the opportunity to catch up with some of the friends she never seemed to see these days, have long, unhurried lunches, or indulge herself in afternoons at the Sanctuary. She had told Stephen not to give it a second thought. Then, she could not have anticipated the hot weather, or how huge and uncomfortable she would become. Now that he was about to leave, his departure felt like a betrayal.

'What's up?' Stephen asked.

'I just wish you'd told me, that's all,' she said, trying to think of a reasonable explanation for her sudden feeling of utter despondence.

'Well, we did discuss it—'

'No, I meant the River Café, that's all,' she interrupted. 'I'll never have time to change and I can't go looking like this.'

The sleeves of her black linen jacket were crumpled and she felt damp all over.

'You look lovely. Hot, but lovely ...' he said, reaching over to smooth her hair back from her face. The gesture irritated her further. She pushed his hand away as if she could not bear the additional heat of his touch.

'Perhaps we should just skip the class. I don't know if I can face it,' she said, looking out of the window. There were four lines of traffic on Hammersmith Broadway, all stationary, all pouring their fumes into the steaming air.

'Of course not. You'll enjoy it,' Stephen coaxed, 'we both will, you're right, we need to meet other incipient parents.'

Suddenly the last thing in the world Alison wanted

15

to do was walk into a room full of people she did not know. 'No, I won't enjoy it,' she insisted, 'I feel too anxious.'

'What are you anxious about?' he asked patiently.

'Everything. I don't know . . .' She shrugged.

Stephen could be so infuriatingly pedantic. He behaved as if there was an answer to everything when for the last few months she had been feeling she did not even know what the question was.

'Darling, you're being a bit irrational . . .' Stephen attempted to soothe her.

'Yes, I know that, Stephen,' she retaliated icily, deliberately looking away from him. 'Emotions are irrational,' she repeated his word with heavy emphasis, adding under her breath, 'not that you'd understand . . .'

As soon as she said it, she wished she had not. She turned to look at his face and saw that the comment had wounded him.

'I'm sorry,' she retracted it immediately, 'that was so unfair . . . It's just so hot, I'm stifled . . .'

'It's OK,' he forgave her instantly, 'I knew I shouldn't have said I'd go to the convention, but I'm in the programme now and—'

'No really, it's fine. I'll be fine,' she found herself saying, trying to engage him in a smile, but he was looking straight ahead, perplexed, as if he could see something very interesting on the cab's meter.

Alison stared at the distant traffic lights changing from red, to red and orange, to green. Still the traffic refused to move. Blinking back tears of frustration, she wondered why it was that her relationship with Stephen, which had run perfectly smoothly for five years, had, just occasionally in the past few weeks, begun to snag, as if they were slightly out of sync with each other. It was a bit like the zip on her soft leather shoulder bag, she thought, as her right hand played absently with the charm that dangled from the zipper. The two halves always used to slide together so beautifully, but recently one side had started to catch on the lining, making Alison tug at it with a disproportionate impatience that threatened to destroy the fastening altogether.

Lia was lying naked on the bed. The electric fan hummed as it turned lazily on its pedestal, rustling the drawn curtains, then blowing gently on her skin, blowing on her skin, then rustling the curtains. It was only when she registered Neil's footsteps on the wooden staircase that she opened her eyes and realized that she had been lulled into an afternoon doze.

'Hello, gorgeous.' Neil was beside the bed, leaning over and brushing her mouth with a soft, dry kiss. He knelt on the bed and put his lips to her belly, 'Dad here,' he whispered against the stretched, smooth skin, 'have you been a good baby today?'

He planted a kiss on the dome of Lia's tummy, then turned his face towards hers, his cheek still resting there, smiling bashfully, half embarrassed by his own silliness.

Lia liked it when he talked to the baby. His northern accent was so gentle, and the uncharacteristic soppiness made him seem somehow vulnerable. She stroked damp hair back from his forehead. His face felt like fine sandpaper against her bump; she could smell the saltiness of his sweat. She loved the sheer physicality of the contact of his skin against hers, the weight of his head resting next to their baby. They lay staring at each other, joined in a silent cocoon of peaceful contentment.

'What's the time?' she asked him eventually.

'Sixish, I should think,' he replied, shifting up the bed so that he was lying next to her, clasping his hands behind his head, 'I'm sorry I'm a bit late, but the first team made heavy weather of it at the start.'

Neil was Head of the Sports Department at a local comprehensive. She remembered him telling her that

17

morning that there was a cricket match against the local independent school.

'Did you win?' she asked, turning on her side to see him looking at the ceiling, grinning all over his face. He loved cricket. Playing it was best, but watching the kids win was pretty good too.

'Thrashed them!' he said. 'Four wickets to spare in the end.' He looked at her, beaming.

She smiled at him, knowing little of the rules, but sensing that it had been a good victory.

'And their parents are paying three thousand pounds a term for the privilege . . .' Neil added with further satisfaction. He was a good teacher, a committed teacher, and the inequalities encouraged by private education pained him. He wanted the children he taught to do well, and it gave him additional pleasure when they triumphed over public schoolboys.

'That's the great thing about sport,' he told Lia, as he often did, 'it doesn't matter who you are, or where you come from . . .'

Lia nodded, not really caring one way or the other about sport, but thinking what a good father he was going to be. She remembered watching him kicking a football around with the village kids the day after they met. She had been sitting on the porch of the beach café drinking ice cold beer feeling dazed, wondering how, after the night they had just spent together, he could find the energy to throw himself into the football match with the unguarded enthusiasm of a boy. She noticed the way that he passed the ball around, ensuring that each of the children, however small, got a fair crack at it. He managed to do this without patronizing them, without them even noticing he was controlling the game. She watched, transfixed by the easy, balanced movement of his body as he ran around barefoot in the sand, tackling the village's best player, finally unable to resist having a shot at goal himself. The ball soared between the two beach umbrellas that stood as goalposts, and Neil leapt in the air, fists punching high in triumph, then turned to look at Lia, smiling his endearingly half-embarrassed, self-mocking smile. And as he began to walk up the beach towards her, brushing the sand from his knees with the flat of his hands, she found herself in the grip of one of those defining moments in life where she suddenly knew, with a kind of fated certainty, that she wanted to have his children. The peculiarity of the thought had almost frightened her, because she had never been aware of any maternal instinct before, but as he dipped his head under the yellow Schweppes umbrella to kiss her, she thought, yes, yes, I could handle that.

Lia shifted on to her side and snuggled her head next to his. He turned his face and kissed her slowly. Her mouth and then her whole body opened to his touch and she felt the familiar wave of arousal, like warm syrup suffusing every cell of her body. Their love-making had not diminished until recently when the doctor had advised against penetrative sex, but they had discovered almost as profound satisfaction in the exquisite tenderness of restraint. She held his face in her hands, looking into his eyes, eyes that were turquoise, so pale she sometimes felt she could see beyond, into his soul. Then suddenly a stray thought brought her back to the realm of the mundane, as she remembered why she had wanted Neil to come home early.

'The ante-natal class . . . we're going to be late for the class,' she said.

'Oh, do we have to go?' Neil sighed, drawing her closer. 'It's really hot out there.'

'Have a shower, come on,' Lia scolded him, laughing, pushing against his body, trying to roll him off the bed.

'You first,' he whined.

'No, I've had mine. I was just lying here wondering what to wear when I dozed off.'

'Wear that dress,' he said, finally heaving himself to his feet, realizing that Lia was determined. 'That green dress. You look really beautiful in that.'

She blushed at the unexpected compliment. 'But is it practical? What if they make us do exercises or something?'

'Exercises? You told me we were just going to meet people,' he said, looking up warily as he began to strip for his shower.

'Oh, all right, I'll wear the dress,' she said quickly, not wanting to put him off the idea of the class altogether.

The tarmac path was melting in the sun. The stickiness of it pulled Alison's shoes away from her feet with each step. Even the porch, with its dark ivy and cool floor of orange and black tiles, offered no shade. The sun seeped relentlessly into every corner.

A petite woman opened the door and ushered them, with bossy jolliness, into the large living room, then strutted off to the kitchen to fetch refreshments.

Late 1980s provincial hotel, Alison thought, making a quick critical assessment of the chintz-covered furnishings and swagged and tailed curtains. It was the kind of décor she absolutely loathed, and its fussiness seemed to make the heat almost worse indoors than out. Stephen immediately detached himself from her side, as if drawn by a magnet to the faux-Victorian bookcase, and stood inclining his head to read the titles, pulling out volumes at random. The two other women who were in the room were asking each other tentative questions about when their babies were due; the men exchanged different words for the heat – barbecue, furnace, inferno.

Alison stood stranded in the middle of the pink carpet, wishing she was the type of person other people found approachable. She was aware that her

business-like appearance and make-up were somehow putting the others off including her, but she
didn't know how to ease herself in to the conversation. It was so hot. She wished she could just flee,
but it was too late now that they were there. Anger
with Stephen began to well up inside her. How could
he abandon her as soon as they arrived?

The hostess returned with a large frosted jug from
which she poured water into highball glasses, plop-
ping an ice-cube into each. She handed one to Alison.

'Thank you,' Alison said with relief, scooping out
the ice-cube with her fingers and running it along the
back of her neck.

'What a good idea,' said one of the other women,
following suit and smiling sympathetically at her.

Alison smiled back, feeling slightly better.

'Well, that's broken the ice,' said their hostess, and
they all laughed again, politely. 'Now, women on the
floor,' she instructed, explaining that it was best for
their babies' position if they did not slouch.

To Alison's amazement everyone, including herself, obeyed, lowering themselves onto the dry wool
pile, pretending that they were comfortable. The men
slipped into chairs behind their partners.

'We've one or two missing, but let's begin anyway,'
said the hostess. 'I'm Judith. I've been through what
you're going through twice! My children are now five
and three. I've been leading ante-natal classes for the
last two years. Now, which one of you's going to go
first – just tell us your name, and anything you think's
important about you?'

Her eyes flicked round the faces and came to rest on
Alison.

'Alison,' she said. 'I'm editor of the Lifestyle section
of a Sunday newspaper . . . er, what else?' She looked
at Judith, suddenly at a loss.

'When's the baby due?' Judith asked.

'Oh right . . . in five weeks' time.' Alison realized
instantly she had given the wrong reply. As a mother,

you defined yourself in terms of your baby, not your job.

'And your husband is . . .' Judith led her on.

'Stephen,' Alison replied, stretching her slim manicured fingers back over her shoulder to catch his hand, but grasping air. She twisted round and saw that Stephen was staring into space paying no attention to the hand she had offered him, or to anything else in the room.

'Stephen's a professor,' she attempted to explain, flicking her stranded fingers through the ends of her bob.

The ghost of a murmur of laughter wafted round the room. She had meant the words to be light and faintly humorous, but it had somehow sounded like showing off.

'So, it's Stephen, is it?' Judith asked, pointedly directing her voice at him.

'Yes, it is.' Stephen suddenly turned on a smile of such unexpected brilliance, Alison forgave him for his earlier distractedness.

'So who's next?'

Tap tap tap.

Everyone turned to look at the window where a very pretty, cheeky face was waving at them.

Judith got up and went to answer the door.

'Shit, I'm so sorry I'm late!' the new arrival seemed to tumble into the room. If she hadn't been pregnant she would have looked like a child herself. She slipped a small black patent rucksack off her shoulders and sank gratefully into the last available armchair.

'Mums on floor,' Judith waggled a finger at her, 'for baby's position.'

'Sod that,' said the girl, 'I've given up alcohol and Brie, but I'm buggered if this little sod is going to get me sitting on the floor.'

'Could make labour more painful,' Judith warned.

22

'Not with all the drugs I plan to take.' Laughing, the girl looked round the room.

Alison smiled at her, instantly warming to her irreverence.

'And you are?' Judith asked.

'Ginger, short for Virginia, ironically,' said the girl, pushing a hand through her short peroxide crop.

'Baby due?'

'Yes . . . oh, in August.'

'And your partner's coming separately?'

'Don't they always?' Ginger said, her bright blue eyes flicking from lap to lap registering with dismay that the others were wearing wedding rings. 'Oh, you meant . . . No, I'm doing this on my own, actually. My twin says she'll breathe with me during labour. Perhaps I ought to have brought her along?' she added, belatedly making a concession to conformity.

It was clear that Judith had no training in dealing with single mothers with attitude. If a stare could have moved the newcomer's bottom from her seat, she would have hit the floor at high speed, but Ginger stared back defiantly, and stayed put.

'Yes, well,' Judith said, 'we were just introducing ourselves.'

She looked at the remaining two couples who gave their names meekly and said that their babies were due in September and October. Judith nodded, grateful for their no frills approach, then she started handing out pencils and scraps of paper.

'Now, I've got a little exercise, just to warm things up, not that we really need it any warmer!' She paused to underline the weak humour. 'Divide into mums and dads and then write down what you like about being pregnant, and what you don't like about it. And for the dads,' she smiled at the men, 'write down what you like about your wife being pregnant, and what you don't like. I'll just go and get another jug of water.'

As soon as she left the room, Ginger said, in her loud voice, 'Well, one of the things I absolutely hate about this business is the way people treat you as if you're a child. I mean games, for God's sake, and those ghastly dungarees that look just like a huge version of what toddlers wear . . . er—' She stopped as she noticed for the first time that the other two women were wearing maternity dungarees. 'Well, you obviously don't need to pee as much as I do,' she added quickly.

'All the clothes are horrible, aren't they?' Alison contributed, eager to rescue someone she had immediately sensed was a kindred spirit.

The two women in dungarees eyed her black suit disbelievingly.

This is the one smart thing I could find after trailing up and down Bond Street for a day, Alison wanted to explain, and it's costing me a fortune in dry-cleaning bills. But she said nothing.

'Well, shall we start writing things down?' one of them suggested.

'Ugh,' Ginger flopped back into her armchair. 'Do we really have to? I mean, what's to like? I pee when I laugh, for Christ's sake!'

'Quite,' Alison agreed.

But the woman persisted, pencil in hand. 'I'll write all our answers down,' she said, like a games captain at school, then, as if she were choosing her team, she pointed at her comrade in dungarees: 'You first.'

'I *hate* my ankles swelling, but I *love* wandering round Mothercare, looking at all the little vests and things.'

'They're so tiny, aren't they?'

Ginger and Alison exchanged glances. Far from easing things, Alison mused, the exercise had instantly divided the women into two pairs, them and us.

The games captain solemnly noted 'vests', then, with barely concealed hostility, she stared at Ginger.

24

In the hall, the doorbell rang again, and they could hear Judith tapping down the corridor to answer it.

'Oh, all right then, if I must,' Ginger said loudly. 'Well, I *hate* having – what's the polite word? – haemorrhoids . . . and actually,' she went on, 'the only thing I *like* is the fact that I'm going to have a baby. Well, sometimes I like it, the rest of the time it scares the shit out of me, or it would do if it weren't for the haemorr—!'

Alison felt the nervous giggle she was trying to suppress turn to acid bile in her throat. The heat and the almost palpable confrontation in the air were making her feel nauseous.

A stunningly attractive woman walked into the room. She was wearing a green sundress which seemed to float on the transient breeze created by the opening and shutting of doors. Her face was fresh and lightly tanned, her long wavy hair held back by a pair of Lolita sunglasses with white plastic frames. She was like a Pre-Raphaelite vision of Summer, with her meadowy dress and the mist of light fragrance that seemed to waft in with her.

'Hello,' she said, 'I'm Lia.'

'You?' The games captain was pointing at Alison with her pencil.

Alison tried to remember what she was being asked. Something about what she liked and what she didn't like. She was going to have a baby. Suddenly she felt very, very sick. What she liked. Baby. Baby. The words whirred round in her head. Baby. She must say what she liked about it. The room swam out of her reach and back. Baby.

She could hear a man's voice, a soft North Country accent, talking pleasantly to Judith in the hall. It was like an echo in her head. She looked towards the door, just able to make out his profile. Then he turned and walked into the room, smiling.

Baby. Baby. What she liked and what she didn't. Baby. Baby. She struggled to maintain her composure, but it was too late, she was going to faint. The last thing she saw before nausea and dizziness overwhelmed her, was the man's smile vanishing as the room misted over, then disappeared.

A couple of hours later, Neil, Lia and Ginger sat down at a marble-topped pavement table in the centre of Richmond.

'Extra cheese for me, and pepperoni, and olives, oh God, I'm so hungry, I want extra everything on mine!' Ginger put down the cardboard menu and grinned at the waiter.

Neil was uncomfortable. He didn't know why he should feel that it was slightly improper for a woman at such an advanced stage of pregnancy to be flirting so overtly, but somehow he just didn't like it. He tried to catch Lia's eye, but she was entranced by her new friend, laughing at every exaggerated utterance. At least he had done the right thing asking the blonde to join them for supper. They had found themselves walking in the same direction after the class, with Ginger pushing her bike along beside them. He had issued the invitation on the spur of the moment.

'Lovely bum!' Ginger said, watching the waiter post their order at the serving hatch.

Lia laughed. It was a female laugh, half conspiratorial, half knowing. She was very good at passing the time of day with people, moulding herself to the shape of another character straightaway, becoming what they wanted her to be. Sometimes it unsettled him and made him wonder whether that was the way she was with everyone, whether she was just as fluid when she was alone with other men, even whether she was like that with him. But he thought of the intensity in her eyes when they made love, the pure, honest expression of love that seemed to sweep his being like radar, demanding nothing less in return. That, surely, was just for him.

As if she had heard what he was thinking, Lia put

her small warm hand over his and, catching the moment when Ginger was fishing around in her patent rucksack for something, smiled at him with an intimacy that chased away his momentary doubts. He wanted to pull her to her feet and run away with her.

'That poor woman . . .' Ginger said, pausing to look at her reflection in the plate-glass window of the restaurant. She made an O with her mouth, touched up the shocking-pink lipstick, then snapped the top back on and threw it back into her bag. The people who were sitting at the table behind the glass stared at her, taking a moment to realize that they were effectively behind a two-way mirror, and that the peroxide blonde either couldn't, or didn't care to see them. Then they went back to their pizzas, not quite knowing whether to be offended.

'Do you think it was the heat?' Ginger continued.

'I don't know. I barely saw her before she passed out,' Lia replied.

'Actually, she seemed quite nice,' Ginger revealed, eager to fill them in on the first part of the meeting they had missed. 'Unlike the other two,' she added.

'Did we miss much?' Lia asked, unwilling to be drawn into criticism.

'I don't think so. We had barely started with that ridiculous game, or teaching aid, or whatever it's called. I hate things like that, don't you? I mean, we're all grown-up, for heaven's sake. What on earth is the purpose of answering moronic questions?'

'It sometimes helps give people confidence.' Neil felt obliged to defend his profession.

'Really? I don't see how.'

Well, you wouldn't since you've obviously never lacked it, he wanted to say. She was beginning to get on his nerves. He finished his beer and wondered whether to order another. It was only weak Italian beer. He held up the empty bottle and waved it as the waiter passed.

'Do you think you'll go again?' Lia asked Ginger.

27

'To the class? I don't think so, do you? I'm not really into all that natural birth stuff. I just thought it would be good to meet a few people in the same boat. It somehow helps to know that other people look like whales,' Ginger said. 'For the first time in months, I wasn't the fattest person in the room!'

'You're pregnant, not fat,' Lia protested politely.

'Well, at least yours is all where it should be.' Ginger looked at Lia's thin bare arms. 'Mine seems to have laid down fat deposits all over. And I've never worn a bra before, and now I need a suspension bridge.'

Neil looked away pretending to be interested in the traffic. He felt as if he were eavesdropping on a conversation in a changing room. It always amazed him how freely women talked about their bodies when they were alone together, the shared laughter, as if they were all in on the same private joke, the way they understood how to give each other confidence. Even though Lia and Ginger had known each other less than three hours, they were already building a rapport. It was as if they were performing an odd, quintessentially female courtship ritual, literally sizing each other up, revealing points of vulnerability in the hope of a reciprocation that would be called friendship. It was a dangerous game, trading weak points like this. Perhaps that was why men didn't play it. If two men had known each other for this length of time, he thought, we would still be discussing the weather.

'Do you think we'll go again, Neil?' Lia attempted to draw him in to the conversation.

'If you want to,' he said, guardedly.

'Yes, how was it for you?' Ginger leant across the table, putting deliberate sexual innuendo into her question and pausing for effect. 'I mean, was it at all useful to talk to other fathers-to-be, or should I say "dads"?' she said, mimicking Judith's voice exactly.

Neil shrugged. Ginger was the kind of person, he

realized, who always slightly misjudged the boundaries between people. She was trying to draw him and Lia into the gang she wanted to form of those in the class she judged to be acceptable, according to some rules of behaviour that only she seemed to know. He didn't want to join her gang. Not yet, anyway. Everyone said the way to meet other first-time parents was to do ante-natal classes. The idea had appealed more to Lia than it had to him because they knew virtually no-one as a couple, and no-one nearby who had children. It was the beginning of parental responsibility, Neil had joked, lining up playmates for your foetus. He reminded himself that he was meant to be nice to Ginger for the sake of his child.

'Like you said,' he eventually replied to her question, 'it's good to know some people in the same boat.'

'Well, at least we've met each other,' Ginger said, 'so it wasn't an entirely wasted evening. Oh good, I think this is our order.'

She picked up a slice of pizza, folded it, then opened her bright pink mouth very wide and bit. A streak of tomato sauce attached itself to her left cheek.

She must be upper class, thought Neil, to have the voice and table manners of a fishwife, and not to care what people think. He noticed that Lia had a slice of her pizza in her hand too. He swigged his beer. Perhaps it was the trendy way to eat it, but it didn't feel right to him. He picked up his knife and fork.

'I do hope that woman is OK,' Ginger said, her mouth full.

'If you're so worried about her, why don't you ring?' Neil said impatiently.

As they were leaving, Judith had issued everyone in the class with a list of telephone numbers and due dates, encouraging them to become friends.

The sharpness of his tone seemed to cut through the balmy night air.

'Maybe I will,' Ginger replied, slightly defensively,

conscious of the reprimand in his voice, 'tomorrow, if I have a minute. They're making me work very hard for my maternity leave.'

'You said you worked for the BBC,' Lia said, asking the right question, smoothing the atmosphere. 'What do you do, exactly?'

'I'm a secretary. I type letters and get shouted at. Everyone told me that it was the quickest way to get on in television, but they didn't tell me that you had to be a *good* secretary . . . What do you do?'

'Anything that's on offer, really,' Lia said, 'I was waitressing, but my blood pressure's high, and the doctor told me to stop.'

'I teach. Sport,' Neil replied, as Ginger nodded at him.

'Teacher, mmm, I might have enjoyed sport if I'd had a teacher that looked like you, rather than a dreadful old dyke wielding a hockey stick like the statue of Liberty,' Ginger said.

Neil looked quickly at Lia, to see whether she was as offended as he was embarrassed, but she was smiling and perfectly at ease.

Alison stood at the bottom of the garden with a cigarette in one hand and a cook's box of matches in the other. On the day the test result came back positive, she had thrown away the smooth flat silver lighter that had felt like a cool pebble in her palm, but she had never quite managed to quit the smoking.

Stephen watched her from the conservatory as she deliberated whether to light up. He knew she still smoked on occasion, but probably not often enough to make it dangerous. Sometimes she came home with the taste of Listerine on her tongue which was more of a giveaway than the smell of smoke in her hair, which might only have meant that she had lunched in a City wine bar. He never remarked on it, because he did not want to add to the stress she bore so heavily, combining the job with the whole business of being pregnant, the doctor's appointments, the exhaustion and the hormonal changes that seemed to make her lose her temper so readily. He turned away from the window and sat down at the piano.

Finally, she put the cigarette in her mouth, and struck a match. The first drag made her feel slightly light-headed. She drew again, inhaling deeply as if the smoke were pure oxygen. She flicked ash on to the patio, dispersing it with the toe of her black patent pumps, then looked at the cigarette in her hand, observing that her lips had left a scarlet imprint on the filter.

It made her think of her mother. Margaret's subterfuge had been shopping for groceries she had mysteriously forgotten to buy. 'I'm just slipping out for a tin,' she would call, closing the front door, walking down the garden path, her pace quickening as she neared the end of their road. One look round to check her husband wasn't following, then cigarette would come out of one pocket, lighter out of the other. And then the hit. Watching from her bedroom window, Alison would see her mother's features changing from pinched to smooth in an instant, the addiction of the nicotine strong enough to overcome even the tremendous impropriety of smoking in the street. Surely her father must have known? Even he must have sometimes glanced in the cupboard next to the sink and wondered why they kept such a large stock of Heinz spaghetti. Could her mother really have believed the adverts on the back of the Sunday colour supplement – vigorous pearly-toothed youngsters climbing up a waterfall – which implied that menthol cigarettes kept your breath clean? Cool as a mountain stream.

I'm turning into my mother, Alison thought with horror, and threw down the butt, grinding it into the concrete. Ash and tobacco disappeared into the dust, but the scarlet-stained filter remained, like an undeniable accusation.

A cigarette that bears a lipstick's traces, she

thought, as the pit of her stomach began to wobble again and she walked slowly back to the house.

Stephen was playing the 'Moonlight' Sonata, quietly. She could not tell from his expression whether or not he had seen her smoking.

'I cancelled the restaurant. Didn't think you'd want to go out,' he said, taking his hands off the keys for a moment.

She looked at him blankly, then remembered. The River Café.

'Right,' she said, 'I'll cook something then.'

She walked past him to the kitchen and began to prepare supper.

There was something therapeutic about the sheer monotony of chopping vegetables. She decided to make a ratatouille. She sliced thick rounds of aubergine and salted them, piling them up in a colander on the draining board, then poured boiling water over fresh plum tomatoes in a bowl, and took them out, one by one, scalding the tips of her fingers, slipping off the skins, delighting in the soft, almost furry, quality of the warm pulpy flesh underneath; realizing, too late, that she had forgotten to put an apron on over her black suit. Thick green olive oil turned clear and golden in the bottom of a heavy pan. She threw in a couple of garlic cloves. The scent brought Stephen into the kitchen.

'Do you need any help?' he said behind her, draping his arms over her shoulders, his hands resting on her bump.

'No, I'm fine . . . really,' she said, wishing he would go back to his music.

The preparation of food gave her mind just enough to think about, just enough to stop it darting forwards in time to the yawning, terrifying unknown, or, worse, backwards, to events she had wrapped in the grey gauze of memory, but which had suddenly become vivid and agonizing, all over again.

32

'Perhaps I should rebook?' Stephen suggested. 'I didn't think you'd be hungry.'

He was trying so hard to be kind, she knew she should be grateful, or reassured, or whatever it was he intended her to be, but she didn't seem to be able to feel anything, not disappointment, nor even irritation. Just numb and exhausted.

'No, I'm quite enjoying this,' she said.

'As soon as I get back, then. Shall I make a reservation?' he asked.

Do whatever you want but leave me alone.

'We ought to make the most of this time, you know,' he said, wandering into the living room and picking up the phone. 'It won't be the same after.'

Alison fished the garlic cloves out of the oil with a slotted spoon then added careful layers of aubergine, courgette, and the dripping, falling-apart slices of tomato. She sealed the pan with a tight lid, and turned down the flame. She could hear Stephen speaking to the restaurant, and suddenly she wished they were going out. She desperately needed the distraction.

'Say we'll come this evening, after all,' she shouted through to him, but he had already put down the receiver.

'No, you're quite right, I'm sure it's better if we have a quiet time tonight, after your . . .' He walked back across the sanded boards.

'I'm fine now. Really.'

'The table's probably gone,' he said, obviously reluctant to ring again. 'Anyway, it smells delicious, what you're making, far better.'

'It'll be nicer tomorrow, ratatouille always is,' she said, knowing somehow that she had already lost. She couldn't push too hard. He would begin to think her crazy or guess at reasons for her strange behaviour. 'Oh well, next week, then,' she said.

'Yes, next Friday. I said eight. Is that OK?'

'Fine.' She felt like a stranger fixing a lunch

appointment on the phone. She turned back to the kitchen.

'Alison?'

'Yes?'

'You *are* all right?'

'Yes,' she said, glad she was facing away from him, and that he could not see her face.

'You hated her, didn't you?' Lia said, as they watched Ginger cycle slowly away, the shiny rucksack reflecting the orange neon street-lamps long after her silhouette had merged into the night.

'Not hated,' Neil replied, cautiously, 'I just thought she was arrogant, and a bit crude.'

Lia laughed. 'I liked her,' she said. 'Under all that shouting, there's quite a scared little rabbit, I think.'

Lia was one of life's observers. She had the ability to put people at their ease, chatting for hours about nothing at all, and yet her observations were always pin-sharp. He loved the way she sometimes used language slightly oddly, after living abroad so long. Bunny, he thought, is what most people would have said, a scared little bunny, but Lia said rabbit. He imagined Ginger with rabbit's ears sticking out of her peroxide stubble of a hair-cut, and somehow she became easier to deal with.

'Shall we get a taxi?' he asked, taking Lia's arm.

'No, let's walk. I like walking in the dark and talking to you,' Lia said.

He thought of the evening they met, how they had walked along the beach together in the moonlight, saying very little, convention demanding that they mark some time between first setting eyes on each other, and making love.

'Don't you want to go to that class again?' he asked her.

'I don't know. I thought I wanted to know all that stuff about the stages of labour, but now I'm not sure. I felt a bit funny when that woman passed out as soon as we walked in. It felt like an omen.' She looked sideways at him for reassurance. He pretended not to notice. 'I don't know,' she continued, 'I think I'd rather have an open mind.'

He breathed a sigh of relief. He most definitely did not want to go again, but he didn't know how to begin to explain why. He should, he realized, have said something straightaway, rather than waiting, putting it off, asking the blonde out to dinner with them to give him time to think.

'I'll see how I feel next week,' she added.

He felt a small seed of anxiety in his stomach take root. Again, he said nothing. It was easy to be silent in the dark, when she couldn't see his face. It wasn't lying, he told himself. He didn't want to say anything to upset her, not with her blood pressure. And anyway, he reasoned, there really wasn't anything to say. To mention it would give it a significance it did not deserve, make it seem like a problem. Which it wasn't. Not at all.

Ginger got off her bike at the bottom of the hill and began to push. At times like this, she wished somebody would invent a kind of ski-lift for cyclists where you could sit on your bike, hook a T-bar behind the saddle and be dragged up to the top. Strategically placed on the inclines of London, they would really encourage people to cycle to work. It would be a far more sensible way to spend money than painting ineffectual cycle lanes on the main routes, which motorists ignored, and that suddenly disappeared when the streets got too narrow and you actually needed them. And if more people cycled to work, the fumes that hung over the Thames on hot, hot nights like this might not be so acid. Why didn't politicians ever think of things like that?

As the hill grew steeper, and she grew more breathless, she found herself visualizing her lungs. They looked like a yellow floor-sponge grown crusty with age, which she had once found at the back of the cupboard under the sink. Ginger told herself to think of kinder images. The people who said that the pregnancy hormones made you relaxed were lying. Just as they lied about so many aspects of it. From the day the circle turned dark blue in the window of the white plastic pee-wand, Ginger had been plagued by nightmares and grotesque images of almost surreal proportions. No wonder they advised you not to drink or take 'recreational' drugs, she thought, although sometimes, in the early hours of the morning, on the seventh or eighth visit to the lavatory when she was desperate for an uninterrupted sleep, she had got as far as unscrewing the cap off the half-drunk bottle of Stolichnaya that stood at the back of her cluttered mantelpiece. But she had always resisted, worried enough that the embryo had spent its first few hours of life swimming in her vodka-laden blood the night it was conceived.

Ginger was actually looking forward to labour. She didn't care how painful it was because at some stage, within a day, or two days, of it starting, surely no longer than three days, it would be over. Her GP had chuckled when she told him that at the last check-up, telling her, 'Babies are much more trouble when they're out,' which she had thought was one of his more stupid remarks. Of course she realized that it would be more difficult to care for another person, especially a tiny weeny person who couldn't talk or eat bacon sandwiches, than it was for a bump. But at least she would be herself again, with a functioning memory and bladder.

Ginger stopped for breath. She could feel her pulse beating against the inside of her skull. Away from the hot tarmac of the busy high street, the air seemed a degree cooler, and a slight breeze cooled the sweat that trickled down her temples. As if woken by the slight change in temperature, her baby started kicking. She watched as a tiny fist, or foot, pummelled inside, rippling across her tummy, like a mouse under a carpet. He (she was sure it was a boy) always woke up at this time, just as she was thinking of turning in. He didn't kick much during the day when she was on the move. But when she let herself stop and rest, he seemed to wake up and demand to be noticed. And even if she were on the verge of feeling desperate, it never failed to make her happy, to sense the vigour of the life inside her, knowing that this was a child who really wanted to be born.

Ginger smiled, pulled the bike from the railing where it was resting, and started on her way again. Her flat was in the terrace of houses right at the top of the hill. She always kept her eyes on the pavement as she walked, saving the exhilaration of the view as a reward for reaching the top. She had only lived on the Hill for a few months. Her beloved grandmother, Hermione, had died suddenly in the spring and surprised everyone by leaving the ground-floor flat she had lived in since she was widowed to Ginger. It had made Ginger very sad that Hermione had not lived to see her first great-grandchild, but she felt so perfectly at ease living in her flat, amongst her heavy Victorian furniture and ornaments, that she sometimes felt that something of Hermione had remained and was watching over her.

It was dark as she let herself in, but her answerphone on the dining table was blinking like a Christmas-tree light.

She pressed playback.

Bleep.

'It's just me,' said her twin, Patricia, nicknamed Pic. 'You haven't rung for ages. Are you all right? Give me a bell, but not too late. Byeeee!'

Ginger turned on the kitchen tap and stuck her head under it. The dribble of water felt icy on the nape of her neck.

Bleep.

'Virginia, it's your mother. Just to remind you that

37

Daddy's having his operation on Thursday. He would love to see you, darling . . .'

Ginger sighed and turned up the tap. Her mother made it sound so easy.

Bleep.

'Pic again. I meant to say that I'm going to see Daddy tomorrow lunch-time and I wondered if you'd like to come with me for moral support. If you're not back till late, then ring me at work.'

Ginger held up her arm to look at her watch. It was too late. Why did Pic and Ed always go to bed so early? She simply couldn't understand it.

Bleep.

'Ginger? It's Charlie Prince here. Why don't you give me a bell sometime?'

Ginger stood up so quickly she caught the back of her head against the tap.

Bleep.

'Darling, I do wish I didn't always have to speak into this awful machine . . .'

Ginger didn't wait to hear the rest of her mother's second message, she pressed rewind.

'Ginger? It's Charlie Prince . . .'

Shit!

Her mind raced through all of the good reasons he might be ringing: perhaps he'd been abroad for a few months and he hadn't been able to stop thinking about her, so as soon as he touched down at Heathrow, he called. Possible, she thought, but given the efficiency of international telecommunications, very unlikely, and anyway, she'd seen his picture recently in *Broadcast*, at a British awards ceremony so . . . Perhaps he and Lucretia had split up for good this time, and . . . No, Charlie and Lucretia were like a lesser version of Hugh Grant and Liz Hurley, they were together, then they were apart, then they were together again, but they were always really together, because one was diminished without the other, so . . . Maybe he was clearing out his Filofax, and he came across her name, and he remembered the night they had spent together, smiled, and picked up the phone? No, because she had moved since then and had a different number ... and anyway, that was pure fantasy.

She started to run through the bad reasons he might be calling. Maybe he had bumped into Robert and they had talked about her, and Robert had told him. No, he couldn't have. She had sworn him to secrecy. But, she thought, Robert was inclined to be untrustworthy when there was a good-looking man within fifty feet. And why else would Charlie call after all this time? Oh God, perhaps Charlie had AIDS, and they had told him to contact everyone he had slept with, and he had told them that he always used condoms, but then he remembered that night and ... No, it couldn't be. Surely that would be just too unlucky ...

Ginger jumped as she caught her reflection in the gilded mantel mirror above the black marble fireplace. It always took a split second to remember that she actually was the round lady who seemed to lean backwards from the waist like a wobbly toy. If I'm making myself jump, I'm never going to sleep, she thought, and picked up the phone.

'Pic? You weren't asleep, were you? I'm sorry ...' She waited as her twin sister, on the other end of the line, got out of bed, kissed her grumbling husband on the cheek and took the cordless phone downstairs. 'I've just got in ... No, I was at the ante-natal class and I went out to dinner with one of the couples ... Yes ... Well, the man was a bit po-faced, but the wife seemed nice, I mean, not my type of person really, but it's funny how anyone who's pregnant becomes my type of person these days ... No, I didn't ring to tell you about that, sorry ... No, it's just that when I got back there was this message ... Yes, I got yours ... No, I'm not ringing about that ... Oh for God's sake, Pic, I'm trying to tell you, if you'd let me get a word in. *He* called ... Charlie Prince ... Pic ... No, I haven't spoken to him ... That's why I'm calling you, for heaven's sake!'

The next day, as Ginger pedalled up to the grimy red-brick entrance of the hospital, she thought how out of place her sister looked standing amid the dust and discarded cigarette butts, like a fragile orchid growing on a landfill site. From the earliest age, Pic had looked freshly laundered and ironed. She was the sort of person who walked off a long-haul flight with tights unladdered, clothes uncrumpled, and make-up unsmudged.

'I've never understood how you work in a laboratory and still manage to look like that,' Ginger said, greeting her with a kiss.

'I do most of my work on computer,' Pic replied, kissing her back enthusiastically, 'and if I'm in the lab, I wear an overall.'

'Yes, and I bet that it's Persil-white and creaseless too,' said Ginger, who had no idea what her sister actually did, just that it was very high-powered and important scientific research.

Pic giggled.

'You've got smuts on your face,' she told Ginger, taking a clean white cotton hanky out of her bag and dabbing at her sister's shining pink cheeks. 'Do you really think you ought to be cycling in—'

'My condition?' Ginger interrupted crossly.

'I was going to say "this weather", but yes, in your condition too.'

'Actually, I mostly push the bike around these days. It's a kind of cross between a shopping trolley and a zimmer frame for the pregnant woman, but it's better than sweltering on public transport.' Ginger bent to lock her bike to the iron railing. 'I haven't the patience for public transport. I don't just mean the time, but the people. I get so hot and bothered trying to stop myself leaning forward and asking, "What possessed

40

you to wear that tie?", and things like that . . . Deep breath,' she said, as she straightened up.

'Does that help?' Pic asked, concerned.

'No, silly, I'm just preparing myself for seeing Daddy. It's the first time since I told him.'

'Well, I'm sure he's got over the shock,' Pic said, sounding more confident than she felt, and wondering whether it had after all been such a good idea to encourage Ginger to visit a man with severe heart disease. Her belly was so large, she looked as if she might go into labour at any moment, even though she still had several weeks before she was due.

When Stephen caught sight of the twins walking down the corridor to their father's private room, he was reminded of those figures painted on a board at a seaside pier, cartoon outlines with holes for faces, which people stood behind to pose for photographs, squashing their features into the blank ovals and giving themselves joke bodies. The twins each had exactly the same face framed by different hair-styles and perched on top of different bodies. Even if their faces had not been visible, an observer would have known they were related, and not just because they were holding hands. They were exactly the same height and they walked in exactly the same way, with their toes turning outwards like children in a ballet school. Stephen smiled to himself before turning away, realizing that the face was familiar to him, though he could not think why.

'Darlings!' Their mother swept out of their father's room. She always looked elegant but somehow distracted, as if her mind was on other things. 'Oh, darling!' she said, her voice plummeting in disapproval as she took in Ginger's appearance.

Ginger was wearing black and white spotted cycling shorts and a sleeveless shirt made of the same cotton jersey fabric that fastened over her bulging front with large white plastic buttons. A bright pink scarf was tied in a bow round her bleached crop. On her feet, she sported black and white trainers with the laces untied, and on her back, the black patent leather rucksack.

In contrast, Patricia wore a cream linen tailored suit, with a lemon silk vest under the short-sleeved jacket, and a single string of graduated pearls. Her shoes were cream leather and so was her handbag with its tortoiseshell clasp that exactly matched the small buckle on the narrow cream leather belt.

'Oh darling what?' Ginger challenged her mother, loudly.

Her mother's eyes flicked over her daughters' pretty heads and to each side, establishing whether anyone else was within hearing range.

'It's just, darling, you know,' she said, with a pained expression on her face, 'you look so . . .' She searched for a word that wouldn't be too derogatory. 'So bright!'

'Well, I'm sorry, but I don't see why I should slop around in a hideous romper suit or a workhouse dress of faded denim, which are the only alternatives,' Ginger replied defensively.

Beside her, Pic giggled.

'Oh Patricia, don't encourage her,' their mother reprimanded, which made them both laugh, since she had been saying the same thing for as long as they could remember, with very little effect.

'How is Daddy?' Pic asked, regaining control of herself.

'Well, he's having a rest, which he badly needs,' their mother said, standing back so they could go into the room. 'Now, I know he'll be so happy to see you, but you really mustn't tire him,' she said, looking sternly at Ginger.

Their father was dozing. The slatted blinds at the window were down, shutting out the worst of the sunlight, and in the still, warm gloom of the room, his face was grey. That is how he'll look when he's dead, Ginger thought, shocked to see how old and ill he had grown in the months since she had seen him last. She felt a rush of fear and affection welling up inside her. Please don't die hating me, she thought, grasping her sister's hand for support.

They approached the bed tentatively, side by side, and as if he sensed them there, he opened his eyes. For a second they lit up with undisguised delight, and then, as if he had suddenly remembered himself, narrowed slightly into a frown.

'Well, well, well,' he said, 'my heavenly twins.'

Ginger braced herself for the put-down that was sure to follow, and was surprised when he merely waved his hand at the hard chairs on each side of the bed. They both sat down.

'I don't know whether to be honoured or alarmed,' he finally said, 'to have visits from long-lost relatives before I go under the surgeon's knife!'

Ginger bristled, but forced herself to keep quiet.

'Oh Daddy, don't be silly,' Patricia said, quickly, 'the reason you never see us is because you're always away in Brussels or somewhere, and I've given up ringing you because I'm sick of leaving messages with your secretary.'

'I was only joking, my dear Pickles,' he replied, making her blush with embarrassment.

You bastard, thought Ginger. No wonder he was a politician. He loved control. Usually, it would be Ginger who walked into his traps because she was far more inclined to fly off the handle and speak without thinking. She felt slightly guilty now for hanging back, because her silence had made Pic jump in, eager to ease the palpable tension in the room, and now they both looked stupid. Her father was smiling. What kind of a man could extract pleasure from the most petty of power struggles, she wondered, feeling a kind of revulsion towards him, then hating herself for it, because he was ill.

43

'And Ginger, are you well?' he turned to her side of the bed, 'You look—'

'Don't say blooming,' Ginger interrupted him, 'it's only a euphemism for fat. I'm fine, thank you, but I certainly picked the wrong summer . . . Now I know why they call it a bun in the oven. It's so bloody hot. Even when the weather cools down, I feel like a boiler with the thermostat on high.'

Her father laughed.

She was grateful that he had decided to acknowledge her condition straightaway. Maybe it was easier for him now, she thought, since she was so obviously with child. She had noticed people at work now treated her with a little respect, opening doors, jumping in to help if she attempted to shift anything heavy, and her boss had even stopped making her re-do the letters with minor punctuation errors.

The air in the room seemed to have cleared and she felt able to ask him about the operation, knowing that he wouldn't go into any meeting without being fully briefed, particularly not into a meeting with a surgeon holding a knife. He described the procedure in detail, the extraction of arterial matter from the thigh, its transposition to the heart, by-passing the area that was failing. She hadn't realized that the operation had such a literal name.

'These days, it's pretty much routine,' he told her, and even though he sounded confident, she knew that he was frightened, and that the words were for his reassurance as much as hers.

A nurse came in to monitor his pulse and blood pressure. Pic nodded at her and they both got up to leave.

'Good luck!' Pic said, leaning over him and kissing his cheek, 'I love you, Daddy.' She walked out leaving Ginger alone with him.

Ginger stood awkwardly beside the bed. 'I hope it goes well,' she said.

'Yes,' he replied.

'Right, then,' she said, unable to bring herself to kiss him. As she turned to go, his hand, firm and bony, stretched out and grasped hers. She looked at him and saw that his eyes were full of tears. She squeezed his hand and said, 'You take care. I'll see you soon.'

He nodded at her, silently, his mouth pursed, then let her hand drop back by her side.

'I think there's a cafeteria,' Pic said, taking her arm as they emerged from the ward, having said goodbye to their mother.

'No,' Ginger replied, 'let's go somewhere else. I hate hospital canteens, they're always full of sad people.'

There was an Italian sandwich shop across the road with two tables at the back obscured by an enormous glass-fronted refrigerator-unit filled with mounds of sandwich fillings in oval stainless steel dishes. They ordered cappuccino and Ginger found she couldn't resist an avocado and bacon on brown and a doughnut oozing confectioner's custard.

'Thank you for making me go,' Ginger said.

'I didn't make you,' Pic said, neutrally.

'Well, you did actually. I thought I was quite prepared for him to die without making my peace, but actually that would have been horrible.'

'He's not going to die,' Pic said.

'No?'

'No,' Pic replied firmly; then, as if unable to bear any more morbid talk, she asked, 'Now, what are you going to do about Charlie Prince?'

Instinctively, Ginger looked over her shoulder. The name Charlie Prince was one of the few secrets she had ever kept. She had trained herself not to say it, however much she was tempted, and it felt odd hearing the words in public.

Only two people in the world knew the identity of the father of her baby. Her best friend, Robert, because it was his party from which they had disappeared together. Robert who, a few months later, had guessed

45

the reason that she had suddenly stopped drinking, and deduced the rest of the story. There had been no point in denying it, because as well as being hopeless at keeping secrets, Ginger was also very bad at telling lies. And Pic. She had told Pic because she told Pic absolutely everything, and trusted her far more than she trusted herself.

'I suppose that I'd better ring and find out what he wants,' she now said to her sister. 'It's probably just something like the direct-line number of someone at the Beeb who's avoiding his calls.'

She had spent the night running through increasingly Byzantine fantasies about the reason for his phone call, but at six in the morning, it finally occurred to her that Charlie simply wanted something from her, because that was the only reason independent producers ever turned on the charm. After that, she'd slept for two unbroken hours, and woken up feeling relatively calm.

'What if he wants to see you?' Pic pressed on.

'I'm sure he won't,' Ginger said.

'Well, if he does, you will tell me,' Pic said, concerned.

'What, are you thinking of slumming it in some of my pre-pregnancy clothes, bleaching your hair and playing me?' Ginger asked, biting into her doughnut.

'Now, there's an idea . . .'

When they were little, they had sometimes managed to trick people by swapping clothes, but although they had looked identical, even then they were such different personalities that the pretence normally only lasted a few minutes.

'I knew I shouldn't have told you how brilliant he was in bed . . .'

Now, Pic blushed bright red. 'Oh, I didn't mean . . .'

'I know you didn't. Listen,' Ginger said, looking at the large black diver's watch on her wrist, 'I've got to get back to work.'

* * *

The buddleia bush was alive with butterflies and the warm honeysuckle-scented air hummed sporadically as a bee mooched lazily from one bloom to another. Lia lay on a sun lounger in the dappled shade of the apple tree, drifting in and out of sleep, wondering, in her conscious moments, what it was about the antenatal class that could have upset Neil.

On the way there, he had been in such a good mood, looking forward to the end of term and the summer holiday that stretched before them, but on the way back, an impenetrable cloud of gloom seemed to have settled around him. At first she thought that he was angry that she had got on so well with Ginger, whom he clearly had not liked, but it was not that. When he had come to bed, eventually, after pacing the long, narrow garden for an hour, believing her asleep upstairs, she had turned to him, and seen in his eyes a strange mixture of emotions: distress, fear, and something unfathomable, like loss. Silently, she had opened her arms and drawn him in and held him, his head on her chest, his body curling round her belly, until his breathing became slow and even, and he turned away in sleep.

Perhaps the class had frightened him. Not just the stark physical way Judith had described labour, but reality finally dawning, that their lives were about to change irrevocably. Perhaps he had only just experienced that stab of foreboding she had felt months before, when, standing shivering in their freezing bathroom at six o'clock one Sunday morning, she had watched the pregnancy test turn undeniably dark pink in front of her eyes, suddenly terrified that they were tempting fate by choosing to change something between them that was so perfect. Breathing deeply, she had kept the information a cherished secret for just a few seconds, then she had rushed into the bedroom to awaken him with the news, and they had held each other silently for a long time, shocked by the enormity of what they were doing.

47

Lia stretched her arm out to grasp the Evian bottle from beside the sun lounger. She took a sip of the sun-warmed liquid then splashed a little over her face. From time to time, a breeze picked up children's shouts and splashes from a nearby paddling pool and wafted them into the garden. It was so hot that if she closed her eyes, she could imagine herself back on the beach by the ocean, the sound of children playing in the waves, the kindly warmth of the late-afternoon sun on her face.

She remembered being in bed with him one evening that first week, lying entwined in a slick of sweat and sex as if they were one creature – a beached octopus – with eight limbs.

'You know that I love you,' he had suddenly said, softly, almost under his breath, 'I want to be with you for ever . . .'

'Yes,' she had replied, simply.

Afterwards, she had thought how strange it was that she hadn't even considered asking him *how* he knew, or how often he had said that in his life, or why, or any of the questions that would normally have gone through her mind. And she realized that the reason was that she felt the same way as he did. There had been men she thought she loved before, but no-one like Neil. It was not just that he was incredibly gorgeous, nor that he had a wry smile in his eyes that made her wet whenever she looked at him, it just felt as if they were meant to be together. She had drifted between countries, between men, for ten years, but now she had found the person she wanted to spend the rest of her life with.

She had quit her job that day. They climbed on his motorbike, drove away from the village and roamed along the coast, pitching his tent on deserted beaches, bathing in sea that looked like molten metal in the moonlight, but was as cold as ice. They had exchanged vows at the far western tip of Europe under a sky brilliant with stars, and then they had come back to England. She had never thought about returning before, but with Neil it had felt like coming home.

Lia sat up slowly, easing herself to standing. As she walked up the garden and opened the back door, she heard the stutter of the motorbike as Neil turned off the main road into their street. She watched him through the front window as he locked the bike and removed his helmet, then he unlocked the box behind the seat and took something out, a bunch of carnations, wilting in the heat. He walked the few steps to their door slowly, his shoulders stooped in contemplation. When he saw her watching him from behind the lace curtain, his face lit up in a smile and he waved the carnations at her. And she opened the door to greet him, wondering why he had bought her flowers.

'So how was your photographer last night?' Ramona asked, her mouth full of sandwich.

They were sitting side by side on a park bench in a dusty triangle of city park they frequented at lunchtime because it was just a few streets away from the newspaper's office. For a moment, Alison didn't understand what she was talking about.

'Oh, it wasn't him. It was Stephen. He came to take me to the class.'

'Sweet of him. How was it?' Ramona asked.

Alison was about to take a bite into her sandwich. She paused for a second, her mouth wide open, wondering whether to tell Ramona what had happened.

'Fine,' she said, biting down.

'So what was it the editor wanted to say to you so urgently on your last day in the office?' Ramona asked.

That morning, when she had arrived at her desk, Alison had found a message from the editor asking her to pop in to see him before the end of the day.

'Not happy with the number of baby items over the past few weeks,' Alison said, dabbing at the corners of her mouth with the paper napkin. 'I hadn't realized I was so obsessed, until he listed four Test Cases in the last six weeks: car seats, slings, Moses Baskets and cot mobiles.'

'Well, at least you've equipped your nursery,' Ramona said drily.

'Yes, but how many Moses baskets can you use at once? I think I'll donate the others to the hospital.'

'Does it worry you?' Ramona asked.

'What?' Alison replied. 'Temporary loss of brain cells?'

'No, you know, maternity leave . . . going off for four months when the paper's in such a mess . . . who knows who'll be sitting at your desk when you come back, that sort of thing . . .'

'I don't really see that I have much choice,' Alison said diplomatically, looking at her bump.

Ramona was a good friend, but she always wanted to know just slightly too much. She had a way of tapping into insecurities you didn't even know you were feeling. One part of Alison did feel it was slightly odd that today of all days the editor should choose to make his first criticism after three years of working for him. But another part of her had almost wanted him to suggest that she should not return after her leave. What a relief it would be, to be given breathing space, an excuse to relax and decide what she wanted to do with her life, and a generous redundancy cheque. The trouble was, she was too good at the job. He had spoken to her gently, masking his criticisms as mere comments, telling her how much he valued her. She hated the kindness accorded to women in her condition, like fleshy Madonnas, to be whispered at and revered.

Sometimes Alison wished that she were brave enough to quit. She just wasn't enjoying the job any more. The first year had been fun. She had spent the salary, gone on all the freebies, bought a lot of expensive new clothes, had her hair cut to look like a real power-dressing female executive, and relished the achievement and the recognition she had worked so hard for. The second year, she found it easier, more routine, still pleasant, but less demanding, which at the time had suited her fine. But in the last year, it had begun to drive her mad. To have her life mapped out by meals: if it's August it must be barbecues and garden furniture, November comfort food and fireplaces, the endless search for something new to eat and put on your tree at Christmas. If she hadn't been, finally, pregnant, she would have been looking for another job, where she could write more, or at least edit something more worthwhile than beautifully written and illustrated articles about food and drink and gardens and interior decoration.

In daydreams, she entertained fantasies about training to be a nurse, a charity administrator, someone who made a basic, useful contribution to society. As each month went past, and she planned yet more fatuous features on the style dilemmas of the middle classes – wallpaper or paint, colours or monochrome – she became more and more frustrated with her life, more and more critical of herself, her job, her whole existence.

She had assumed that the prospect of a baby would give meaning to it all. But it wasn't so. Sometimes she lay awake at night wondering why on earth she had been so keen to conceive, why it had become an obsession after three years of trying and failure, and what could have persuaded her to subject herself, twice, to the strange, unnatural process of *in vitro* fertilization. She asked herself why it was she was such a perfectionist, always desperate to succeed at whatever she did, but never content when she had achieved it. The job, the baby, it was all part of the same thing. Something drove her on, never allowing her time to pause and ask herself what she wanted.

51

Her first reaction to the positive pregnancy test had been pure triumph, her second, utter panic.

As they lay next to one another in the dark that night, Stephen had asked her why she was trembling, and she had told him in a whisper, as if saying it quietly would make it untrue. 'I don't think I want to have a baby.'

'Well, it's too late now, my love,' he had replied, and she had heard the gentle smile in his voice. He had thought she was joking.

Alison's baby moved, jutting its head into her pubic bone, making her wince.

'Ouch!' said Ramona, seeing the look on her face. 'It's not like it is in the movies, is it?' Ramona had two grown-up children. It was only women who had been pregnant themselves who came close to understanding the discomfort of the condition.

'I suppose it depends which movies,' Alison replied with feigned joviality. 'I've seen movies where women die in childbirth.'

She felt better having made a joke, declining the option to share her pain with Ramona. One of the things she most hated about being pregnant was the loss of privacy. As soon as you started to look pregnant, you became a kind of public property. Even if you tried to behave as if nothing were happening to you, people, sometimes people you didn't even know, felt they had a right to touch you, or speak to you. They were only trying to be nice, but she hated the intrusion, and if you dared to object or retaliate, you were automatically placed under an invisible sign that everyone else could see which said in large glowing letters, 'HORMONES', although it might just as well have said, 'STUPID AND FAT'.

'Anyway,' Alison said, scrunching up the waxed paper in which her sandwich had been wrapped, 'I'd better be getting back. I'm going to have to rethink my 101 ways with formula milk, re-jig the Test Case on bottle sterilizers and pull the design feature on

nursery decoration . . . Only joking. Jesus, Ramona!
I'm joking!'

There was a small impromptu party at six o'clock.
The editor opened a couple of bottles of Australian
Chardonnay, called the staff into his office and
presented her with a giant teddy bear, far too big to
wrap, with a ribbon and card tied around his neck.
Then everybody started kissing her and wishing her
good luck, and, surrounded by such unusual bon-
homie, she almost cried, until Ramona whispered,
'It's always the ones who are gunning for your job
who are nicest to you, isn't it?'

It felt very odd and very final checking her desk,
signing off from the computer, and taking the lift
down to the ground floor, alone, except for the bear.

He sat beside her in the taxi, his great furry head
next to hers, his beady brown eyes staring straight
ahead as blind to his surroundings as she was blind,
mesmerized by the strangeness of leaving work, no
longer able to judge how she felt about it. It was only
when she became aware of the three small children
on the back seat of a Volvo that was crawling along
next to the cab in the traffic jam, that she realized how
odd she and her companion must look. She took the
bear's paw and made him wave at them, regally. It felt
good to see their faces light up with surprise and joy
at the simple gesture.

Stephen was waiting in the hall, his case and suitbag
packed. 'I'm glad I didn't miss you,' he said, failing to
acknowledge the bear, leaning awkwardly over him
and kissing her on the cheek. 'You're late.'

'Yes, they had a little party for me,' she replied.
'Good.'

'Have you ordered a cab?' she said, looking behind
her. 'You could have taken mine . . . I'm sorry, I didn't
think.'

'No, there's one on its way,' he said, glancing at his
watch again.

She wondered whether he would have waited to say goodbye if his cab had arrived before hers.

'When's your plane?' she asked him.

'Nine-thirty.'

'Plenty of time, then.' She tried to be reassuring.

'I suppose so, if the traffic's OK.'

It always surprised her how nervous he was about flying. Here was a man who could cut and stitch a man's arteries with a perfectly steady hand, and yet shook visibly as he walked on to a plane. Perhaps it was because he understood how close life was to death.

She put the bear down at the bottom of the stairs and walked into the kitchen. 'Shall I make some tea?' she asked, running the tap.

'Not for me, thank you.'

She knew that the brusque, staccato conversation was only a product of his fear, but it irritated her. He was going away for a week of fine dining and animated discussion with his peers. The least he could do was be a bit cheerful about it.

'Sir James Prospect is in for open-heart surgery,' Stephen said, conscious of the need for him to fill the space that yawned between them.

'I didn't know he had one,' Alison said. 'A heart, I mean.'

Stephen laughed drily.

Then a car sounded its horn outside.

'That's my cab,' he said.

'Yes,' she replied, flicking the switch on the kettle.

He strode across the kitchen and kissed her again, chastely, on the cheek.

'Have a good time,' she said, sullenly, conscious of the ugliness of her self-pity, but unable to alter her behaviour.

'Please take care of yourself. You have all my numbers and I'll ring as soon as I arrive.'

She did not follow him to the door, but when she heard the car door slam outside, she suddenly thought how awful it would be if his fears were realized, the plane crashed and she never saw him again. How terrible it would be if his last image of her was of her back. She raced out into the hall and flung open the front door, but the cab was already at the end of the road and she could see that Stephen was sitting very straight in the back seat, and he did not turn round to wave.

Neil watched as Lia turned lamb chops on the barbecue, drops of fat flaring, making her step back quickly. On the white plastic table beside her, two places were set, a bowl of salad, a basket of cut baguette. The carnations he had bought had been trimmed and placed in a tall glass vase, the pink, yellow and red blooms looking somehow out of place against the subtle shades of the garden, like plastic flowers in an expensive bouquet.

He tried to remember why he had come into the kitchen. Beer. He opened the fridge to see if there were any cans cooling, and took out a four-pack of Stella Artois. Sometimes he found it odd that someone else did his shopping and remembered the things he liked, probably better than he did. He became overwhelmed in supermarkets, either feeling he must buy something from every shelf, or wanting to dash out with nothing at all. He had shared his house with several women over the years, but none of them had ever shopped for him or made the place comfortable. Perhaps none of them had dared to change things, scared that he would resent their nesting instincts.

Neil smiled, remembering what a bastard he had been to anyone who tried to get too close to him, until the day he had discovered Lia, sitting like a beached mermaid on the porch of a Portuguese seafront bar. She was the most beautiful woman he had ever seen, with her long, soft hair, and skin that tasted of salt. And she cast a strange spell on him, making him feel suddenly replete with love, fierce in his desire for her,

55

and yet gentle towards the world. He had brought her home, like a fisherman returning with treasure, and she had transformed his house in the year she had been there, making it a warm and welcoming home, not somewhere hard and male, to sleep and screw.

There were soft colours and soft things, like cushions and curtains and a duvet cover with a design that looked as if it had been painted, not engineered. In the kitchen, articles appeared to make life easier: a tall plastic bin, instead of a plastic carrier bag hung on the handle of the back door; a bowl for washing vegetables; an oven glove for removing trays of curry from the cooker without burning fingers, and fridge magnets for lists of things to buy and things to do, and, Neil closed the fridge door, of names of other couples about to have babies. He stared at the list for several seconds, wanting to tear it down, but not knowing how to explain if she asked why he had done that. Then he checked the garden again. Lia was still leaning over the barbecue.

He snatched the phone from its holder and dialled the first number on the list. It rang, once, twice; he was about to put it down, then it was answered.

'Hello?' Alison said.

He listened to her breathing for a few seconds, then, unable to believe what he had done, he replaced the receiver.

A week after the ante-natal class, Lia ran into Alison again.

The first thing she noticed was the dress. It was a Madras cotton check, purple, turquoise and black. There was something about the depth and clarity of the colours that made it look expensive. She was just wondering whether she dared to ask where the woman had bought it, when she turned round. The second thing she noticed was the bump. It was as huge as her own. The woman pulled the last items out of her shopping trolley and straightened up wearily. The third thing she noticed was the face, and she knew it was familiar, but could not immediately think why, but she thought they had enough in common to say, 'Hello.'

Alison looked up. 'Oh . . . hello.'

'I love your dress. Where did you get it? Or is that a rude question?' Lia said, remembering now that it was the woman who had passed out.

'No, not at all.' Alison's face broke into a smile. 'Actually, Harvey Nichols, but I kicked myself because they have some almost the same in Monsoon.'

'It's lovely, so bright,' Lia said. 'Are you well?' she added.

'Yes. Thank you,' Alison replied, but she looked wary, perhaps not wanting to be reminded of the incident.

The check-out girl took Alison's credit card and swiped it through the till. Lia put her own purchases, a bottle of fresh ginger lemonade and a pound of sausages, on to the conveyor belt, and began to help Alison pack her bags.

'It's OK, really, thanks,' said Alison, signing the receipt and loading the bags into her trolley.

'Did you come by car?' Lia asked her, paying cash for her drink, and following her towards the exit.

'Yes.' Then, as if remembering her manners: 'Did you?'

'Er, no, we don't have a car.'

'Can I give you a lift?'

The invitation was polite rather than meant.

'No, thanks. I haven't got much to carry!' Lia smiled at her, swinging her plastic carrier bag like a pendulum.

They came to a halt beside the lift to the car park.

'Hey, I was just going to go and sit by the river and drink this . . . Would you like to join me?' Lia made one final effort.

Instead of responding, Alison simply looked at her laden trolley.

'You could put it in the car first,' Lia suggested.

'Oh, well, OK, then,' Alison finally replied, not able to think of another excuse.

The pavement in the narrow street leading down to the riverbank was only wide enough for one pregnant woman. Lia led the way and, walking behind her, Alison noticed how the people who stepped into the road to let them pass couldn't help smiling at her natural beauty and the enormousness of her bump that looked almost out of place on such a slender body.

They sat down on a bench. Lia twisted open the seal on the bottle of still lemonade and offered Alison first sip. For a few minutes they were both silent. By the pier, a riverboat started its engines, making a lot of noise, that faded as it chugged away, until the put-putting seemed to melt into the background hum of the city and the lapping of the wash on the shore took over.

'Sometimes I forget how nice it is to be beside water when it's hot,' Alison said, scuffing the gravel tow-path with the leather soles of her slim Italian shoes. 'It's ridiculous, isn't it? You buy a house in a lovely part of town by the river, and then you're so busy you never even see it. I think of how I longed to live in London, and now I do, I spend all my time in two rooms, my bedroom and my office – three if you count the weekly trip to Waitrose!'

'I've been spending a lot of time in our garden,' Lia said, 'but when I get lonely, I come down here.'

The slightly wistful admission of loneliness sent a jolt of guilt through Alison for her earlier reluctance to be friendly. She looked quickly round at her companion who was staring out over the river.

'You've got a great tan,' Alison said, admiring her thin arms.

'I've never been this brown before, even in Portugal. I think it must have something to do with our "condition",' Lia said, stretching her arms out in front of her. 'Well, at least there are some advantages . . .' she added.

'Name another . . .' Alison demanded, smiling.

Lia put her chin on her hand and pondered with exaggerated seriousness. 'No, that's it!' she said, laughing.

'Absolutely!' Alison said, beginning to relax, 'whereas the disadvantages . . .'

'How long have you got?' Lia asked.

They began to swap lists of the things that irritated them: the way everyone, from family to shop assistants, felt obliged to make some comment about your size.

'I've been asked twice already today whether it's twins,' Alison confessed, 'it's as if because you're pregnant, you haven't got feelings about your body any more. Can you imagine asking someone who wasn't pregnant why they were so fat?'

'And the way people keep banging on about the baby's sex,' Lia chimed in. ' "Do you think it's a boy or a girl? Which would you prefer?" As if there's anything you could do about it!'

'Yes, and then, "Have you decided what to call it?" ' said Alison.

'And I am so sick of lying around . . . I haven't been able to work for the last six weeks, they thought I was a high pre-eclampsia risk . . .' Lia explained.

'God, you poor thing. I'm complaining after less than a week!' Alison laughed.

She already had itchy feet. It was too hot to do anything much, and she felt she was just wasting her time sitting at home in front of a fan, when she could have planned all the issues up to Christmas in the refrigerated office. In the absence of anyone to talk to, she had found herself going over old conversations in her head. Ramona's hints about people trying to oust

59

her from her job, for instance, repeated in her brain like indigestion, until she almost picked up the phone to the editor to ask for assurances. At work, she had longed for the peace of their house, relishing the prospect of time to herself, time that was due to her, time that stretched ahead far longer than any holiday she had taken since university. Now that she was at home, she seemed unable to relax even for a second. She simply did not know what to do.

'Sounds like there's a lot of pressure in your job,' Lia said.

'Yes, but I suppose I kind of love that,' Alison confessed. 'I think I was born to be in an office, although if you'd asked me last week, I would have said I'd give it up like a shot!'

It was a relief to talk to someone about it. She found the words bubbling up inside her and tumbling out, and was surprised by how easily she could articulate what she had been feeling to someone she did not know. Perhaps it was just because she did not know her that she found it easier to talk, Alison thought. Or perhaps, she thought, distrusting herself, she was in fact revealing very little of any importance, lulling the girl into a false sense of security, in the hope that when she dared to ask her all the questions she wanted to, Lia would automatically respond without considering why she wanted to know. It was a technique she had used effectively when she was doing interviews. It always worked with women. Few could resist a trade of intimacies. With men, the information was sometimes more difficult to extract.

And yet, she found that when opportunities arose, she was deliberately avoiding asking Lia any of those questions. Lia volunteered that she had met her partner in Portugal just a year before, and instead of asking for details, Alison had steered the subject away with questions about her job and what it had been like to live in Portugal.

'Portugal's great,' Lia replied simply, 'better than Málaga, where I was before.'

'Have you lived abroad a lot?'

'Since I left home,' Lia said. Then, as if she had never worked out the figures before, she frowned and added, 'Must have been about ten years, in various places. I started off in Majorca. I was eighteen and it was my first foreign holiday. Me and my friend just decided to stay. We did a bit of waitressing, then she got fed up and went back to England. I moved on.'

'What did your parents think?' Alison asked, mentally calculating Lia's age. It was so difficult to judge when a woman was pregnant. Twenty-eight. Almost ten years younger than she was. A stab of jealousy.

'I've no idea,' Lia said.

Alison tried to imagine what it must feel like to be so convincingly separate from your parents. She had never really been able to shake herself free from her mother's embrace. It was the pay-off for the only child – to have the mother's undivided attention as a child, but to continue to have it as an adult. Whenever Margaret took her arm when they were out shopping, and squeezed it in that crushingly intimate best-friend kind of way, Alison felt herself shrinking away, not wanting a friend for a mother. Sometimes, as they strode down South Molton Street together, she would look at her mother in her smart coat and high heels, flipping through the racks on the designer floor, and wish that she would just knit, or watch television, or do what older people were supposed to do, rather than trip around boutiques, trying on the same clothes, and often looking as good in them as Alison did.

Alison sighed. Margaret would ring this evening, as she did every evening when Stephen was away, and almost every evening when he was not, demanding to know about her day. Alison would begin by replying cautiously, non-committally, but somehow, through persistence, or judicious use of the hurt silence, her mother would persuade her to part with her thoughts, and Alison would ring off, finally, feeling as if she had been bled. It was no use leaving the phone to ring, because her mother would immediately assume that she had gone into labour and drive up in a panic to check that she was not giving birth on the kitchen floor. She had tried switching on the answerphone, but the guilt she felt listening to her mother's messages always made her ring back and spend twice as long as she would have done if she had taken the call straightaway. If you picked up the phone when somebody called, you could always pretend that you were cooking, or entertaining, or in the bath, but if you rang back, it was assumed that you had all the time in the world to chat.

Suddenly, she was aware that she had been silent for a long time, lost in thought.

'I *always* know what my mother thinks,' she said, remembering the starting point, and Lia laughed.

The lemonade bottle was empty. Lia stood up and walked over to a rubbish bin. 'I'd better be getting back,' she said.

'Oh.' Alison had enjoyed Lia's company much more than she had expected to.

'It's just that Neil usually gets in around five,' Lia explained, sensing Alison's slight disappointment, 'and we eat early . . . Would you like to join us, since you're on your own?'

'No, no, thank you,' Alison said quickly, then, realizing that might sound rude, she added, 'but I'll give you a lift home, if you like.'

It was a small terraced cottage in one of the cheaper areas of the borough, but it stood out from its neighbours. All three windows had window boxes spilling over with red geraniums. A hanging basket, a great ball of pink flowers and trailing blue lobelia, almost obscured the small green-painted front door.

Alison began to slow down even before her passenger had told her where to stop.

'It would be lovely to meet up again, sometime,' Lia said, opening the car door.

'Yes—' Alison was about to suggest a day, when the roar of a motorbike speeding down the road behind them interrupted her. Instinctively, she glanced in the rearview mirror.

'Perfect timing!' Lia said, pulling herself out of the car. 'Are you sure you won't come in for tea with us?'

Alison leant over and slammed the passenger door shut.

'I'll call you,' she said, and started the car, just as the motorbike came to a halt behind her.

In her mirror, she saw Neil take off his helmet and watch as she drove away down the street. And she could see the image of their two faces surrounded by bright flowers long after they had become dots in the distance.

She wondered why he had not told his partner about her. She knew that he had not, because she was sure Lia would have mentioned it. Perhaps, Alison thought, hoping wildly, he had forgotten all about her, or just not recognized her. But she knew he had, because he had rung her the next day.

She had dialled 1471 after the silent call, suspecting who it was, and checking the caller's number against the list of names Judith had given them as they left the ante-natal class, which Stephen had pinned to the cork board in the kitchen.

It had made her sad picturing Neil staring at the receiver in his hand and wondering why he had called.

A telephone that rings but who's to answer?

Surely he could not still be angry, or hurt. Not after twenty years?

'Who was that?' Neil asked as they watched the car pull away.

'Her name's Alison,' Lia told him, putting her key in the front door. 'She was the woman who fainted at that class.'

'Oh . . .' He paused, not daring to say anything more.

'I ran into her in Waitrose. She was a bit cold at first, but we ended up having quite a nice chat.' Lia smiled, remembering how intimidated she had been by Alison's unfriendliness at the check-out.

Alison was older, taller, and had the kind of poise that came from a university education. She had a high-powered job, and a thick shiny bob of hair the colour of a newly opened conker. She was the sort of woman who wore subtle expensive perfume for a casual trip to Waitrose, rather than saving it, in its pretty glass bottle on the dressing table, for an evening occasion. They were very different. But very soon Lia had seen cracks just under the glamour of the surface grooming, and, from time to time, a vulnerability, that emerged as uncomfortable brittleness or self-deprecating wit. She had found herself warming to her, wondering if they had enough in common to become friends.

Living an itinerant life gave you the ability to form intense friendships very rapidly. Sometimes you made friends with people because you had gaps that they could fill, and sometimes it was the other way round. Abroad, there were always other drifting ex-pats whom you became close to for a month or two, before they, or you, moved on: the forlorn, middle-aged, gay tennis coach who talked you through the catalogue of beautiful boys who had exploited him; the bartender who looked but did not touch, because you were good for business sitting on one of his high stools and passing the time of day; and there were other girls who had run away from England, because of a bad marriage, or an abusive step-father, or just because they thought there must be more to life than the boredom of being a secretary in a no-hope job, with nothing to look forward to except a new suit each season from the Next catalogue.

Since she'd come back to London, Lia had found it more difficult to meet people. There were a few colleagues from Neil's school they occasionally bumped into when doing the week's shopping, and there were the lads at his sports club and their wives and girlfriends, but she hadn't met anyone she thought of as a soul-mate for herself.

'What about?' Neil asked, breaking into her thoughts.

There had been such a long silence since she spoke, Lia didn't understand what he was asking her. She looked at him perplexed,

'What did you chat about?' he pressed her.

'Oh, this and that, you know,' she replied, walking through to the kitchen. 'Will sausages be all right for you?'

Alison swerved to avoid a car that was pulling out of a parking space in front of her house. She had not seen it. It was lucky there was nothing coming in the opposite direction, or there would have been a crash. Shaking, she pulled into the drive and switched off the engine. She sat gripping the steering wheel for several minutes, desperate to silence the whirring snatches of guilt that seemed to be screaming at her from inside her skull. Breathing slowly, trying to calm herself, she began to examine possible scenarios in her head.

The first option was to go inside, pick up the phone and talk to him. Look, this is ridiculous. I'm sorry about breaking your heart, but it was twenty years ago, and can't we just be friends? What if he silently replaced the receiver again?

She could ring and ask to speak to Lia, and yet that did not feel right. You could only tell someone something like that if you knew them very well, or not at all. It was impossible now that she knew her a little.

Hey, I don't know if he's mentioned it, but I was your husband's first love. Don't be jealous, you were only eight years old at the time. No.

At the very least, she could tell Stephen. You know when I passed out at the ante-natal class? Well, it wasn't just the heat. No, I had a bit of a shock when my first boyfriend walked into the room, and he looked just the same as he did when I fell in love with him. But Stephen was in the States, and it wasn't the kind of thing you could say on the phone.

Perhaps Neil had examined all the possibilities too, and come to the conclusion she was beginning to reach, that it was better to do nothing at all. If she hadn't fainted, they would probably have said hello quite naturally and courteously, introduced their partners, and behaved like grown-up people. But since that had eluded them, it was probably best just to carry on as if they were strangers, which, after all, they were. Now. Twenty years was a long time. They knew nothing about each other.

Alison got out of the car and opened the boot. She carried the bags of shopping one by one into the kitchen and dumped them on the floor, too tired to start unpacking. She took a bottle of chilled mineral water from the fridge, wandered into the conservatory and lay down on the chaise longue, stretching out a languid arm to switch on the fan. Closing her eyes, she tried a relaxation exercise, focusing on the fan's monotonous hum, letting her arms feel heavy and drop by her side, visualizing her toes, her calves, her knees, her thighs.

She was almost asleep when, suddenly, as if startled by sudden noise, she opened her eyes and sat up.

On the top of the sideboard, neatly stacked in alphabetical order, were Stephen's CDs. Safely hidden in the cupboards below lurked her untidy piles of old LPs. With difficulty, she knelt on the floor, opened the doors and began to rummage through

66

heaps of records she had forgotten she owned, examining each cover, making a pile of those she would play: *Ziggy Stardust*, the Beatles *Red* and *Blue* albums, *Transformer*, which she had hidden when she first bought it because her father thought Lou Reed looked as if he was on drugs. She decided to spend the evening in delicious nostalgia, with not a thought for Stephen's good taste nor his look of polite bemusement as she bounced the needle from track to track, picking out her favourite tunes and playing them again and again.

Finally, she found the album she was looking for. Bryan Ferry posing on a sky-blue background, his name in plain red lettering. She turned it over. There was the title. *These Foolish Things*. She tugged the cover off, pausing only to look at the white paper sleeve, on which she had written her name, very seriously, in blue fountain pen. Then she put the record on the turntable and dropped the stylus on to the last track on side two.

A familiar crackle. The needle bobbed over the scratches, then Bryan Ferry's plaintive voice and a quiet crescendo of notes played on a distant piano.

> *'Oh will you never let me be?*
> *Oh will you never set me free?*
> *The ties that bound us are still around us,*
> *There's no escape that I can see . . .'*

It must have been 1974 that Neil Gardner arrived in the town. It was the year before the town was runner-up in Britain-in-Bloom. Alison pictured the sign on the road in, with the town's name and a phoney crest above the proud words 'Britain-in-Bloom Runner-up 1975'. Before the Gardners arrived, no-one in the town had even thought of entering the competition.

She had often wondered whether Neil's father had become a professional gardener because of his name, like one of those word jokes her own father had been so fond of:

Teacher to small boy: 'What you are going to do when you grow up, Gardner?'

Small boy can't think of anything.

Teacher: 'Gardner?'

Small boy: 'Yes, sir.'

Her father might even have said something like that to her, the day he came back from the council meeting and announced as they sat down for tea, 'We've finally got someone for the park. He's a northerner so he's grateful for the pay and the roof over his head.'

Her father's notion of northerners was only slightly more respectful than his notion of West Indians, whom he always referred to as 'coloureds', as if that were a politer way of describing their skin. Her father liked to think of himself as refined.

'You get a better class of person on this side of town,' he would say as he showed potential buyers properties in their road, 'I live here myself.'

It was only a couple of miles away from the tiny keeper's lodge beside the park gates where the Gardners were to live, but the social distance was much greater.

Alison had always assumed that the dilapidated, dark-brick, Hansel and Gretel house was a kind of folly, a bit like the Ruined Arch near the overgrown rose garden, or the Thatched Cottage, which was really nothing more than a rain shelter where couples went to snog, and, it was said, a man had exposed himself. She could not remember a time when the park lodge had been inhabited. When she was a child, she had frightened herself by imagining that a witch lived there, who malevolently spied on children playing in the sandpit from behind the black, curtain-less windows. Once, a small boy had drowned in the paddling pool, although it was less than a foot deep, and Alison had shivered, thinking of the witch, and wondering if she herself had somehow caused the child's death by conjuring up a wicked presence in a place that was meant to be happy.

After the Gardners moved in, the lodge looked almost less like a real house, and more like one made of gingerbread and sugar. Mrs Gardner put frilly gingham curtains up at the square little windows, and Mr Gardner repaired the low picket fence, painted the carved boarding round the eaves, and planted tubs of flowers either side of the front door. Sometimes, in the summer, when the windows were open, the delicious warm smell of baking cakes would float around the house, mingling with the scent of lavender from the herbaceous borders.

People in the town congratulated themselves on their choice of park-keeper, and were even prepared to reserve judgement on the less welcome addition of Mr Gardner's two tall, leather-jacketed sons.

Unlike their diminutive father and mother, who seemed to fit the lodge exactly, like the little man and woman who pop in and out of a children's weather house, Pete and Neil Gardner were both over six feet tall. Pete, the elder of the two, was coarser-looking and had greasy hair. Instead of finishing his education at the boys' school, he got a job at a garage, and soon moved out of the lodge into a caravan, with his newly pregnant girlfriend, who sliced bacon behind the counter in David Gross, and had bright blond hair with black roots. Neil, who was quieter, more intelligent, a fine all-round sportsman, and heart-breakingly handsome, entered the sixth form and instantly became an idol.

Suddenly the park was the most popular meeting place for teenagers in the town. There was an unseasonal demand for the tennis courts, and mothers with small children were surprised by how often their sulky older daughters volunteered to take their little brothers and sisters to the playground. If Neil was aware of the stir he was creating, it did not show. The park had been without a keeper for several months and needed a lot of tending. Each weekend, when he couldn't be glimpsed playing cricket at the town club,

Neil was to be seen helping his father tidying the flower-beds, turning the earth, putting in winter bulbs, pruning roses. On the odd occasion a giggling adolescent girl dared to speak to him, he replied quietly and laconically, leaning on his spade for a moment or two, sometimes honouring her with a direct look, before going back to his digging. The fact that he neither smiled, nor associated with the other boys of his age, made him seem like the coolest thing on earth. In the evenings, he sat pillion on his brother's Yamaha 250, with a gang of other bikers who rode side by side in a roar of throttle and exhaust, and struck terror into the hearts of the town's older residents.

Like a hundred other girls, Alison watched him from a distance, until her friend Sally's brother threw a party.

'You came, you saw, you conquered me.
When you did that to me, I somehow knew that this had to be . . .'

It was her first real party and she was hating every minute of it.

There were couples everywhere – pressed up against the fridge, sprawled on the sofa, entwined under the dining-room table, buried beneath the pile of jackets on the parents' double bed. Every time Alison opened a door, she heard a girl's shriek, or a boy shouting, 'Sod off!' She stood outside the door of the bathroom for ages until she realized that a couple had locked themselves in there too.

Her father had insisted he would pick her up at eleven. She had protested but had to agree when he threatened to come in and look for her if she kept him waiting in the car outside more than five minutes. Now she wished she had said ten.

She was wearing a summer dress in striped seersucker, and everyone else was in jeans, or loons, with tie-dyed T-shirts or cheesecloth shirts. She sat on the top step of the stairs, holding a plastic cup of warm cider, pretending she was queueing for the loo, pressing herself into the moulded wallpaper when anyone stepped past her. She felt as out of place as she did at her parents' Christmas cocktail dos, when she was expected to hand round peanuts until bedtime, then disappear upstairs, where she would sit on the landing in her dressing-gown, listening as the men's laughs got louder and the rich burnt-vanilla plumes of cigar smoke wafted into the hall. Here, the smell was cigarettes and patchouli oil, and the sound was Mott the Hoople, pounding out of the speakers Sally's older brother Simon had built in their garage.

'You waiting?'

At school, the girl who had asked the question wore her hair in one long plait down her back. She was a prefect.

'No,' Alison replied cautiously.

'Well, get out the bloody way, then.' The prefect tossed her loose golden hair over one shoulder.

Obediently, Alison stood up and walked downstairs. With relief, she noticed the telephone in the hall and picked up the receiver, but after dialling the first two numbers, she put it down again. She would have to shout to be heard over the record, and she couldn't bear her father's triumphant sneer. She looked at her watch again. Less than five minutes had passed since the last glance.

She decided to sit on the floor by the window in the living room. It was dark in there, and the music was so loud, no-one would even notice her. She could peep behind the curtain and see her father's car draw up. She didn't really trust him to stay sitting outside for five minutes before coming in to retrieve her.

'Have you seen Diana?'

Suddenly Neil Gardner was standing in front of her blocking the way into the living room.

She felt a blush shooting to the surface of her skin, as surely as blotting paper soaking up red ink.

If Woolworths had stocked posters of him alongside the ones of Robert Redford and David Bowie, they would have sold out in one Saturday morning. Half the fifth form had his initials engraved on their desk. Girls who had previously walked home now caught the bus, just for the chance of waiting next to him at the bus stop. It wasn't just his looks (James Dean with longer hair), it was his smile, his voice, his black leather jacket. Everything about him spelled total hunk. And now *he* was speaking to *her*! On Monday, I'll be able to say I spoke to him, she thought.

She knew that Diana was the prefect with long fair hair. He had been spotted kissing her in the entrance to Hepworths. It was only fitting that the best-looking girl in the town should be going out with the best-looking bloke. Even the dozens of love-sick fifth-formers had to admit that there was a certain inevitable symmetry to the arrangement, whilst also wishing Diana would get run over by a bus.

'I think I saw her leaving.'

Afterwards, Alison couldn't imagine what had made her tell such a lie. Was the look that crossed his face anger, relief or indifference? She didn't even know whether he had heard her. The rush of blood to her head seemed to have filled her ears, muffling everything. Suddenly she realized he was actually looking at her, not through her, or past her, but at her, trying to engage her eyes as they darted everywhere at all but at his. Then, unbelievably, he said. 'Wanna dance?'

No, I'm wearing a dress my mother made me, I'm a friend of Simon's sister, and I'm only in the fifth form. If you knew these things you wouldn't even dream of speaking to me, she thought. Not trusting herself to speak, she nodded and followed him into the living room.

He swayed about in front of her, and she attempted to mimic his actions, knowing she was in time to the music, but feeling as if she had one joint too many. As her sleeve brushed his arm accidentally, she inched back.

'*All the young dudes!*' wailed Mott the Hoople.

The song was really too slow for dancing, it was more for striking poses. Her face felt so red, she was sure she was glowing like neon. She risked a quick glance round the room. Everyone else was too busy snogging to notice.

Then Sally's brother put on the new Bryan Ferry album he had just bought. The first track was a cover of the Stones song 'Sympathy for the Devil'. It was a faster beat. She began to dance, becoming more confident, almost enjoying it. Neil smiled at her. Unable to believe her luck, she kept dancing, track after track, until the tempo changed. Sally's brother grabbed his girlfriend and pressed his body into hers. Alison stopped dancing abruptly and began to sidle towards the door. But Neil caught her hand, and pulled her back.

'Where are you going?' she thought she heard him say, then he raised his eyebrows, just slightly, as if tacitly asking her permission to draw her closer. She froze, terrified that she was reading the signals wrongly. He pulled her gently towards him, resting his hands at the back of her waist.

'*I know that this was bound to be . . .*'

Bryan Ferry sang, and she thought, as she finally dared to rest her head on Neil's shoulder, I shall remember this moment for ever.

The song was fading away. Alison got up, walked over to the turntable and put the track on again.

> '*And still those little things remain*
> *That bring me happiness or pain . . .*'

Alison closed her eyes and swayed with the music, remembering exactly how it had been the first time she had heard their song. She could almost feel Neil's hands still on her waist, the heat of his skin through his black T-shirt, the exotic smell of his aftershave. Brut, she later discovered. For a long time after, she had not been able to pass a man in the street who was wearing it, without having an almost Proustian memory of Neil. The fragrance must have been discontinued in the 1980s, she thought, making way for Lynx or Denim or some other aftershave with lurid adverts at Christmas, or perhaps she had just stopped noticing.

> *'Oh, how the ghost of you clings!*
> *These foolish things*
> *Remind me of you.'*

For Alison, the memory triggers were the smell of engine oil when you walked past a garage, leather jackets, the taste of lager and lime, pubs with horse-brasses round the bar, John Player Special cigarettes, French kissing.

The song faded away again.

She wondered whether Neil remembered the same things, or different things, or nothing at all. Men didn't remember like women did.

Alison put the track on again, smiling this time, remembering how they used to sit on the low wall outside the youth club kissing, just kissing, and how it had felt to be sixteen, and wildly, deliriously, in love.

Chapter 2

AUGUST

Lia wanted to call the baby Natalia or Anouska, and she couldn't understand why there was a problem with that. They had not discussed names before. It was something she felt superstitious about, thinking it would not be right to choose a name until the baby was alive in the real world. Then, she had thought, the baby would look like a name. And she did. With her damp dark hair and her pinched, delicate face, her tiny daughter looked like a miniature ballet dancer.

Neil said that fancy names led to teasing at school. He wanted something simple and plain.

'How about Anna?' he offered as if he thought that sounded something like Anouska.

For the first time in their relationship, Lia felt anger flash through her.

'No,' she said firmly, 'anyway, you're thinking of boys. Girls don't get teased for having pretty names. I never was.'

'But you were always pretty, weren't you?' Neil argued. 'We've got to think about if she's ugly or fat, then she'd really suffer if she was called Anouska.'

The way he said the name annoyed her, his voice going up on the second syllable, making it sound impossibly pretentious. She looked at the baby in her arms. Couldn't he see that she was beautiful? Lia cradled her protectively.

'She looks like a little old woman, doesn't she?' Neil said, touching the baby's cheek. The baby started, as if she had heard and understood.

'I'm going to feed her now,' Lia said, turning away from him with the baby resting in the crook of her arm. She wondered whether he had secretly wanted a boy. He would have known what to say to a boy.

Neil watched her bare a breast that was round and taut with milk, murmuring quietly, coaxing the tiny creature to suck. He saw the concentration on her face, her total engagement with the baby, the gentle way she talked to her constantly, as if it were the most natural thing in the world. It made him feel utterly superfluous.

He did not seem to know what to say to the baby. It embarrassed him to say anything, especially when there was a nurse in the room too. He realized with shock that he felt no connection whatsoever with the little wrapped bundle of flesh and bones and vest and nappy. When he looked at her, he simply did not recognize her as he had expected to after all this time imagining the baby and talking to it through the smooth curve of Lia's belly.

It was stifling on the ward, the hot stale air smelling sweetly of talc and women's blood and baby shit. He decided to go outside.

Sitting on a sloping bank of brown grass outside the maternity unit, he watched the toing and froing of visitors and hospital staff. From time to time, the unnerving siren of an ambulance would rise up in the distance, becoming more and more urgent as it drew nearer, then cutting off suddenly, as the vehicle turned into the hospital, its blue light twirling manically as it raced up the ramp to Accident and Emergency.

It was the smell of hospitals that he hated most, the cloying stench of human decay, that could never quite be disguised by the sour odour of disinfectant. The smell even managed to seep into the maternity unit, which was supposed to be a place of innocence and life.

The birth, that he had thought would be wondrous, had been darkly terrifying. Seeing his lover's body racked by the force of the contractions, he had wanted to run from the room, but had known that he could not. It was his duty to stay with her and watch her suffer as he would never suffer. And then, suddenly, it was over. One minute she was screaming for help, on the very edge of life, the next, she was perfectly calm, gazing at the gore-streaked infant, with a beauteous smile on her face. But the fear had stayed with him, and he could not seem to shake it off.

He lay back on the slope, staring at the cloudless blue sky, trying to feel what he thought he ought to feel. But he couldn't seem to feel anything except tired and thirsty, as if he had been crying for a long time. He sat up, and took a deep breath, then forced himself to go back inside. He told himself that everything would be fine as soon as he could take Lia and the baby back home.

In a private room at the far end of the ward, a party was going on.

'I've decided that you can be his godfather, Robert,' Ginger said, loudly humming the music from the film, 'as long as you promise faithfully to have nothing to do with his moral upbringing.' She took another gulp of champagne from a paper cone she had stolen from the stack beside the water-dispenser.

'Honestly, Ginger,' Pic interrupted, 'are you sure you should be drinking?'

'I'm not ill, I've just had a baby,' Ginger retorted.

'Yes, but doesn't the alcohol go into your milk?'

'God, I never thought of that. Do you suppose it does? Oh hell, he'll have to get used to it soon enough,' said Ginger holding out her cone for more.

'And why do I receive this great honour?' asked Robert, sarcastically.

'Because you're the only friend with the presence of mind to buy me lots of champagne and not horrible blue flowers.' Ginger waved at the baskets of carnations and irises that were wilting in the heat on the windowsill. 'Oh Pic, I'm sorry,' she added, seeing her sister's hurt face, 'I know that you didn't choose the ones you sent, and the outfit you bought is the sweetest thing I ever saw, really.'

Pic smiled with relief. 'Don't be silly,' she said, looking at her watch. 'Listen, I must go, but I'll be here tomorrow at ten. They've given me the whole day off as sorority leave! Bye, little Guy,' she said to the sleeping baby, kissing her finger and touching it against his cheek.

'I suppose I ought to be off, too,' Robert said, picking up his newspaper.

'Oh no, you can't go,' Ginger wailed. 'Pretend you're the father. They're allowed to stay until eight.'

'But would anyone believe me?' Robert responded in his most camp voice, glancing at the checked shorts suit he was wearing which simply would not have been worn by a heterosexual man. 'Talking of the father,' he added mischievously, 'did he ever call you?'

'As a matter of fact he did, a couple of weeks ago,' Ginger replied.

'And yet I remember you saying quite clearly that men never called after one-night stands,' Robert joked.

'Sssh, not in front of the child! Well, it was almost nine months later, which is way beyond the statute of limitations on such things . . .'

'What are you going to tell him?' Robert said, looking at the baby with a kind of nervous curiosity.

It was one of the few times, Ginger thought, that Robert had been lost as to the correct etiquette for the situation. Should he pick the baby up, kiss him, touch him, or just ignore him? It was rather sweet to see him so undecided.

'Tell who?' Ginger asked.

'My godson.'

'About Charlie? I've no idea. I'm sure I'll think of something,' Ginger said, holding her cone out for more champagne. 'Goodness me, you're getting horribly responsible-sounding all of a sudden. You can't be his godfather if you're going to be a boring old fart, you know.'

Although she masked it with her light tone, she was annoyed. Robert was absolutely the last person she had expected to introduce a serious note into the celebrations.

'What did he say, then?' Robert asked.

'Who?' she asked again.

'The father.'

'I do wish you'd stop calling him that,' Ginger said, huffily. 'He just wanted some information.'

'What?'

'Oh, I've forgotten. Anyway, what on earth does it matter?' she asked impatiently.

She hadn't forgotten, she remembered every word of the conversation they had had when she returned Charlie's call. It had begun in confusion. When the receptionist had asked her name she had said, 'Virginia Prospect.'

A computer-generated 'Greensleeves' played in her ear for a few seconds.

'Could you tell me your name again?' the receptionist came back to her.

'Tell him it's Ginger,' said Ginger, resigned to the fact that her attempts at gravitas rarely succeeded.

'Ginger!' Suddenly he was on the line, and she found all the hours she had spent preparing for the conversation with Pic, and all the rehearsals she had done in front of the mirror had been a waste of time. She had no idea what to say.

'Yes?' she finally replied, because somebody had to fill the silence.

Immediately, she realized she should just have said 'Charlie!' in the same tone as he had, but the opportunity had now passed.

'So how are you after all this time?' Charlie asked.

Was this his way of saying that he knew?

'Fine,' she said, circumspectly.

'Work?' he asked.

So he *was* calling about work. She began to relax. 'Work's OK. What can I do for you?' she asked, crisply.

'I was wondering whether you've got any lunches free in the next week or so?'

Lunch. It must be a very big favour he was after. Charlie was the sort of person who booked lunches months in advance. Ginger had a sudden attack of dignity. How dare he imagine he could bribe some precious, no doubt confidential, information out of her for the price of a seared tuna steak?

'I'm sorry, I don't,' she replied, amazed to hear herself speaking the words.

'Oh come on!' Charlie was used to getting his own way. 'Can't you cancel something?'

Ginger, whose diary was completely blank for her last week in the office, was beginning to enjoy herself. 'I'm sorry, no. I'm very busy for the next week, then I'm on leave for a while.' She remained enigmatic.

'Oh. Are you going away?'

'No. Anyway, what did you want to ask me?'

'I'd rather not say on the phone,' Charlie said, 'it might be difficult for you.'

'Oh, for heaven's sake,' she replied angrily, 'I'll tell you if it's difficult, and you'll have to smarm your way round someone else for the information.'

'What information?' Charlie asked, and then, as her words sank in, 'Listen, forget it. Bye!'

Ginger had put down her phone feeling rather pleased with herself. It wasn't exactly the conversation she had planned with Pic, but it had achieved the same result. She didn't think Charlie Prince would bother her again. The next time he decided to screw a secretary after a party, lavishing her with compliments and alcohol, maybe he would think twice before slipping out of bed while she was still sleeping, using one of her best lipsticks to draw a heart on the living-room mirror, and never even calling to see whether she had recovered from her hangover.

'Oh come on, tell me,' Robert was wheedling, 'what did he say?'

'No,' Ginger replied sulkily.

'I just wondered . . .' When Robert had his claws on a potential piece of gossip, he wouldn't give up.

'Well, wonder somewhere else,' she snapped, 'this is a maternity ward, remember? You're not meant to upset me.'

'It's just that I had lunch with him a while back, and I had the distinct impression that he was trying to extract information from me about you.' Robert casually threw the bait into the conversation.

'You didn't tell him about—?' Ginger asked, nodding at the perspex pod in which her child was sleeping, and feeling slightly panicky.

'Of course not,' said Robert hotly. 'In any case, he seemed rather more interested in your professional performance than your personal one, magnificent though I'm sure the latter is.'

'Oh, do shut up!' Ginger said, finding herself suddenly unable to bear his teasing.

'Temper, temper. You are touchy today.'

'I'm allowed to be. I've just had a bloody baby, haven't I?' Ginger shouted, just as the midwife walked into the room to monitor the baby's breathing.

Alison was propped up in bed with silent tears rolling down her cheeks.

Her son had eventually been delivered by emergency Caesarian section, after she had spent hours in agony and terror, hooked up to machines and screens, listening to every irregular electronic bleep, certain that her baby would never be born alive. As she emerged from the anaesthetic, Stephen pointed to the perspex bowl in which a baby was sleeping, and her first thought had been to wonder whether it was really hers. Stephen recounted every step of the operation, in such detail that she wondered if he had been taking notes, but she still could not quite believe that the well-formed little boy had emerged from inside her.

Her mother visited, and told her that she was proud of her, which was peculiar, because Alison felt she had done absolutely nothing except make a terrible fuss. The only positive feeling she was able to experience was a kind of vague pleasure that everyone else was so delighted with the baby, and, when she did not seem to be able to produce milk, she had become very quickly distressed. From time to time a midwife would come into her room and position the baby at her breast. When Alison looked down at it, rooting around, she felt totally detached, until it clamped its mouth on her nipple and its soft gums were like a knife slicing the tender flesh. They told her that her hormones were probably upset by the medical intervention and that the milk would come once she settled down. Just relax, the midwives said, as her face contorted in pain each time the increasingly thirsty baby latched on.

Whenever Stephen visited, he insisted she try again. The baby was becoming desperate and her nipples were blistered. On the third morning, when the baby would not stop screaming, and she felt she could not stand the pain and noise any longer, she requested formula. Stephen arrived to find her sitting up in bed with the grateful creature slurping contently from a bottle. Despite his best efforts to contain himself, Stephen went white with fury. The room became airless with tension.

'What were the midwives thinking of?' he finally said, with the contempt of a consultant.

'It was me,' Alison replied, 'I asked. The baby was starving. And now, he's not.'

Stephen's mouth pursed with disapproval. 'All the research indicates that breastfeeding is far better . . .' He spoke as if she were one of his students who had fallen behind on an assignment.

'Yes, but he was screaming,' she faltered, feeling a complete failure.

She had seen Neil walking past several times, and wondered whether he would look in her direction, but he never had. She knew that Lia was booked into the same hospital, but not until a couple of weeks after her. Their baby must have been premature, she thought. Fate seemed determined to bring them together, and in the alien pale green world of the hospital, it didn't seem to matter any more. This time, when he passed, she called out.

He stood in the doorway as if reluctant to cross the threshold of her private room. They looked at each other for a long time. His face was tense, almost troubled, and she saw that he registered her unhappiness and her recent tears.

Finally, he said, 'Hello, Ally,' in a soft, serious voice, that bore no trace of recrimination, and she sighed with relief.

Nobody had ever called her Ally, except him.

'Hello, Neil.'

It felt good to say his name at last, as if a spell had been broken.

She pointed at the baby sleeping in the bassinet beside the bed.

Neil took one cautious step into the room and leaned forward to get a better look.

'It's a boy,' she told him.

'He's big,' Neil replied, 'he looks like a proper baby. Ours is only five and a half pounds. How long have you been in here?'

'This is my fourth day. I had a Caesarian, and the wound's not healing very well,' she explained, gratified to see the wince of sympathetic pain that crossed his face. 'How about Lia?'

'Last night. Four-hour labour. I think we were lucky. They say we can go tomorrow, although she's very small.'

'You had a little girl! Congratulations!'

'Yes,' he said, then remembering his manners, 'and to you.'

She had to make a huge effort not to start crying again.

'Well, I'd better get back,' he said, awkwardly.

'Yes,' she said, and as he turned away, she added, hastily, 'I haven't told him and you haven't told her, have you?'

'About us? I couldn't see the point,' he replied.

'Quite,' said Alison.

'Quite,' he imitated her middle-class accent, and for the first time in twenty years, they smiled at each other.

That evening, there was a sunset, a glorious flaming sky, that quickly faded to grey leaving just a sliver of ember on the horizon, which burned bright for a few seconds and was gone. The air was still hot, but it was bearable now that the noise of the city had followed the sun away, leaving only the plaintive cooing of pigeons on some nearby rooftop, and the faraway rumble of traffic.

'I hear you met Neil at last?'

Alison woke from her doze. Lia was standing in the doorway to her room wearing a long white short-sleeved cotton robe. For a second, Alison couldn't work out whether she had actually spoken to her or whether she had just dreamt the words. She had not seen Lia since the afternoon they spent by the river. Although it was only a couple of weeks before, it seemed to have happened in a different life. A lifetime ago, literally, Alison thought, glancing at the baby sleeping beside the bed.

'Hello,' she said, blinking to accustom her eyes to the gloom, then pulling herself up on the sloping rack of the hospital bed, she added, 'come in!'

Lia pushed a trolley into the room.

'You don't mind if I bring Anouska with me? She's sleeping but I just can't leave her. I even take her into the loo! I'm so frightened someone will steal her.'

'No, of course, bring her in. What a lovely name!' Alison switched on the lamp above her head.

'I'm so pleased that you said that,' Lia said, perching on the end of Alison's bed. 'We haven't actually agreed on it yet, but I think that if I say it often enough, Neil will come round . . . especially if other people say that they like it.'

'We haven't chosen a name yet,' Alison said, glancing at her baby, who appeared to be sleeping contentedly.

'Neil said it was a boy.' Lia peered over the bed to have a good look. 'Oh, he's lovely! So big!' she exclaimed.

'Yes.'

'And you had a Caesarian. Poor you! That's why I came down to see if you needed anything. I thought it might be difficult for you to walk up and down the ward.'

'Yes,' Alison smiled wanly, 'thank you,' she added.

In the pale light, Lia looked very beautiful with her long rippling hair, flawless skin, and delicate features. Her brown eyes were huge from lost sleep. They shone like the eyes of a startled deer. Her body was fine and slight. Only a few hours after giving birth, it was difficult to believe that she had ever been pregnant.

'So, your little girl arrived a bit early,' Alison said, struggling to make conversation.

'Yes, but she was just over five and a half pounds, so they didn't make her go to Special Care, thank heaven! How much does he weigh?'

'Nine pounds,' Alison sighed.

'Wow! How's the feeding going?' Lia asked.

Lia had been a mother a shorter time than she had, and yet she seemed to know what you were supposed to say and how you were supposed to be. Perhaps that was the advantage of being on the ward rather than stuck in a private room. Alison had had no contact with anyone except the midwives, Stephen and her mother. It was like being in an isolation cell. She felt that something strange had happened to her, not just to her body, but to her brain, which made her unable to do the things she normally did, like smile or make a joke to mask her unhappiness. Suddenly, she started crying, not quietly, nor prettily, but in great gasping gulps.

Lia's response was instant. She slid up the bed and put her arms around her, allowing Alison to weep on to her thin shoulder, and murmuring soothing words into her hair.

'It's just, it's just,' Alison sniffed, 'I don't seem to have any milk, you see, and Stephen's so cross with me . . .'

'It's OK,' Lia said, patting her back gently.

'But it's not . . . if the baby's ill, it'll be my fault . . .'

'Of course he won't be ill!'

She sounded so sure, Alison thought. How could she be so sure?

'Are you breastfeeding yours?' Alison sniffed again, blew her nose into a tissue and allowed Lia to wipe her eyes.

'Yes, I am, but I seem to be the only one who is, on the ward.'

'Really?' Alison brightened instantly, taking consolation from the simple fact that she was not alone. Her breathing became quieter. 'How are you managing. Does it keep hurting?'

'No. It's all about positioning. Judith told us about it at class. You must have missed that bit. You should get her to come and see you. I'm sure she wouldn't mind . . .'

'Wouldn't she? I'll give her a ring then . . .' Alison said, inwardly squirming at the idea of subjecting herself to the bossy ministrations of the ante-natal teacher. Suddenly she felt embarrassed by her outburst and Lia seemed to sense her discomfort and she slid back down the bed. They both sat for a few moments in silence.

'Is this a private party, or can anyone join in?' a loud voice at the door called out. 'I'm Ginger,' she explained, in case Alison had forgotten her, 'we were all at that ghastly ante-natal class together, until you did what we all wanted to – fainted with the boredom of it.'

Alison smiled and beckoned her in.

Ginger pushed another trolley into the room. It contained a fluffy rabbit at one end, a baby in the middle bit and, at the other end, a bottle of champagne.

'I'm making up for lost time, while there are trained staff around to make sure that this little person doesn't come to any harm,' said Ginger, pulling the wire off the top of the bottle. The cork shot across the room and ricocheted off a window into a twig basket of forget-me-nots.

Lia's hand shot out instantly to protect her baby's face.

'Nice flowers,' Ginger remarked, giving the room a once-over, 'mine are all disgusting dyed carnations. All blue, so you must have had a boy.'

Then she turned her attention to Lia.

'How on earth can you wear that beautiful white robe? I'm bleeding like a stuck pig!'

She stood at the foot of the bed, poured a paper

cone of champagne and handed it to Alison, then offered one to Lia, who took it but did not drink. Then, cautiously, and without invitation, she lowered herself on to the other side of Alison's bed.

'This is what is called sitting down *gingerly*,' she said. 'They don't tell you anything, do they? You think when you've actually had the baby, your stomach will go back in, but I still look nine months' pregnant. I weighed myself, and there's no difference. I'm beginning to wonder whether I actually had a baby, or whether this is all a pethidine hallucination . . . that's until I try to sit down . . .'

Alison laughed. She was beginning to see why people said that having children was a great leveller. The three of them had very little in common, and yet at that moment they had everything that mattered in common. It was strangely reassuring to know that someone else had blithely assumed that once the baby was born, her body would immediately return to its normal shape.

The champagne bubbles prickled in her mouth, taking away the taste of hospitals. She took another sip, feeling the alcohol seep through her capillaries like warm anaesthetic. It made her want a cigarette, or lots more alcohol, or both. She held out her paper cone for Ginger to refill, feeling peculiarly at ease. It was nice to have the girls sitting at the end of her bed. It reminded her of *What Katy Did*, which had been her favourite book when she was about ten. Reading it in her bedroom at home, she had longed for sisters who would sit on her bed when she was ill, chatting and bringing her things they had made. But she wasn't ill, she reminded herself now. She had just had a baby.

'Who'd have thought that something that starts so pleasantly could end in such pain . . .' The champagne was making Ginger garrulous and she regaled them, loudly, with the story of her decision to become a single mother.

She had become pregnant by mistake – a Durex

broke, but she hadn't been too bothered because her periods were incredibly irregular and she had never even considered being fertile, only realizing three months later when she kept piling on weight. She told them how she had booked herself in for an abortion but changed her mind as she sat reading *Hello!* in the waiting room of the clinic. There was a spread of photos of an ex-model's latest offspring. Even the Agnès B. clothes and the pastel paradise that was its bedroom could not disguise the fact that this was an incredibly ugly baby. For the first time, Ginger had found herself imagining how her own baby would look. She thought about the father's curly black hair and wicked smile. He had been the undoubted star of their year at Oxford, and she had fancied him from the minute he walked into their first lecture but she had always assumed he was out of her league. She imagined how beautiful their child would be.

'So,' she concluded, 'I just put down the magazine and walked out of the clinic. How many people can honestly say that *Hello!* magazine fundamentally changed the course of their life?' she asked them, with bright, laughing eyes. 'Anyway, I was on the shelf.'

'How could you be on the shelf at your age?' Lia said, laughing with her.

'Oh, I was, believe me,' Ginger said, 'I may only be twenty-seven, but I've had enough men to know that they never like me for very long. They think I'm fun for a night or two and then, when I start showing signs of being human, they take me back under the trades-descriptions act.' She put on a deep voice and held up her hands: 'Hey, I thought you were a good time girl, and now you're asking me whether I'm going to be free next week. I don't need this kind of pressure . . .'

Alison laughed loudly. She was enjoying the performance enormously, but she also noted the quest for approval behind the entertainment, and she guessed that Ginger spent a good deal of her life defending herself. It didn't surprise her when Ginger went on to describe the heated row she had had with her father when she had announced her pregnancy.

'So, does he know you've had the baby?' Lia interrupted.

'Daddy? Yes, but he's recovering from open-heart surgery himself, so he can't come to the hospital. That's his excuse, anyway . . .'

'I meant the baby's father,' Lia said.

'No way!' Ginger looked at her as if she were mad. 'Doesn't even know I got pregnant. I didn't want him trying to change my mind.'

'Perhaps he wouldn't have done,' Lia suggested.

Alison began to switch off from the conversation. It was getting just a little too uncomfortably intimate. She watched the two women at the end of her bed in their animated discussion. They were both so much younger than she was, and they had the moral certainty of people in their twenties. It was only as you grew older that you seemed to realize that nothing was clear cut.

'He would. He's got a girlfriend,' Ginger argued. 'Anyway, what man would really want to know about an accidental baby?'

'But what man wouldn't want to know that he was going to be a father?' Lia asked.

'Practically every man I know, except Robert, who would be amazed, because he's gay . . . you must know some very nice men,' Ginger said to Lia. 'Well, of course, your man is to die for.'

A proud smile flashed across Lia's face.

'Have you met Lia's dish of a man?'

The question hung in the air for a few seconds until Alison realized it was directed at her. 'Yes,' she said, feeling herself flushing and trying to sound natural. 'Yes.'

'He's gorgeous, isn't he?' Ginger persisted.

'Yes, I suppose he is,' Alison said, looking out of the window.

It was completely dark now. All she could see was her own reflection staring back at her. The fact that Ginger so obviously fancied Neil made things easier to deal with. If Neil had the same effect on everyone, then it wasn't anything particular and special between the two of them.

'Your bloke is pretty tasty too, if I remember,' Ginger went on shamelessly. 'Where did you find him?'

Alison laughed. She had never heard Stephen described as a bloke before. It was so very at odds with his bookishness and his unworldly looks.

'At a New Year's Eve party . . . I literally saw him across a crowded room,' Alison began, suddenly eager to join in. 'I suppose I was on the shelf too and just when I thought that there were no attractive men left in London, there he was . . . It was a complete fluke, actually, the reason it was a crowded room was that there were two parties going on. The club had double-booked, and they didn't bother to tell anyone, which was good, really, because being ever-so polite and English about it, nobody realized until quite late on and by the time they found out, everyone was enjoying themselves so much, nobody wanted to make a fuss.'

'So, he wasn't at the party you were at?' Ginger said.

'Well, he was and he wasn't, if you see what I mean. His party were mainly doctors, and the one I was at were mainly journalists, and you know how everyone becomes so cliquey . . .?' She looked up at her companions. Ginger was nodding emphatically, Lia was just listening. 'We all spent the evening thinking what interesting people our hosts must be to know such a diverse crowd of people . . .'

Alison had noticed him as soon as he walked into the gathering. He was very tall and he was wearing a long black coat and a fedora hat. When he took the hat off and bent to kiss an acquaintance, Alison had been startled to see that he was completely bald. Oddly, it made his violet eyes seem larger and more piercing, increasing his attractiveness, rather than diminishing it. He had caught her looking at him and smiled. They had spent most of the rest of the evening talking, and when they had swapped telephone numbers, standing outside the club in the freezing cold, and she went to get into her cab, she had not known how to say goodbye.

'I like your hat,' she remarked in the awkward silence.

'Thank you. It does keep my head warm. Someone gave it to me for Christmas. She thought it would be less tickly on my scalp than the bobble hat,' he told her, quite matter-of-factly.

And as the car drew away, Alison had found herself wondering about the someone who had given him the hat, and feeling quite extraordinarily jealous of her.

'So he's a doctor?' Ginger asked.

'He's a cardiac surgeon,' Alison replied, 'a professor, actually.'

'Really, where?' Ginger asked.

Alison named one of London's big teaching hospitals.

'But that's where Daddy was . . .' Ginger's voice suddenly trailed off.

'What's your father's name? I'll ask Stephen if he saw him. He doesn't do private work, but I'm sure he'll have known about him.'

'No, I'm sure he didn't . . .' Suddenly Ginger, who, moments before, had been quite happy to describe in great and unnecessary detail the state of her torn perineum, looked awkward and lost for words.

Alison and Lia exchanged looks, then both raised their eyebrows at Ginger, soliciting her response.

'No, well, if you must know, my father is Sir James Prospect, but please don't hold it against me,' she pleaded, looking genuinely worried.

'For heaven's sake, you don't choose your parents,' Alison said, reassuringly, 'I certainly wouldn't have chosen mine.'

'Nor would I,' Lia agreed.

Ginger breathed a loud sigh of relief, at which point her baby awoke and started crying.

'Poor little boy,' she said, picking up her screaming child, 'you wouldn't have chosen me either, would you?' Then she looked up at the two other women and said, as if the thought had just occurred to her, 'Perhaps I've named him Guy because, subconsciously, I want him to blow up Parliament?'

They both laughed, and then the other two babies woke up crying and suddenly the room, which had been a quiet sanctuary of champagne and girls' talk, reverberated with the noise of inconsolable infants.

A midwife came in and shooed Lia and Ginger to bed. It was only ten o'clock but that was a whole hour past lights-out in this particular dormitory. She handed Alison's baby to her and screwed a teat on to a ready made bottle of formula, shaking the liquid on to her wrist to test the temperature.

The baby drank voraciously. Alison rewrapped him and returned him to the perspex pod. Then she remembered that she was supposed to make him burp. She leaned over, feeling the strain on her stitches, picked him up again and placed him against her shoulder, gently patting his back and wishing that she could feel some connection with the child, as Lia and Ginger so obviously did with theirs. She tried talking gently to him, but the words that seemed to tumble so naturally from the others' lips sounded false and silly when she said them.

She lay awake, trying to shut out the sound of babies crying on the ward, and thinking of those first few weeks with Stephen. In the beginning, the powerful attraction she felt for him was not simply the pure physical high his presence seemed to give her, but the sheer interest she found in his work. It was stimulating to talk to someone with such a different background, who spoke to her in a language she hardly recognized as her own. She had also relished the perplexed way he greeted the insanely shallow preoccupations of her world. Why were shallots so crucially preferable to onions, he wanted to know, and could people really tell whether their olive oil was cold-pressed? For him, lunch was a cheese sandwich eaten at lightning speed as he marched from operating theatre to ward, if he was lucky. For her, it was a way of life.

They had taken it in turns to educate each other on their first few dates. She taught him about food and media gossip, he took her to concerts and talked to her afterwards about the music, using words precisely, explaining the technicalities of structure and harmony. She had noticed that he never used the verb 'to feel'. In her world, people felt. In his, they reasoned. But when they went to bed with each other for the first time, in his characterless flat in the Barbican, she found that he was an extraordinarily gifted lover, who immediately sensed what she liked and needed, and brought her to climaxes on a different plane to anything she had achieved before. This was truly grown-up sex, she had thought, lying back and watching his fingers playing her body like an instrument.

She had not been fair to Stephen in the last few months, she realized. It was she, not he, who had changed. His cool and rational approach to things was the reason she had fallen in love with him. If he had not been as supportive as she would have liked over the whole business of conception, it was because to him it was just a medical procedure that either worked, or didn't. If she had not told him about the baggage of unresolved fears she carried around with her, that was because she thought he would not understand what she was talking about, but it did not make it his fault. It was the same with the breast-feeding. He was good at separating statistics from emotions. In his job, he had to be.

Tomorrow, she promised herself, it will be different. We love each other. We have made a beautiful, healthy baby together. This is what we wanted. This is what it has all been about. We will be happy.

The next morning when Stephen popped in early on his way to work, she was trying to feed the baby. He rewarded her with a delighted smile, and she felt she knew what it must be like to be one of his favoured students.

'Can you bring me some nice food when you come back?' she asked, putting the baby down and picking up a triangle of hospital toast with disdain. 'I don't think this is helping.'

'Of course, what would you like?'

'Parma ham, unsalted butter and fresh French bread,' she told him.

'Fine. I'll try not to be too late,' he said, kissing first her forehead, then the baby's.

While she remained in hospital, he saw no reason to take leave, reasoning that it would be better for them to spend the time together when she came out, when she would need him. She saw the logic of that, but as he left the room, she found herself wishing that he would just stay and sit beside the bed and chat to her about nothing in particular. Time passed so slowly in hospital. She picked up a book from the top of her locker and tried to read it, but could not concentrate. Her brain felt like cotton wool. She wished she had asked him to bring her some magazines too. She toyed with the idea of paging him, but resisted, imagining his face if she were to disturb him with such a flippant request in the middle of something important.

'How's your head this morning? Mine feels like a band is playing inside it.' Ginger was standing at the door dressed to go home. Beside her stood a woman who looked so exactly like her it was almost disturbing. She was carrying Guy strapped into a brand-new car seat.

'This is my sister Pic,' Ginger said, stepping into the room, 'and this,' she told Pic, 'is my friend Alison and her son. Did you tell me his name?'

'We haven't decided yet ... perhaps Benedict,' Alison replied, 'but we keep changing our minds ... Don't you like it?' she added, seeing the look of undisguised horror that flitted across Ginger's face.

'Sounds a bit too much like a saint, or a monk, or something, but I suppose Ben's all right,' Ginger replied.

'Honestly, Ginger,' her sister scolded, 'it's a lovely name,' she assured Alison.

Alison, who preferred Ginger's frankness, explained, 'Well, I like the name Ben ... but then there's the question of Benjamin, or Benedict, and Stephen tells me that Benjamin is traditionally the youngest son. I hope that doesn't mean he wants another one ...' she added with a short, dry laugh.

'That, at least, is one thing I don't have to worry about,' Ginger said, a frown puckering her impish face.

Ginger was so blasé and confident, it was difficult to envisage her worrying about anything at all, Alison thought, and yet she must be incredibly frightened. She was finding it difficult enough to imagine how she would cope when she left hospital, even with Stephen there. She began to see Ginger in a new light. The previous evening she had thought her funny and precocious, she now appeared rather brave.

'Let me know when you're home,' Ginger said, casually approaching the bed and landing an unexpected kiss on Alison's cheek.

'I will,' Alison said, surprised by the show of affection, and rather moved. 'Good luck!' she called, as the twins disappeared.

96

Minutes later, Lia came in with her tiny infant wrapped in a white cellular blanket. 'Neil's waiting in the car,' she explained, 'so I can't be long, but do ring me when you're home, won't you . . . and best of luck with the feeding . . .'

'Yes,' was all Alison could say, because all the kindness was suddenly making her want to cry again.

The air was still stiflingly warm and the thin patterned curtains did little to keep out the sun. She wanted to lie on her side, but her stitches were too painful to move. She could feel sweat trickling down the back of her neck and her nightie sticking to her back. She lay gazing at her son, expecting at any moment a sudden rush of love for him, but feeling only the ache of loneliness.

Mrs Gardner had pale blue eyes, just like her son, but in her face they looked old, watery and critical. Lia wished that she would go away and leave them alone.

When she first arrived, Lia had found it companionable to have another womanly presence in the house. Although she had never before felt comfortable with Neil's mother, sensing she was suspicious of the whirlwind romance with her younger son, now that they had the profound experience of birth in common, Lia hoped they could be friends. Mrs Gardner had also been very helpful with the housework. It was all very well Neil insisting that he would do everything, but it meant that the washing had piled up, the lino on the kitchen floor was sticky with dropped bits of hurriedly eaten food, and the rubbish bin brimming and smelly. Lia hadn't been able to think of a way of tackling the problem without offending him, sensing that he was already feeling slightly excluded from the bonding process with the baby. Within an hour of Mrs Gardner's arrival, the kitchen was cleaner than it had been for months and white babygros and tiny vests were flapping about on the line like a string of celebratory bunting.

Lia had even enjoyed listening to Mrs Gardner's tales of what Neil had got up to when he was a little boy. She envied those stories that families owned, like albums of memories to be brought out, told again, and relived whenever they were together.

It had all been fine, until Mrs Gardner had begun to feel at home and started to offer advice, and now, as Mrs Gardner peered into the carrycot where Anouska lay sleeping on her back, Lia was certain she was about to grant yet another pearl of wisdom.

'We always used to put them on their front,' Mrs Gardner said, for the third time that morning.

'The advice is now to put them on their backs . . . look, it's even in this book they give you,' Lia replied, hoping that if she saw the advice in print it would settle the matter.

Mrs Gardner looked at the book with contempt. 'We never had any books,' she said, as if that was something to be proud of.

'Well, anyway, it's what all the doctors say,' Lia said, patiently.

'She'll choke on her vomit, if she's sick,' Mrs Gardner warned ominously, almost as if she were willing the baby to do just that, in order to prove her point.

Lia decided to ignore her. The silence yawned between them for several minutes, then Anouska began to cry. Lia was almost relieved to hear her. She picked her out of the carrycot and put her to her breast.

'She'll get into bad habits if you keep feeding her every time she cries,' Neil's mother opined.

Lia bit back her anger, stroking the top of her baby's head to calm herself down.

'Once every four hours. That's what we did, and if she cries, let her. It's a good lesson to learn. You can't always get what you want when you cry.' Mrs Gardner smiled, congratulating herself on her good sense.

Oh shut up you old cow, Lia wanted to shout, but said nothing.

'It's a pity your own mother can't see you now,' Mrs Gardner remarked.

Lia looked up, surprised. She had always had a nagging suspicion that Mrs Gardner held her responsible for her childhood, as if it had been somehow her fault that she had been brought up in a home. Lia stared at her watery eyes, trying to see whether she had meant to hurt her, or whether she was just being even more insensitive than usual. Either way, she thought, she was going to have to go.

'I'm not planning to rest in bed any longer. The midwife says I'm fine, so tomorrow I'm going to get up and your mother can go home,' Lia announced to Neil that night, in a whisper, conscious that Mrs Gardner was in the next-door room, and no doubt straining to hear every word.

'But she's really enjoying being here,' Neil protested out loud.

'Maybe she is, but I don't want her here any more,' Lia hissed.

'Just tomorrow, so you won't be on your own when I'm at the match ...'

She had forgotten about his regular Sunday cricket match.

'Oh, we couldn't let anything like the birth of a baby interfere with that,' she said, only half joking, and then added, more kindly, 'I'll be fine, honestly.'

'What's wrong, love?' Neil asked her, finally sensing her agitation.

'It's just ... oh, I've had it with her advice, so-called advice. She seems to think she knows better than the health visitor and all the midwives put together.'

'Well, she has had two children,' he defended his mother.

'Neil, for God's sake, things have changed in the last forty years,' Lia said angrily, her voice rising, 'and

99

anyway, I'm Anouska's mother. I want to get to know her by myself.'

'But she's only trying to help—'

'No!' Lia began to shout, then stopped abruptly. 'No,' she repeated, more softly.

It wasn't very close, but it was the nearest they had ever come to a row. She saw that confrontation was not the way to deal with it. There was no point in setting up in competition with his mother. He loved her and it was right that he should. But she knew she couldn't stand having Mrs Gardner in the house another day, and she also thought, but she wasn't sure why, that on this occasion it was important that her will prevailed. In desperation, Lia burst into tears. He had never seen her cry before, and she knew he would not be able to bear it.

'I just want us to be a little family on our own. I just don't want anyone interfering,' she sobbed.

'OK, love, it's OK,' Neil said, bewildered, holding her, then patting her back, 'I'll get Dad or Pete to come and collect her first thing tomorrow . . . OK?'

Sometimes, Lia thought, you could get what you wanted when you cried.

In a tree-lined street just a couple of miles away, a solitary rectangle of light shone pale lemon in the darkness while inside the newly decorated nursery, Alison tried to feed her baby.

'Come on, let's try again,' she said, trying to get him to latch on as Judith had shown her, but he was used to a bottle now, and didn't want to work for his food.

Tears trickled down Alison's face. The pain of his sporadic sucking and the hard discomfort of the milk coming down were almost bearable, but not his bleating rejection. She was so tired, she felt her head slump forward, then jerk back out of sleep.

'Oh, don't, please don't,' she pleaded as the baby began to cry again, 'you must try, please try . . . Oh for

God's sake, please . . .' she said, returning him to his rocking crib, with extra care, shocked by her sudden desire to throw him hard against the blue-and-white-striped nursery wall with its frieze of marching geese. She pushed the crib backwards and forwards with her foot, hoping the rocking movement would soothe him, but the noise did not subside. Nobody told you how awful it was to hear your baby crying, how it sliced right through your skin and flesh and bone, leaving your nerves raw and exposed. Nobody told you how cold it could feel, even on the hottest night, at three in the morning, when you had had no sleep for days.

'Alison, Alison, love . . .' Stephen stood bleary-eyed at the nursery door.

He walked across the room and began to stroke her hunched shoulders, willing her to stop crying, then he picked up the baby and went downstairs. She was too tired to follow him.

A few minutes later he returned with the baby and a bottle of formula. He sat on the floor and put the teat into the baby's mouth.

'I'll do the night feeds from now on,' he said, 'I'm used to less sleep.'

'But . . . formula . . .' She was too exhausted to form a sentence.

'Oh, plenty of babies grow up perfectly OK with the stuff,' he said as nonchalantly as he could, and although her body flooded with relief, his concession made her feel more inadequate than ever.

Ginger was looking at her baby, wondering how many other women in London were awake watching over their children. Probably hundreds, she estimated, and the thought of them made her feel less alone. It was her first night by herself with Guy, and she kept getting up to check that he was breathing.

Pic had stayed the first night, then their mother had come up from the country but after spending one night on the camp bed she had remarked, 'I don't know what Hermione was thinking of when she left this place to you.'

Her grandmother and her mother were so different, Ginger sometimes forgot that they were mother and daughter too.

'She wanted me to have a roof over my head without having to kow-tow to Daddy,' Ginger retorted, remembering fondly Hermione's open contempt for her son-in-law.

'Well, it's entirely unsuitable for a baby, so I've decided to hire you a maternity nurse,' her mother replied.

What she meant, Ginger realized, was that the flat was entirely unsuitable for her to stay in, and that she had no idea what to do with a baby, since she had always employed staff to look after her own twins. But Ginger didn't point this out, because she thought any help would be more useful than her mother's aggrieved and mystified expression each time the baby cried.

Jeannie was plump and middle-aged, and, with her uniform and stern expression, looked like a character from *Prisoner Cell Block H*, but she had turned out to be really kind, encouraging Ginger through the first tiring days, and cooking her nice, wholesome meals like shepherd's pie and milk puddings. She taught Ginger all the rudiments of caring for a new-born with efficiency and good humour, which took the panic out of scary things like bathing him for the first time. Her no-nonsense approach had given Ginger confidence, so that when she had waved her goodbye that morning at the end of their week together, Ginger hadn't even thought about whether or not she would cope on her own.

'I think we've done OK, considering,' she said to Guy, evaluating their day. She folded a blanket diagonally, just as Jeannie had taught her, wrapped him, and placed him back in the Moses basket, smiling at the incongruity of the pale wicker basket with its soft pastel blue lining perched on top of a dark mahogany chest of drawers. She got up again, picked up the basket and put it on the bed beside her. Jeannie had warned that if you allowed a baby into your bed you'd never get him out, but it felt nice having him right there next to her. She snuggled down alongside the basket and turned out the light.

'Now, let's see if we can get at least three hours,' she whispered in the darkness to her sleeping son.

As they walked through the Gardens, Alison could not suppress the recurring feeling that she and Stephen, who were both so tall they had to bend to push the pram, looked as if they were just playing at Mummies and Daddies. She wished now that she had not chosen the red pram, which she had liked in the shop because it was different, but had settled for a navy one, like all the others, which would not have stood out and looked so very new.

'Do you feel silly?' she asked Stephen, linking her arm through his.

'Silly?' he repeated.

'Well, odd, you know, different . . . It just feels so different, pushing a pram and everything . . .'

'Would you like me to go back and get the sling?' he asked.

'No, no, of course not,' she said, disappointed that he had not understood. A sling would be worse. She had seen couples walking along with their babies bound to them like Red Indians with a papoose. They looked ridiculous.

As they passed a group of families with babies in prams picnicking together on the lawns outside the Orangery, she observed that Stephen smiled joyfully, and said, 'Good afternoon,' whereas she deliberately avoided making eye contact. It made her think of the scene in *Gone with the Wind* where Rhett Butler is determined to introduce his daughter to polite

103

society, while Scarlett skulks along beside him, embarrassed by his proud-parent act. It was as if she had not yet made the switch of self-image from woman to mother, as if her identity was lagging behind the reality of the situation.

'I know, let's have tea at the Maids of Honour,' Stephen suggested, as they approached the Main Gate. He was in an expansive mood, clearly enjoying his freedom from work, and his new status as a father.

'Yes, all right, let's,' she agreed, not feeling particularly hungry, but hoping that any minute she would be swept along by his enthusiasm.

There was a cricket match on Kew Green. They paused for a few moments by the low fence, admiring the near-perfect English scene, the cricketers clad in white against the backdrop of the church and the row of tall trees, the gentle patter of spectators' applause. A bowler ran up. The batsman at the crease hooked a soaring six. The sound of leather on willow seemed to hang for a moment in the air as they watched the ball fly high in the air and drop out of sight.

'Good shot!' Stephen cried. He took his hands off the handle of the pram and clapped.

Beside him, Alison was trembling, unbalanced by the force of the *déjà vu*. True *déjà vu*, she thought, because she *had* seen it before, that determined movement of shoulders and bat. She had seen it a thousand times. One simple swing at a cricket ball and a whole summer of memories dazzled her vision.

Then, too, the grass had been brown, scorched by weeks of relentless sun. Neil was regularly one of the town's opening batsmen, and they said if he kept on playing like this, he would be selected for the county before he was twenty. She watched every match, loyally, and when he came off the pitch, his tan and the cricket whites making his eyes seem brighter and bluer than ever, they would climb on to his bike and ride out to the Blue Lagoon, the romantic name they had given the flooded gravel pit a couple of miles from the town. It was dangerous to swim there. The surface of the water was warm, but underneath it was deep and cold and treacherous. Everyone knew that strong swimmers had drowned there, but that didn't stop them stripping off, diving into the water, desperate for relief from the heat.

In the evenings, a whole gang of bikers would ride out to country pubs and drink cider, and one night, during his parents' annual fortnight in Scarborough, Neil's brother Pete had unlocked the park gate and let everyone in to lie on their backs in the shallow children's paddling pool, gazing at the stars.

Neil sent another four flying over the dry brown stubble.

'That batsman's not bad at all,' Stephen remarked.

'Did you play cricket when you were at school?' Alison asked, looking at her husband, trying to distract herself.

'A little. I was a half-way decent spin bowler once upon a time,' Stephen replied.

How strange it was to know nothing of how the man beside her had spent that dreamy summer, and yet to recall every minute of it with the man in the distance.

'Let's go home,' she said, turning away from the match.

'No tea?' Stephen asked.

'Yes, of course, if you like,' she said, hurriedly, not wanting him to think she had forgotten.

'Tired?' he asked, turning the pram in the direction of home with one hand, and putting his other arm around her.

'Yes,' she said, weakly, 'very tired.'

Chapter 3

SEPTEMBER

On Neil's first morning back at school after the summer break, Lia watched him unlock his motorbike and put on his helmet and gloves. He turned round and waved at them. She held up Anouska's tiny arm and made it wave back. He sat on the bike, checked the road, and was gone. She heard the roar of the engine long after it had disappeared as she stood at the front door, distractedly picking dead flowers from the hanging basket. There was a slight chill in the air. The hot summer was finally coming to an end.

Lia went back inside and put the baby into the carrycot on the kitchen table. Then she made herself a cup of coffee and sat down, turning the radio on, then off, a couple of times, undecided. She told herself she was feeling peculiar because it was the first time she had been alone since the baby was born. Not alone, but the only adult, in sole charge of Anouska. But she knew it wasn't that. The image of Neil's face as he had looked up and ridden off remained in her mind. He had been smiling, not at her, but at the road ahead. He had been happy, she realized, to get away from them.

Mrs Gardner's abrupt departure had left a feeling in the house, a scent of mild recrimination that remained long after Pete had arrived to take her back home. Lia felt that her relationship with Neil had not quite regained its equilibrium since. He was very quiet, and if she asked him if something was wrong, he answered no, but his eyes said yes, and she should know, without having to be told. She had read about new fathers feeling rejected, especially if the mother was breastfeeding, but she would never have believed that Neil would conform to that stereotype. On a couple of occasions, she had inadvertently criticized the way he handled Anouska, as he tried to play with her like an older baby, not a new-born. There wasn't time to be polite about it. She saw her child distressed, flailing in his strong, large hands, and she shouted at him to stop. He had handed the baby back to her and marched silently out of the room.

Lia herself had been surprised by the way that her love for Anouska had immediately overridden any thought for his feelings. It was almost as if she had a kind of primitive instinct to protect her child. Her tiny daughter needed her totally, and beside her, Neil sometimes seemed like a great big thing who could look after himself. She tried to be sensitive to his needs, but when he continued to sulk, she became impatient too, feeling she had quite enough to do caring for the baby without the additional worry of tiptoeing around his sensibilities.

Lia drank the last of her coffee. The day stretched ahead of her and she had nothing to do and no-one to worry about except her tiny sleeping baby. She felt her shoulders relax as she exhaled a long pent-up sigh and then, catching sight of the list of telephone numbers stuck to the fridge door, she picked up the phone.

From the stone steps of the doorway, Ginger watched the last nanny she was interviewing that morning walk away down the hill. She was stout and she wore sensible shoes and a belted beige raincoat. She did not look back.

'I thought she seemed very good,' her mother said, as Ginger returned to the living room.

'Did you?' Ginger replied, wandering through the large ragged, rectangular hole in the wall into the incongruously modern kitchen area.

The flat hadn't changed much since Hermione had lived there, except that Ginger had got a builder to knock down the wall dividing the huge living room from the tiny, old-fashioned kitchen and scullery that adjoined it. Her mother had given her the money to have a modern kitchen installed before the baby was born, but the walls around the units and sink remained unpainted and untiled. The knocked-down wall between the two rooms was supported by an RSJ, but otherwise unfinished. Ginger switched on the kettle. 'I'm afraid I couldn't stand her,' she said.

'Well, what are you looking for?' her mother asked, tapping the toe of her alligator shoes on the dusty Persian carpet that covered Ginger's living-room floor, the disorder of the flat clearly offending her fastidiousness.

'I suppose someone I feel a kind of empathy with,' Ginger said, peering over the edge of the Moses basket that was resting on one of the kitchen work surfaces. Guy was sleeping. His implausible mop of hair stood up in a spiky style it would have taken hours for a punk rocker to achieve.

'Oh really, darling,' said her mother, continuing the post-mortem on the nanny in a weary voice, 'you're not going to find a friend, you know. In my experience, nannies are usually down-to-earth girls, not high-fliers, otherwise they wouldn't be nannies, you see.'

'Is bringing up a child such an undemanding skill then?' Ginger asked her provocatively, stirring sugar into her instant coffee, then adding spitefully, 'I don't suppose you'd know.'

'You know exactly what I mean, Ginger.' Her

mother sighed in exasperation, declining the invitation to row.

'Anyway,' said Ginger, picking up the Moses basket and sitting down in an armchair opposite her mother,' I don't want a friend. I just want someone I kind of click with. Jeannie was fine for a week, but I don't want someone middle-aged around me all the time.'

'Well, I thought it would be better for you to have someone with experience, someone reliable,' said her mother, giving herself away.

'So you particularly asked the agency for older ones?' Ginger said, outraged. 'Oh, I get it, what you're really trying to do is employ someone to spy on me and report back to you, just like you did with all our nannies when we were children.'

'Don't be ridiculous, Virginia, you loved your nannies.'

'I hated them without exception,' Ginger told her. 'They probably told you I loved them, but you never bothered to ask me, which rather proves my point.'

'Well, I don't think this is the time to rake over the past, do you, darling? We're looking to the future now, and if I'm paying for this nanny, then it is only reasonable that I have a say in what kind of person I employ to look after my grandson.'

'You sound exactly like Daddy,' Ginger said, staring straight at her mother, who looked away, slightly sheepishly, unable to meet her daughter's challenge.

'Oh, I see. It was Daddy's idea, was it?' Ginger suddenly understood. 'I wonder why it took me so long to twig. Sleep deprivation must be affecting my brain. Anyway, you can tell Daddy to stuff his plan. I've just decided that I won't have a nanny at all, and there is absolutely nothing you can do about it . . .'

'Ginger,' her mother said, 'you are so ungrateful. Daddy's been under such stress—'

'Because of me? Go on, say it. Look, if Daddy didn't have such mean and disgusting views about single mothers, then he wouldn't have been caused any embarrassment, would he? Maybe he should change the way he thinks, if the idea of his own daughter going against his principles is so very difficult for him.'

'I've come all this way to help you but you're obviously not in a mood to be reasonable,' her mother said, picking up her handbag and tying her silk scarf in a knot. 'I'll be at the flat one more night, but then I'm going home. There, now you decide what you want to do.'

'I just have,' Ginger said sulkily, slumping back in the chair.

'I'll see myself out,' her mother said, giving her daughter an exasperated look before leaving the room.

'I'll see myself out,' Ginger mimed behind her back, and then the phone rang.

'How are you getting on?' Lia said.

'Don't ask,' Ginger replied.

'Well, listen, Anouska and I are about to go for a walk in Kew Gardens and we wondered whether you'd like to meet up . . .?'

The Year to Remember hour on the radio was 1974.

'Alvin Stardust coming up,' shouted the DJ, 'w-i-t-h' – his rising voice gave the word at least four syllables – '"My Coo Ca Choo" . . .!'

The first jamming notes of bass guitar bounced around the kitchen where Alison was washing up the night bottles. She swayed her hips from side to side with the music, staring through the window into the garden. Her mother was pegging out washing. Alison dropped the bottle brush back into the water and twirled, enjoying the pounding beat, wondering why it was that every tune from the seventies seemed to carry such a specific memory for her.

The Monday afternoon following the party where she had met Neil, she and Sally were walking down the hill after school listening to Sally's trannie. Alison remembered how deliciously wicked they had felt

110

turning the volume up high, almost daring any of the prefects to confiscate it, and bopping together side by side on the path when this record came on. They had finished their 'O' levels and they felt as if they owned the world. Then they returned to their highly serious discussion about what clothes they would wear on their first day as sixth-formers when uniform was no longer required.

How weird, Alison thought, putting her hands back into the hot, sudsy water, that nowadays she had to write down ideas for features immediately or risk forgetting them, but she could remember exactly what she and Sally had been talking about that day, more than twenty years ago.

Sally had spotted Neil before she had. He was standing at the bottom of the hill.

'Hey up!' she said, nudging Alison hard, 'Your dancing partner is waiting for you.'

'Don't be silly,' Alison replied automatically. She had spent the whole of Sunday assuring herself that there was no chance that he fancied her, deciding, finally, that he had just taken pity on her because she looked so stupid in her dress. He couldn't be waiting for *her*.

It was the way his face lit up when he picked her out from the sea of other girls in their green shirtwaister dresses that gave Alison the confidence to stop instead of just shuffling past in Sally's shadow.

'Hello, Ally,' he said.

Ally? He had said Ally, not Sally, hadn't he? She couldn't trust her hearing.

He did not have to wear a blazer because he was already in the sixth form. He looked more gorgeous than ever in his clean white school shirt, the knot of his school tie casually loosened.

'Hi!' Alison replied, her voice croaking with anxiety.

'Where are you going?' he asked them.

'To get the bus,' Alison said.

'We're going for a coffee in the Wimpy,' Sally lied simultaneously.

'I'll come to the bus stop with you then,' he told Alison, ignoring Sally's implied invitation.

He walked along beside them, saying nothing.

'Good party, wasn't it?' Sally chattered on, 'I was just saying to Alison, it was a pity she had to leave so early, wasn't it?'

Alison wished she would go, and yet she didn't know what she would do if left on her own with him.

'Yes, it was,' he said neutrally, and smiled at Alison.

'Oh well' – Sally finally conceded defeat – 'I think I'll go to Boots. I really need some new eye-shadow,' she said.

'Friend of yours?' Neil asked Alison, as they watched Sally saunter across the road, her head held high, looking as sophisticated as it was possible to look in green gingham.

'Well, yes, she's my best friend,' Alison replied honestly, which, for some reason, made him laugh.

Then, almost immediately, her bus drew up beside them, and she thought it would look really stupid to let it go. Anyway, she had already run out of things to say to him and the four-pence fare in her palm was wet with sweat. The line of schoolgirls in front of them started clambering in, some of them whispering to each other and sneaking quick glances back at him. He walked along slowly next to Alison as the queue moved up.

'Would you like to see *The Great Gatsby*? It's on at the Odeon,' he finally said.

'Yes,' she stated, still not sure whether it was an invitation or just a question.

'Friday night?' he said, as she stepped on to the bus. 'It starts at eight. I'll meet you outside. OK?'

'OK,' she agreed.

Then he was gone. He just turned and walked away, and she wished that Sally had still been with her to confirm that she had heard him correctly and not dreamt it all.

'What on earth has happened to you?' her mother asked as Alison tried to get upstairs without giving her a chance to notice her tell-tale sparkling eyes.

Her mother had a way of extracting information. It was never stated, but Margaret's support was crucial if Alison wanted to go out in the evenings, and she always expected something in return. Her mother was bored. Life with her father was an emotional black hole, except for the occasional violent row. She relied for succour on her daughter's experiences. Margaret looked so young, and chatted like a girl, not like anyone else's mother, and she had encouraged Alison from the earliest age to think of her as a confidante. Whenever Alison attempted to be non-committal, her mother sniffed a secret like a truffle hound, and nudged and worried until she dug it out.

With a sigh, Alison deposited her satchel at the bottom of the stairs and went into the kitchen to share a pot of tea and a packet of Jaffa cakes with Margaret. When she told her, as calmly as she could, that a boy had asked her out to the flicks, her mother was immediately as excited as she was, and so, carried away by her enthusiasm, Alison told her who it was. Her mother frowned and remarked that he was perhaps a little old. Daddy would worry. How did she meet him? So Alison revealed that she had danced with him at the party, that, unbelievably, he had been waiting for her at the bottom of the hill, and within minutes her mother had heard the whole amazing story.

Alison watched her mother dead-heading a couple of roses on her way back in with the washing basket. She still found it very difficult to resist being drawn into intimate chats with her, which she invariably regretted afterwards.

'This morning's Year to Remember is 1974,' the DJ

113

broke into her thoughts, 'and now The Drifters and "Kissin' in the Back Row of the Movies" . . .'

Their first date had been a huge anticlimax. It was raining, and the waves she had spent ages struggling to coax in her long hair with her mother's Carmen rollers had fallen flat before she even set eyes on him. *The Great Gatsby* was a good film. She knew because she saw every moment of it. When the lights came up, they walked out, discussing the beautiful 1920s costumes and the Charleston music, wondering whether it would start a fashion. Alison remarked that she would love to wear one of those flapper dresses, and he had commented that it would suit her. It was the nearest they had got to intimacy.

He saw her to the bus home, but did not attempt to kiss her, or even put his arm around her shoulders. She spent the ride home wondering what she must have said or done wrong. Other boys who had taken her to the cinema could hardly wait for the lights to go down before an inevitable battle to get a hand up her jumper. Neil obviously wasn't interested any more. It had finally dawned on him that he was way out of her league. She stared at the bus window watching the droplets of rain join up with each other like globules of mercury on the bench in the Physics lab, speeding in wet trails down the glass.

Her mother was waiting for her, drinking Cinzano Bianco alone at the kitchen table. She offered Alison a glass, eager to hear every detail of the evening, but Alison told her she was tired, and went straight up to bed.

But the next Monday, Neil had been waiting at the bottom of the hill again.

'You must give me your telephone number,' he said, 'we can't go on meeting like this!'

It wasn't that funny, but Alison had laughed for an inordinately long time, feeling the tension and nerves bubble out of her body, and then he had asked her to go with him to the end-of-term disco at the Boys' school.

'And now ...' said the DJ on the radio, quietly, slowing the tempo and attempting to make his voice extra-husky, 'let's chill out. Why don't you all stop what you're doing and take a deep breath of "The Air that I Breathe" by the Hollies ...' He paused for the first chords, then spoke softly over the intro, 'I bet some of you can remember having a last dance to this one back in 1974, The Year to Remember ...'

Alison emptied the bowl of washing-up water down the sink and flicked on the kettle, then she sat down at the table, pretending to read the paper, but listening, wallowing in the corniness of the tune.

It was hot and dark at the sixth-form disco. The faint smell of boys' feet and school dinners mingled with the feminine, artificial citrus scents of Aquacitra bubble bath and Silvikrin lemon-'n'-lime shampoo. A revolving disc in front of coloured lights threw patterns of slithering oil onto the faces of past headmasters. Neil and Alison sipped non-alcoholic shandy from paper cups, agreeing that it was too embarrassing to dance in front of the teachers, even though a couple of them had donned jeans in a vain attempt to appear trendy and relaxed.

'Let's get some air.'

When Neil took her hand, she felt the envy of every girl in the room like a cold breeze on her body. Outside, he took a quick look back to check that nobody was following them, and then pulled her arm. They began to run fast across the playing field, into the dark shadows beyond the fall of the light, keeping their bodies as low as possible so that no-one would witness their escape. The coloured lights from the hall flooded through the high arched windows half-way across the field. From their hiding place beneath the row of poplar trees at the far end of the grounds, they could see dark figures coming out of the hall to share surreptitious cigarettes. From time to time, a teacher on duty would emerge. They could tell from the orange arc of a burning cigarette butt quickly discarded, and the shadows shifting along the wall, as the smokers moved away from the evidence. The warm evening air carried snatches of music across the field. The grass smelt of earth.

He lay down looking straight up at the sky, pointing out the constellations. She lay back next to him, an arm's length away, pretending to see the patterns of stars he was naming. Her heart was racing so fast she was sure he could hear it, or see it pumping under her cream cheesecloth smock. She was sure he was about to kiss her.

The heart-tugging chorus of 'The Air that I Breathe' drifted across the cricket pitch.

'Do you like this song?' Neil asked, breaking off from his dissertation on the stars and rolling on to one side. He propped himself up on his elbow, his head resting on his palm, and looked down at her.

'. . . Er, I don't know, really,' she replied, nervously, not knowing what he thought, not quite daring to commit herself.

'It's a bit soppy, isn't it?' he said plucking a long piece of grass from beside her face and tickling it under her chin.

'Yes, I suppose it is,' Alison agreed, giggling a little.

'But then, I'm feeling a bit soppy about you,' he said, his face dipping closer.

And before she had a chance to say anything, his lips were on hers.

Oh God, that kiss! His mouth slightly open, pressed hard and dry against hers, his tongue flicking between her teeth. She didn't know how to breathe, but she felt she would rather suffocate than stop.

In her 1990s designer kitchen in Kew, Alison inwardly scolded herself for behaving exactly like the sentimental housewife the DJ on the radio imagined as his listener, whom he was now patronizing over the last wailing echoes of the song.

'. . . Well, ladies, I'm sure that brought back some memories . . . You're listening to 1974, The Year to Remember, back in a moment with Sparks, their one-hit wonder, "This Town Ain't Big Enough for the Both of Us" . . .'

The Hollies faded into an advert for mobile phones.

'Do we have to have this awful rubbish on, darling?' Margaret asked, carrying a basket of dry washing in through the conservatory.

'No, of course not,' Alison replied, and turned the dial off with a click.

'I'll just fold this lot away,' Margaret said. 'I think we could get at least another load out today. It's lovely weather for drying.'

Her mother was really helping, Alison was slightly shocked to realize. Instead of roaming round the kitchen as she usually did, running manicured finger-tips along surfaces, complaining about Alison's clean-ing lady, she now rolled up her sleeves and mucked in, cooking, loading the steam-sterilizer, even don-ning a pair of yellow rubber gloves to transfer the baby's washing from its pail of Napisan to the washing machine. It was as if the presence of a child had turned her back into the model fifties housewife she had been when Alison was born.

The dynamic of her relationship with Margaret had shifted slightly since Ben's birth. The ambivalence was still there but had taken on surprising new forms. Alison could not have anticipated the transparent joy that the baby would bring to her mother, or the delight that that in turn would give back to her. It was a bit like having chosen the perfect gift – a scarf she knew Margaret really liked because she wore it all the time – but about a million times better. At the same time, she was determined not to allow Margaret a vicarious second motherhood with Benedict. Her baby was not going to be another aspect of her life for Margaret to requisition.

Before she had the baby, Alison had been sure that her mother would keep as quiet as possible about being a grandmother, but she had been surprised to find that she was positively eager to walk the pram up and down the street boasting about her new status to anyone who would listen. Perhaps the neighbours responded with feigned disbelief that she was old enough to have a grandson. Alison didn't know, but whenever she ventured out with the pram herself, she was amazed by how many people recognized Benedict, and knew his name.

'Why don't you take him out for a walk today?' Margaret suggested, looking into the pram that was parked in the kitchen. 'You're looking so peaky, I'm sure it would do you good.'

Alison didn't really feel like going out, but there was no point in refusing. Once her mother had decided something, it was easier to get on with it. Advancing age had made her want to dominate more than ever. If Alison didn't go out now, as advised, the fact that she had not would be brought up every hour for the rest of the day. It would become the reason why Benedict wasn't hungry, or was crying, or wouldn't sleep, so she obediently went to get her jacket while Margaret tucked a blanket round her grandson.

It was a beautiful September day. The sun was still warm but there was a new crispness in the air that seemed to make the sky a clearer, brighter blue than it had been since spring. The leaves on some of the large trees were already fading to yellow after the long, dry summer. As she strolled past the Temperate House towards the lake, Alison wondered whether there had been a sudden baby boom, or whether there had always been so many women pushing prams, and she just hadn't noticed them before. Everyone she passed

118

seemed to have a baby or toddler in tow. She still did not feel part of this community of mothers, but she was more used to pushing the pram now. It gave her a convenient prop to remind her that she was not playing truant from work on such a lovely morning. As she neared the lake, she spotted two women sitting on the grass, with prams parked a couple of yards away in the shade of a big oak tree. Then suddenly one of them started waving at her, beckoning her over to where they were sitting. Alison manoeuvred the pram off the tarmac path and pushed it onto the grass.

'I was just saying that you feel like bloody Mary Poppins pushing these things around, don't you?' said Ginger, with her uncanny knack of pinpointing what it was that they all thought.

Alison parked Ben's pram beside theirs and dropped onto her knees next to Lia.

'And why does everything have a ridiculous name?' Ginger went on, 'it's a complete nightmare even *asking* for what you want in Mothercare, and that's before you get to opening your wallet. When we were little we had a pushchair, but now it's called a buggy, and you have to buy something called a Cozy toes to go with it, if you can bear to say the word, and then there's babygros . . .'

'Yes, well, that's just short for baby-grows-out-of-it-so-quickly-you-can't-believe-you-just-spent-fifteen quid-on-two,' said Alison, 'Ben was too big for the new-born size on day one, and we couldn't take them back because my mother had insisted I wash them before going into hospital.'

'Don't even start me on mothers,' said Ginger. 'I find it so frightening that I *am* one now. Just think' – she waved in the direction of the prams – 'in twenty years' time, these three will probably be moaning about us. God!'

'Mine's been surprisingly OK, actually,' Alison said, with a sudden, unexpected feeling of loyalty to Margaret, 'apart from knowing best about everything.

I don't know what I'd do without her. There's so much to do, isn't there? And Stephen sometimes works so late, I don't think I'd like to be on my own with Ben just yet . . .'

'You've got your mother staying with you?' Ginger said, amazed. 'I drove mine out after one night, I'm afraid, but then she does kind of live in another world. I've just resisted her attempt to impose a nanny Stormführer on me. What about you?' she asked Lia.

'Neil's mother came up for a few days,' Lia said, lifting her eyebrows. 'Nightmare! Like you said' – she nodded at Alison – 'she knows best about everything.'

'She always was a bit of a busybody— I expect . . . What about your own mother?' Alison asked, quickly covering her slip.

'I don't really have one. Well, maybe I do, out there somewhere.' Lia plucked grass from the lawn considering whether or not to reveal her past to the other women. People in England were never really happy until they knew where you came from, but sometimes, when they found out, they weren't happy either. There was a kind of closeness developing between the three of them that made it seem as if they had known each other far longer than they really had. She decided to take the risk.

'My mother couldn't cope, so I grew up in a home. I was one of the last Barnardo's girls,' Lia said finally, looking up at her companions. They reacted exactly as she expected they would.

'You poor thing,' Alison said, her face going through a familiar series of expressions: surprise, horror, pity, embarrassment that she had asked.

'What was it like?' Ginger asked, sitting forward with eager curiosity.

'It wasn't that bad,' Lia said, after a moment's thought. 'When I hear other people going on about their parents sometimes I think I'm lucky not to have all that . . . Sorry, I didn't mean that to sound rude,' she added as Ginger shifted position uncomfortably.

120

'Some of the time, it was fun. We lived in a cottage, with a house-mother. We went to school. They tried to make it as much like a normal family as they could. It was a bit lonely sometimes – that sounds funny because you were always surrounded by people – but I expect everyone gets a bit lonely when they're growing up.'

Alison thought of childhood holidays on the beach in Cornwall, sitting in the shelter of her parents' windbreak, watching the other children making castles in the sand and wishing she had the courage to ask if she could join in. She would have to pick her way alone around the slippery rock pools, occasionally finding a tiny crab or a pretty shell, and running back to show her mother, who huddled behind the windbreak in her silk scarf and raincoat, trying to keep sand out of the sandwiches.

'. . . It wasn't so great when you got a bit older,' Lia was saying, 'when you became aware that people thought of you differently because you were Barnardo's.'

'Oh, I'm sure—' Ginger began to protest.

'Yes, they did,' Lia interrupted firmly. 'It's not that they say it to your face, but you know when you walk past, if your hair's a mess, or your school blazer's a bit small, there's that exchange of looks . . . There's a kind of expectation that you're going to be bad, and if you're not, there's surprise. "She's very nice . . ."' – she mimicked an upper-class accent – 'and then those unspoken words, "*considering where she comes from* . . ."' She looked up for a second as if to reinforce her point.

Alison's liberal instincts made her want to object, but she knew that what Lia was saying was true. She could hear her mother's voice in every word she quoted.

'You get used to it,' Lia went on, 'you learn to keep very quiet about where you come from. You listen really hard to the other girls at school so you know

121

what it's like to be in a real family; the sort of things real families do, like eating your tea in front of the telly, going to the shops in the car at weekends, uncles and aunts sending you cards on your birthday, Dad taking you sledging when it snows . . . I suppose that one of the things that appealed to me about having a baby was being able to do all that properly.'

The way she said it was as if the thought had just occurred to her. Lia had a kind of instinctive intelligence which was rather attractive, Alison thought. The combination of unsophisticated freshness and resilience had made her hard to place, and the description she had just given of her growing up provided answers to questions Alison hadn't even realized that she had asked herself. Lia seemed to know herself far better than she herself did, even though she was ten years younger and had had none of the benefits of a middle-class home and education.

The three women fell silent for a few moments reflecting on the enormous change in their lives.

'Does anyone fancy lunch?' Ginger asked, getting to her feet.

'Good idea,' Alison said.

'Yes,' Lia said, glad that the moment had passed, and that she could detect no shift in the companionable atmosphere between them.

They agreed to head for the restaurant on the other side of the Gardens.

'Let's walk briskly,' Ginger commanded, leading the convoy of prams. 'I've still got over a stone to lose!'

There were tables outside beneath trellises strung with vines with wizened bunches of small, sour-looking fruit. Ginger reached up, plucked a grape and popped it in her mouth to see if it was real.

'Hmm,' she said, making a face, 'they are real, but not edible. So,' she continued as they settled down, 'now that we're all experienced mothers, let's have a vote on what's the worst thing about it.'

'Lack of sleep,' Lia volunteered immediately.

'I agree,' Ginger said. 'If Guy were a South American country, Amnesty International would have a campaign about him. It's torture, right?' She looked at Alison for confirmation.

Alison nodded, smiling. The answer she had been going to give was something to do with the over-whelming sense of responsibility for another human being, the feeling that she wasn't up to it, but it was easier just to agree. The lack of sleep was awful, and even though Stephen was now doing most of the night feeds, she felt she hadn't yet caught up the hours she had lost in the first couple of weeks.

'And the best thing?' Ginger asked her.

'Not being pregnant,' Alison responded immediately.

'Not working,' Ginger said, with a sigh.

'I think the best thing is just holding her,' Lia said, and Alison noticed with a slight shock that Lia had her baby at her breast, almost hidden under the simple white cotton T-shirt she was wearing. She looked completely at ease, her long hair falling about her shoulders, her dark brown deer's eyes smiling.

'Don't you like your job, then?' Alison said, quickly turning to look at Ginger, embarrassed that her own response to the question had been so negative.

'What's to like?' Ginger said, 'I make coffee and tell lies on behalf of my boss. She's a chain-smoking bitch who can't make up her mind whether she'd rather be powerful or liked, so one minute she's flirting with the big boss man, and the next she's moaning on about glass ceilings to her lipsticked feminist friends over a crate or two of Chardonnay, before coming back to the office, spraying a bit of breath-freshener about, and telling me she's too busy to take any calls . . .'

When Ginger had first gone along for interview, the woman had been disconcertingly matey and Ginger, who had not had much experience of interviews, and was desperate for the job which everyone told her would be the first step on the ladder to a career in television, naïvely handed over a list of programme ideas she had painstakingly typed the night before. She never saw the list again, but she noticed, a few months later when she was filing the minutes of a meeting with the head of department, that a number of her suggestions had been discussed without reference to their source. When she plucked up the courage to raise this, her boss put on her cloying, I'm-so-grateful-for-all-you-do voice, and promised Ginger a nice long boozy girls' lunch where they could talk about her promotion prospects. After several months waiting for the lunch to happen, Ginger's naïvety turned to disillusion and she realized that she hadn't a hope of getting any further unless her boss got run over by a bus (an event she fantasized about often, as she typed tape after tape, made coffee after coffee, and particularly as she stood in the queue to collect her boss's dry-cleaning).

'I was looking for another job, when this happened,' Ginger pointed into Guy's pram, 'but there didn't seem to be much point in losing my maternity leave, and I didn't think anyone would want to take me on if they knew that I was pregnant . . .'

Ironically, the whole purpose of going to Robert's fateful Christmas party had been to schmooze herself another job. Buoying herself up with a couple of quick glasses of champagne, she had made a bee-line for Charlie Prince. Renowned during their time at Oxford as a director of OUDS, he had been arrogant enough to set up as an independent producer straight after coming down, and had quickly made his name producing several successful youth-orientated programmes. His perpetually expanding company had also produced a low-budget feature film that had been a hit in the States. He was media flavour-of-the-month, and he knew it. Ginger had introduced herself slightly nervously. They had been at Oxford together, she told him, and she was amazed when he volunteered he had loved her Beatrice in the garden production of *Much Ado About Nothing* in New College cloisters.

It was the one great role she had been offered at university, and then only because the willowy beautiful girl who was down for the part had come back from her Easter vacation in Kenya with malaria. Usually, Ginger had got what the directors called the character roles, and what she called the very small parts, because they were either children, or dwarfs, or, occasionally, court jesters, if there were no short men available. Girls who auditioned with her were normally at least a foot taller than she was, had long hair, husky voices, and looked as if they would be ready, at a moment's notice, to perform a memorable Ophelia.

The fact that Charlie Prince had seen Ginger's one moment of acting glory called for more champagne and then more, and somehow she hadn't got around to talking to anyone else at the party.

'Trying to sleep your way to the top?' Robert had asked bitchily as he sidled past with another bottle of Bollinger.

Three months later, exasperated by her decision to have the baby, he had been crueller.

'There are a lot of women who sleep their way into jobs, but you're the only one I know who slept her way out of a career.'

'All my friends thought I was bonkers,' Ginger told Lia and Alison, 'or that I was just using it as an excuse because I don't have what it takes to make a brilliant career in television. Perhaps I don't,' she said, unusually forlorn.

Sitting eating a sandwich in Kew Gardens on a sunny September morning, it was difficult to imagine going back to the oppressive atmosphere of the BBC. That great ugly building in the wastelands of White

City, with its dismal curving corridors and closed office doors, was about as conducive to creativity as the characterless floors of a Communist hotel. But she knew she had to, or she wouldn't qualify for the maternity pay, which she needed even more now that she had decided to reject her parents' conditional offers of assistance.

'What about you?' Ginger turned to Lia. 'Are you going to go back to work?'

'I haven't really thought about it,' Lia said, 'but then I don't have a brilliant career.'

Ginger smiled, acknowledging the echo of her words.

'I've done loads of jobs, but they were all pretty crap – you know, waitress, cook, standing outside discos trying to lure blokes in, whatever was going really. I even taught English a bit in Portugal, but there's not much call for that here. Anyway, I'm not qualified. If I went back to waitressing, it wouldn't be enough money to pay a childminder to look after Anouska . . .'

'I did a bit of waitressing once,' Ginger said, 'until I tipped sour cream over a customer's Versace. Well, she said it was Versace, but I think that was just for the insurance claim . . .'

'Can be quite a laugh,' Lia said, 'but I think I'd prefer to look after Anouska.'

To have no job, no income, no independence, sounded like hell to Alison, and yet, she thought, as she bade the others farewell and pushed her pram slowly down her street, past the large detached houses with their gravel drives and expensive cars, Lia seemed perfectly serene and contented, sitting there feeding her baby like a Madonna of the Vines. Had she always been like that, Alison wondered, trying to suppress the eruption of jealousy in her gut, or was the key to happiness being with Neil?

I could have been with him, Alison thought,

remembering, with almost excruciating clarity, the moment he had proposed to her.

It was one of those hot, hot evenings almost exactly two years after they met. They were sitting on the swings in the middle of the eerily deserted park. The perfume of tobacco plants filled the air and the chains of the swings creaked rhythmically as they rocked backwards and forwards side by side.

'You won't laugh at me if I tell you something, will you?' Neil suddenly said.

'Depends what,' she replied, fixing her gaze resolutely on the climbing frame in front of them. She knew it would be something momentous. She had sensed him working up courage in the silence.

'I love you, that's what,' he said.

Her pulse thumped against the hard warm seat of the swing.

'I want to marry you . . .' Now that he had started, the words came tumbling out. 'I want to live with you happily ever after.' He turned and looked at her, suddenly realizing that she had said nothing.

'No,' she said, still looking straight ahead, 'don't say that. That's too far ahead. It's enough to love each other now—'

'Do you?' he interrupted her, desperately disappointed by her response.

She nodded, solemnly.

'Say it, then,' he urged.

'I just did.'

'No, you didn't.'

'I love you, too,' she said, and, on the last word, she turned her eyes to meet his, and they were sparkling with laughter. Then she leapt up and started twirling round and round, arms stretched out horizontally, face tilted, basking in the moonlight as if it were sunshine, and she were a child on a sandy, windswept beach.

They had not been much more than children with their nervous declarations of love, and their hesitant

127

explorations of each other's bodies, which, a few weeks later, two years to the day since they met, had culminated in the loss of her virginity. But who was to say that the love they felt for each other then, that sensation of elation that made it impossible to eat or sleep those summer nights, was any less real than what adults called love later on.

Alison put her key in the door and called out, 'Hello,' to her mother.

'Did you have a nice time?' Margaret asked, picking Ben out of the pram, kissing him and looking at him as if she had missed him during the time Alison had been in the Gardens.

'Yes. I saw a couple of people I know,' Alison said, 'one of them—' On the point of telling Margaret who Lia's partner was, she quickly checked herself, 'works for the BBC.'

'How lovely,' Margaret said. 'Now, you've had a couple of calls: Ramona says to tell you that she's dying to see you, and Stephen will be home early. I thought I'd take myself out, leave you two, you three, on your own for an evening.'

'But what will you do?' Alison asked, concerned.

'I'm not entirely decrepit, you know,' her mother retorted with good humour, and Alison noticed that she was dressed to go out and had lipstick on. 'I thought I'd go up West. Have a look in Selfridges . . .'

'Right, of course,' Alison said, wondering why she felt so dislocated from the world, why she seemed to be a step behind everyone that day.

When Stephen came home, he handed her a flimsy purple carrier bag from W. H. Smith.

'Present,' he said with a beaming smile as he watched her open it.

Mystified, she pulled out a CD of *The Jungle Book*.

'Well, it's for Ben, really,' Stephen said, grabbing it back, and racing to the CD player.

Half-way through 'Bare Necessities', she realized with stunned disbelief that he knew all the words.

Stephen knew every single word to every song in *The Jungle Book* and he was singing, performing all the actions, padding round the conservatory like Baloo the Bear with Ben in the crook of his arm.

Fatherhood had unlocked something in him, releasing a part of him that was childlike and fun. She saw how he must have been as a little boy when he saw the film of *The Jungle Book* for the first time. With typical thoroughness he had absorbed something he liked, remembering all the tunes, the words, the exaggerated cartoon faces. It was wonderful to see him dancing with such abandon, and yet when he beckoned to her, encouraging her to join in 'The Elephants' March', she found she couldn't. Parenthood had chased away Stephen's inhibitions but it had magnified her own. She sat on the chaise longue watching her husband and her son, feeling completely isolated from their enjoyment of one another. She kept telling herself how lucky she was to have everything that she had ever dreamed of having – a successful career, a rich husband, a beautiful house in London, and that most sought-after accessory of middle-class women in their late thirties, a baby – and yet all she seemed able to think about was a time when she had nothing. Nothing except the love of a boy called Neil.

Chapter 4

OCTOBER

Lia woke up, shocked to discover that she had slept until it was light. Her first instinct was to jump out of bed and check the carrycot, but as she became fully conscious she realized that the reason she had woken was Neil's head between her legs, his tongue very gently licking her.

'I'm just making sure that everything's healed down here,' he whispered, lifting his eyes to look at her.

'But . . .' Lia stammered, trying to sit up.

'It's OK, I've checked,' he told her, 'she's sleeping. She's fine, now you just relax . . .'

Lia sank back into the pillows with a sigh, trying to let her body find a response to the delicate stimulation of Neil's mouth. He continued to lap at her, varying the speed and force. She felt a flicker of arousal, like a spark from a bonfire that glows in the air for a second then dies. He sensed her body tense momentarily then relax. He looked up and she smiled at him, wanting him to believe that she was liking it, anxious that he would know she was not.

'Hey.' She inched away from him, taking over, pushing down with her elbows, drawing her body up the bed, then clasping her feet round his neck and dragging him back up the bed with her. 'Hey, come here.'

She kissed his mouth, fervently, disliking the taste of herself on his tongue, drawing him on top of her.

She could feel his penis solid against the loose skin of her stomach.

'Fuck me,' she whispered into his ear.

He drew his head back and looked at her searchingly.

'Please . . .' she said to him, throwing back her head. 'Now, please,' she commanded.

He couldn't resist twice. He was trying to enter her gradually, but the pent-up energy of weeks of restraint suddenly took over and plunged him into her body. She felt him prising her legs wider and wider apart as his penis pushed deeper. She gasped, and writhed beneath him, using all her energy to thrust back at him, ramming their pubic bones together, watching him as his eyes closed and the primal, unstoppable rhythm took possession of his body,

'Yes,' she whispered in his ear, 'oh yes, yes, yes, come on.' She was desperate for it to end.

And he exploded inside her.

They lay breathing each other's breath for a few seconds, then he raised his head from her shoulder and said, 'I'm sorry . . .'

'Why?' she asked.

'I should have waited for you.'

'No, it was lovely,' she said, hating herself for lying to him.

'You are beautiful, did you know?' He stared at her with pure, undisguised love in his eyes. She held his gaze, but it seemed to be asking her so many questions, she had to look away quickly. Then the baby began to cry.

Later, he came up behind her while she was washing-up the breakfast things and put his arms around her waist.

'Hello, gorgeous,' he said softly.

She could feel the whisper of his breath on the nape of her neck. Before, when he had touched her there, almost unbearable currents of sensual pleasure had shot across her shoulder-blades. Often, when he had been about to leave for work, she hadn't been able to stop herself turning round to kiss him, holding her dripping arms away from his chest in order not to ruin his newly ironed shirt and they had ended up fucking quickly on the kitchen table, a marmalade jar beside her ear, her head bashing the cornflake packet with each thrust. The rest of the day, she would feel him inside her, and she would find herself smiling for no reason, as she noted down a customer's order, or waited for a bus, attracting bemused stares from strangers.

Today, she felt almost repelled by his closeness.

'I'm still a bit sore,' she said, wriggling away from him, turning back to the dishes to hide her irritation. Now that she looked the same as she had before the pregnancy, he expected their sex life to be the same. Saturdays meant mornings in bed, eating toast and making love among the crumbs. A long walk by the river, hand in hand, a pub lunch that often stretched into dinner, and home for *Match of the Day*, which they watched lying on the floor together with more beer and rolling into sex again, giggling, and making sure that Neil's head was at the right angle for him to look up and see the goals.

She felt so very different now, not just physically, but in her head, that those weekends seemed part of a long-distant past. She told herself that it was because she was tired, that once she stopped feeding the baby, she would have a different body-image, that Neil's attentions turned her off right now because her body was not entirely hers any more, and certainly not his, as it had been. Perhaps they would discover other ways of making love, as they had in the final weeks of pregnancy. Perhaps.

She was desperate to get out of the house, into the air, away from the oppressive atmosphere that unsatisfactory sex left behind.

'Let's go into town. There are lots of things we need,' she said, pulling the plug out of the sink. The water made a loud noise as it drained away.

'What do we need? Do you mean go with the baby?' Neil asked.

'No, we'll leave her here on her own, I'm sure she'll be fine,' she said, with uncharacteristic sarcasm. 'Of course, with the baby.'

He started looking for excuses. 'I don't think I can bear all the hassle of carting the pram down the tube.'

'That's one of the things we need, a lightweight pushchair, but today we'll use that sling that Alison gave us. You can wear it.'

He pulled a face, then seeing her expression he said, 'OK, OK, it's about time I did my new man act.'

Was she losing her sense of humour, Lia wondered, or was he being unreasonable and then pretending that she was the one who was overreacting? She hated it when men mouthed the letters PMT at each other behind the back of any woman who made a reasonable objection to what they were doing. Perhaps they did the same post-pregnancy as they did pre-menstruation. Women's hormones were a convenient excuse for any amount of inconsiderate male behaviour.

'Oooh, he's grown, he has really grown in the last week,' Pic said, lifting Guy out of his basket. She turned to Ginger. 'Have you been all right?'

'I love your order of priorities,' said Ginger. 'I've just become an adjunct to this tiny person . . . not that I mind, though,' she said, wrapping both her sister and her baby in a tight hug. The close contact with someone her own size felt good. She held on for a long time.

'I'm so used to cuddling this little person, your head seems really huge, almost Brobdingnagian,' she told Pic.

'Well, thanks a lot,' Pic replied, laughing. 'Look, Ed,

hasn't he grown?' She held the baby up for her husband to see.

'I suppose so,' Ed acknowledged, taking a quick glance, then sitting down on the sofa and picking up the financial pages of *The Times* from the scattered pile of unopened newspapers.

'Oh, please don't read all morning,' Pic protested, 'you have all of Sunday to do that.'

Ed looked up and shrugged as if to ask what else there was to do. Ginger noticed that Pic was ruffled by his lack of interest in the baby.

'I'm sorry the place is such a mess, but I just don't seem to have the time to do anything.' She waved vaguely at the floor, in a kind of apology for the newspapers.

'Well, of course you don't,' Pic said, staring intently into the baby's eyes, 'you've got much more important things to do than clear up ... hasn't she, Guy? Oh look, Ginger, he smiled, I'm sure he smiled at me.'

'Oh, he smiles all the time now,' Ginger said, slumping into a chair, 'and he has funny dreams because he often laughs.'

Ed looked up from his paper. 'Isn't that just wind?'

'No, it's not,' the twins said firmly in unison, affronted.

Ed went back to reading.

'I seem to be doing the washing for the entire world,' Ginger said, trying to jolly Ed out of his rather unsociable mood, but when he looked up at her, his expression said that she had only herself to blame, so she got up again, and went to put the kettle on.

'No, no.' Pic suddenly jumped out of her adoring contemplation of the baby. 'I'll do that. You sit down and I'll make brunch.' She looked round in vain for an apron. 'We've brought everything, bagels, cream cheese, smoked salmon, eggs, bacon, even some American pancake mix and real maple syrup ... now, what would you fancy?'

'Everything,' Ginger said, 'I'll start on the bagels, because they're easy while you scramble the eggs.'

Pic looked at her as if she was joking.

'No, really,' Ginger said, 'you have no idea how hungry feeding this baby makes me, and I am so sick of Marks & Spencer ready meals . . .'

She started unwrapping paper bags from the delicatessen, and bit into an onion bagel as Pic began to clear the draining board. One of the good things about a sister saying she'd cook you breakfast was that you knew she would do everything, including the washing-up, if there was any, and there was, a whole week's worth.

When Robert had rung before he visited and asked politely but insincerely if there was anything he could do, Ginger had surprised him by asking for a meal. He had turned up with all the ingredients in a plastic bag from Camisa's, and had proceeded to cook her chargrilled vegetables and porcini risotto. The meal had been delicious, but he had left everything, from the seeds of the capsicum peppers, to the pan caked with arborio rice, for Ginger to clear up. It was one thing asking a friend to cook for you, but it was another to force them to do the washing-up. The next time someone asked the same question, Ginger had said, yes, she would adore a Chinese take-away.

Relaxing properly for the first time that week, Ginger watched her sister tackling the washing-up methodically and efficiently as ever, stopping only to turn the rashers of bacon she had put under the grill which were beginning to fill the room with their mouth-watering aroma. She observed that Ed did not move an inch to help his wife. He was one of those men whose mothers had taught them that it was the man's job to do the washing-up. Once or twice a week, he would rise nobly from the table after eating, don an apron and rubber gloves, and make a huge show of clearing the table. Often, he would complain about the age of the scourers ('How am I meant to clean this properly with this old thing?') or the state of the sink. Then after hours of slow toiling, he would wipe his brow and sigh and expect to be rewarded with a cup of freshly brewed coffee and a mountain of gratitude. His mother obviously hadn't told him that baking trays and saucepans did not miraculously clean themselves if filled with cold, scummy water and left to soak on the work surface, nor did knives and forks towel themselves down and leap helpfully back into the cutlery drawer.

Still, thought Ginger, he was a nice man, a good-looking, clever man, who was probably not imaginative enough to be unfaithful, and who suited Pic very well in lots of ways. The thought crossed her mind, as it had on many other occasions, that she too should probably have settled for a nice man, who might have his little ways and foibles, as all men did, but who would at least be there. But then she reminded herself that she had dated a couple of such men in the past, and just when she had been weighing up whether she could stand the boredom of settling down with them, they had chucked her.

Pic was so thorough, she even cleaned the cafetière, which Ginger had not used since Guy was born, and which had grown a thick layer of grey mould on top of the coffee sediment. 'Hmm,' she mused, with good humour, 'I wonder if this would fit in your sterilizing unit. Or perhaps I should just take it back to the lab. What do you think, Ed? I might even be credited with discovering a new antibiotic!'

Ed looked up and nodded, not really listening to what she was saying.

'Where's your ironing board?' Pic asked, pulling a tablecloth from the clothes horse where it was hanging.

'I've no idea,' Ginger said, 'anyway, it doesn't matter.'

Pic draped the cloth over the large oval mahogany

dining table, trying to smooth out the creases surreptitiously, not wanting to appear critical of her sister's slovenliness. Then she poured three glasses of freshly squeezed orange juice and three mugs of steaming coffee, and called them over, but as soon as Ginger sat down, the baby started crying.

'Don't move,' Pic ordered her, 'I'll deal with him. You eat while it's still warm.'

Ginger was too tired to raise the slightest protest and began to tuck in.

The baby quietened as soon as her sister picked him up.

'There, you see, he's just fine with me, aren't you, darling?' said Pic, putting the baby over her shoulder and patting his back.

'Perhaps he thinks you're Ginger,' Ed observed, with his mouth full of scrambled egg.

The remark seemed designed to deny her a relationship with the baby, and Pic was clearly wounded. For the first time in her life, it dawned on Ginger that she had something that her sister did not. Perhaps Pic wanted a child now, and Ed did not. His lack of interest in Guy was very pointed and there was obviously a sub-text to the exchange of frosty remarks between the two of them. Ginger was suddenly filled with sadness for her sister. She shovelled pancake into her mouth.

'I suppose it must be rather odd for him to have two big people who look the same,' Pic admitted.

'Yeah,' said Ginger, trying to lighten the atmosphere, 'and since you were the second person to hold him, he probably thought that every adult looked like we do!'

Pic laughed weakly.

'Actually,' Ginger said, wiping maple syrup and bacon grease up with a piece of toast, 'they probably can't distinguish people at all at this age. All he can sense is that you love him very much, and that's why he's gone quiet.'

Pic smiled a thank you at her.

'And now I'm going to feed him,' Ginger said, getting up from the table. 'That was delicious, by the way. Now, Ed, if you don't want to see my tits you'd better go. I'm not embarrassed, if you're not.' She began to unfasten her maternity bra,

Her brother-in-law, who had been quite content to dawdle over his breakfast, reading articles between mouthfuls, suddenly shot up and brushed crumbs off his jeans. 'I've got some shopping to do,' he said, making his way to the door, only remembering his manners when he had reached the safety of the hallway, when he called back, 'Can I get you anything?'

'Oh, some nice fruit, if you see any,' Ginger called in reply.

'What sort of fruit?' Ed shouted back, sounding irritated to be taken up on his offer.

'Whatever looks nice,' Ginger said.

'No,' Pic whispered to her, 'you don't understand how to give men instructions. You have to be specific or you'll end up with nothing at all.'

'Forget it, Ed,' Ginger shouted, 'we'll get some later.'

'You sure?' he shouted back, and they heard the front door slam before there was time to rethink.

Then they both looked at each other and started giggling.

'Mummy told me that you argued about a nanny,' Pic said, putting her own breakfast down on the table.

'I'm afraid we did,' Ginger replied.

'But what are you going to do?' Pic asked her, sitting down to eat.

'I'm not sure, but I've got a few months to decide. I'm coping all right at the moment, don't you think?'

'I think you're doing brilliantly,' Pic enthused, 'nobody at work can believe it, especially the ones with children.'

Pic was so serious about her job, Ginger couldn't

imagine her gossiping about her errant twin to the other women, but it gave her enormous pleasure to think that she did.

'Well, unlike most people, I did have Jeannie for the first week, who taught me everything,' Ginger said modestly. 'That was one of Mummy's better ideas. Somehow, I didn't mind her being bossy and old-fashioned, but I can't have someone like that living here all the time.'

'Of course not,' Pic said, 'but it must be such a strain coping on your own.'

'Well, it won't be so bad when he sleeps through the night. At the moment, I'm on autopilot most of the time, but it is OK. And I have friends. Lia told me that if I ever needed someone to talk to in the middle of the night, then I could ring, and I think she meant it, and there's Alison. You met her. Her husband's a consultant. I'm sure I could call her too . . .'

'You could always call me,' Pic said.

'Oh, you're hopeless at night, but thanks all the same,' Ginger said, then some instinct made her look up and see that her casual dismissal of her sister's offer had hurt her. 'I didn't mean . . . It's just that, until you do, you know, have a baby, you just have no idea what it's like in the middle of the night. You're so tired, you can't believe you're alive really . . .'

Pic ate her breakfast in silence.

'Are you trying to have a baby?' Ginger asked her bluntly, wanting to know if her suspicions were correct.

'Well, I'd like to, but Ed wants to wait.'

It was a perfectly matter-of-fact statement, so evenly delivered that Ginger was certain it masked a great deal of pain.

'Oh,' she replied, trying to give her sister space to talk.

'I don't really see why, that's the thing.' Pic's voice began to waver. 'I think it would be so lovely for our

139

children to grow up together . . . but Ed can't understand that.'

'Perhaps he's threatened by our closeness,' Ginger guessed.

'Do you think so?'

'I've no idea,' said Ginger, who wasn't particularly inclined towards the language of psychology. 'Anyway, please don't be sad. It makes me sad to see you sad.'

Pic obediently blinked back her tears and blew her nose.

'Do you know,' Ginger asked, remembering her earlier thought, 'I've never had anything that you've wanted before, and when I realized just now that I did, I was really sad for you. And I thought, God, perhaps Pic's been sorry for me all my life. Have you?'

Pic looked at her in astonishment. 'You're not serious?'

'Yes, I am, for once.'

'That's utterly ridiculous,' Pic said, sipping her mug of coffee, 'you've always had things that I wanted.'

'Like what?' Ginger challenged her.

'How long have you got? Well, you're funnier than I am, you were always more popular at school, you're braver—'

'Am I?'

'Of course you are. In fact, the only thing I can think of that I have and you don't is our parents' approval, and quite honestly, sometimes I wish I didn't have quite so much of that.'

'Oh come on,' Ginger said, 'what about the GCSEs, the "A" levels, the First from Cambridge . . .'

'Only because I worked hard. You had a much better time.'

Ginger had to admit that was probably true. Whereas Pic had slaved away in libraries at Cambridge, Ginger's life at Oxford had involved rather a lot of drinking, experimenting with drugs and a constant flurry of party invitations and popping round to friends' rooms for tea. If there was any spare time after that, she had spent it acting. After a couple of years, she had been sent down without a qualification. The only thing she had gained were a number of good friends, who had allowed her to sleep on their battered old sofas while she looked for work.

Pic had sailed into the fast-track graduate recruitment scheme of a multinational pharmaceutical company, met Ed and bought a house. Ginger had lived in a housing co-op and tried to get acting jobs, supplementing her dole with shifts waitressing in a wine bar. She had done some unpaid work in community theatre and had briefly got an agent through connections in OUDS. But the one real job she was offered, the role of Crackle in a Rice Krispies advert, had fallen through when the manufacturers decided that an animation with plasticine figures would be preferable to real actors. After that, Ginger had decided that somebody was trying to tell her something, and resigned herself to getting a job with a regular salary.

'Well, you have the man,' Ginger continued her list, 'the handsome husband standing in the porch of the perfect country church in the silver frame on the mantelpiece . . .'

'Hmm, well, husbands aren't just for the photographs,' Pic said, seriously.

'No?' Ginger asked, cheekily, ducking out of the way of a friendly swipe.

Ginger laid Guy on a padded playmat on the floor. The bright poster colours looked odd against the deep dark reds and blues of the Persian carpet. He stared up at the twirling shapes of the mobile she had suspended from the chandelier in the middle of the ceiling and she watched him, trying to guess what he was thinking.

For some reason, she found her mind going back to an essay she had once been set in the Philosophy component of her degree. It was one of the few that had interested her enough to make her stay up the entire night before the tutorial, trying to make sense of the articles on the subject in heavy volumes of the *Philosophical Review*. The title, she remembered, had been 'Can people think without language?' At four o'clock in the morning, when the words of Ayer and Russell were dancing around on the page, and her head was lolling and starting, only jolted back from sleep by the pints of black coffee and Coca Cola she kept pouring into her mouth, she had wondered whether a more appropriate question would not have been 'Can people think without sleep?' Now, seeing her eight-week-old son so obviously engrossed in the sparkling rainbows of light above him, she realized why she had never really got to grips with Philosophy. The dry arguments of logic that the academics got so steamed up about in their incomprehensible papers were just completely irrelevant. You need only look at a baby, at the myriad expressions on his face, to know that yes, of course people can think before they have language. She suspected, however, that a one-word answer 'Yes' would have gone down even worse with her tutor than the haphazard scrawl of notes she had handed in.

'Do you think Daddy is ever going to come to see his grandson?' Ginger stood up, walked into the kitchen area, took a tea-towel from the clothes horse, and began to dry the second round of washing-up Pic was starting on.

'He's not very well, you know. He does look awfully weak,' Pic said, diplomatic as ever.

'Oh come on, I know that he voted in the House the other day, I saw him being wheeled in on telly. If he can make the effort for the government . . .' Ginger's voice trailed off.

She didn't know why it upset her so that her father had yet to acknowledge her baby in person. She had been used to his disapproval as long as she could remember, and it often made her angry, but never sad.

Now, she was having to fight back tears that had involuntarily sprung to her eyes.

'Have you invited him?' Pic asked her, pushing back her hair from her face, leaving a crescent of suds on her forehead.

'Well no, but surely I shouldn't have to?'

'Have you thought about taking Guy home, then?' her sister persisted.

'How? I haven't got a car, and I just couldn't carry everything, as well as the baby, and get myself to Waterloo, and then get on a train, I just couldn't . . . Anyway, I haven't been invited . . .'

As soon as she had spoken the words she realized what Pic had been driving at.

'OK, OK.' She held up her hands in defeat. 'Maybe I should do the grown-up thing and invite him . . . not because I want him here, of course,' she added, trying to sound serious, 'but because I feel I must allow my son to make up his own mind about his grand-father . . .'

'How noble you are,' Pic said, solemnly, then arched her back to lessen the effect of Ginger whacking her on the bottom with the frying pan she had just finished drying.

As they were walking up the slight incline to the station, Neil caught sight of Alison who was also on her way to catch a train. She was alone, walking briskly, wearing a light tweed jacket over narrow jeans. Her shiny chestnut hair swung about her face. She had red lipstick on.

Lia spotted her at the same time, and called out her name.

He watched as she halted and looked around, wondering whether she had heard her name, or just imagined it, clearly annoyed that her purposeful stride had been broken. She looked arrogant when she was nervous, he remembered. It had made a lot of people wary of her at school, but it had probably been good for her career. From what Lia had told him, she had a very high-powered job nowadays. When she saw who it was walking towards her, her face softened, just a little.

'Hi,' she said, kissing Lia on the cheek, and nodding at Neil, acknowledging the fact that he was wearing their tiny baby in the green corduroy sling over his black T-shirt, 'you're using it, then?'

'Hello, Ally,' he said.

Her face stiffened for about a millionth of a second then relaxed and he wondered why she was quite so frightened of being discovered.

'Where are you going?' She directed the question at Lia.

'Oh, we're going up to John Lewis, we need so many things. We never really had a chance to get ready before she arrived,' Lia explained.

'No, of course.'

'What about you?' Lia asked her.

'Oh, I'm just popping into Richmond,' Alison replied, 'to have lunch with a friend. It's my first proper outing. I mean, on my own,' she said quickly, adding, with a brittle laugh, 'I feel as if I'm on holiday!'

It was a good effort, but she was lying. Neil could see it in her eyes. It amused him to think that twenty years had passed, and yet he still knew what was going on in her head. She had been about to go into town, but she couldn't bear the awkwardness of sitting with them for the journey.

'Come on, Lia,' he said, 'if we don't get a move on, Annie will want feeding again and it'll be back to square one.'

'You're right.' Lia smiled at Alison. 'Anyway, see you Thursday?'

The three women now met regularly in the Gardens on Thursday mornings.

'Yes, Thursday,' Alison responded, and walked over the bridge to the opposite platform.

A train going into London came in almost immediately. Lia and Neil stepped in and sat down. Then they waited, smiling and waving across the track at Alison, becoming slightly embarrassed, after several minutes, that the train had not left immediately. Finally, the doors closed with a compressed-air sigh, and they pulled away.

Neil wondered whether Alison would wait until their train had disappeared safely down the track, then cross back over to wait for the next one into town, or whether she would actually get on the train in the opposite direction, change platforms at Richmond and then head back towards London. Probably the latter, he thought. She was a hopeless liar and she wouldn't want to take the risk of someone else seeing her and having to explain why she had waited for one train, and then the other. But he was grateful that her efforts had meant that they didn't have to spend the entire journey into town making stilted conversation with her.

'She's Alison,' Lia said, as the train started picking up speed.

'What?' he said, not understanding.

'Not Ally,' Lia explained, 'she's not at all an *Ally*.'

'Oh, right,' he replied, 'sorry.'

'It's OK,' Lia went on, 'I don't suppose she minded. She seems a bit uptight, but she's not at all really, once you get to know her . . .'

'Right,' Neil said, beginning to feel slightly uncomfortable himself. 'Now, what are all these things we need so badly?'

Alison bent and kissed Ramona. 'I am so sorry I'm late, I ran into someone.'

'That's OK,' Ramona said, 'we've got the whole afternoon . . .' She stubbed out a cigarette in the ashtray. 'I thought some shopping afterwards? I love this store. It's the only place I know where they relegate men to the basement . . .'

145

Alison looked at the smouldering stub which Ramona had not quite extinguished. She had promised herself she would not smoke again. She tried to tell herself that the smell was horrible, but it wasn't. It was quite as delicious to her taste-buds as the aroma of freshly ground coffee that wafted over from the Espresso bar. They were grown-up smells that seemed to offer an afternoon's glorious release from the life that smelt of nappies, baby lotion and sickly-sweet spilt formula milk.

'Do you mind?' she asked, fingering the packet of Marlboro that lay enticingly on the table.

'Course not, go ahead.'

Alison lit up and inhaled. Her vision whirled momentarily, then the hit of nicotine coursed into her bloodstream, making her feel complete again.

'Hmm . . . almost as good as gas and air!' she said, exhaling.

Ramona laughed. 'Did you have Pethidine too?'

'I had everything, but listen, I don't want to talk about all that. This is my first proper outing, and I'm not even going to think about babies or motherhood or anything to do with it.'

'Fine by me.' Ramona picked up one of the brightly coloured pieces of card the waiter had handed her and ran her eyes up and down looking for a suitable wine. 'You're looking great, by the way,' she said.

'I'm back to my pre-pregnancy weight,' Alison said proudly. It had taken near-starvation to achieve it, but it was worth it to fit into clothes she had forgotten she owned.

'My God,' Ramona said, 'I haven't achieved that in fourteen years. Are you up for a bottle of wine, or just a glass?'

'Oh, I think a bottle, don't you?' Alison said recklessly. 'So, what's the gossip?'

Ramona told her that there hadn't been any dramatic developments at the newspaper. A threatened

146

take-over had not happened, the rate of redundancy seemed to be slowing.

'But that,' Ramona said, as she poured two large glasses of Californian Cabernet Sauvignon, 'is only because there's hardly anyone left to get rid of.'

An affair between the sports editor and the television critic rumbled on and there was intense speculation about whether he would mention it in the book he was writing.

'It's one of those male-confessional jobs about snooker as a metaphor for life or something,' Ramona told her. 'Actually, I'm beginning to wonder if all that stuff about getting in touch with your feelings was a good idea, if the result is all these bloody men confessing everything. Amazingly, some publisher paid him a fortune, and he sits there all day tapping away, obviously completely absorbed by the story of his own life. Dom managed to hack into the file one day, but all we found was a tedious description about balls kissing each other on the cushion − snooker-language, before you get too excited . . . I miss you, of course, as well as being green with envy,' she added, as their first courses arrived.

'Actually, I can't wait to get back,' Alison told her, staring down at the table top as if she could see something incredibly fascinating on the plain, polished wooden surface, feeling suddenly very close to tears.

'Hey, what's up? Is everything OK?' Ramona asked, trying to manoeuvre a multiple frond of frisée lettuce into her mouth. It fell back onto the plate.

'Oh hell,' Alison said, putting down her fork. A tear threatened to escape from one eye, and she quickly dabbed at it with her napkin, 'Yeah, everything's fine, the baby's fine, he's healthy, he even sleeps through the night sometimes, if that's what you mean. I know I'm really lucky, but, well . . .' She stopped herself, then could bear to hold back the truth no longer.

147

'Sometimes I feel completely miserable, a lot of the time, in fact . . .' She looked up to see what effect the words had had on her friend, and was hugely relieved to see that Ramona's face was concerned, but not critical.

'I don't know what's wrong with me. It's as if I no longer know who I am . . . and I long to be as I was,' Alison went on, wondering how she could possibly be unhappy in this emporium of sensual delights, where everything, from the cutlery to the peculiar bare light bulb chandeliers, worked in a kind of harmony of contemporary design, combining the impression of dining al fresco in Italy with the busy, noisy intimacy of a bar in Downtown Manhattan.

'I just don't seem to be very good at it – motherhood,' she tried to explain, feeling almost energized by her admission of failure. 'I see all these people enjoying their babies and I think there must be something wrong with me – to have wanted a baby so much, and then to feel, well, nothing . . . I mean I know he's very sweet, but . . . That sounds awful, listen, you won't tell anyone . . .?'

Ramona had stopped trying to battle with her salad and was breaking pieces of bread distractedly with her left hand while she listened.

'Of course I won't,' she replied, almost offended, then, probing cautiously, 'What does Stephen think?'

'Oh, he loves it. It's as if he's discovered a whole new dimension to his life.'

An image of her husband playing with her child the previous evening shot through Alison's mind. She had been on her way downstairs when she heard Stephen say, 'Navigator to Captain, over.' He was putting on a nasal voice, with lots of buzzing and crackling noises, like a character in a Battle of Britain movie. 'We're changing course now. Mummy spotted entering airspace, over, and we're coming into land . . . whoosh.'

Benedict's head appeared at eye level round the

door of the living room, followed by his body held horizontal in Stephen's hands. The baby looked perfectly at ease in his Superman pose, being flown through the air by his father.

'He likes flying,' Stephen said, breathless with the exertion of the game, looking rather sheepish as he realized how silly they must look.

'I meant what does he think about the state you're in?' Ramona interrupted her thoughts.

'Oh, I don't know . . . I don't know if he realizes,' Alison said, her smile fading, 'he's out so much, you know, and when he's home, he's either sleeping, or he's with Ben. He's very good about getting up in middle of the night to check him and all that stuff — far better than me, actually.'

'Well, he's a doctor. He's used to broken sleep,' Ramona said, sharply. 'Do you mean you haven't told him how you're feeling?'

'It would only make me feel worse if I did,' Alison said.

'Are you sure? Have you seen your own doctor?'

'I went for my six-week check. Everything's fine.'

'But did you say you were depressed?' Ramona pressed.

'Well, no . . .' Alison admitted, then said, 'Do you think that's what it is — post-natal depression?'

'Sounds like it . . . I had it a bit after Jonty was born, not as bad as you're describing, but I think I know what you're going through,' Ramona said. 'I thought it would be easy for me, especially having had one already, but it all seemed very difficult. I remember Sol and I didn't have sex for months.'

Alison smiled with relief that someone else had shared that experience. At the six-week check, her doctor had asked her whether she and Stephen had had sex again yet, and had seemed surprised when Alison said no. I thought you had a child, Alison had almost joked, but had stopped short of saying it, alarmed that they were abnormal to leave it so long.

'What are you doing about childcare?' Ramona demanded.

'Well, we're going to get a nanny when I come back to work. At the moment my mother comes up during the week, and the weekends when Stephen is working—'

'Oh, for heaven's sake, no wonder you're depressed!' Ramona said, warming to her theme. There was nothing Ramona liked more than the opportunity to prescribe solutions to other people's problems. 'This is what you do. One: get yourself a nanny straightaway. Ring up the agency first thing Monday morning, yes?'

Alison nodded.

'Two: ban your mother from the house.'

Alison giggled.

'Three: book a weekend away with that gorgeous man of yours. Honestly! Now have dessert, you're far too thin.'

Alison took another Marlboro from the box and lit it thoughtfully. There's just one other thing, she wanted to say. I think I'm in love with someone I went out with when I was sixteen. When I see him, I feel alive. So what do I do about that?

But she didn't. Ramona was lovely: kind, bossy, nurturing, the ultimate Jewish mother-figure, even though she was only a couple of years older than Alison. She approved of marriage and she approved of Stephen.

And so do I, Alison reminded herself, guiltily extinguishing the cigarette. And so do I.

After lunch, they wandered round each floor in turn, examining the winter collections, pulling hangers off shining chrome rails and holding thousand-pound coats up against their bodies, but Alison's heart wasn't really in it and she knew a quick fix from MaxMara or Calvin Klein was not going to make her feel better.

What Ramona had said had thrown a whole new light on her feelings. For some reason, she couldn't now imagine what, depression had not occurred to her before as an explanation for the weird way that she was feeling. She knew that something was wrong, but she hadn't stopped to think that maybe the chemicals in her body were unbalanced and making her that way. Post-natal depression was something you read about in books. It happened to other people, not to you.

Ramona was holding a four-hundred-pound Joseph sweater against her body and trying to think of a reason she deserved it, when Alison kissed her and said she had to go. She glided down the escalator and through the scented, mirrored forest of perfumery counters into the slightly acid, exhaust-filled air of late Saturday afternoon Knightsbridge.

Hyde Park was virtually empty. A few warmly wrapped American students were playing softball. A determined Saturday-afternoon father rowed his two small anoraked children in a boat across the wind-whipped Serpentine.

Alison sat down on a bench and stared out over the lake, thinking about the last time she had been depressed, properly depressed, not just sad, or unhappy, or vaguely dissatisfied, but that feeling of pure, bleak isolation from which she had not been able to imagine an escape.

It was during the first term at university. She had been thin, very thin. It was before people started talking a lot about anorexia, but, with hindsight, she supposed that was what she had been suffering. It was only when a friend from her Hall of Residence, who was studying Psychology, suggested talking to a counsellor that she began to break through the cloud that seemed to have turned everything around her grey.

The oppressive hatred she felt for herself began to lift a little each week as she sat in the little room above Gower Street sobbing incoherently for her allotted hour to the Australian counsellor, Mrs Goode. She had always thought how appropriate her name was, because she seemed to radiate kindliness and sympathy. Gradually, Alison began to trust herself to talk. She told Mrs Goode things she had told no-one in the world. Mrs Goode listened, but she wasn't the sort of therapist who sat in stony silence. Sometimes, she offered practical suggestions about how to cope. She was full of good common sense, delivered evenly, with no hint of judgement or prescription, a bit like a less bossy Ramona, Alison thought with a smile.

One day in spring, Alison woke up in the small modern room in Hall feeling different. The sun was streaming in through the unattractive institution curtains with their large swirls of orange and brown and Alison had decided she could not stand looking at them another day. She went to Habitat on Tottenham Court Road and bought stripy fabric that conjured thoughts of deckchairs and summer. Climbing down from her desk, on which she had stood to hook the bright material over the curtain rail, and admiring the marquee effect she seemed to have achieved, she recognized the sensation of hunger in her stomach, for the first time in months. She bought egg mayonnaise on a granary bap and a can of drink, and slipped away from afternoon lectures to Regent's Park. She remembered very clearly sitting on a bench overlooking the zoo munching her sandwich, savouring each taste, the deliciously sloppy egg, the hard nutty grains in the bread, the straw-like cress, realizing that she felt better.

Depression could lift, Alison told herself, sitting in another London park, twenty years later. If Ramona was right, and post-natal depression was what she had, then it would go as soon as her body returned to normal. Just talking about it had made her feel considerably better already. Ramona's advice, whilst perhaps not as professional as Mrs Goode's, was sensible. Of course she must get a nanny and start to live her life again. Of course she and Stephen must spend time together. No wonder she felt so odd. They hadn't had sex for months.

The wind was biting through her shirt to her flesh. She stood up, pulled the edges of her jacket together and headed home.

'Why do we have to have a brand-new pram that converts into a pushchair, with a raincover, shopping tray, sun canopy and foot muff, whatever the hell that is?' Neil hissed behind Lia as the shop assistant demonstrated the benefits of the latest Mamas and Papas range in a sing-song voice.

'Because we only have your brother's old carrycot on wheels, and it's old and heavy to push around,' Lia explained, in a whisper, trying to listen to what the shop assistant was saying.

'But it costs almost as much as a small car,' Neil protested.

'We'll think about it,' Lia told the shop assistant, 'thanks very much.'

She started walking smartly towards the lift.

'Where are you going?' Neil hurried after her.

'Home,' she said, in a clipped voice, not turning round, 'I don't know why we bothered to come if we can't afford to buy anything.'

'Lia, stop,' he said, chastened by her anger. 'Why don't we sit down and work out what we can afford.' He put his hand on her arm. 'Look, there's a café over there, let's have a coffee.'

'All right,' she said, taking a deep breath, 'all right.'

She sat at a table by the windows, looking out over the grand rooftops of Cavendish Square and then back to the counter where Neil was extravagantly sliding two fresh cream cakes onto his tray, and she didn't really notice the woman in an overall starting to wipe her table. The woman paused mid-wipe and Lia could feel her staring. Then a familiar voice said, 'It is, isn't it? Hello, Lesley! How're you doing?'

Lia looked up sharply.

Before she had a chance to answer, Neil was there too, holding the laden tray.

'Hello, Trace,' Lia said quietly, 'this is Neil, and Anouska.' She pointed at the baby sleeping tied to Neil's chest.

'Oooh, she's lovely,' the woman squealed.

'Thanks,' Lia replied, non-committally.

'Well, must get on. Lovely to see you again,' the woman said, and was gone.

'Who was that?' Neil asked, surprised.

'Trace. She's one of the girls from my house,' Lia said. 'She used to be a bit of a bully.'

'She called you Lesley,' Neil said, sitting down.

'Did she?' Lia replied. Suddenly she had no appetite for the chocolate éclair that sat on the plate in front of her.

Neil said nothing, but the air was charged with the unspoken question.

'It's no big deal,' Lia said. 'I changed my name when I went to Spain. Well, I didn't change it, exactly, but the first person who asked me didn't understand Lesley, he thought I said Lia, and I liked the sound of it, so it stuck.'

'Oh,' Neil said.

'What's wrong with that?'

'Nothing, I suppose,' he said.

'Well, you seem pretty pissed off,' she said.

'No, I'm not.'

'Oh, this is ridiculous,' she said, getting up to leave the café. Suddenly the ceiling seemed so low, it was threatening to crush them. She needed air.

They went down in the lift and walked through the ground floor in silence.

'I just don't see why you didn't tell me you had changed your name,' he said as they left the shop.

'But I didn't change it,' Lia said, trying to keep up with him as he fought his way through the Oxford Street crowds. 'I liked it. It seemed easier just to say yes. I couldn't be bothered to put him right,' she defended herself, falteringly, knowing what he was going to say next.

'But when we were deciding on *her* name,' Neil said, pointing at the baby, as if he hated her, 'you assured me that you had never been teased at school, but you didn't tell me that your name hadn't been Lia then.'

She revealed her guilt in a blush. 'All right, I'm sorry about that,' she said as they stepped onto the escalator at Bond Street.

He was silent on the tube home and for the rest of the day. Whenever she tried to talk to him, he walked away. That made her angry. She told him to stop it. He denied he was doing anything. She took Anouska into their bedroom to feed her and slammed the door, fuming.

It wasn't really anything to do with her changing her name, she realized, calming down as she stroked the baby's cheek. It was the combination of weeks of broken sleep, no sex, feeling left out, concern about money, all these things had been building up steam inside him, like a pressure cooker waiting to go off, just as she had a list of different unspoken resentments: why did he take so little notice of the baby, why was he obsessed with what everything cost, why did he have to keep touching her up? They said that having a baby brought you together, but she and Neil couldn't have been any more together, and it seemed instead to be driving them apart.

When the baby finished feeding, Lia put her down and went downstairs.

'I'm sorry,' she said simply.

'So am I.'

He came to her and kissed her face and hair and they ended up making love on the floor of the living room in a sad attempt to achieve reconciliation. But as she lay there, feeling suffocated by his closeness and yet distant, she felt as if whatever it was they had shared was somehow irrevocably diminished.

Chapter 5

NOVEMBER

The vine leaves had turned a deep coppery red, and there was a damp smokiness in the air that carried the yeasty smell of rotting apples. Dry leaves crackled under the soles of Ginger's Doc Marten's like scrunched-up brown paper.

'We always have the same drinks,' she observed, putting the tray down on the table. 'It's rather like that party game – if you were a drink, what would you be? Do you know it?'

Alison looked at the tray. 'So, Ginger, you would be Coca Cola – bubbly and picks you up when you're down, Lia is orange juice – fresh and natural, and I am black coffee – strong and bitter,' she remarked with a dry, ironic laugh.

'No,' said Lia, quite seriously, 'I think of black coffee as smart and sophisticated.'

Alison smiled at her. 'Thank you,' she said, blowing into the plastic cup, then sipping.

Ginger looked around at the deserted restaurant enclosure. A chilly breeze was picking up handfuls of leaves, whipping them into small eddies round the legs of the empty tables. They were the only people sitting outside.

'This restaurant's closing up for winter next week,'

she remarked, 'so where are we going to meet after that?'

'I think the Orangery stays open, doesn't it? Or maybe we could try somewhere in Richmond sometimes,' Lia suggested, conscious of the fact that the Gardens were a long walk from Ginger's flat.

'Like where?' Ginger asked.

'Well, I'm the wrong person to ask,' Lia said, 'because I still don't know Richmond very well.' She turned to Alison and asked her, 'Where were you off to meet your friend that time we bumped into you?'

Alison was just about to reply that she had met Ramona on the Fifth Floor of Harvey Nichols, when she remembered her trek up and down the line. It had made her very late.

'Oh, that wasn't very good,' she said, covering quickly, 'I wouldn't go there again.'

'Well, it'll have to be somewhere they allow three prams,' Ginger said, 'and the only place I can think of is McDonald's.'

'Two prams. I won't be here anyway,' Alison said, 'I'm back at work on Monday.'

'Oh . . . we'll miss you,' Lia said. 'Shall we stick to the Orangery then?' she asked Ginger.

'Fine for me. I love walking. I really miss my bike,' she continued, 'I can't wait for the time when he's big enough to go in a child's seat at the back. You can get them with safety belts now and everything.'

For some reason, the thought of Ginger and Guy on a bike together made them all laugh.

'How's your nanny getting on?' Ginger asked Alison.

'Justine? She's an angel. I think we've been very lucky. Ben seems to like her and my life is transformed . . . she spends hours puréeing organic vegetables and introducing them into his diet, one by one, keeping a diary . . . it's marvellous. Honestly, Ginger, I wouldn't be too quick to refuse your parents' offers of help on this one,' Alison enthused.

'Hmm, but the difference is that I don't want to leave Guy.' Seeing Alison's face, she added quickly, 'Oh sorry, I didn't mean that to sound . . . I just meant that I don't really enjoy my job like you do, and so I can't get enthusiastic about going back. Anyway,' she went on, brightening, 'I don't have to think about it quite yet.' Then she asked, out of the blue, 'Do you think I should go on telly?'

'What do you mean?' Alison asked, still thinking about childcare and jobs and wondering if Ginger was asking about a career move.

'I've been asked to go on telly, you know, one of those awful phoney discussion programmes they have in the mornings.' Her voice put inverted commas round the word discussion. 'A friend of mine's a researcher, and they're doing one of those "Single Parents – is flogging too good for them?" kind of debates.'

Both Alison and Lia laughed at the deep, serious commentator's voice she put on to make her point. Ginger was a fantastic mimic.

'I think you'd be really good on television,' Lia chipped in.

'Of course she would,' Alison said, trying to inject a note of caution into the conversation, 'but would television be good to her? Surely that's the point. I mean, what's in it for you, Ginger? They're bound to have some horrible Tory grandee on patronizing you, someone like . . .' She thought for a moment.

'Like my father,' Ginger finished the sentence for her.

'Well, yes.'

'That's rather why the idea appealed to me. It would annoy him so much.'

Alison laughed. 'Well, I suppose if you could bear to, you'd be a far better spokesperson for single people than a lot of the victims they might get on. I mean you've made a positive decision to do this, you're coping and you're enjoying it . . . aren't you?' Alison asked.

'Oh yes. More than I've ever enjoyed anything. I thought I'd love my baby, but I never realized how much fun it would be,' Ginger said, beaming.

She would become a media star, Alison thought, if she looked on screen as she did now, with her impish face full of laughter, and her eyes sparkling with pride.

'You must let us know when you're on,' Lia said.

'Yes,' said Alison, 'that's one morning programme I wouldn't miss.'

'Oh, I don't know if I could if I thought you two were watching,' Ginger said, suddenly bashful.

'But you wouldn't care about the other two million viewers?' Lia asked.

'Not really, no, it's kind of like the school panto-mime – I was fine until the night when my parents were in the audience.' Ginger stood up, slurping back the rest of her Coke. 'Which reminds me,' she said, banging down her can on the table and tugging back her sleeve with her teeth to check her watch, 'I've got to run now, I haven't cleaned the flat and my father is coming to lunch.' She spun her pram round and walked off at her usual breakneck pace.

'Are you doing anything for lunch?' Lia asked Alison, as they watched Ginger disappear behind some tall conifers.

'Well, actually my mother's coming this afternoon, so I'd better be getting back, too,' Alison said; then, feeling guilty when she saw Lia's face fall, she added, spontaneously, 'but why don't you come back with me, and we'll have a bite together.'

'Are you sure?' Lia asked.

'Of course, if you don't mind bits and bobs from the fridge,' she said, trying to remember what there was to eat. Since Justine, her nanny, had started work and everything for Ben was taken care of, Alison had stopped bothering so much about their shopping and

160

cooking, which she loved to do on occasion, but found boring as a routine. Stephen had even remarked on the fact that they seemed to eat nothing but pizza these days, which they phoned for when he returned late at night, and was delivered by a spotty-faced boy on a moped.

'It's just that Neil's got a football match tonight, so it's a bit of a long day for me,' Lia said as they strolled down the road where Alison lived.

'Yeah, Stephen seems to work all the time at the moment, and I gave Justine today off in exchange for Saturday. Did I tell you we're going away for a night? Just to a hotel down the road, but I'm so excited . . . anyway, I don't want her coming into contact with my mother.' Alison grimaced, 'Well, I suppose that's a bit unfair. My mother was a great help and all that, but, you know . . . Here we are.'

They manoeuvred the prams into the large hall. Both babies were still sleeping.

'I love the coloured glass in the door,' Lia said.

'Oh, thank you,' Alison smiled. 'It's not original, I'm afraid. When we bought the house, we had to strip virtually everything. It had all been "improved" in the seventies. The panelled doors had hardboard tacked over, can you believe it?'

Lia made a suitably surprised face, although she knew she wouldn't be able to distinguish a panelled door from any other kind of door. She followed Alison into the large room that stretched from the front of the house to a conservatory at the back. It looked like something out of a Sunday magazine, she thought, with its bare polished boards and rugs. Books lined the walls of the living area and there was one huge sofa covered in loose terracotta canvas, heaped with richly patterned cushions. The kitchen area was mainly dark green, with a great solid wooden table, on which sat a large blue glass bowl of lemons. She found herself reaching out to check they were real.

Alison filled a kettle, also dark green, and pulled open the door of an enormous American-style fridge. 'Would a salad and some pâté be OK?' she asked.

'Fine,' Lia said, trying to contain her awe, then pulling out a chair and sitting down.

'Would you like a glass of wine?' Alison asked, conscious of the slight awkwardness that always accompanies the first time someone visits your home.

'Yes, please.'

Lia watched as Alison uncorked a bottle she had taken from the fridge and poured white wine into stemmed green glasses, then began to prepare the salad, tearing lettuce leaves and pink-veined chard over a giant bowl the shape and colour of a cabbage leaf. Even the vegetables went with the colour scheme, she thought.

'Fantastic kitchen,' she said.

'Thank you. Do you cook much?' Alison asked.

'I used to, nothing fancy, but there never seems to be the time now. I don't know why. Your life changes, doesn't it, in all sorts of ways, that nobody ever tells you about.'

'I think they probably do,' Alison said, 'it's just that you can't imagine what it's like until it happens.'

Lia laughed weakly and took a sip of her wine. 'Is Stephen good with Ben?' she asked, and saw surprise on Alison's face.

None of them ever mentioned their partners, which was odd because when they were together it felt as if they could say anything. Sometimes one of them, usually Ginger, would admit to a fear of a failing that both the others had felt, and it was such a relief to think you weren't alone. It was always something to do with babies, Lia realized. They were all equal as mothers, but in every other way they were so different. Perhaps it was out of respect for Ginger that they didn't mention the men, because she didn't have one.

'Yes he is,' Alison replied, 'he's a much better father than I thought he would be, if I'm honest.'

162

'Really?' Lia said. 'It's just the opposite with Neil . . .'

'Oh?' Alison turned away, rummaging around in a cupboard and pulling out a half-empty jar of sun-dried tomatoes in oil. Suddenly, she wished she had not invited Lia for lunch.

'I thought he would be brilliant, but, well, perhaps he'll be better when she's a bit older,' Lia went on.

'I believe a lot of men are like that.' Alison breathed a sigh of relief. Subject closed. She dribbled vinegar into the jar.

'Perhaps I'm to blame,' Lia continued, 'so much of me is taken up loving Anouska, I don't have enough time for him—' What she couldn't understand was why, when they had a beautiful little girl and she was as happy being a mother as she ever had been, Neil seemed to be trying to spoil it for all of them.

'It takes a bit of adjustment,' Alison interrupted, feeling dreadful that she was not prepared to recipro-cate with her own problems. The conversation was beginning to remind her of the long, agonized talks she used to have at school with Sally, when they would tell each other everything that was on their minds, except that she had never really believed that Sally told her as much as she told Sally. And now she understood why that was. It gave you quite a sense of power to be the confessor rather than the confidante. But it was a power she did not want.

'I hate having to rely on Neil for money,' Lia went on. 'I mean, I know that what I'm doing is a full-time job, but I'm just not used to not paying my way, it makes me feel funny somehow . . . I didn't think it would affect our relationship, but it has, do you know what I mean?'

Alison listened, holding the jar of dressing in mid-air, ready to be shaken. Why are you telling me this, she wanted to ask Lia. I don't want to know so much about you. Don't draw me into your life.

'I'll have to face the different problem of guilt . . .'

163

Alison tried to divert the direction of the conversation.

'Guilt?'

'Leaving Ben with someone else when I go back to work . . . although,' Alison continued, as they began to eat, 'I think you feel guilty as a parent most of the time anyway, don't you?'

'Guilty?' Lia repeated.

'Responsible would be a better word. There's this terrible weight of responsibility that descends on you, that you've brought this being into the world and if anything happens it will be your fault,' Alison said.

Lia took another sip of her wine. 'I know that I want to give Anouska the best possible life I can, if that's what you mean,' she said, thoughtfully, 'I look at her and I love her so much, I can't imagine how anyone abandons their child . . .'

Suddenly Alison felt a tremendous surge of sympathy for her, remembering the calm, straightforward way she had told them about her childhood. 'Do you remember your mother?' she asked, gently.

'I think I can just remember her,' Lia said quietly, 'but I never know whether I'm just imagining it. I used to have this dream about her leaving me at the gate and I walked up this long, grey drive, all on my own, but that can't be right. There wasn't a drive like that. I probably got the picture from a book. There was a book about orphans . . .' She tried to remember the title.

'*Madeline*?' Alison suggested. It had been one of her favourites. She used to wish she was an orphan too, she remembered, because they seemed to have so much fun.

'Yes, that's the one. They all used to walk along in two straight lines.' Lia brightened at the memory of it.

'Have you ever looked for your mother, I mean, tried to trace her, now you're grown up?' Alison asked.

164

'I don't think she'd want to be reminded, do you? No, it wouldn't be fair,' Lia replied.

Alison felt chastened by the selflessness of Lia's answer to her question. It was not at all the way she would look at it, she thought.

'Stephen tried to find his real mother a while ago,' she told her, anxious to appear to understand. 'He was adopted. Funnily enough, one of his half-sisters turned out to be a journalist I vaguely know . . . but his mother had died. It wasn't a very satisfactory experience.'

They both ate mouthfuls of salad.

'You move on, don't you?' Lia said, eventually, 'you don't always want to be going over the past.'

'No,' Alison agreed, not trusting herself to say more.

Then first Ben, then Anouska woke up, and as they ran into the hall to pick them up, Alison's mother arrived.

A black Rolls-Royce drew up at the top of Richmond Hill, and the chauffeur jumped out and ran round the car to open the kerbside back door. Sir James Prospect rose, with some effort, from his seat, and stood on the pavement. The driver listened to his instructions, tipped his peaked hat, then walked back round the car, got in and drove away.

Ginger watched from the window of her ground-floor living room, hoping that none of the neighbours had witnessed her father's arrival. They were used to limousines – a famous rock-and-roller, now grown respectable in his middle age, had recently bought a whole house in the terrace – but her father was such a hated figure, she had wanted to keep her relationship to him a secret.

He looked at the window and saw her standing there. She waved to him without returning his smile and went to open the door.

'I haven't got very long, I'm afraid,' were his first words as she opened the door.

She felt like slamming it back in his face.

He bent to kiss her, but she stepped back, unwilling to act out the meaningless ritual of greeting.

Leaving him to close the door she marched back into the large, high-ceilinged room, reminding herself she had promised she would be charming and courteous to him. She was a parent herself now, and she must be polite, if only because she owed it to her son. But the moment she had heard the car draw up outside, a fiery impatience had begun to wind up her body. It was the sensation that used to precede a tantrum when she was a child. Now she was older, she knew how to suppress her temper, but the effort made her tense and tight-lipped.

She picked Guy up from his mat on the floor, holding him to herself, relishing the warmth of him, the sweet smell of his hair, the comfort of his small, sturdy body that fitted so snugly against hers.

'This is Guy,' she said, turning round so her father could see him, but not offering the baby to him to hold.

She watched Guy's face as he became aware there was another person in the room. Sometimes he stared at people with such undisguised suspicion it made her want to laugh.

'Hello, young man,' her father said.

The words grated. He sounded like an uncle visiting his nephew at Eton, not wanting any nasty un-English displays of emotion. She half expected her father to try to give Guy's hand a good firm shake.

She waited for as long as she could bear for him to say something nice about her baby. Recently she had started feeling warmer towards people who said he was gorgeous, than towards those who remarked on his size. Handsome was good too, and once, when she had bumped into Lia and her partner walking along the tow-path, Neil had peered into the pram and said what a good-looking chap he was, and she found the words had made her warm to him a great deal more than she had previously done.

'Well, what do you think?' she finally demanded of her father.

Her father sniffed the air. 'I think there's something burning.'

'God, the quiche!' Ginger thrust the baby into his stiff, besuited arms, and ran to the oven.

The Marks & Spencer broccoli and tomato quiche was a rather darker brown on top than the colour of the serving suggestion on the packet. She grabbed it, then dropped it on to the work surface as the hot foil case burned her bare fingers. Miraculously, the quiche landed the right way up.

'I thought perhaps you were being a little over-ambitious inviting me to lunch,' her father laughed. 'Come on, let's call Colin up on the mobile and he'll take us somewhere nice.'

Holding Guy under one arm, he extracted a mobile phone from his pocket and began to press buttons.

Ginger was seething. 'No,' she said, trying not to shout.

'Really, darling, it's no trouble, he's only driving round and round the block till I need him.'

She didn't know whether his treatment of the chauffeur, his casual dismissal of her hospitality, or the way he was holding her precious baby like a spare overcoat that made her more furious. She became all the more determined to see him putting the dried-up quiche with its burned cheese crust into his supercilious mouth.

'Certainly not,' she said, taking Guy back from him, 'I haven't got a car seat for Guy and I don't want to take him out again today. It's too cold.'

'But the car's very cosy and surely you can hold him on your lap. We always did.'

'It's illegal actually,' she said to him, 'and we wouldn't want a government minister breaking the law of the land . . .'

His face registered the potential of a *Daily Mirror* reporter snapping him with his single daughter and her brat, and she knew that she had won this particular showdown.

Ginger put Guy in a bouncy chair. Then she opened a bag of salad, emptied it onto two plates, cut the quiche in half and slid one piece on her plate and one onto her father's. While he ate, she spooned a jar of organic vegetable purée into Guy's mouth, feeling cruelly triumphant as she watched her father masticating the unappetizing dry food, knowing that every mouthful served to remind him that his arrogant, smiling white teeth were not his own.

Sir James dutifully drank the cup of instant coffee she made him, then took out his mobile phone again. 'OK, Colin, if you'd be so kind.' Then he switched it off, and said to Ginger with the false note of regret she had heard him use so often on television, 'So sorry it had to be such a short visit, but it is heartening to see you looking so well.'

'Aren't you going to say anything about my baby?' she asked him as the car drew up outside.

'Well, I'm sure he's very sweet, darling. I was never very good with small babies. I'm sure we'll be great friends when he's a little older . . .'

The Kawasaki 900 let rip at the second roundabout of the A1. Neil opened up the throttle and glimpsed the speedometer flickering above 100. It was fantastic getting up speed, leaving the suburbs of London behind, shooting past fields still white from the morning frost, unwarmed by the city's neon. A mist rose from muddy patches of damp turf, merging with the pink-washed grey of the sky, as the pale sun slipped away to his left, and darkness quickly followed. He felt as if he had been released.

Pete lived in a village not three miles away from the municipal park lodge where they used to live. It was a large pebble-dashed council house built in the sixties, with a big garden that served as workshop, spare parts warehouse, and adventure playground for the boys. Neil propped his bike up next to the wheelless, rusting old Zephyr which Pete had owned for years and was always planning to restore to its former, pale pink glory. He had promised to drive his oldest daughter Wendy to her wedding in it, but when the time came, they had had to hire a white Jag instead.

The bare hundred-watt light bulb that hung from an extension lead strung from the rafters of the shed was blazing. Neil took off his helmet and wandered in. 'Hello?'

'Jesus, mate, I didn't hear you drive up.' Pete slid out from under a van on a mechanics' trolley. His smiling face was covered in oil. 'Hang on a minute and I'll be with you.'

'Finish what you're doing,' Neil said, pulling off his gauntlet gloves, 'I'll go in and see Cheryl.'

He walked over to the frosted glass door at the side of the house, knocked and went in.

His sister-in-law looked up from the stove where she was frying sausages, and smiled at him. 'Hello, stranger!'

'Hi there,' he said, inhaling the warm fug of kitchen air, loosening the long scarf that was wound several times round his neck.

'You ride down?' she asked, unnecessarily. He was wearing leather biker's trousers with ribbing at the knee and his battered old leather jacket. His face was ruddy from the wind. 'Turned pretty cold, yeah?'

'Yeah,' he said, pulling out a chair and sitting down.

'You eaten?' she asked him.

'Not since lunch.' He smiled at her as she piled four sausages onto a plate and pointed with the fork she had in her hand at the wrapped loaf of bread on the table.

'Make yourself a sarnie,' she said, 'there's HP and ketchup by the toaster.'

He set to work spreading thick slices with margarine from a family-sized tub, layering the hot sausages on top so that their grease melted the yellow fat and the delicious brown oily mingling seeped into the pappy white bread. He picked up the sandwich in both hands, admiring its construction, and opened his mouth wide.

Cheryl put a cup of hot strong tea beside his plate and sat down opposite him. More sausages spat and sizzled in the large black frying pan.

'What brings you down on a night like this then?' she asked him.

'Fancied a ride,' he said, his mouth full.

'Lia OK?'

He nodded.

'And the babe?'

'Fine, yeah . . . What about your lot?'

'Don't see much of the boys these days. Football. If they're not playing, they're watching Sky at one of their friend's. They're at the fireworks tonight. They helped with the bonfire. We're going along later, if you fancy it. Wendy's all right. She's got another one on the way . . . Has Pete told you?' she added, putting her hand on her stomach.

'What?' he said, taking a glug of tea.

'I'm expecting again,' she smiled. 'We were a bit careless after Pete's fortieth . . . I'm happy enough. Maybe this time we'll have a chance to enjoy it.'

'Well, then,' Neil said, nonplussed.

'Just think,' Cheryl said, 'one of my grandchildren will be older than my own baby!'

It was impossible to think of her as a grandmother. She looked more or less the same as she had when she had married his brother twenty years before. A few lines round her eyes, a more natural blonde tint in her hair, and, he thought wryly, she didn't look as pregnant now as she had then.

It must have been tough bringing up a baby in a caravan. He couldn't imagine how they had coped.

170

Wendy had spent much of her babyhood with his mother in the lodge, while Cheryl and Pete worked all the hours they could so that they would be able to furnish their council house nicely once they reached the top of the waiting list. They had waited a few years before having more kids – two boys in quick succession, and now after all this time, they were going to have a fourth child.

'Be nice for Anouska to have a cousin her own age, though, won't it?' Cheryl was asking him.

He suppressed the irritation that niggled him every time he heard or spoke his child's name.

'Suppose so,' he said, trying to get some enthusiasm into his voice.

The back door opened and his brother walked in. He went to the sink, dipped his fingers in the huge tin of Swarfega on the windowsill and rubbed his hands together, sluicing off the worst of the grime under a running tap. Then he came to the table and sat down.

Pete had always been tall. Now he was big too, burly. Not surprising, Neil thought, watching him wolf down half a loaf of bread wrapped round a pound of sausages.

'Nice snack,' his brother said, licking his lips, 'now what's for dinner?' He laughed.

With his long hair tied back in a pony-tail, his huge frame almost bursting out of the once-white, all-in-one, oil-stained overalls, and the good-humoured smile on his face, he looked like a friendly giant.

'Tell him he's got to watch his weight,' Cheryl urged Neil, trying to be cross, but unable to stop herself smiling back at her cheerful husband, 'he snores something terrible.'

'Fancy a beer, mate?' Pete wandered over to the fridge and pulled out a four-pack.

'Oh, take him down the pub,' Cheryl said, 'I don't want you filthy great louts cluttering up my kitchen.' She shot Pete a meaningful glance.

She had guessed that he wanted to talk to him on

his own, Neil realized, appreciating Cheryl's intuition.

'OK, mate?' Pete asked.

'OK,' Neil replied, and gave Cheryl a quick hug as they left.

'You take care,' he told her.

'And you too,' she said, wondering what it was that was so preoccupying him.

'What's up then, mate?' Pete asked, as he plonked two straight pint glasses down on the small round table in the corner by the fire. He picked one up and tasted it. 'Ugh, that's your one, mate, I don't know how you can drink it with lemonade.'

'I'm on the bike and it's better than those non-alcoholic lagers,' Neil said.

'Yeah, well, a can of Tango'd be better than that crap,' his brother observed, taking a long draught from his glass. A moustache of foam appeared on his upper lip. He licked it away.

He was voracious in everything he did, Neil thought, half repelled and half fascinated by his brother's appetites. He looked around the pub. It had changed since the days they used to ride out from the town and drink cider that hot, hot summer of 1976. Then, there had been horse brasses round the bar, plain wooden floorboards and a dartboard. If you were hungry you ordered a packet of pork scratchings pulled from the card next to the till, or a bag of crisps from the boxes under the bar. Now, all the seats were plumply upholstered in red fabric with covered buttons. There was carpet, and printed menus poked out of silver holders on every table, offering Yorkshire puddings with a variety of fillings or something called Surf-'n'-Turf. He preferred it how it had been.

'Cheryl's pregnant, did she tell you?' Pete said.

'Yeah, congratulations!' Neil knocked his glass desultorily against his brother's.

'What about you? Going to have another one?'

172

'No way,' Neil said quietly, adding, for the sake of politeness, 'not for a long time, anyway.'

The experience of being a father was so very different from what he had expected, he had found it very difficult to get used to, and there was no pleasure in it. When Lia looked at the baby she seemed to see things that he could not. She talked about her as if she were a person. We had parsnips today, but Anouska says she prefers sweet potato; she liked this rattle so much in the shop that I just had to buy it for her. It wasn't that he thought she was imposing a personality on the child, but when he looked at the baby he could only see a tiny creature with a startled face, who had just two ways of expressing herself: a toothless grin, or, more frequently, a roar of discontent. If he had not heard it at least twice a night, he would not have believed that such a small, frail body could produce so much noise.

'Seems so much work,' Neil expanded in the silence that had followed his statement, 'well, it does for Lia. I don't know, Cheryl seems to take it all in her stride, but Lia spends her whole life making pear purée . . .'

'Yeah, well, Cheryl and me've had a lot of practice, haven't we, though, mate?' Pete took another mouthful of beer. 'Takes a bit of time getting used to it, you know. For ages you're getting nothing back, but it's great when they're older. You loved it when Chris and Ryan were growing up, didn't you?'

'Maybe I'd know what to do if we had a boy,' Neil said, despondently.

'Not really at that age, mate,' his brother, the man of experience, informed him, 'I think men find it pretty scary how small and helpless they are. Women are better at that bit. They've got the equipment. I don't just mean tits . . .' he added.

'Yeah, well,' Neil said, looking into his glass.

'That's not it, is it?' Pete asked him.

'What?'

173

'Come on, mate, you come all the way down here on a cold dark winter's night when you haven't been for months, you've got a face like a man who's lost his winning lottery ticket, don't tell me you've just come to see the fireworks.'

Neil smiled. His brother wasn't the subtlest person in the world, but he had always been able to sense when something was bothering him. That was why, he supposed, he had needed to come and talk to him.

So, he bought him another pint, and told him slowly and hesitantly that he felt everything had changed since the baby was born.

'It happens, mate,' Pete said. 'What else?'

So Neil told him about the row they had after he discovered that she'd changed her name.

'So what's the big deal? It's only a few letters.'

'I don't know ... I just feel like if she's lied to me about that, then how many other things has she lied about?'

'But you just said she never lied, she just never told you. What's wrong with that?'

Perhaps he had been stupid to think that Pete would understand. It seemed so fundamental to him, but to Pete the distinction was merely semantic.

'I don't blame her for changing it myself, Lia's a much classier name. Perhaps that's it,' Pete said, nudging Neil's arm, trying to jolly him out of his mood, 'you prefer a bird with a classy name. You always did have a thing for snooty girls, there was that silly slag, you know, who lived up in the Willows ... Daddy's an estate agent and who's for tennis, all that. What was her name?'

'Alison, and she wasn't a slag,' Neil said defensively, twirling a beer mat around on the table top. 'I met her again recently.' He attempted to keep his voice light and casual, but as soon as he'd said it, he wished he hadn't.

'Oh yeah.' Pete put down his pint and stared at him. 'So, finally we get the reason ...'

174

'No,' Neil protested, 'no, she's married, she's got a kid, for heaven's sake.'

'Those are reasons why you shouldn't, not reasons why you don't want to.'

'Well, I don't want to . . .' Neil said emphatically.

'I hope not, mate,' Pete said, finishing his beer, ''cause I'll tell you something for nothing. Lia is class, mate, real class. Shines out of her. She's the real thing. That Alison, well . . . anyway, I'd better go and see this bonfire my kids have spent the last week building.' He began to rise from the table.

And Neil felt certain that if their conversation had continued for a minute longer they would have ended up exchanging blows.

His brother shook his hand before he got on the bike, but he didn't say anything more, nor did he turn back to wave goodbye as his huge outline merged into the night. Neil roared off, almost performing a wheelie in his haste to get away. He drove much faster than he should, taking risks on corners of the country lanes where ice was already forming, his anger daring him to the limits of danger.

Speeding through the last village before the A1 roundabout, he saw a child run into the road, not thinking about traffic in her excitement to get across to a firework party. Neil was too close. As he braked, the world seemed to stop and go into slow motion and he realized he was going to hit the little girl. He swerved and skidded to a halt, miraculously keeping control of the bike and just avoiding her. Her mother ran over and scooped her up, shouting curses at him.

'You should hold her bloody hand, then,' he shouted back, dusting himself down, and roared off.

A hundred yards up the road, he stopped again, realizing he was shaking too much to drive safely. He sat down in the freezing grass on the verge of the road, and pulled a packet of cigarettes out of his top pocket. There were only two left. He'd given up when Lia became pregnant. Seemed a good reason, and for a while he'd been feeling the catch in his lungs when he was refereeing the boys' games at school. But he had always kept a packet for emergencies. The psychology of knowing you had a choice worked well against the strangely powerful grip nicotine exerted on your mind. Recently, there seemed to have been a lot more emergencies than usual, and he was getting through a packet a week. Lia didn't seem to have noticed. They hadn't been close enough for her to smell his breath.

Pete was right, he thought, taking a long, determined drag, blowing out smoke that froze in the icy air. His brother had seen through him straightaway. And his criticism was fair enough. He knew himself that he shouldn't be having the thoughts about Ally that he had been having, but he didn't seem to be able to find a way of stopping them.

The memory of the exquisite moment their bodies had joined was too clear. He couldn't get it out of his mind. First the heat of their skin touching, and then her legs parting underneath him, and as he pushed, the slight resistance, like the flesh of an almost-ripe fruit suddenly ripening under his touch, flooding with sweet juice, and closing again around him. It had felt as if he were being sucked into her soul. He had never really left.

Stop it, he thought, throwing down the half-smoked cigarette, repeating the familiar mantra in his head. She left you. She went away and didn't even tell you that she wasn't going to come back. You waited, like an idiot, for a long time, but she never even bothered to find out whether you were still alive.

Everyone had told him that time healed wounds. It had taken nearly twenty years, but he had eventually found a better woman to love. Go home, he told himself. Go home.

Lia lay in bed listening to the distant whoosh and bang of fireworks exploding. From time to time there

176

was one like a scream that cut out at top pitch and sounded disturbingly like someone being strangled. Each time it happened, she sat up with a start, unnerved, then lay back down again feeling the race of her pulse against the pillow. She couldn't sleep. Sleeplessness had become a habit and even though she had come to bed early, relishing the prospect of a few hours' oblivion before Anouska woke up, she had not been able to drift off. Now that they had moved the baby's cot into the other bedroom, Lia found it more difficult to relax, feeling almost lonely without her. She was half tempted to take the duvet and lie down on the floor next to the cot, but she knew that if Neil found them like that he would be annoyed. He said it was good for Anouska to get used to being on her own, and he was probably right, although Lia thought the decision to move her out of their room probably had more to do with Neil's sleeping patterns than the baby's.

Where was Neil? She glanced at the alarm clock. It was after ten and he still wasn't home. She knew that he wasn't at the football match, because Bill, his junior in the sports department, had rung earlier to tell him that the team had won the match 3–2 in extra time. The result meant that they were now at the top of their league, he had told Lia excitedly, and asked her to pass on the message when Neil returned. She was sure that Neil had said he was taking the team this evening, but she had probably misunderstood, Lia thought, looking at the receiver as Bill rang off. He'd probably gone up to his sports club, or for a drink with another teacher, but it was strange that he hadn't rung to tell her. Perhaps he had gone for a spin on his bike. He often did that when he wanted to clear his head. When something was troubling him, his impulse was to work it out on his own. Hers was to talk to someone about it.

In the past few weeks she had longed for a friend to talk to. She had thought about confiding her anxieties to Ginger, but she sensed that Ginger did not like Neil, which would make her biased, and she didn't need that. In the end, she had found herself telling Alison, but that hadn't helped. As soon as you thought you were getting close to Alison, she seemed to veer away, as if embarrassed by intimacy. Meeting her mother explained a lot. A middle-class Tory who bought her suits from Jaeger and thought that style was anything with a Louis Vuitton logo, she had looked Lia up and down, making a quick judgement about whether she was a suitable lunch companion for her daughter, and, Lia felt, decided that she wasn't. Lia had never felt so conscious of the scuffs on her ankle books or the splashes of carrot purée on the big Arran jumper of Neil's she was wearing over leggings.

Where was Neil? It was cold out. The weather map of England had three large letters over the whole of the south-east. ICE. It was dangerous to be racing round on frozen roads. Oh God, perhaps he had had an accident! She looked at the clock again. Half past ten. Too early to ring the police. They would think she was totally neurotic. She imagined two uniformed coppers on the desk. Poor sod's not allowed out on his own at night, they'd say, cutting off her phone call. Silly cow, perhaps hubby's somewhere he shouldn't be. Who could blame him? No. Lia tried to stop the thought gathering momentum. Surely he couldn't be seeing someone else? Surely things hadn't got that bad between them? Surely there would be signs? And yet, another part of her whispered, it would explain so much: his inability to engage with the baby, his moodiness, his overreaction to the revelation of her real name. It was almost as if he had been looking for an excuse to be nasty to her. Men who felt guilty often took it out on their partners, trying to make it their fault. If he was seeing someone else, it would explain why she had felt since almost before Anouska was born that there was a little piece of him he had closed off, that she could no longer touch.

When he got in, she was going to ask him where he had been, she decided, as the clap, clap, clap, whizz of the end of the fireworks bounced from house to house in the street outside. It was the not knowing that she hated. But it was only one evening, the other side of her said. What had happened to them if she didn't trust him just to stay out one night for a few hours without telling her where? It was far more likely that he had had an accident. She pictured him lying in a mangled heap of blood and metal by the side of a motorway and shuddered. She would wait until midnight, she decided, then it would not be unreasonable to ring the police. The moment she had made the decision, she heard the bike coming down the street and a minute later, his key in the lock.

He called out, 'Hello.' She could tell by his footfall on the narrow wooden staircase that he was in a good mood. He was taking the steps two by two, eager to find her. The flood of relief that he was safe was quickly replaced by irritation at his lack of consideration for her feelings. Couldn't he have rung? Didn't he realize she would worry? She pulled the duvet up protectively over her ears and closed her eyes. He leapt onto the bed and lay beside her, still clad in the cold biker's leather.

'Are you asleep?' he whispered.

'Not any more,' she said, tightly.

'How's the baby?'

'Fine.'

'I'm sorry I'm so late,' he said, then he put his arms around her and whispered, 'I'm sorry about a lot of things . . .'

She felt her resolve melt. 'That's OK,' she said, turning towards him, 'didn't you go to the match?'

He had forgotten he had told her that he was taking the football team to an away game. For a second, he

179

hesitated. It was such a silly thing to have said, when all he had wanted was a chance to think about things. If he had said he was going down to Pete's, she would have wanted to come too.

'No, I just went for a ride around,' he told her.

'Well, good night then,' she said, turning away from him, knowing that there was something he wasn't telling her.

The morning of Ginger's screen début, Charlie Prince was early in to the office. He had already made half a dozen calls when he chanced to look up through the glass wall that separated his office from the reception area at the television set that was positioned above the receptionist's head.

On the screen, a girl's face was talking animatedly and rapidly, although he could not hear a word because the glass blocked out the sound. It took him a few moments to realize that he recognized her. He put down the phone and stood up, but by the time he reached his door, the camera had zoomed in on another person's face.

'What's it about?' He pointed at the screen.

The receptionist jumped. Charlie rarely spoke to anyone without the aid of a handset under his chin. Sometimes she wondered why he didn't get a pair of earphones with a microphone attached like she sometimes used when she had typing to do as well as answering the phone.

'Haven't been paying much attention, really,' she told him, 'it's been busy.' She pointed at the switch-board.

He frowned.

'I think it's something about single parents,' she added.

'Turn it up,' Charlie ordered, sitting down on the edge of one of the low-slung leather chairs. Somebody he recognized as a Tory Baroness had just finished her sentence and was looking distastefully at the girl sitting opposite her in the circle of invited guests. The camera followed her gaze back to Ginger.

'Look,' Ginger said, trying to keep her voice reasonable, 'you're the type of person who doesn't like single mothers, and you object to abortions, right? So, what's the alternative?'

There was a flurry of applause from the audience behind.

'You could control yourself,' the Tory lady suggested.

A few of her supporters clapped.

'Oh get real!' Ginger said.

The camera zoomed in on the host of the show, who was smiling with a kind of smug pleasure that the discussion was getting a little controversial.

'Well, if I may say so, it's all very well for people like you who have money—' the Tory lady began.

'Oh, so it's OK for the rich, like so many other things,' Ginger interrupted her, 'yeah, that's really great, isn't it? So, next step eugenics and then you'd be happy . . .'

The host smiled even more broadly. A few more comments like that and his show would make the front page of the *Sun* the next morning.

'No, I'm certainly not saying that.' The Tory lady looked flustered. 'All I'm saying is that people with the means to do so can get proper, trained help, whereas those who don't—'

'Are forced to look after their own kids . . . oh dear!' Ginger finished her sentence for her. 'So it's fine to have a well-paid nanny, but if you're a single mother in the poverty trap and have to bring up your child yourself then that's wrong. Look,' she went on, gathering momentum as she spoke, 'I'll tell you what's wrong: one, single mothers who are poor don't have the freedom to choose whether to work; two, they don't have the money to buy their children the things they need, like decent food and shoes. People like you think it's fine, preferable, in fact, to get a stranger to look after your children until they're old enough to be sent away for months to public school . . . and you're the good parents?'

Charlie laughed out loud.

'We're going to have to leave it there . . .' said the host, as the titles started to roll. He looked very seriously at the camera. 'Tomorrow: does anyone have the right to tell *you* where you can walk *your dog*?'

Charlie mimed drawing a knife across his neck, indicating that he wished the television set to be turned down again. The receptionist complied.

'Get me Robert Preston,' he instructed her, and went back into his office.

The room was still dark, but outside the sun was shining. There was a bright sliver of light, white, like a moonbeam, breaking through the gap where the curtains were not quite properly drawn. The room smelt unfamiliar – of pot pourri and beeswax – and the covers on the bed were heavy and reminded her of wintry mornings at home in the pre-duvet days of her childhood. Alison felt like Sleeping Beauty waking up in a palace after sleeping for a hundred years.

Stephen was propped up on a bank of white pillows looking down at her. She stretched her arms in a huge, waking-up yawn.

He dipped his head and kissed her lips. She tasted mint and soda. He had already brushed his teeth.

'Did you sleep well?' he asked her.

'Blissfully . . . did you?'

'Oh, you know how I am,' he said. As a junior hospital doctor, Stephen had trained himself to do without sleep, and now that learned ability almost amounted to insomnia. 'I watched the video,' he added, 'it's the great advantage of having a suite. You could put that in your piece.'

' "A suite is preferable if your partner wants to watch television all night . . ." I don't think so.

182

Anyway, what video?' she asked, laughing as she pummelled the pillows on her side of the bed into a comfortable white cotton mound behind her.

'They gave us a video when we arrived, their version of a brochure, I suppose. It tells you what you can do.'

'And what can you do?' she queried, amazed at the kind of clinical thoroughness he brought to everything he did, even an away-from-it-all weekend in one of the most luxurious hotels in the country, where the only rule was to relax.

'Oh, everything – riding, swimming . . .'

'In the pool where Profumo met Christine Keeler?' she asked.

'Well, that's outdoor, so I think not, in this weather, but there's an indoor one, too.'

'You have done your research,' she teased him.

'Another alternative is to make love to the very beautiful woman in your bed,' he said matter-of-factly, putting his hand on her arm very gently.

'That's on the video, too, is it?' she bantered, his flattery making her shy.

'Well, I suppose they might have hidden cameras' – he looked at the drapery above their heads – 'but I don't think they'd give a film of what we did last night away for nothing . . .'

She smiled at him, the memory of the previous evening making her immediately wet.

He slid down the pillows so that the whole length of his body was touching hers.

What a good fit we are, she thought, shivering with the pleasure of his warm skin against hers under the fresh-smelling sheets and the heavy counterpane. She clasped her hands behind his neck, reaching up to kiss him deeply and felt him harden against her thigh. She rolled over on top of him, pausing while he adjusted the bedclothes to keep her bare back covered. He spreadeagled his legs and she lay perfectly still between them, her head inclined on his shoulder, the tip of his penis nestling against her belly button. Then she raised her bottom and knelt above him, and he rested his hands, his beautiful slim surgeon's hands, on her pelvic bones and guided himself into her.

Last night it had been for her, all for her. She still felt tender where his fingers had tickled and coaxed and rubbed her hard through soft undulating ripples to sublime torrents of orgasm. It was a delicious tenderness, quivering on the edge of pleasure and pain, and now he was inside her again, her flesh seemed to be remembering, responding, retracing again the unfamiliar ascent of sensation to climax.

We can do it, she wanted to scream with joy, we can still do it!

'I must buy Ramona some flowers,' she remarked, spooning fresh fruit salad into her mouth. A drop of the cold, light syrup fell between her breasts and she watched fascinated as her nipples contracted. She felt as if her body had been given back to her. Every inch of her skin was alive and responsive to the sensual touch of each new surface it made contact with – the sheets, the ice-cold syrup, the soft, cold carpet under the soles of her feet as she walked barefoot to the bathroom, her husband's silky, warm skin.

'Why's that?' he said, his mouth full of scrambed egg and buttery toast.

His passion for breakfast never ceased to amaze her. It was so out of kilter with his fastidiousness. If he were a breakfast, she recalled the game she had played with Ginger and Lia in the Gardens, then he would be Earl Grey tea with a sliver of lemon, and a dry biscotte. In fact, he was devoted to greasy spoon cafés, and full English breakfast with everything. She looked at his plate – it was the five-star hotel version: home-made pork sausages, lean bacon, perfectly scrambled eggs, superior black pudding the texture of a chocolate mousse, with none of those horrible white circles of fat, and dark, chewy slices of sautéed chanterelle mushroom.

'How is it?' she asked him, pointing her spoon at the plate.

'I prefer a bit of streaky bacon,' he said, looking up for a moment, then laughing at himself.

'Well, it was really Ramona's suggestion,' she went on, continuing her earlier thought, 'to get away and be grown ups again.'

'I thought it was a freebie?'

'You must be joking – you don't get a suite like this on a freebie. No, I'm afraid it's me being extravagant . . . Well, I am going to do the restaurant column about our dinner in Waldo's last night, so I can claim that back . . .'

'I like your extravagance,' Stephen said decisively, wiping his plate with the soft centre of a piece of toast, 'I shan't even begin to think about the price.'

'Good,' she said, sipping her glass of freshly squeezed orange. 'So, what are we going to do for the rest of the morning?'

'Well, first I think we should ring Justine and see how Ben has fared without us,' Stephen said, picking up the phone.

For over an hour, she realized, she had been so deeply entranced by the fairy-tale ambience of their sumptuous room, she had not had a thought, not even a fleeting one, about their son.

'Good idea,' she said quickly, dabbing at her mouth with the heavy damask napkin.

There was a free appointment in The Pavilion. She decided to indulge in a seaweed body wrap while Stephen went for a walk in the gardens. They agreed to rendezvous in their suite at eleven. It seemed wasteful not to spend as many minutes there as possible before they had to let it go.

She was there before him, sitting at a Georgian desk writing a postcard to her mother.

'I've booked us into the Terrace for lunch,' he said.

She turned round and beamed at him. Passing one of the dining rooms on her way back from being pampered, she had toyed with the idea of booking lunch, desperate to extend this fantasy time before going back into the real world again, but she had guessed that Stephen would consider it one extravagance too many. She was delighted that he had surprised her.

'How does my skin look?' she asked him, inclining her face towards the window.

'Just the same as ever,' he said, putting his finger under her chin and examining her face, then turned the bleak statement into a compliment by adding, 'you always have lovely skin.'

'Not on my tummy,' she said, pinching at the loose fold under her black woollen Nicole Farhi dress. 'Do you think I ought to have a tummy tuck?' she asked, only half seriously.

'What is a tummy tuck?'

'Cosmetic surgery – to get rid of that stretched bit above the scar.'

'I believe plastic surgery without a sound medical or psychological reason to be quite inappropriate,' he pronounced in his consultant's voice, then, hearing the pomposity of his words, he added, 'Anyway, I love that loose skin, and your scar, and everything they tell me about you. It's what's inside that is beautiful – the bit that no surgeon can "improve", the bit that even when I have my hand inside a person's heart, I cannot touch . . .'

'Ugh, you're putting me off the idea of lunch,' she said playfully, but his words had moved her, and she wondered, as she often did when he surprised her by saying something totally unexpected and inadvertently poetic, what she had done to deserve the love of this good man.

Chapter 6

DECEMBER

'He asked me why you had suddenly become a spokesperson for single parents, so I told him that you had a baby,' Robert was saying.

'But that programme was weeks ago,' Ginger said, thinking how weird it was that so many people had seen her on television. She had been inundated with calls ever since. It appeared that almost everyone she knew had time to watch morning television, despite the fact they were always moaning to her about how hard they worked.

'Yes, well, we kept missing each other's calls, you know how it is,' Robert told her, adding sarcastically, 'Perhaps you weren't at the very top of his agenda?'

'Are you sure that's all you told him?' Ginger persevered, refusing to rise to his cattiness.

'Of course,' Robert said, sounding slightly huffy at the implication that his integrity was being called into question.

'Well, thank you for telling me. So, when am I going to see you?'

'Well, I've got a terrible attack of the busies at the moment,' he said archly, 'and it's such a bore to always keep trekking down to Richmond. Why can't you come up to Soho?'

'Robert, you've only been here twice since Guy was

born, and you know perfectly well how difficult it is for me to get up to town while I'm feeding the baby,' Ginger protested.

'Are you still breastfeeding?' His tone made it sound as if she was doing something utterly perverted.

'Yes, I'm going to stop in the New Year,' she replied, through gritted teeth.

It never ceased to amaze her how many people felt they had a perfect right to criticize the way you reared your child, especially, she had found, people who knew absolutely nothing about children, but had some slight acquaintance with psychoanalytic theory.

'But you *are* coming to the party?' Robert said, picking up the annoyance in her voice.

'If Pic will look after Guy, yes . . . Oh, but Charlie'll be there,' she remembered.

'Well, you're bound to bump into him some day. Better in familiar surroundings, and without a miniature *doppelgänger*,' Robert advised.

'I suppose you're right,' she admitted.

'Gotta go, bye!'

'Oh, OK then, bye!'

Ginger stared into the handset. Now she was on the receiving end of it, she hated the hasty way that media people exited their conversations, a finger cutting off the call after the most perfunctory farewell, immediately tapping out another number, the receiver constantly wedged under the jaw.

Suspended from the door-frame in a baby-jumper, Guy jingled as he bounced happily up and down. She waved at him and his face lit up with a smile of pure, undiluted joy. She had always known that character must be genetically determined and there from the start – how else could it be that she and Pic were so different given exactly the same upbringing – but it had still been a delightful surprise to meet this tiny, robust and co-operative person who had been dozing in her tummy for a while, and find that he was exactly the sort of friend she would have chosen.

I do not want to go back to work, she thought, and sighed loudly.

Immediately sensing a change of mood, Guy stopped bouncing.

'No, it's OK, I've just got a few things on my mind,' she explained to him, taking his hands and dancing him up and down. He smiled again. With his improbable mass of dark curls and his determined square face, she had to admit that he was unmistakably Charlie's son.

When she was pregnant, she had been so sure that not telling Charlie had been the right thing to do, but since Guy's birth, she had been having occasional doubts, that grew stronger as Guy increasingly stamped his personality on the world. She caught herself imagining the first conversation they would have about it, and knew already that she would not be able to lie to her son, and yet she did not want to mix him up by being truthful about things he could not understand until he was much older. She wasn't even sure that she herself really understood the reason she had decided to go ahead with the pregnancy, because when she made the decision, she hadn't had the slightest idea that it would be the best thing she had ever done.

It was all very well talking at dinner parties about *Hello!* magazine changing your life. She had even managed to convince herself that the anecdote was true, but sometimes, at two o'clock in the morning after a glass or two of wine, in those lonely moments of uncompromising honesty, she wondered whether her motives had had more to do with angering her father than anything else. That wasn't the whole truth, she would assure herself, but she had to admit it was a good part of it.

She bent to pick up her son. 'Come on, let's have a look in the wardrobe for a party outfit.'

She pulled Guy out of the bouncer, held him on her hip and walked down the passage to the bedroom at the back of the flat. She propped him up on her bed, surrounded by pillows, and threw open the carved wooden door of the huge oak wardrobe that looked more like furniture from a church than a bedroom. A deluge of jumpers and T-shirts cascaded from the top shelf onto her head. Guy shrieked with laughter.

'What do you think?' she asked, pulling a stretchy black minidress over the jeans and T-shirt she was wearing, and twirling round like a model at the end of a catwalk.

'No, I agree,' she said, seeing the baby's perplexed expression, 'even with more suitable underwear, it doesn't work now that I have tits.' Discarding it, she reached up, took a shiny lime-green shirt off its hanger, and gave it a long, hard look before rejecting it. She flipped increasingly desperately through the hangers that stuffed the wardrobe. There were things she could not bear to part with even though she suspected that she would never wear them again — cut-off clingy T-shirts, a fake leopardskin miniskirt, a bright pink linen shorts suit she had worn to Pic's wedding. But there was nothing suitable for Robert's Christmas party.

'I've absolutely nothing to wear!' she said, putting on the voice of a weary débutante. Guy laughed again.

How could he tell, at such a young age, which was a comic voice and which was a normal one, she asked herself, amazed at his intelligence.

'Come on,' she said, picking him up again, 'let's find the credit cards and spend some more money we don't have. Mummy has to wear something nice for meeting Daddy.'

Alison was hurrying past the Early Learning Centre when she noticed that a small crowd of toddlers had gathered around a bigger child who was prowling on all fours around the play area near the window. It was only when the older child looked up and waved at her that she saw it was Ginger, who had discovered a display of model zoo animals and was demonstrating to her son the noises they made. Guy sat in his pushchair solemnly watching his mother trumpeting like an elephant, roaring like a lion and barking like a seal.

'Now,' Ginger asked herself out loud, picking up a rubber penguin, 'what noise does a penguin make?'

'I don't think they make much noise, do they?' Alison said, under her breath, as she walked into the shop.

'Oh, I know.' Ginger's face lit up. 'When it's feeding time, they kind of gollop a whole fish down in one go, like this . . .' She threw her neck back, dangled an imaginary fish above her mouth, and made an appropriately loud gobbling noise. One of the toddlers started clapping.

Alison laughed, and mimed drinking a cup of coffee. Ginger got to her feet, explaining to Guy what they were going to do, put her jacket back on, and followed Alison out.

'I can't wait to go to the real zoo with him,' Ginger said, breathless from her performance, as they walked down the street together.

'To add to your repertoire?' Alison teased her.

'Can you imagine what it must be like to see an elephant for the first time?' Ginger said excitedly, 'or a giraffe . . . You'll be so surprised,' she leant forward to tell her son, 'they don't look at all like they do in books, and' – she wrinkled up her nose – 'they really smell. How's Ben?' she asked.

'Fine, thanks,' Alison said, 'he's having a male bonding session with his father. Actually Stephen was feeling guilty so he's taken him out.'

'Why?' Ginger asked.

'Why guilty?' Alison had temporarily forgotten how direct Ginger could be. 'Oh, because he's got a seminar in New York over New Year and in a fit of great altruism, I said I could cope on my own.'

'Couldn't you go, too?'

'I could, but it wouldn't be the same, would it? Babysitting in a hotel and watching Times Square on television – I could do that at home . . . Anyway, can you imagine getting everything you need for the baby into a suitcase? Our car is completely full if we go down to my mother's for the day.'

'True,' Ginger conceded.

'And anyway, it's freezing there. I can't imagine it's much fun slithering round Central Park with a buggy while Stephen gets wined and dined and comes back at night dying to tell me all about the latest technological advances in ventilators.'

'At least they wouldn't have bagpipes on television there,' Ginger said laconically. 'So where have your boys gone?'

'Swimming. Apparently Ben loves it. Have you been?'

'Yes, we all go on Thursday mornings now that they've got their inoculations. It's getting a bit cold to meet in the Gardens. Actually, we were meaning to ask you whether you thought Justine and Ben would like to come with us. It seems a shame that we don't see him these days. I kind of like the idea of all three of them growing up together – when they're older, they can say that they've been friends from before they were born.' She was only half joking.

'What a sweet idea,' Alison said, surprised at feeling slightly left out. She liked the other two mothers well enough, but she hadn't been aware until now of missing their Thursday mornings together. 'It hadn't occurred to me . . . must be being a twin that makes you think like that.'

'Oh!' said Ginger, delighted by the suggestion, 'perhaps it is.'

'I'll ask Justine, but I'm sure she would love to come.'

'Tell her to get him a Floatie,' Ginger said enigmatically, then, seeing Alison's expression, 'It's like a baby lifebelt.'

'I'll buy him one on my way home,' Alison said. 'So, shall we have a coffee?'

'I'd love to, but . . .' Ginger hesitated. 'Could you do me a favour first? I've got to get something to wear for a party and it's so difficult taking the pram into changing rooms . . . I just wondered . . .'

'I'd love to,' Alison said enthusiastically, 'any chance to shop . . . What are you looking for?'

'Well, that's another thing . . .' Ginger said tentatively, wondering whether she dared ask Alison for advice. She was always so beautifully turned out in expensive clothes with exactly the right accessories. 'I would appreciate some help. I kind of feel I've grown out of black miniskirts and Doc Martens, and I don't just mean my shape. I want something kind of . . .'

'. . . more sophisticated?' Alison finished her sentence for her.

'Yes,' Ginger said, pleased with the word, 'more sophisticated.'

In the next hour, she was taken into shops she would never have thought of entering. It was an experience almost akin to the time when she and Pic first found their way to the attics at home and opened up trunks of Hermione's 1930s ball dresses.

It took a while for Alison to convince Ginger to try on anything that wasn't black or fluorescent, but after some coaxing, she began to enjoy having different colours and fabrics picked out for her. Alison found it was like being back at her first job in journalism, assistant to the fashion editor of a glossy women's magazine, where she often found herself helping out on photographic shoots. Except that Ginger was far better company than most of the pouting bitches of models she had worked with in those days. She had always felt comfortable with Ginger. She was open and honest and told you what she was thinking whether you wanted to hear it or not.

'What do you think about red?' she asked her, flipping along a shiny rail of dresses. The hangers sounded like knitting needles clicking against one other.

'I don't really. I've never worn it,' Ginger said, not really paying attention.

'But your colouring is perfect for red . . .' Alison said, appraising Ginger's flawless pale skin, her forget-me-not blue eyes and dark eyebrows.

'D'you think so?' Ginger said, distractedly, 'I thought that red was for dusky brunettes.'

'It can look wonderful on blondes too.'

'I'm not really blonde, though,' Ginger admitted, unnecessarily pulling up a strand of her hair which was platinum at the tip and light brown at the root.

'Well, your skin is very fair . . . and I think you should cut off those ends before the party,' Alison said, taking her job as advisor very seriously indeed. 'You would look really good with a kind of French hair-cut like Juliette Binoche – do you know what I mean? You've got the bone structure for it, and your face is so feminine, you wouldn't be mistaken for a boy.'

'OK,' Ginger said, dubiously.

Alison held up a short dress in crimson crushed velvet, and laughed as Ginger's eyes widened.

'Go on, try it on, it'll look superb.'

The amazing thing was, it did. The shape was simple, just two rectangles of fabric joined by the merest stitch at the shoulders, but the cut was so expert that the material fell in softly draping horizontal folds from the neck. The fabric was gorgeously rich, and shimmered as Ginger's slight frame moved uncertainly beneath it.

'You look like a million dollars,' Alison said.

'That's because that's what it costs, almost,' Ginger said, looking at the price label, and seeing that it was approximately ten times as much as she had ever paid for a dress.

'But I'm sure you'll wear it to lots of parties,' Alison said, adding helpfully, 'When I buy something expensive, I always divide the cost by the number of times I wear it, and then it doesn't seem so much.'

'On that calculation,' Ginger said, 'I reckon my jeans owe me money, but . . .' She was tempted, and Alison was so eager for her to have it, she almost felt it would look ungrateful to turn it down. She tried to rationalize the purchase in her head, but could not come up with a persuasive excuse. 'You see,' she whispered, 'it's Robert's Christmas party, the one where last year . . .'

'Oh heavens!' said Alison, understanding immediately, 'and . . . *he* will be there?' She didn't know quite how to refer to him. With uncharacteristic restraint, Ginger had never revealed his name.

'Yes . . . Will I do, do you think?' Ginger said.

She looked so very vulnerable standing bashfully slightly knock-kneed and staring at herself in the long mirror, Alison wanted to hug her.

'You'll be perfect. It's a very sexy dress, but it's not overt. He won't be able to take his eyes off you, if that's what you want . . .'

'I don't know what I want, really,' Ginger said, 'I suppose I just want to look grown-up.'

'Well, you do.'

'That settles it, then.' Ginger did a little skip as she went to get changed.

She stood by the till trying to look casual in the agonizing wait as the machine read her card and decided whether to allow or decline her credit. After a few moments' hesitation, it coughed and spluttered and miraculously started churning out a receipt. Ginger stared hard at the supercilious shop assistant, and signed the slip with a flourish.

'Now, shoes,' said Alison, as they stepped out into the street.

'No, I've already gone to my limit . . .'

'But you can't wear Doc Martens with that dress.'

'I know. Look, perhaps I've been silly.' Having second thoughts, Ginger peeped into the carrier bag where the beautiful dress nestled in white tissue paper. In the cold, wintry natural light outside, the colour seemed to glint like liquid. She could not bear to take it back.

'Let me buy you a pair for Christmas,' Alison suggested.

'No, of course not,' Ginger said quickly, then smiled unexpectedly. 'I'd forgotten about Christmas, though . . .'

Later, as they sat on bar stools in Prêt-à-Manger drinking heavy white china cups of *cappuccino*, a pair of black suede square-toed pumps with chunky high heels in a carrier bag hanging from the handle of Guy's pushchair, Alison issued further instructions.

'Now, I know that you're thinking you should wear black tights, but you absolutely mustn't. That would look tarty. Choose a sheer, natural colour,' she said with a smile, realizing that she sounded exactly like the copy she used to write, 'and make sure your legs are waxed. Absolutely no jewellery,' she concluded firmly, 'except possibly some plain earrings. You do not want to look like a Christmas cracker.'

How odd, Ginger thought as she pushed the push-chair up the hill, that Alison should turn out to be such a girlie girl. She had always thought her the kind of person who liked to keep her distance. There was an almost tangible buffer zone of space around her, and whilst she sometimes appeared to reveal personal details about herself, on closer inspection, Ginger had noticed that they always turned out to be trivial things, like an irritation with her mother, which almost everyone might feel. Her dress-sense and grooming added to the effect. She was as sleek and unknowable as a Burmese cat. And yet, today, she had been animated and relaxed like an old friend from school. Perhaps it was a matter of confidence. Alison knew about clothes and clearly enjoyed them, to the extent that she had even offered to pay for shoes to make the outfit look right, and Ginger had sensed it was a genuine offer, with no obligation to repay or reciprocate attached, issued with spontaneous generosity in the sheer enthusiasm of the moment.

A wave of elation washed through Ginger's body as she reached the top of the hill and paused to look at the view. She had a new dress and new shoes suspended in chic cardboard bags from thick cotton cords over her shoulder, and she felt she had made a new friend too. It had been a good morning.

As soon as she had taken Guy from his pram and put him on his mat on the floor, she picked up the phone. 'Pic, I've chosen what I want from you for Christmas – you'll approve. Actually I've bought it too. You couldn't put some money in my account, could you? Er, well, today, if possible . . .'

There were at least three football matches in progress on the playing fields. From a distance, it was difficult to tell where one stopped and the next began. The grass was swarming with small masculine figures in poster-coloured shirts and black or white shorts. Eventually, Lia picked out Neil's outline, in a black tracksuit, running up and down the farthest pitch. She breathed a sigh of relief, then was ashamed of herself for checking up on him, wishing that she had been strong enough to resist the pull of suspicion. Of course, he wasn't seeing someone else, she told herself. When would he have the time?

His arm shot into the air. He was too far away for her to tell whether he was awarding a penalty, or waving at her. In any case, she had come too far to turn around now. She pushed the pram slowly along the frozen muddy edge of the field.

His face lit up when he recognized that it was her. It

197

was such a spontaneous expression of pleasure, she smiled back, blushing with surprise. The moments when he looked at her just as he had done when they first met made her wonder how she could ever doubt his love, but they were rare these days. He pointed at his wrist, then held up both hands. Ten more minutes.

She watched the game, trying to work out which team he was in charge of, realizing she didn't even know his school colours. She worked out that the boys in red and black stripes were probably his. He was much harder on them when they fouled, and they looked at him with familiar exasperation as he held up a yellow card, authoritatively and seriously, just like a referee of a Premiership match, brooking no argument and showing no trace of humour. It made her want to giggle.

'Sir, is that your wife, sir?' A short, cheeky-looking boy of about twelve danced round Neil's legs as he strode towards her after blowing the final whistle.

'Yes, Sean,' Neil replied, briskly.

'She's ever so pretty, sir.'

'I know that, Sean.'

'Is that your baby, sir?'

'Yes,' Neil replied wearily, winking at Lia as they approached.

'Your wife's not wearing a wedding ring, sir, are you sure she's your wife, sir?'

'Don't be cheeky, Sean,' Neil said evenly but firmly.

Lia liked the way he responded directly to his pupils' curiosity, even though, strictly speaking, he wasn't quite telling the truth. She still retained humiliating memories of the sneering sarcasm with which her teachers had greeted every question. You are nosy today, Lesley, what a shame you don't show the same curiosity about your science homework. That kind of thing.

'Hello, Mrs Gardner,' the boy said, grinning at Lia.

'Hello! What's your name?' Lia asked, smiling at him, which made him blush to the roots of his cropped red hair.

'Sean, sir, I mean, miss,' he stuttered, then ran off back to his team-mates.

'Hello, gorgeous,' Neil said, leaning forward to kiss her quickly on the lips. A few yards behind him a cheer went up, and Sean, confident again amongst his peers, put two fingers in his mouth and whistled.

'We'll have an audience till we reach the gate,' Neil said, 'then most of them won't be able to resist the temptation of nicking something from the newsagents.' He hung his arm around her shoulder, and she had the definite feeling that he was proud of her and glad she had come to meet him.

'My street cred just went up a few points,' he whispered to her, and laughed.

A pale, lemon-silver sun slipped towards the horizon, and the air was suddenly cold. It was getting very wintry.

'What shall we do for Christmas?' Neil asked her, as if the whiteness of the ground had triggered a Christmas-card snow scene in his mind. He held open the gate and she pushed the pram through. There was a chorus of goodbyes from the boys behind as they passed the corner shop.

'Well, I'd like to spend it at home . . . a real family Christmas together,' she said, looking at Anouska, whose cheeks, the only part of her not covered by a padded snow suit, were pink from the cold.

'At our house?' he asked, surprised.

'Yes,' she said.

He was silent for a few minutes evaluating the suggestion.

'I suppose we could . . .' he said.

'Your parents could come up for the day,' Lia volunteered. She was anxious to avoid a repeat of the previous year, when they had gone to Neil's parents' house, and Mrs Gardner had refused to let her help cook the dinner.

'It would be a lot of work for you,' Neil said.

'Well, better me than your mother,' Lia replied.

'If you're sure . . .'

On this occasion, Lia was grateful to his mother for her whining Christmas martyrdom, which had clearly inculcated into her son the notion that preparing Christmas dinner was an enormous sacrifice for the woman of the family.

'Of course,' she said, then, capitalizing on his positive reaction, 'Neil, could we afford a car?'

'A car?'

The surprise in his voice could not have been greater if the question had been, Neil, can we buy an elephant? Why was it that men thought in straight lines? Everyone else had a car, and yet it obviously hadn't occurred to him that she might need, or want, one.

'It's just . . . well, I seem to spend my whole life trailing backwards and forwards to the shops with the pram, and I worry about Anouska catching cold after swimming, and I could do things, if we had a car . . .'

'What things?' he said eventually, a long exhalation of breath turning to white mist in front of him.

'Go places that I can't walk to,' she faltered.

'I'll have to have a think,' he said, retreating into gloomy silence for the rest of the walk home.

Lia unwrapped the baby and sat her in a bouncy chair in front of the playgym she had made her. It was a simple construction, just the frame of an orange box, which Neil had sanded to remove splinters, with coloured ribbons stapled on, from which she attached objects of different shapes and sizes. Today there were some painted cotton reels, a balloon whisk from the kitchen drawer, a matchbox with rice inside. For Anouska, it was as enthralling as a soap opera.

Neil picked up the phone and dialled his parents.

She tried to listen in, but the noise of the kettle boiling made eavesdropping impossible.

'Well, I think retirement must have gone to my dad's head,' he said, coming into the kitchen after his call.

'What?' She poured him a cup of tea and handed him a plate of biscuits.

'They've booked a time-share in Lanzarote for two weeks over Christmas. They're taking Pete's boys with them. Dad always said he fancied going away at Christmas. I never thought he would get round to it.'

'How lovely,' Lia said, almost unable to contain her smiles of relief. This was surely a good omen, to have the credit for offering to 'do' Christmas, but to avoid entertaining the in-laws after all.

'Shall we invite Pete and Cheryl instead?' Neil suggested.

She was pleased that he seemed keen on the idea of making a family Christmas out of it, and she liked his brother and sister-in-law. 'Yeah, ring them now,' she said. 'Let's get a big tree . . .'

'OK, and I'll tidy up the garden, maybe string up some lights out there,' he joined in, walking towards her, and for the first time in weeks she felt herself relax into his embrace rather than stiffen away from it.

The last Monday before Christmas, the postman arrived just as Alison was leaving the house. She threw the bills and circulars back on the doormat, but took the envelope that was addressed to her in handwriting and stuffed it into her heavy leather bag. As she drank her first coffee of the day at her desk, she opened the letter and read it.

Sarah-Jane, the woman who rented her old flat in Islington, was writing to tell her that she was getting married at Christmas, and to ask whether Alison would mind if she gave less notice than the lease required. Alison sighed. If Sarah-Jane had been planning a wedding, she must have known for some time.

Why on earth had she not informed her earlier? She supposed she would have to agree, although it was a nuisance.

It was ironic that after four months spent doing nothing more demanding than counting the correct measures of formula into bottles of cooled, boiled water, now, suddenly, there seemed to be new demands on her every time she turned around. Employing a nanny took away the boring menial grind of caring for a baby, but it meant getting to grips with employment law, setting up standing orders for Justine's salary, making decisions about how much money to allow her to decorate her room as she wished, as well as ensuring there was always enough cash for the playgroups and other activities she attended with Ben. The week before, her cleaning lady had announced she was retiring, and although she had agreed to stay until they found somebody else, Alison was aware that she would not be able to test her patience beyond Christmas. Then there was the whole business of buying presents and getting in shopping for the days after Christmas, when both Stephen and Justine would be away, and she would have to do everything herself. That, as well as her job, finding time to have her hair cut, dropping clothes off at the dry cleaner, and now, all the business of having to interview prospective tenants for the flat.

Still, Alison reminded herself, it was far better this way than mooching around at home with all the time in the world, and nothing to do except think.

She read the letter once again, wondering whether it would be sensible to sell the flat. The market was said to be moving again, but even that option would be stressful. She remembered the endless conversations with estate agents and solicitors when they were trying to buy the house in Kew. Stephen's hours meant that he was rarely any help on these matters, and, as he constantly told her, she was far better at it, which was his charming way of saying that he couldn't be bothered.

Unlike everyone else she knew, Stephen had not heard and meekly obeyed the Thatcherite call to property in the early eighties. Instead, he had chosen to rent an apartment in the Barbican and keep the money he had inherited from his parents in a normal building society account, without even bothering to ascertain whether he was receiving the maximum amount of interest. He was relaxed about finance, because he could afford to be. His parents had been rich and generous. Sometimes, his casual indifference to money irritated her, but it had at least given her an excuse not to sell her flat in Islington when the market was so poor.

The idea of selling the flat came reluctantly. She had never seriously considered moving back, but the option was always there, which was important to her. If you had choices, life could not imprison you.

'Bad news?' Ramona asked, dumping down her bag on the opposite desk.

'No, not really, but I can't decide what to do.' Alison explained her problem.

'Sometimes I find the best thing to do when you can't decide, is decide to decide some other time,' Ramona suggested. 'At least then you've made a decision of sorts, you see.'

'Like Scarlett O'Hara – I can't think about that today, so I'll think about it tomorrow.'

'Exactly, though you need to work a little on that Southern Belle accent.'

'You're right,' said Alison, resolving to take Ramona's simple advice by not doing anything until the New Year.

'I have to have a system for everything,' Ramona expanded, 'I'm such a control freak – I can't have anything in a mental pending tray, so I diarize it and file it away for later. Hey, I'm beginning to sound like a management guru. At this rate, I'm going to have to start charging for my ideas . . .'

'All right, I'll give you a fiver if you can come up with something original for Valentine's Day,' Alison said, replacing the letter in her bag and getting back to work.

'And you're the one married to a heart specialist,' Ramona quipped.

Alison made a face.

'Everyone does *coeur à la crème* with raspberry coulis, but have you ever tasted one? What man is really going to want to eat white mush with watered-down jam?' Ramona asked. 'Last year, it was Shrove Tuesday at around the same time, so I made pancakes and cut them into heart shapes with a biscuit cutter – sprinkle of cinnamon and lemon, delicious!'

'You old romantic,' Alison said, 'but it's a lovely idea, simple. Do you mind if I do use it?'

'As long as you don't suggest bloody raspberry coulis as an alternative topping . . . I've also cut smoked salmon into heart shapes and added it to tagliatelle with pesto, if you're interested. Make sure you rinse the biscuit cutter well, though, otherwise you'll get fishy pancakes. Actually, I don't know why we don't just swap jobs,' Ramona suggested wearily, 'you always have better ideas for my bit . . . I mean you even *look* like the fashion editor, and I look like the one who tries all the recipes.'

'No way,' Alison countered firmly, 'I've done my bit in fashion. If I moved, I'd want to be doing something more interesting, like reporting on the women's movement in Guatemala or something.'

'Mmm, Guatemala, they have some lovely cardigans, there's a shop in Camden . . .'

'I didn't mean what they're wearing!' Alison protested. 'Which reminds me,' she added enigmatically, chewing the end of a biro, 'I have to buy some tights at lunch-time. Don't let me forget.'

It was the kind of sunny, exhilarating winter day

that feels as if the crisp air is breathing you, rather than the other way round. Alison hugged her charcoal grey cashmere coat around her waist and lifted her face to the sun. It was impossible not to feel optimistic on a day like this. The sunshine made Cubist mirrors of the surfaces of the tall buildings, and the sky was solid blue. Even the roar of traffic seemed invigorating, like the whoosh of a magnified heartbeat, throbbing through the City's arteries. She infinitely preferred the urban landscape with its hard angles and grime and noise to any amount of fields and soft, honey-coloured stone cottages with roses round the door. On days like this, London could still give her an adrenaline rush of escape from the dreary, stifling atmosphere of the small town in the Home Counties where she had grown up.

It was a day like this, she remembered, that she and Neil had come up for the day to Biba, the first time she had ever been to town without her parents. He had encouraged her to try on amazing clingy purple dresses, even though they hadn't even enough money to buy a meal in a Golden Egg. They had spent everything they owned on tickets for Bryan Ferry at the Rainbow, where they had arrived far too early, having no idea of the speed of the tube, feeling like country bumpkins as they wandered around the neighbouring grey streets to kill time before the gig.

Even Finsbury Park had seemed glamorous then, shops that smelled of spices with boxes of weird-looking vegetables outside, okra and knobbly sweet potatoes, still caked in Caribbean mud.

Bryan Ferry in his white lounge suit had symbolized everything that London was, and their town was not. Sophisticated, cool and distant. Observing the stylish, metropolitan Ferry-clones around them, they had both made a silent vow never to wear faded denim again, and when he played 'These Foolish Things', they did not dance or kiss, but reached discreetly for each other's fingers in the dark, hoping no-one would see them holding hands. At the end, they had clapped and cheered, preferring to miss the last train rather than the encore. Reality had only dawned on her again as they sat next to the fumy gas fire in the waiting room at King's Cross, shivering with cold, fear and the certain knowledge that her father would never allow her to go to a gig again.

Alison sat down at the counter of the sushi train above Liverpool Street Station. How satisfied they had been then with so little, she thought. A cup of coffee from a stainless steel jug that had been boiling bitterly for hours on its hot plate; an oval platter (never plate) of spongy pancakes with maple-style syrup, and one of those little pats of ice-cream that melted to yellow foam, these had been their treats. Now, people casually swapped their allegiance from Thai to Japanese to Australian cuisine, chose the blend of their *cappuccino* from an international range of freshly ground coffees at the station kiosk, and bought yams and wasabi sauce from Tesco. She wondered whether egg and chips would ever make a come-back, or Brown Derby ice-cream sundaes, that exotic combination of a doughnut, a whip of bright white shaving cream and dribble of chocolate-flavour topping.

Perhaps she should make a feature of it – ask some celebs their favourite teenage food, call it *Noshtalgia*, or something like that. She leant down from her high stool, took her Filofax from her bag and wrote it down. Then, remembering her errand, she wolfed down two pieces of maguro sushi and a cup of green tea, and hurried off to Sock Shop to buy tights.

On the evening of Robert's party, Ginger's taxi pulled up outside the little Victorian terraced house in Sheen.

'You look fantastic,' Lia told Ginger as she paid off the taxi and hurried into the house, carrying Guy like a rolled-up carpet under her arm.

206

'Well, I almost didn't . . . luckily I had decided not to get myself ready till the last minute, this boy threw up all his last feed. He's fine now, but I feel sick about leaving him. Are you sure you'll be all right?'

'Yes, of course we will, won't we, Guy?' Lia held out her arms to take the baby from Ginger.

Pic had called the night before, with a temperature of over a hundred, and a sore throat so acute it was almost impossible to understand what she was saying except that Ginger would have to find another baby-sitter. Ginger had resigned herself to missing Robert's party, but Lia, who had called shortly after, had insisted that she go. She had offered to take Guy for the whole night so that Ginger could be out as long as she wanted to be, although her stated plan was to have one glass of champagne, say hello to a few people, and leave.

Lia put Guy on the floor beside Anouska. The two babies stared at one another.

'Here's his changing stuff, water, food, not that he'll need it . . .' Ginger divested herself of a number of bags strung around her shoulders and took off her coat.

Lia gasped as she saw the dress. 'Oh my God, it's the most beautiful thing I've ever seen!' she said. 'Neil, come and look at Ginger.'

Neil walked through from the kitchen, an open packet of crisps in his hand. 'Very nice,' he said laconically between crunches, then smiled at her.

He was extraordinarily good-looking, Ginger thought, blushing slightly as she did an embarrassed twirl, especially when he smiled. There was something about his eyes. With his colouring, they should have been brown, but they were blue, a kind of light, dull turquoise, and they made him look soulful. What must it be like to wake up each morning and look at his face? she wondered.

'What do you think of the tights?' she asked Lia,

conscious that she had been staring a little too long at her husband.

'Perfect,' Lia said.

'Yes, they are, aren't they? Alison sent them to me, can you believe it? She told me not to wear black. Of course I immediately forgot, then this morning a Jiffy bag arrives with not one but two pairs of Christian Dior Nude. She must have guessed, correctly as it happens, that I always put my fingers through the first new pair.'

Lia laughed. 'That's so sweet of her.'

'She's really lovely,' Ginger said, as if she were speaking of a fairy godmother, or a much-favoured aunt. 'Is she coming?'

'Well, I said that we were having a Christmas drink together before you went to the party, and she said she would try,' said Lia, who had rather nervously called Alison at work earlier that day to invite her over.

The last time she had met up with Ginger, they had discussed whether Alison might be missing their get-togethers. Ginger said she thought Alison's stand-offishness could actually be nervousness and she told her how helpful she had been about choosing the dress. They had jointly decided to try to invite her to things they did together, if her work schedule per-mitted.

Neil wandered back into the kitchen and called out from behind the fridge door, 'Do you want a beer?'

'No thanks,' Ginger called back. 'I've bought a bottle of pop,' she said to Lia, pointing at the heap of bags by the staircase, 'it's in one of those.'

'Oh, you shouldn't have,' Lia said, pulling out a boxed bottle of Veuve Cliquot.

'Of course I should,' Ginger replied, 'it's the least I could do when you're looking after Guy.'

'Oh, I don't mind at all. If he's asleep when you go, it'll be fine, even if he isn't, I've got Neil here to look after Annie.'

208

Ginger noticed that Anouska's name was being shortened more and more often these days. Apparently Neil didn't like it. Ginger guessed that he was quite a difficult character, prone to moods. Lia was very loyal and Ginger had never heard her utter a word against him, but there had been times, recently, when she had detected the glassiness of tears in Lia's eyes and suspected that she might be on the verge of pouring her heart out to her. Ginger, who wasn't very good at being a shoulder to cry on, had moved the subject along swiftly or made a bad joke, and the tension of the moment had quickly dissipated.

There was a knock at the door. Lia went to open it, looking relieved to hand back the champagne to Ginger.

'Will you open it? Ask Neil to get some glasses.'

Suddenly the small, low-ceilinged room was crowded with people. In a blast of cold air, Alison came in carrying Ben in a car seat, followed by Stephen who was holding another bottle of champagne.

Alison kissed Lia on the cheek. 'I hope you don't mind me bringing Stephen,' she said, lightly, 'he hasn't met the other babies, and he's heard so much about them.'

'Of course not,' Lia said, thrilled to be the hostess of an impromptu party. 'Here, give me your coats . . . God, is that what you wear to work?'

Under her grey coat, Alison was wearing her black Nicole Farhi woollen dress simply adorned with a large swirling silver brooch. It made her look particularly slim and elegant. Lia suddenly noticed the shapeless blue jumper she was wearing over her jeans and wished that she had changed into something that was at least clean. She didn't have a lot of smart winter clothes. She hadn't really needed anything warm living in Portugal, and everything got so messy looking after Anouska, she had never really thought about buying anything nice, even if there had been any spare money.

From the kitchen, there was a loud pop and the splash of champagne on lino.

'No, hold it at forty-five degrees,' Ginger instructed. 'There, you see, for some reason it doesn't spill like that.'

'You're obviously more used to opening this stuff than I am,' Neil replied, with a slight edge to his voice, and then they both came back into the room.

'So, this is the dress,' Stephen said, looking appreciatively at Ginger, 'you were right, darling, it looks fabulous.'

Sometimes Stephen's memory took Alison by surprise. She hadn't even been aware that she had told him about the dress she had helped Ginger choose. Without thinking, she took his hand and squeezed it, grateful for the grace of the compliment, then released it noticing that Neil's eyes were fixed on the place, mid-air, where her fingers had just clasped Stephen's. She was so used to seeing Lia and Ginger together, it hadn't occurred to her that he would be there. He shook his gaze away, avoiding direct eye contact with her, and stepped forward to shake Stephen's hand in a friendly, masculine way.

'Champagne?' said Ginger, who had registered the slight awkwardness from her position by the door.

There were two sorts of good mothers, Alison decided, the champagne making her feel oddly flat. There were the ones like Ginger, who had many childlike qualities of their own. Ginger didn't have to get down to Guy's level, because in some sense she was already there, with her uninhibited imagination and delight in simple games. As Ginger had left for her party, Alison had seen how much of a wrench it was for her to be parted from her son for just a couple of hours, even though he was already asleep.

Then there were the ones to whom mothering came

naturally, like Lia, who seemed to know instinctively what children wanted, and who could transfer a certain sort of calm within themselves onto the child.

And then there were the mothers who didn't really know what to do at all, and didn't much care, she thought, taking another slug from her glass. Perched on the arm of the chair in which Stephen was sitting, she watched with envy as Lia took first Guy, then Anouska, upstairs, humming soothing snatches of lullabies, enveloping them in warmth and care.

'That was quick,' she said, as Lia returned.

'Well, Guy was off anyway, and I put Annie down awake now.'

'You put her down awake, and she goes to sleep?' Stephen asked, incredulously.

'Yes – she has a thing that lights up and plays a tune and she just drifts off.'

'We must get one of those, darling,' Stephen said to Alison.

'I shouldn't think it would make much difference,' Alison said, slightly resenting the implication that Ben was not as good at going to sleep as the other children.

'Where did you get it?' Stephen persevered.

'At a jumble sale . . . it was only ten pence. We had to buy batteries, of course. I sometimes wish they made them for grown-ups,' Lia elaborated, 'it must be nice to fall asleep with all these little pictures going round on the ceiling, like magic . . .'

'I can't imagine it,' Stephen said, 'will you show me when she's asleep?'

Lia smiled. 'Of course, do you want to come up now?'

'May I?' Stephen stood up. 'I love watching them sleep . . . they are so exquisitely beautiful and inno-cent.' He looked lovingly at his son, asleep in his car seat.

Alison exchanged glances with Neil. Neither of

them said a word but she knew that they were thinking the same thing. Then he got up and went into the kitchen for another beer, and she glanced at her watch, wondering how much longer she could bear to be there. She was tired and hungry, having skipped lunch because it was press day, and when she finally arrived home after being stuck in a defective train for twenty minutes, the last thing she had wanted to do was go out.

Unusually, Stephen had been home before her, and when she mentioned Lia's invitation for a drink, he had been keen to go. She had assumed that he would quickly tire of baby talk and they would have an excuse to make a quick getaway, perhaps even go out for a meal together. It was one of Justine's babysitting nights, and it seemed a shame to waste the rare opportunity to spend some time together. But Stephen seemed blissfully contented playing with the babies, and discussing developmental signs with Lia. She appreciated his charm with her friends, but she was now getting impatient.

'What are you doing for Christmas?' Neil asked her, less out of interest than obligation to fill the silence that gaped between them.

'We're going down to my mother's,' she told him.

'Oh . . . does she still live in . . . ?'

Alison glanced nervously at the staircase. 'Rustington, yes. It's by the sea,' she added, unnecessarily.

'And your father?'

'Died, a while ago . . . just before I got married.'

'I'm sorry.'

'Thank you,' she said, wishing Stephen would come downstairs. 'It's a big house for her now, but she has friends . . .'

'Right,' he said.

She realized politeness probably required her to ask about his parents, but she was finding the woodenness of the conversation almost unbearable.

'So, you're a teacher?' she said finally.

212

'Yes. It's a bit of a long way from opening for England, but it pays the bills, just,' he said.

It was the first direct reference either of them had made to things that had been said in the past, and she was thrown off-balance.

'Yes, well, we've all come a long way,' she said, fighting a sudden urge to ask him whether he remembered seeing Bryan Ferry.

Her words sounded trite and patronizing, she realized, repeating them in her head, especially since he was talking about being a long way away from his ambition, and she meant something completely different.

'You still play cricket though, I saw you – on the Green . . .' she faltered, feeling almost shabby admitting she had watched him without him knowing she was.

'Yeah, but it's never been the same since the accident. I came off my bike back in the winter of '76,' he said, staring meaningfully at her, and she suddenly felt as if his failure to achieve his ambition had all been her fault.

With relief, she heard Stephen and Lia's footfall on the wooden staircase. '. . . but what's Alison going to do?' she heard Lia say to him.

'Oh dear, you are making me feel guilty,' Stephen replied. 'You'll be all right, darling, won't you?' he said, dipping his head to avoid the beam at the bottom of the staircase.

'Yes, of course,' she replied, assuming they were talking about New Year.

'Well, if you've nothing better to do, you and Ben would be very welcome here on New Year's Eve. It's horrible to be on your own,' Lia said, adding, as Alison hoped she wouldn't, 'Neil?'

'If we're here,' he said bluntly.

'Well, where else would we be?' Lia asked him, surprised.

'Oh, I don't know, sometimes people go to parties

213

on New Year's Eve, I believe,' he said, attempting a joke to mask the gracelessness of his remark.

Everyone laughed a little nervously, and Alison leapt up to hand Stephen his coat before he could settle down once more in the armchair.

The narrow streets of Soho were pulsating with people. Ginger couldn't decide whether it had always been like this and she had been so used to it she hadn't noticed, or whether there had been a sudden restaurant boom that coincided with her confinement in the suburbs. As she approached the modish new club she had not been to before, she began to feel really excited. She was out on the town and she was going to have a good time.

There was a public phone in the lobby, but she forced herself to walk past it. The only thing she would achieve by ringing Lia now would be waking the babies. Guy would be fine, she told herself. In a funny kind of way she had felt happier leaving him with another mother than with Pic, who might panic over something trivial, or ignore something serious.

She slipped into the Ladies and stared at herself in the mirror, still surprised by the slicked-back new hair-cut. She reapplied her lipstick and blew a kiss on to a thoughtfully provided tissue. Then she replaced the lipstick in the side pocket of her black patent rucksack, wishing she had had the foresight to empty it of clean nappies and babywipes. Imagining Alison's horror at the notion of taking the bag into the party, she reluctantly checked it into the cloakroom, with her coat, feeling naked without it and not quite knowing what to do with her bare arms. At times like this, she wished she smoked. She took a deep breath and walked into the room, the height of her heels making it easier for her than it usually was to spot familiar faces in the crowd.

Robert's Christmas parties were famous for two things – the unlimited flow of champagne, and the hordes of beautiful, single men who were sadly uninterested in the almost equal numbers of attractive, single women.

'You can look, but you can't touch,' Robert said, handing her a glass and watching her eyes follow a slim Keanu Reeves clone across the room.

'Why do you do this to us?' Ginger asked him, 'it's like forcing someone on a diet to spend an evening staring into the window of Pâtisserie Valerie.'

'Well, I just don't know that many heterosexual men,' Robert told her.

'I'm beginning to wonder if there are any left,' Ginger said. 'I've just walked down Old Compton Street and I'm telling you, there are men sitting drinking Amaretto and espresso on the freezing cold pavement, as if it's Rome in the spring, but I didn't get a single look, not even a hiss.'

'I thought you hated that kind of building-site mentality,' Robert said.

'It's worse when you feel you're getting in the way of the spot-the-best-looking-motorbike-messenger show . . .'

'Well, if it means anything from an unreconstructed old poof,' Robert told her, 'I think you look quite lovely tonight.'

'Thank you, Robert,' she said, smiling gratefully at him. He could be the most infuriating person in the world, but, sometimes, when you least expected it, he could make you feel completely wonderful. That was why she couldn't help being extremely fond of him.

'He's not here, yet,' he added, seeing her glancing anxiously round the room, 'but there are lots of people dying to see you . . .'

'It's been *ages* . . . What *have* you been doing . . . Have you been away?' Suddenly she was surrounded by people she hadn't seen for months asking her questions. On the tube, she had rehearsed a number of cool responses, but now she found she couldn't resist announcing immediately, 'I've had a baby!'

She noticed several of the faces set in a kind of false, embarrassed grin, before turning away. A couple of Robert's ex-lovers began to witter on about changing the law so that gay couples could adopt, two female journalists started telling each other how awful it was that everyone assumed, once you reached the age of thirty, that you were hankering to conceive, and an advertising executive began to explain how impossible it was to sell anything these days, from razors to toilet roll, without the prop of a baby. It was the ultimate designer accessory, he assured Ginger.

'What, like a genuine crocodile Hermès Kelly bag?' Ginger asked him.

He thought for a moment. 'Almost better,' he pronounced, hedging his bets in the style stakes.

She found this so amusing that her desire to scream evaporated.

I'm not talking politics, pressure or PR, she wanted to explain, I've actually created another human being. Is that so very dull? I'm not interested in discussing colic or nappies either, but have you ever considered how wonderful it must be to see a shiny helium balloon for the first time, floating above your pram, when you have no idea about gravity, or light, and yet you still somehow know that something special is happening?

It wasn't worth it. Motherhood was simply not a career option for an educated woman in her twenties. They would only assume that pregnancy had shrunk her brain. She contented herself by thinking of the expression on Guy's face as he woke each morning, anticipating all the fun the new day would bring, and it saddened her that it wasn't a fit topic of conversation for polite society. What a strange, child-hating nation we are, she thought.

Ironically, it was only Lucretia whose face registered the slightest interest in her news.

'Is it absolutely awful?' she drawled, blowing a

cloud of smoke from her cheroot vertically into the air, then leaning towards her with a theatrical air of confidentiality.

Up close, Ginger was pleased to observe that there were distinct lines around her eyes, and the breath that escaped her blood-coloured lips was sourly stale. Her character, Ginger thought spitefully, was beginning to show in her face. She was still undeniably beautiful, but the hardness that had earned her the soubriquet La Borgia at university was creeping into her features.

Ginger instinctively shied away from her. 'No, I love it. It's the best thing I have ever done,' she announced determinedly, seeing the derision in Lucretia's eyes as they swept over her shoulder, searching out someone more interesting to talk to.

'Hello, darling!' Charlie Prince's unmistakable London voice behind her sent a shiver of panic down Ginger's spine.

She looked around for help. Robert was smiling into the eyes of a man in slate-blue Armani, and everyone else she knew seemed engrossed in animated conversation.

For God's sake, she wanted to hiss, look who I'm with, but then she realized that it was Lucretia he had been addressing. He hadn't even noticed that she was there. To add to the humiliation, his hand shoved her gently out of the way as he went to kiss his girlfriend. Ginger sidled off in the direction of the bar, wishing that she had worn black, and could pass herself off as a waitress.

'You looked very beautiful this evening,' Stephen said, lying back in their big bed as Alison undressed in front of her dressing table later that evening.

'No,' she protested modestly, 'I looked exhausted.'

'Well, pale and wan seems to suit you,' he said, 'your friend's husband couldn't keep his eyes off you.'

'Don't be ridiculous, Stephen,' she said, a little too

quickly, she thought, turning away to brush her hair and wondering what had made him make such an uncharacteristic remark. Did he know something? Was he testing her? In the mirror's reflection, she saw him pick up a tabloid section from one of the Sunday papers and start to flick through it, absent-mindedly. No, she decided, it must have been a chance remark.

'I feel terribly inadequate beside those two,' she said, suddenly.

'Which two?'

Upside down, she saw that Stephen was focusing on an article about garden pergolas. His concentration amused her, given his minimal interest in gardening.

'Ginger and Lia,' she said.

He put down the paper. 'What do you mean?' he asked her.

'They're such good mothers,' she said, climbing into bed next to him, 'and I'm hopeless.'

'Hopeless? Have you seen the look on Ben's face when you come in from work?'

'Yes,' she said, smiling, 'it's like a sunbeam, and it makes me feel terribly guilty for leaving him all day.'

'Well, you mustn't,' Stephen said categorically. 'The most important thing for him is that you are happy. That we are all happy,' he added.

'We are happy, aren't we?' Alison said in a small voice, snuggling down beside him, like a child after a nightmare, needing his warmth and his protection to send her off to sleep.

'We're very happy,' Stephen assured her, squeezing her tight with one arm, and switching off the light with the other.

She felt calm and secure listening in the dark to his even breathing, feeling the strength in his arm around her body slacken after just a few seconds as he fell asleep. She lay watching the patterns the street-light made on the wall, thinking of the magic lantern in Anouska's room, with its stars and animals that twirled around the ceiling to the decelerating ping of

Brahms's lullaby. She was in bed with the man she loved, who loved her, she told herself, turning over, trying to settle. But she did not seem to be able to wish away the frisson of excitement that had shivered through her body when Stephen had implied that Neil still fancied her.

'Why on earth didn't you say something to him?' Robert asked Ginger crossly, when he discovered her sitting on a crate of champagne, looking as if she were reserving it entirely for her own consumption, and insisting to the bemused bartender that he really did look just like Mickey Rourke.

'Like what?' Ginger scowled at him to go away. She rather fancied her chances with Mickey, even though designer stubble wasn't usually her thing.

'Like, can you give me a job?' Robert said.

'In lieu of child support, you mean?' Ginger asked, the alcohol loosening her tongue. She was finding it suddenly exceptionally difficult to work out the meaning of anything anybody said to her. Even Mickey's, 'Would you mind getting out of my way?' had taken several minutes to be processed by the sluggish computer that appeared to have been swapped for her brain.

'He thinks you're an original – God knows, he wouldn't if he saw you in this state – and he's looking for a development person, but every time he tries to ask, you're either rude to him, or don't return his calls. Honestly!'

'Well, for your information,' Ginger said, with what she thought was great dignity, 'I don't want to be a development person, so there. Come on, Mickey, let's go,' she said, standing up.

'It's Gary,' said the bartender, 'and I'm not going anywhere. I've got to clear this lot up.'

'Have you eaten anything?' Robert asked her.

'Only a couple of those bits of toast with stuff.'

'Crostini,' he said.

'Crostini,' she echoed, mockingly.

'You are intolerable when you're drunk, but I feel it is my duty to my godson to buy you dinner. I can't send you home to him in this state,' Robert told her, offering his arm.

She looked longingly at the bartender, but he was studiously ignoring her as he busied himself collecting glasses from around the room.

'All right, but I must call my baby-sitter,' she agreed, finally.

'You will not call anyone until I say so!' Robert said, adding, more kindly, 'It's OK. It's not even midnight yet. God, Ginger, not even midnight, and my party's over, I must be losing my touch . . .'

'It's your party and you'll cry if you want to,' Ginger sang, out of tune, and for no logical reason, as he walked her downstairs to the restaurant.

'Does Charlie really want to give me a job?' she said, after Robert had made her eat a lot of bread to soak up the alcohol.

'I don't know. I think so,' Robert said. 'I can't think why else he'd be interested.'

'Thanks a lot.'

'Oh, you know I didn't mean it like that, I meant, well, you know Charlie, he's all work. Yes, we do.' He flashed a sudden smile at the waiter who had asked if they cared to order, and handed him back the menus. 'Hamburger and chips twice.'

'Hamburger? I thought you invited me for dinner, not bloody fast food.'

'Oh, suddenly she's sober enough to tell the difference . . . actually, hamburger is what you eat here. It's well known to be the best this side of the Atlantic. I think they use Argentinian beef — anyway, it's BSE free. Even vegetarians come here for the bloody hamburger,' Robert snapped at her.

'Can I have a glass of red wine?' she asked him.

'Certainly not,' he said.

The hamburger was very good, cooked so rare, it

was almost steak tartare, and served with a dollop of thick, yellow *béarnaise* sauce with capers in.

'Do you have ketchup?' Ginger asked the waiter as he set down two large plates and a wooden bowl filled with thick slices of potato, their skins still on, dusted with crushed chillies.

'Er, I'll have a look. I know we have salsa, and sour cream and guacamole . . .'

'Ooh, yes please, all of that,' Ginger said, enthusiastically.

'God, you are unbelievable,' Robert hissed at her, 'I buy you decent food and you ask for ketchup. Have you no manners?'

'Actually, if you had any manners yourself, you would know that the classiest places always have what the customer wants, and if they don't, they consider it their failing, not the customer's, so they run out to the Seven-Eleven to get it,' Ginger countered equally aggressively. 'It's like if your guest uses the wrong fork, then you're supposed to too, but I don't expect they teach you these things at grammar school,' she added, amusing herself by pulling rank on someone who considered himself such an arbiter of taste, and knowing full well that Robert's friendship with her was to some small extent propelled by his fascination with her aristocratic background. He was the most terrible snob.

The waiter returned with a big squeezy bottle of Heinz.

'Thank you.' Ginger smiled regally at him. 'Now, you don't have one of those little condiment trays with that wonderful sticky sweetcorn relish and mango chutney in, do you? You know the sort I mean, kind of stainless steel and they twirl around . . . only joking,' she added, sticking her tongue out at Robert, who had put down his knife and fork and had his hands in the air in mock-surrender.

'Oh my God, don't look round,' Ginger said, spotting Charlie Prince eating at the other end of the room.

He had been hidden by Lucretia's back, but as she bent to light a cheroot from the candle in the middle of the table, he caught sight of Ginger and smiled at her.

She couldn't smile back, because she knew that if she did, she would reveal half-masticated mince instead of teeth. Chewing quickly seemed to make her mouth become fuller and fuller, and by the time she had swallowed, the moment had passed and she found she was smiling at Lucretia's sinuous spine. You could see the vertebrae through the black chiffon silk she was wearing, Ginger noticed. She looked away, knowing that her face had turned red enough to match the smear of ketchup she could feel on her cheek.

'What does he see in that bitch?' she asked Robert, not very quietly.

'She's a wonderful actress,' Robert replied, having a quick look around to see that there was nobody he knew within earshot, 'and they've been together for ever, although I think it's pretty open.'

'But she's so—' said Ginger exasperated.

'Oh, underneath I expect she's a frail little flower like the rest of us.'

'Really?'

'I don't think so, but there is something quite fascinating about her ruthlessness. For someone as ambitious as Charlie, anyway.'

Nobody ever talked about Charlie without using the word ambition. He was always quoted as saying that class did not matter, but somehow everyone knew that he had grown up in a tower block in the East End, and was the only boy from his comprehensive school ever to have gained a scholarship to Oxford.

'Is he really looking for a development person?' Ginger asked, vaguely remembering their earlier conversation, and relieved that Robert had insisted on sobering her up.

'Yes, he is.'

'Oh well, if he ever mentions it to you again, maybe you could tell him to call me.'

'That's not how it works, Ginger,' said Robert, telling her what she knew already.

'I know,' she said with resignation, helping herself to the last chip in the bowl. 'Actually, I don't think I was destined to have a brilliant media career, I can't do the small talk.'

'You could if you weren't so ... so ... truthful,' Robert said finally.

'Well, I'm not sure I want to, anyway,' Ginger said.

'What are you going to do, then?' Robert asked her impatiently.

Media people hated any implicit criticism of their world, she realized, because it was underpinned on shifting foundations, like whim, style, and irony, and they were terrified of it all collapsing around them.

'I'd like to have more children,' Ginger said, partly because she was enjoying winding him up.

'She doesn't want to be in the media, she wants to be Mia Farrow,' Robert sneered. 'Excuse me while I go for a slash.'

The waiter handed Ginger a dessert menu, and she was so engrossed in deciding between the marquise of chocolate, or the *tarte tatin* on a puddle of vanilla-scented custard, she didn't bother to look up when he came back to take her order.

'Would it be too greedy,' she asked, her forefinger jumping between the two desserts she wanted, 'to have the chocolate marquise with a bit of the vanilla-scented custard?'

'I expect you could get anything you wanted, wearing that dress,' Charlie Prince told her.

She looked up, startled and embarrassed, but relieved to see that he was on his own.

'Where's Lucretia?' she asked abruptly.

He looked slightly perplexed.

'She's powdering her nose,' he replied.

'Oh.'

'You've changed,' he said, 'I hardly recognized you.'

'Oh?' She wasn't sure whether that was good, or bad. Was this his way of saying sorry for pushing her out of the way earlier?

'Great hair-style,' he went on, looking appreciatively at her head.

Her hand went nervously to her temple. Why was it that she always thought people were setting her up when they said something nice about her appearance? For some reason, she thought of Alison, and the way she responded to compliments. It was more grown-up, she realized, to accept gracefully than to protest.

'Thank you,' she said, as serenely as she knew how.

'I hear you've had a baby . . . I saw you on the box,' he said.

Her heart had started to beat so loudly, she was sure the whole restaurant could hear it. 'Yes,' she said, trying to divert the subject, 'a lot of people seem to have seen me.'

'Not mine, is it?' he joked.

So he did remember they had done it. She had never really been sure. 'Yes!' she said, finding it impossible to lie, but making it sound as if she was joking.

He threw back his head and laughed.

'How would you feel if it were?' she asked him, marvelling at her almost Shakespearean wit. It was as if, in her heightened state of nervousness, one of those plucky transvestite heroines, like Viola from *Twelfth Night*, had temporarily stepped out of doublet and hose and into her red velvet dress.

He stopped laughing suddenly and looked at her as if he sensed a hidden meaning behind the words. She held her bluff, light-hearted expression just long enough to keep up the pretence.

'Alarmed,' he said, grappling with the concept, 'and, I suppose, rather proud.'

What could have possessed her to ask, she immediately wondered, because now she wanted to know more, and the Shakespearean heroine had disappeared from the stage to be replaced by a hapless girlfriend in a John Osborne play.

'Listen, we must have lunch and catch up,' Charlie told her, catching sight of Lucretia at the door, her coat on, ready to leave.

'OK,' Ginger said, despondently.

'And I shall make sure I find somewhere that serves chocolate pudding and custard,' he said, pointing at the dessert menu, and vanishing as swiftly and silently as he had arrived.

'The thing is, in your head, you plan every single scenario, what his question will be, what your answer will be, all that . . . then, bang, he says something you never thought of, and you hear yourself saying something you had absolutely forbidden yourself to say, and you wish the floor would just open up and swallow you,' Ginger told Alison the next morning when she rang to ask her how the dress performed on the night.

'Oh dear,' Alison sympathized, 'but these things are never as bad as you think they were.'

'How about this: I told him Guy was his child—'

'But that's good, I'm glad you did that,' Alison interrupted.

'No, wait – then I pretended it was a joke.'

'Oh . . .'

'But the dress was great. He remarked on it, said I'd changed, which must be good, I think, and, oh hell, what am I going to do?'

Alison thought for a minute. She found herself envying Ginger her guileless honesty, which she herself had lost long before. Nowadays, her bantering conversations with Ramona were about as close as she got to girls' talk, and she rarely revealed anything of importance.

225

'I think you should have lunch with him – give him the benefit of the doubt. I know it's hard to believe, but some men are nice, you know.' She had in mind a picture of Stephen's face, the night before, as he carefully straightened the bow-tie on Benedict's enormous teddy bear.

'Oh, he won't call,' Ginger said, resignedly.

'I think he will,' Alison said, hoping she was right, 'probably not before Christmas, though, so don't be all miserable,' she added, thinking back to her single days, so many of which seemed to have been spent watching the stubbornly silent phone, willing it to ring.

'I can't promise that,' Ginger said, surprisingly brightly, 'I'm spending it in the country with the family, and Daddy hasn't spoken to me since the programme.'

'Christmas is always awful,' Alison agreed, 'the only one I've ever enjoyed I was away. It was just after I met Stephen and we escaped to the Seychelles – even then I spent most of Christmas Day feeling guilty because I couldn't find an international phone to ring my parents.'

Ginger laughed. 'Oh well,' she sighed, 'have a good one, anyway.'

'I'll try,' Alison said, adding on the spur of the moment, 'Listen, what are you doing at New Year?'

'Pic and Ed are having a dinner party, why?'

'Doesn't matter.'

'Hey, but I thought you were going round to Lia's,' Ginger said, interpreting Alison's question.

'I may do,' she said, non-committally, bristling at the idea that Lia and Ginger had already discussed it. 'Anyway, big kiss to Guy,' and she put down the phone.

It was Christmas morning and everything was as it should be. The turkey was in the oven, the sprouts were peeled and washed, the potatoes and parsnips had just come to the boil. Lia turned the gas off and drained the water away, shaking the colander hard to get rid of all the moisture, then carefully dropping the vegetables into a baking tray of hot fat, and turning them to ensure they were coated on all sides. She slid the tray into the oven and silently counted off the tasks still to do on her fingers: lay the table, gravy, bread sauce, feed Anouska and change her into the pretty tartan dress she had wrapped in Santa Claus paper the night before and unwrapped excitedly this morning.

Neil had built a log fire in the grate for the first time that year, and then fallen asleep in front of it, the new cricket jumper she had bought for him by his side, his hand still perilously closed around a half-full can of lager. She tidied up around him as quietly as she could, taking the present he had bought her upstairs, trying to suppress the vague sense of disappointment she had felt when she opened it. If you had to receive underwear for Christmas, she supposed camiknickers in burgundy silk was about the nicest you could get, but it was such an unimaginative present.

Still, everything else was perfect. The tree was almost as tall as the room and decorated with sparkling white lights, silver balls and little wooden toys she had found reduced to half-price the day before. There was a string of coloured lights outside, and a sprig of mistletoe suspended above the kitchen door. It was her first ever real family Christmas.

She tied a matching tartan ribbon around Anouska's head to hide the patches where her hair was very thin. When she was born, she had fluffy hair like down, but most of it had now gone. There was hair coming through underneath now, but at the moment she had to admit Neil was right, it looked a mess. But she did look cute in her Christmas dress and white tights, Lia thought, kissing her baby on the nose and being rewarded with a big toothless smile.

There was a loud knock at the door and Lia looked

out of the bedroom window to see Cheryl standing below, a poinsettia in one hand and a carrier bag full of gifts in the other. She wondered why she had parked just down the road from their house. She lifted Anouska up and took her downstairs.

'Where's Pete?' Lia asked, giving her sister-in-law a hug.

'He's following later,' Cheryl said, not looking at her as she very deliberately pulled parcels out of her bag. 'Let me put this lot under the tree.'

Lia registered a peculiar exchange of glances with Neil, but thought nothing of it. Pete and Cheryl had been known to arrive separately on many occasions. He often had to test-drive a car he had repaired, but liked to have Cheryl as back-up.

'You're pregnant!' Lia said, as she took her coat.

'Yes, it's really beginning to show now,' Cheryl said. 'Didn't Neil tell you?'

'No . . . Honestly, Neil,' she scolded him.

'Sorry,' he said, slumping back in his chair after the effort of getting up to open the door, 'I forgot.'

'Men!' said Cheryl, following Lia into the kitchen and bending down with difficulty to admire the turkey in the oven.

'Are you drinking?' Lia said, opening a shiny blue box and taking out a bottle of Harvey's Bristol Cream.

'Well, just a little bit. Hey, let's stay out here for a while, just the two of us girls . . . sorry, Anouska, just the three of us girls,' she corrected herself.

'Good idea,' Lia said, propping Anouska in the pram which she kept in the kitchen so that the baby could watch her work in safety. She wished they could afford a playpen with net sides like the brightly-coloured one that so jarred against the muted décor of Alison and Stephen's kitchen. One of the many things nobody told you about having babies was that you had to have somewhere to put them. Soon she would be crawling, and she had no idea what she would do then, she told Cheryl.

'It'll be summer,' Cheryl said, 'you can put her on the lawn and watch her from in here. Your garden's perfect for that, unlike our scrap-heap.'

Lia smiled at her, and sipped her drink, its treacle-sweet taste quintessentially Christmassy.

'How are you all getting on, anyway?' Cheryl asked her, never one to beat about the bush.

'Fine,' Lia continued staring into the garden.

'It's just, we haven't seen you for ages, and, well,' Cheryl hesitated, 'well, Neil seemed a bit down the other day . . .'

'On the phone?' Lia asked, surprised.

'No, when he came down, you know, that cold spell. I remember thinking, I hope he's all right going back in this ice . . .'

'I didn't know he'd been to see you. When was that?'

Cheryl thought about it. 'I know. It was bonfire night – of course it was: the boys were out building the fire on the green.'

So that was where Neil had been that evening when he had come home so full of energy. Why on earth had he lied? Lia wondered.

'Things are fine,' Lia said, feeling an enormous weight of anxiety lift from her shoulders. 'We have our ups and downs . . . well, we all do, don't we?'

'You're telling me . . .' Cheryl replied, laughing, and then there was another knock on the door. 'That must be Pete,' and they both stood up to greet him as his bulk filled the kitchen door-frame, his head squashing the mistletoe against the lintel.

'Happy Christmas!' he said. 'Er, Lia, Neil's got something for you . . .'

She could hear the crackle of wrapping paper, and as she walked through into the living room, Neil handed her a small twist of the red and gold paper she had used to wrap his present. She took it, nervously, and unravelled it.

Inside was a car key. For a moment she did not

229

understand, and then she saw Pete glance at the window. A red Peugeot 205 was parked outside their house.

'It's not new, but it goes . . . they're good engines, those diesels,' Pete informed the room, but Lia wasn't listening, she was in the street, trying the key in the lock. It slid in. She opened the door, got in, started the ignition and drove.

The streets were almost empty of traffic. She switched from lane to lane, remembering the mirror, finding the indicator, testing the accelerator. The last time she had driven was in Portugal. She found her right hand going for the gear lever each time she pushed the clutch in, but corrected herself quickly. She drove up Richmond Hill, beeping the horn outside Ginger's house, before remembering that she had gone to the country, then on to Richmond Deer Park. There were deer there! She had thought it just a name left over from the past. She slowed the car as a small, frightened herd ran across the road in front of her. Then she pulled the car over to the verge, slumped against the steering wheel and burst into tears. She had woven Neil's silences and moods into a fabric of deceit and disillusion, but all he had been doing was planning a surprise gift for her! She wiped her eyes and nose with her sleeve, recalling with a stab of shame the times she had snapped at him, or turned away from his affection. Even this Christmas morning she had been distinctly underwhelmed by his gift of lingerie. She would make up for it, she promised silently, starting up the engine and driving home.

'Lunch will be ready in about half an hour,' Margaret announced, 'why don't you two go out for a walk. Give yourselves an appetite. Benedict and I will be fine together.'

She looked at her grandson who was sitting perfectly upright on the peach and eau-de-nil Chinese carpet. He smiled at her, clearly proud of himself for achieving this new goal, then keeled over sideways.

Margaret bent down, propping him up again with a couple of peach damask scatter cushions, and put the activity cube she had bought next to him, determined that by the end of the day it would be his favourite present. He looked away, and picked up the Fisher Price mobile phone instead.

'His mother's son,' Stephen commented, taking Alison's hand.

'Come on, Benedict,' Margaret urged, 'look, if you press this, it squeaks . . .'

Alison was rather enjoying her son's resistance to his grandmother's techniques of persuasion. She smiled at him encouragingly, and waved bye bye as they pulled on their coats and left the house.

'Have you noticed she will not call him Ben?' she said to Stephen as they walked down the gravel drive to the small, private road that led to the sea. 'She thinks it's common to shorten names. She used to take it as a definite sign of somebody's class if they started to call her Maggie . . . that was before Thatcher, of course. I don't think she would have thought it quite so bad if her heroine could tolerate it.'

She recalled the way Margaret's nose had twisted just slightly to the side when Neil had called her Ally on one of the rare occasions he had been invited to their house for tea.

'Well, actually, I've never much liked being called Steve,' her husband replied, 'there were three Steves in my class at school. People thought I was a snob for insisting on my full name.'

Alison had never been able to imagine him as a schoolboy. He seemed so grown-up, and because his parents had both died in a plane crash long before she met him, she had seen no mantelpiece of photographs, like the one at her mother's house above the coal-effect gas fire, which captured her own youth, and gave a pretty accurate record, she always thought, of girls' hair-styles throughout the sixties and seventies.

She knew that he had hated school, and that he had been mocked because he had suffered from asthma. A lot of children who had been sick in their youth became doctors, he had once told her.

'To save other people from suffering?' she had enquired.

'Or perhaps to inflict the same pain on others,' he had suggested, with his usual candour.

When they had discussed having a baby together, the only thing he had insisted was that they would never send the child away to boarding school, and his troubled face had spoken of the pain he still experienced remembering it.

There was a stretch of grass, the width of half a field, between the high garden fences of the last row of houses in the estate and the shingle beach. They walked along protected from the full force of the wind coming off the sea by the scrubby bushes behind the row of clapped-out wooden huts.

'We should do this more often,' Stephen remarked, threading his arm through hers and putting his gloveless hand into the pocket of her coat.

'Come to the sea? Yes, we should. I love it.'

'Well, I meant come to see your mother,' he said.

She pulled a face.

'She's getting on,' he argued patiently, 'it's good for her to see her grandson. He's the only one, after all.'

For the first time, it occurred to Alison that having just one child was probably a very bad idea. The pressure on an only child could be crushing. When she was young she had wished for sisters to play with. Now she wished there was someone else to share the inevitable burden of her mother's ageing. She dared not think what she would do if her mother became helpless and senile. How could she contemplate imposing a similar burden on her son, or an even greater one, because, as Stephen had pointed out, he would be the only grandson too? But I will not be like Margaret, she promised herself, trying to banish the thought and the unpalatable chain of consequences it set in motion.

'I'm going down onto the beach,' she announced, detaching herself from his arm and running off.

The wind blasted her hair back from her face, numbing her ears. The crunch of shingle underneath her feet and the smell of seaweed and salt made her want to race into the dull green spumy sea and wash away all the anxious thoughts that seemed crammed to overflowing inside her head. She chased a wave down the beach, then struggled up a ridge as a bigger, better one crashed about her feet, soaking her jeans and boots. Stephen watched from beside a pale pink beach hut, smiling at her as she twirled and screamed into the wind.

They always walked back across the fields after the Christmas morning service in the village church. Poor Ed was still new enough to the family to feel obliged to listen politely to their mother's dog anecdotes. A few steps in front of them Ginger walked slowly along the bridle path arm in arm with Pic pushing the pram. In the distance their father marched ahead briskly, never able to slow his pace to anyone else's. Ginger remembered all the times she had puffed along beside him trying to keep up with his speed, and how once, when she was quite small, she had stumbled and hurt her knee and cried, 'Please wait for me, Daddy,' but in his haste, he had not heard her.

There were a few rosehips still clinging to the brambles, and some early snowdrops at the foot of the hedgerow.

'At this rate, we're going to have two sittings for lunch,' Ginger told her sister as they paused to look over the ploughed fields, their ridges iced with frost, towards the Palladian house they had grown up in, that shone pale gold in the chilly winter sunlight. 'Daddy hasn't spoken a word to me since we arrived.'

'Has it ever occurred to you,' Pic asked cautiously, breaking off a branch of holly with an abundant cluster of berries, 'that you are both very similar?'

'In what sense?' Ginger challenged her, rising immediately to the perceived slight.

'Well, you're both so stubborn and unforgiving . . .'

'But I'm not vicious and nasty!' Ginger said.

'No, but I doubt he thinks he is either. You're both so sure that you know what's right, and you're both so proud . . .'

'Well, happy Christmas to you, too.' Ginger started to walk quickly on ahead.

'Oh, don't be like that,' Pic called after her. It was impossible to push the pram at any speed on the unmade path. 'You know that I love you the most,' she said as she caught up, putting her arm through Ginger's and looking anxiously at her face which had columns of tears flowing from each eye. 'I didn't mean to upset you.'

'Well, take it back then, say that I'm not like Daddy,' Ginger demanded.

'In lots of ways you're not . . .'

'But in others I am?' Ginger sighed. 'I suppose you're right . . . I'm not really crying about that, by the way,' she added, never able to use emotional black-mail for long, even on her suggestible sister.

'So why?' Pic asked, concerned.

'Because my life's a bloody mess, that's why . . . You're right about being proud. I was too proud to accept their financial help and now I've got to go back to work and I haven't got a clue what I'm going to do with Guy.'

'Have you thought about selling the flat and buying something smaller? I mean, it is lovely, in a way, with all that dark furniture and chandeliers and things, but it's a bit impractical, isn't it?'

Pic lived in a neo-Georgian townhouse in Swiss

234

Cottage. It had a garage, two bathrooms and dimmer lights. It was furnished with modern Scandinavian furniture, and was always spotless. Ginger sometimes wondered whether it was made of the same stuff as one of those modern ovens that cleans itself, and never smells of last Sunday's roast.

'No. Hermione wanted me to have it,' Ginger said, 'and I love it there. There must be something else . . .'

'Well, how about if I give you some of the money I got from Hermione,' Pic said, 'I'd really love to.'

'No,' said Ginger, 'that's yours. It's bad enough that she left me so much compared to you. Anyway, when you have children, they'll need it.'

'Not all of it, there's loads. I'm sure she thought she was leaving us exactly the same. Anyway, I'm sure she would want Guy to have it.'

'No, that's why she left me the flat. Don't you remember, the will actually said: for Virginia and her child?'

'Well,' Pic said, knowing there was no point in trying to persuade her, 'let's think about what you could do. How about a childminder?'

'The trouble with that is Lia and I sometimes overhear one when we're out in the Gardens, and honestly, if the parents knew the way she treated them . . . It's a bit of a risk . . .'

'She wouldn't look after him, I suppose?' Pic asked.

'Who?'

'Lia.'

Ginger stopped walking. 'My God, that is a brilliant idea!' She picked her sister right off the ground in the enthusiasm of her hug. 'I could afford to pay her what a childminder gets. She needs the money. She loves Guy. She's fantastic with children . . . Why on earth didn't I think of it?'

'Perhaps she wouldn't want to,' Pic said, suddenly nervous that Ginger might be about to be hugely disappointed. 'Presumably, she would have volunteered . . .'

'No, she probably just hadn't thought of it. I'll ring her and ask.' Ginger started to run towards the house.

'Wait, are you sure . . . ? Make sure you remember to say happy Christmas!' Pic shouted after her, knowing how rude her sister's directness could sometimes sound.

Lia had just poured brandy on the pudding and struck a match to light it, when the phone rang. In her surprise she dropped the match and the dessert was immediately engulfed in a halo of blue flame.

'You blow it out, Neil, or whatever you're meant to do,' she giggled, and went into the kitchen to answer the phone.

He heard her giggling a lot more, and then a long silence, then another giggle, and then she said, 'Yes . . . No, I'm sure, of course. It would be lovely. Are *you* sure, more to the point? Of course he won't.' More giggling.

In his head he totted up the number of glasses of sherry and wine she had consumed. No more driving for her today. He wondered if the licence she had got in Portugal was valid anyway. It had alarmed him to see her accelerating up the road without looking back, and she seemed to be away a very long time. He had been very relieved when she finally returned, looking different, somehow, almost as if she had been crying.

She laughed again, said, 'Merry Christmas,' several more times, and then came back to the kitchen table, which he and Pete had dragged into the living room for the occasion.

'Well,' she said, 'how about that? I just got myself a job!'

'Congratulations!' Cheryl clinked her glass against Lia's.

'What job's this, then?' Neil asked her.

'That was Ginger. She's asked me if I would take care of Guy when she goes back to work.' She turned to Cheryl to explain. 'Ginger's a friend we met at ante-natal. She's really nice and she's got a terrific little boy, hasn't she, Neil?'

She was smiling at him down the table. He couldn't work out what he felt. In his head, he knew he should be pleased, but the overwhelming sensation in his body was like a low grumble of anger. His face seemed unable to respond with the encouragement she was seeking.

'And you said yes, of course.' The words were neutral, but his voice was surly. He noticed Pete and Cheryl exchange glances.

'Of course I did! I love Guy. He's called Guy,' Lia informed Cheryl, happily.

She was drunk, Neil realized.

'I don't suppose you bothered to ask her how much she's paying for this nannying service,' he said, turning to his brother as if to enlist his support. 'She's a poor little rich girl, who's got this amazing flat on the Hill, but is always telling you how little money she has. My heart bleeds . . .'

'Actually, that's not true,' Lia said, becoming aware that the atmosphere in the room had changed.

'Actually . . .' Neil mocked her use of Ginger's favourite word.

Lia looked bewildered. 'I know you don't like her, but it's a great way of me earning some money, isn't it?' she argued, 'and she says she will buy a playpen, a double-buggy, whatever I need . . .'

'Hasn't she got enough servants?' Neil asked.

'Redistribution of wealth, mate,' Pete intervened, attempting to diffuse the tension between them as he scraped his plate clean of pudding and brandy butter. 'Are you going to save that last bit?' he added, waving his spoon at the remaining wedge of pudding.

'No, go ahead.' Lia pushed it across the table to him, grateful for the change of subject.

They had always played charades in the long drawing room after Christmas lunch, dividing into teams with one weak and one strong player, Ginger and their mother, Daddy and Pic. Now there was Ed, the balance was upset.

'You go with Daddy, Ginger,' Pic suggested, 'the two of you must be about equal to the three of us.'

'But . . .' Ginger shot her a look to kill.

'Come along, Ginger,' their father said, rising from the table and hurrying in to grab the comfortable sofa for them, 'we'll knock this lot into a cocked hat . . . Now' – he raised his voice like a teacher – 'rules: books, films, plays, songs, how about three of each to start with?'

Pic and their mother followed in while Ed went to get the box of Belgian chocolates he and Pic had brought.

Daddy was so competitive, he wanted his team to win whoever he was playing with, even though he had not made eye contact with her since she arrived, Ginger realized.

'Television,' she added, 'you forgot television programmes.'

'Well, none of us watch it, do we?' her father said.

'Only when their wayward daughters are on,' Ginger said under her breath, reeling at the slight to her chosen profession, and retaliating without thinking.

'As a matter of fact, I, unlike the rest of the world, did not see you. I was informed about your appearance by colleagues who had. Fortunately, just before that Labour yob made his joke at PM's questions,' her father told her in his most cold, patronizing voice, adding, 'I presume you did it to embarrass me. You succeeded. Are you satisfied now, and can we get on with the game?'

'Why do you think that everything I do has something to do with you?' Ginger asked him, trying to keep her voice equally chill, but she didn't have the stomach for a major row, partly because she secretly suspected that, on this occasion, he was probably right about her motives. She had agreed to do the talk show the day after her father had come to lunch, she recalled.

'How about *Casablanca*?' said her father, choosing to ignore her question, and get on with the game of charades.

'No,' she said, inwardly admitting defeat, 'we had that last year, and anyway it's easy. How about *Men Behaving Badly*?'

'Well, that's too easy too,' her father said, 'all they would have to do is stand there and point at me . . .' He turned to face her, his eyes twinkling with humour.

She saw it was his attempt at a truce. It was pathetic, but he had made the effort. Reluctantly she smiled back at him. She could almost hear Pic's sigh of relief from the other side of the enormous drawing room.

Standing in his baby-walker, the present Ginger had bought him for Christmas, Guy chuckled. He had not yet worked out how to push himself along, but he was enjoying being upright, supported by the tray at the front, as if leaning against a bar, fascinated by his new perspective on his favourite toy, a set of stacking rings.

'He's a very jolly chap, isn't he?' her father suddenly remarked, watching him with interest, as if it were the first time he had seen him. 'Darling,' he called to his wife on the other side of the room, 'doesn't Guy seem rather advanced? I can't remember the girls doing this at his age.'

'Oh yes, he's very advanced,' their mother agreed absently.

Ginger had not known before where the expression swelling with pride came from. She definitely felt somehow bigger as she basked in her parents' praise of her son.

Her father turned back to her and winked. 'Next year, Ginger, we'll have him on our team.'

It was as if Daddy had finally welcomed his grandson into their family.

When Pete and Cheryl came to go home, Lia watched Neil hand over his helmet and the keys to his motorbike to his brother. Cheryl got into the car she had driven up that morning and Pete sat astride Neil's bike. They both sounded their horns.

'Why's Pete taking your bike?' Lia asked, waving as they drove away.

'Part-exchange for the car,' Neil told her, turning back into the house, unable to watch the bike that was no longer his disappear out of sight.

Lia followed him in and burst into tears. 'But I didn't mean you to sell your bike,' she sobbed, 'why didn't you discuss it with me?'

He said nothing. There was nothing to cry about. It was only a bike. Didn't she have any idea how much a car cost? Where were they going to get that kind of money? He went into the kitchen, got a beer from the fridge, then came back and sat down in front of the television, can in one hand and remote control in the other.

Upstairs Anouska woke up. Lia went to her. When she came back down she had stopped crying and was wearing his dressing-gown.

'Are you watching this?' she asked.

'Not really,' Neil said, without taking his eyes from the screen.

She slid onto his lap, sitting with one leg at each side of his waist, facing him. Then she untied the dressing-gown and shook it from her shoulders. She had put on the dark red camiknickers he had given her that morning. Her skin looked golden in the light of the dying fire. He realized that she was still slightly drunk.

'It was a good day, wasn't it?' she said, smoothing his hair back from his face.

'Yeah.' He peered under her arm to watch the

motorboat chase on the screen. 'Yeah, you cooked a good lunch.'

'Not bad for a first attempt.' She smiled at him, wriggling her hips, then leant forward to kiss his neck, and began to unbutton his shirt. She traced a wet line down the centre of his chest with her tongue, then she knelt on the floor, and he felt her unzipping his jeans. With his eyes still fixed on the screen but not watching, he put his hands on her shoulders and pushed her gently away.

'What's wrong?' she asked, her eyes filling with tears again.

It feels as if you're doing it in return for me giving up the bike, he wanted to say.

'I don't feel like it,' he told her.

'OK.' She joined him on the sofa, trying to look as if it didn't matter. 'I think Anouska liked the wrapping paper better than everything else,' she said, attempting to make neutral conversation.

'Yeah.'

'Are you cross about my job?'

'No.'

'I love you, Neil,' she said, snuggling down beside him, her head on his shoulder.

'Yeah, I love you too,' he said, relaxing a little, planting a kiss in her sweet-smelling hair.

'Will you marry me, then?' she asked.

There was laughter in her voice, but he knew she was deadly serious. It was a kind of last-ditch desperation to make everything all right on Christmas Day. He thought of all the times he had asked her the same question, when she had smiled serenely and asked why change something that was so perfect. And now they both knew it wasn't perfect, but he instinctively knew that getting married would not fix it.

'If that's what you want,' he replied eventually.

'No,' she said, quietly, 'you had to think about it. You wouldn't have done before.'

Then she started crying again, but this time they

241

were sad tears, wrenching her like grief. He let her sob into his chest, stroking her, trying to find the right words to comfort her.

'Let's talk about it in the morning,' he said, 'you've had a lot to drink. You wouldn't want me to take advantage of you when you're pissed, would you?'

It was New Year's Eve and, for the first time in her adult life, Alison was not going out, but she was damned if she was going to spend the entire evening sitting on the nursery floor next to Ben's cot.

The moment she carefully withdrew her hand from the cot, silently inching it away in case he sensed the slightest disturbance in the air above him, and began to tiptoe in slow motion towards the door, like someone playing grandmother's footsteps, the phone rang. Ben woke up immediately and began to scream. She was torn between answering the phone and trying to soothe and comfort him until it stopped ringing. It didn't stop ringing, so she picked him up out of the cot and took him with her to their bedroom. As soon as he was in her arms he fell back to sleep, snuffling against her shoulder.

'I'm sorry, were you in the middle of something?' Stephen asked.

'I'd just got him off to sleep,' Alison said, the fury and frustration making her voice flat and cold.

'Oh dear . . . and have I woken him?'

'What do you think?'

'Sorry, my love.'

'How are you getting on?' she asked him, her voice softening a little.

'I'm fine, but how are you?'

'Desperate . . . I know that it only makes it worse when I lose my temper, but I just can't help it,' she admitted, feeling bad as soon as she had said it.

Now Stephen would worry and feel guilty, and although his name had numbered among the people she had been silently swearing at earlier, she didn't really want him to be miserable on New Year's Eve, a long way from home.

'Oh dear,' he said, sadly, 'has his cold improved?'

'Not really. That's half the problem. His nose is blocked so he can't suck his dummy and breathe at the same time. I know I should feel sorry for him, and I do, but I've had no sleep for two days, and I'm frayed at the edges . . .'

'It's bad luck that he got his first cold now,' Stephen said, full of sympathy.

'Probably inevitable,' she replied resignedly.

'But he hasn't got a temperature?'

'No,' she said wearily, knowing it was childish to begrudge his concern about Ben's state rather than hers, but resenting it anyway.

'So, how are you going to see the New Year in?' he asked.

'Oh, I thought I'd go to the ball at the Savoy . . . How do you bloody think?'

'I'm sorry,' he said again.

'It's all right. You just caught me at a bad moment. What are you going to do?'

'Some of the guys have a table at a place in Little Italy. I thought I might join them.'

'You sound awfully American – guys! Watch out for the men with violin cases,' she joked.

'Why?' He sounded mystified.

For someone so sophisticated, he could sometimes be amazingly ignorant.

'It's where the Mafia hang out,' she told him. 'When I went there, I couldn't believe the number of stretch limos with tinted windows. It was almost clichéd – or maybe I've just seen too many films.'

'Really?' he said, as if assimilating an interesting fact, 'goodness, well, the restaurant is owned by the father of one of my colleagues here. I wonder if that means . . .'

'Well, do whatever he tells you, otherwise you might wake up sharing your bed with a horse's head.'

'A horse's head?'

'Oh, Stephen, honestly,' she said impatiently, but unable to resist a smile. How could anyone have reached the age of forty without seeing *The Godfather*? Stephen was completely untouched by popular culture.

'Why don't you go over to Lia's?' he asked, sensing her mood lighten a little.

'I doubt if they would appreciate Ben's screaming either,' she said.

'He'd probably fall asleep in the car on the way there. He did before.'

'I don't think so,' she said. 'Look, don't you worry, I'll be fine.'

'Shall I ring you at midnight?'

'I don't think I could be responsible for the consequences, if he happened to be asleep by then.' Alison sighed, 'It doesn't matter – we're grown-ups now, aren't we? Quite honestly, if I manage to get this child to sleep, I don't think I'll even bother to stay up till midnight.'

'I will make it up to you.'

'You certainly will,' she laughed, 'I've already picked out what I want in the Harvey Nics' sale.'

'I'll get you one in every colour,' he said.

She was touched that he remembered something she had once said about liking a garment so much, she wished she had bought one in every colour. Stephen's precise memory for detail was one of his special charms.

'I love you,' she said, suddenly really missing him.

'I love you too,' he told her. 'Happy New Year!'

She put the receiver back on its rest and looked at it for a long time, thinking of him sitting on the bed in his hotel room on the other side of the world doing the same thing, with the faint noise of traffic on Park Avenue rumbling fifteen floors below.

Then she stood up and walked back into the nursery, shifting Ben gingerly from her shoulder to the cradle of her arms and lowering him almost imperceptibly slowly into his cot. The moment his face touched the cold sheet, he woke again.

'Go to sleep, my darling,' she whispered, stroking his head.

His roars sliced through the cocoon of calm the conversation with Stephen had spun around her.

'Go to sleep, please,' her voice became pleading, then, 'Oh SHUT UP!' she screamed, as loudly as the baby, and was instantly filled with shame as she heard herself.

It was no good. She walked out of the nursery, trying to collect herself. Maybe Stephen's idea about the car wasn't so stupid. The only reason against going to Lia's, she reasoned with herself, was the sense of panic she experienced whenever she saw Neil, but that was ridiculous. They were both adults with jobs and responsibilities, both in happy relationships with partners who suited them. The only things they had in common were children of the same age, and a juvenile love affair that had finished twenty years before. It had been a mistake not to announce that fact the first time they met, but it was idiotic to let one mistake become an uncontrollable spiral of fear. The way to stop being afraid was to confront it. It was New Year, and her resolution would be not to spend another second wallowing in the past, she told herself strictly. Then without further ado, she picked up the telephone and dialled Lia's number.

'Hello?' Neil answered the phone.

'Oh hi! It's Alison, umm . . .'

'I'll get Lia.'

'No, wait,' she said, determined to give him the chance to put her off if he wanted to. 'Look, I've got a baby that won't sleep here and I'm going mad. I know it's late, but Lia said—'

'Yeah, come round. She'll be glad of the company. I'm off up to the cricket club for a drink. We tossed for who went out,' he said, sounding unusually cheerful,

'I lost the first time, but we decided best of three was fairer!'

She laughed. 'OK then,' she said, putting down the phone.

Confront it, she said to herself, looking into the dressing-table mirror and smiling. There you see, that was easy enough.

'It is cold out there, it took me ages to get the car started,' she said, stepping over the threshold, half an hour later. She glanced over Lia's shoulder to see whether Neil had departed. The room was empty. In the far corner, silver decorations on the Christmas tree sparkled in the light of the fire. 'What a lovely tree!' she added, putting down the car seat, in which Ben was sleeping soundly.

'Do you want to put him down on our bed?' Lia asked, 'that's what I did when Guy was here.'

'Oh, I daren't move him now,' Alison said.

'But he's all scrunched up in there. Here,' Lia said kindly, 'let me see if he'll go down.' She took the car seat upstairs and was down again within minutes.

'Is he OK?' Alison asked, feeling grateful, but slightly irked at the competent way Lia had taken over.

'He's fine. I need the practice,' Lia said, as if sensing Alison's irritation, 'I'm going to be looking after Guy when Ginger goes back to work. She asked me at Christmas.'

'Is that legal?' Alison asked. 'I thought that child-minders weren't allowed to look after more than one child under one year old.'

'Well, I'm not really a childminder, am I?' Lia faltered.

'But what are you going to do if there's an emergency?' Alison wanted to know.

'Call an ambulance, I suppose . . . or drive to the doctor's. We've got a car now,' she announced proudly.

'That's fantastic,' Alison said, suddenly realizing that her reaction to the news had been less than generous. 'I bet Ginger's delighted.'

She saw Lia's taut and anxious expression melt with relief.

'I've got the video of *When Harry Met Sally*,' Lia suggested.

'Brilliant!' Alison enthused, making herself comfortable on the sofa, 'I loved that film.'

'It's set on New Year's Eve, well, the last bit,' Lia added.

'I don't remember much about it,' Alison said, taking the can of Diet Coke that Lia was offering her. 'All we need now is popcorn . . .'

Neil nursed his pint of beer. On the way over to the club he had weighed up the advantages of having two pints of shandy as opposed to one pint of bitter, but decided on the latter. You couldn't go out on New Year's Eve and not have a proper drink.

'Where's Lia tonight?' the captain of his team asked him. He was also on his own.

'At home with the baby.'

'Yeah, it's impossible to get a baby-sitter at New Year, isn't it?'

'Yeah,' Neil agreed, knowing that even if they could have found one, Lia would not have wanted to leave Anouska.

He was pleased that in the end Alison had rung. Now he could relax and not feel so bad about leaving Lia on her own. It wasn't an ideal way of doing things, but it was better, he reasoned, than both of them staying in with only the baby-listener for entertainment.

He would be glad to see the back of this year. Towards the end, as the days grew shorter and shorter, it had begun to feel as if the world were closing in around him. He had looked at Lia and not recognized her. When he met her, she had been something natural, ethereal, like the wind or the sea, more sprite than human being; but now, as he watched her endlessly shopping for Christmas, and cooking, and preparing the house, she seemed solid and materialistic, like a housewife. When he met her she wore bikinis or floaty dresses and now she always seemed to slop around in leggings and his sweaters that were miles too large for her. And she was always crying. The first time he had seen her crying he had not been able to bear it, but it seemed to happen so often these days, he was becoming immune to it. Neither of them had referred to the conversation they had had on Christmas night, but it was there, unspoken in the air. He had been relieved to escape from the room that seemed to stifle him with the heat of the open fire and the constant wink of tinsel.

He finished his pint, savouring the taste of hops and malt, feeling the scrape of bitterness in his throat. It made him want to smoke. He tried to cadge a cigarette from the wicket keeper in the second team.

'I would, mate, but I've only got two left and I'm giving up at midnight,' he was told, so he swapped a note for pound coins at the bar, and went to the machine, looking at his watch. He was going to give up at midnight too, but there was probably time for two or three before that.

His friends were swapping resolutions. Drink less, no spirits, jog, use that exercise bike from two Christmasses before.

'Give up smoking,' Neil said, offering round the full packet of Marlboro.

They laughed.

'How many New Years have you had that one?'

'Oh, about twenty-five.' He had started buying cigarettes at fifteen he realized, shocked at the calculation that he had spent more years of his life smoking than not.

He realized too that he had spent nearly all the New Years in the last twenty-five years in sports clubs rather like this one, drinking and smoking, making the same resolutions and having the same conversations. The names of the cricketers and footballers they talked about changed, but nothing much else. And this year he would be forty. It was a pretty depressing thought.

Tomorrow it will be different, he promised himself as he drove through the deserted streets. A New Year and a new life. Maybe he and Lia had made a mistake having a child so soon. Maybe they should have got to know each other better first. But it had happened. It had seemed right at the time, and now they were stuck with it. They couldn't go back to how it was before so they might as well make the best of after.

It was a film about two people who meet when they are very young and meet again years later and fall in love. No, it wasn't really, Alison thought, taking a paper handkerchief from the box that Lia offered her, it was really a film about being with the right person and refusing to believe it. Frank Sinatra was singing 'It Had to be You', and she wished she was in New York right now, and could run downtown, just as Billy Crystal was running uptown, to the restaurant where Stephen was eating, and burst in and sweep him off his feet.

'That was great,' she said, smiling through her tears.

She glanced sideways at Lia's face and wondered why she was crying too. Perhaps everyone read their own meaning into it, or perhaps it just made everyone cry, just like the fake orgasm scene made everyone laugh, and that's why it was such a good film.

Lia flicked to BBC 1 just in time for the last three chimes of Big Ben. A cheer went up in the studio and the presenter started singing 'Auld Lang Syne', just as they had done in the film. Lia and Alison exchanged slightly embarrassed glances, then got up from the sofa, held hands and joined in. By the end of the song, they were both laughing.

'Happy New Year!' They kissed each other on the cheek.

Then Lia went up to check on the babies.

Alison settled back down into the sofa half watching the Scottish dancing on television, and was startled by the sound of Neil's key in the lock.

'You just missed the chimes,' Alison informed him as he came into the room. 'Happy New Year!'

'Yeah. Happy New Year!'

Clearly he hadn't expected her still to be there.

He bent forward hesitantly, and they both turned their faces at the same moment, making the kiss intended for her cheek land awkwardly against the side of her mouth. He jumped back and her lip felt as if it had been stung by a bee.

'Lia's upstairs,' she told him, determinedly staring at the television.

He took the stairs two by two, and she sat glued to the sofa, feeling utterly helpless as she tried not to hear them embrace above her head. She decided the best thing to do would be to get the car warmed up and take Ben home as soon as they came downstairs again. She went outside, let herself into her car and put the key in the ignition. The battery warning light lit up red indicating that it was completely flat. She hit the steering wheel hard with the palms of her hands and turned the ignition again. Nothing. Now she was stuck. It was impossible to get a minicab in the early hours of New Year's Day.

They were both downstairs again when she went back in, and Neil was about to open the bottle of champagne she had brought to their Christmas get-together.

'My battery's flat,' she announced.

'I'll give you a lift,' he offered immediately, putting down the bottle, clearly as anxious as she was for her to go.

She hadn't registered when Lia told her that they now had a car.

'Oh, right, well, if you're sure . . .' she agreed hastily, 'I'll just get Ben.'

Neil drove fast, as she had known he would.

She remembered the day he passed his test. He had beeped the horn of his dad's Hillman Imp and she had run out of the house to congratulate him. They had driven to a pub miles away with the windows down and Capital, which they could only just pick up, crackling on the radio. They sat outside at the table nearest the car park, drinking Britvic Orange with lemonade from pint glasses, and his eyes kept wandering to the car, as if unable to believe he had charge of it. She had presented him with a key-ring with a miniature Ferrari marque attached to an oval of black leather, and 'One day!' stamped in gold letters on the back. He had turned it over and over in his palm, smiling and proud.

'Made any resolutions?' he now asked politely, as they turned into her road, breaking the silence that hung between them.

'Yes,' she replied, looking sideways at him, 'to stop thinking about you, and what might have been.' She tried to make it sound as if she were joking.

His face betrayed nothing. She wasn't even sure that he had heard what she said.

Calmly, he pulled the car into her drive, and switched off the engine.

'Ally, don't . . .' he said, staring straight ahead at the wall of her house, and sighing.

In the darkness below the dashboard, she sensed his hand searching for hers, and when their fingers touched, it was as if all the pain and joy she had ever felt gathered into one great wave that broke over her body, drenching her with emotion.

He shifted, just an infinitesimally slight movement towards her, and she fell against his chest, shaking. She could smell beer and smoke and the tang of some aftershave she did not know in the soft prickliness of his Shetland jumper. His fingers very tentatively

251

smoothed her hair away from her wet face, as if she were a crying child.

'I'm sorry,' she said.

He said nothing.

She did not know how long she wept.

Eventually, as her breathing began to quieten, she allowed herself one, two, three inhalations of his jumper, trying to imprint the smell of it in her memory. Then she drew away. But as she lifted her head to smile, and say goodbye, his grasp on her shoulders became firmer.

He dipped his head and his lips found hers as easily and naturally as they had ever done. Her head dropped back against the seat like a rag doll, as his mouth pushed against hers, his tongue coaxing, finding the softest tender place just inside her lips, pausing there, tasting, sighing, pressing harder, more urgently.

She opened her eyes and saw that his were closed, concentrating, as if he were searching for memories inside her. Her body turned to liquid. Then he pulled his head back and looked at her.

'Come in,' she whispered, trying to melt every inch of her body against his.

'No,' he said, sitting up automatically, and starting the engine, as if her words had woken him up from a dream.

His eyes were pleading with her to be strong. To go. Now.

She released her door, got out, wrenching her spine in her haste to get Ben in his seat out of the back.

Then he reversed out onto the road in a cloud of exhaust and roared away.

Chapter 7

JANUARY

The call, when it came, was as brief as she had expected, although she had not expected him to find out her work number and ring her there.

'We have to talk.'

'Can you meet me tomorrow?'

'Where?'

She told him.

He was sitting on the steps up to the main part of the house, his back against the railing, reading the *Evening Standard*. She was late, but he did not look up as she turned the corner into the street. He was confident she would arrive, she thought, wondering how long he would have waited for her if she had changed her mind. She could still duck out, she realized, but each footstep towards him made the risk of getting away unseen far greater. Eventually, he sensed her presence, and stood up.

'It's the basement,' she said, taking out a set of keys and pointing. He followed her silently down the narrow wrought-iron steps.

'What is this?' he asked, looking around the room as she switched the light on and turned up the thermostat on the central heating.

'It's my flat,' she said, 'I used to live here, but

it's been rented since . . . and my tenant left early.'

'Nice,' he said, taking in the bright pine furniture and Impressionist posters she had once loved that now embarrassed her.

'Shall I take your coat?' She sounded like her mother hosting afternoon tea.

'Not yet,' he said, clasping the open edges of his leather jacket together, 'I think it's colder in here than out.'

'I'll make some coffee,' she said, needing to do something with her hands.

She opened up her bag and took out a small jar of Nescafé and a tin of dried milk she had bought at lunch-time. She filled the electric kettle, wondering why she had not bought fresh milk. It seemed such a strange thing to do. She had not drunk coffee made with Marvel since her days as a student. She found mugs in the cupboard over the sink and clattered two teaspoons into them.

'Don't!' He was suddenly behind her, so close that she could feel his breathing, even though he was not touching her.

She turned around, and they stared at each other, then suddenly, they were on the floor wrestling for access to each other's skin, through the layers of winter clothing, on the freezing cold tiles. He was all zips, she laces. He gave up trying to remove her boots, throwing her backwards, her skull cracking hard against the floor, and knelt above her. She closed her eyes, her head swimming with pain and lust, her limbs flopping in submission to him. She heard his intake of breath as he found stocking tops and suspenders and fragile silk underwear that tore with a rasp as he tugged it to one side and plunged himself into her. He felt huge inside her, the top of his penis banging mercilessly against the neck of her womb. She imagined her insides, raw and red, as if every nerve in her body led there, carrying all the pain and pleasure to a single point, as if a stiletto knife dipped in cocaine were stabbing at her core. Then, the hot, soothing wash of his sperm pouring into her and his body sagging onto her, as if he had been gunned down. Her senses returned slowly, she became gradually aware of the engine smell of his leather jacket, the bite of the heavy-duty zip against her chest, the tiny high whistle his lungs made close to her ear. When he lifted his head, she saw the pale blue irises, that looked as if they had been outlined with smudgy brown pencil, and she felt the drip of his tears on her cheek.

'We have to talk,' he said, helplessly.

She put an index finger against his lips.

They stared at each other a few more seconds, then he pushed himself up to kneeling, and she wriggled out from under him, stood up and held out her hand. She led him to the bedroom, relieved to see pillows and a duvet on the bed, snow-white without covers.

'Shouldn't we . . . ?' He pulled a three-pack of Durex from his inside pocket, and reading the look of alarm on her face, admitted, ashamed, 'I bought them today. I don't make a habit of this – and I've had a test before . . .'

'Did you?' she asked. 'So did we. I thought it was only because—' she couldn't say her husband's name, 'because he's a doctor . . .'

'Every concerned would-be parent does it now,' he said, drily, 'it's part of the courtship ritual, a bit like buying an engagement ring.' His eyes travelled to her left hand and the diamond there. She hid it quickly behind her.

'I can't get pregnant,' she told him, 'not by natural means, anyway, so you don't have to worry.' She enunciated the difficult words staccato, not looking at him as she began to take off her clothes.

'So how did you . . . ?' He pointed at her tummy, the faint white line of the Caesarian scar, cutting through the goosebumps.

'I'll tell you later,' she said, jumping under the duvet, half embarrassed to let him see her body, half eager to be warm.

She watched his methodical, male way of undressing, the way he folded his trousers over the back of a chair, rolled his socks together, hung his shirt on a hanger. She could almost hear his mother telling him before he left home that clothes don't pick themselves up off the floor and iron themselves, you know. It was advice he had taken very seriously.

His body was a sportsman's body, firm, with no excess fat, and strong long muscles in his back and legs. It was somehow bigger than she remembered. Not a boy's body any more. Sometime in the intervening years his physique had thickened a little and he had become a man, even though his chest was still almost hairless. The way he stood at the foot of the bed, with no clothes on, was endearingly awkward. He had never been aware of his beauty.

She pulled back the duvet, like a bird offering shelter under her wing. He climbed in beside her. They lay on their backs, looking at the white wood-chip paper on the ceiling, the Japanese paper lampshade, the fine gauze of a spider's web that quivered in the slight draught from the window behind them.

'What did you think when you first saw me?' Alison asked, eventually.

'That you'd cut your hair, and you were thin.'

'But I was eight months' pregnant!' she exclaimed.

'Yeah, but you looked like a thin person who was pregnant . . .'

'So, I used to be fat?' she protested.

'No . . . you just weren't what I'd call really thin.'

He had never been able to turn a compliment, she remembered fondly. It used almost to be a joke between them. After a few months' going out with him, she had given up asking how she looked when the gamut of replies ran from 'OK' to 'Nice' with only 'All right' in between.

'What did you think, then?' he asked her.

'I thought: of all the ante-natal classes, in all the middle-class suburbs, in all the world, he had to walk into mine . . .'

He laughed. 'Yeah, that's about it,' he said, then turned his face to look at hers, and kissed her slowly, his eyes closed, his hands coming up to touch each of her features, like a blind man reading a long-forgotten text in braille.

She climbed onto him and lay still for a moment, sandwiched between the soft warmth of the duvet and the hardness of his body, feeling as if she would melt over him in the heat. Then she sat up, straddling his thighs and bent her head to lick the round helmet of his penis. He writhed under her, almost unable to bear the pleasure until the moment she knelt up hovering over him and he grabbed her bottom and pulled her down onto him, arching his back, thrusting into her as if to break her in half. She screamed. He stopped, alarmed.

'No, it's all right,' she said, 'please, please go on.'

He smiled, wickedly, taking control, rolling her onto her back again gently, and looking at her, his large hands tracing soft circles on the inner part of her thighs. She squirmed with gloriously sensual pleasure.

'Please . . .' she said, staring back at him with wide-open, sex-drugged eyes, but he would not be hurried.

His fingers flicked over her clitoris, almost accidentally, and continued their slow caress, then flicked again and again, then settled there and began to rub very, very slowly.

'Oh please . . .' she moaned.

'I'm controlling you,' he whispered, 'you're not sure whether you like that, are you?'

'Yes . . . I do . . . please . . .' She tried to sit up, each time he touched her there, she jumped as if touched by a current. He pushed her down again.

'When I say so. You're hard. Your clitoris is really hard. You really want to come, don't you?'

'Yes,' she whimpered, feeling the flood of juices in her vagina as he spoke to her.

He put his finger there, in the wetness, then went back to her clitoris.

'Oh God!' she said, feeling the rise of orgasm, 'please!'

'When I say so.' He slipped another finger inside her, she felt her muscles contract around it. 'You really like it, don't you?' he hissed into her ear.

She closed her eyes and began to fantasize. She was lying on the scrubby grass banks of the Blue Lagoon, that hot, dry summer of 1976, and Neil was on top of her thrusting in and out. She could see his face, the pink determination to come, and suddenly she was coming too, fantasy blending with reality, a perfect sexual alchemy, that left her reeling and shaking with shock.

Afterwards, she could not stop kissing him, wanting to taste each inch of his body, to touch every pore and make it hers again, then, suddenly exhausted, she fell back into the pillows, and listened, when her breathing had slowed, to the distant sounds of the city and muffled notes from the piano in the sound-proofed room above their heads.

A tinkling piano in the next apartment . . .

'I must go,' he said, eventually.

'Have a coffee first.'

She got up, pulled on her cashmere coat like a dressing-gown and went to the kitchen, leaving him to dress alone.

She felt his kiss on the back of her neck as she poured boiling water into one of the mugs and spun round, but he was almost at the door.

'We didn't talk,' she said.

'No,' he said, simply, leaving her there holding the steaming mug helplessly in her hand.

* * *

As she locked up the flat, Friedrich, the ancient pianist who lived in the house above, was tottering at the top of the steps on his way out, his Scottie dog yelping at him to hurry.

'My dear! How lovely!' His old, papery face lit up as he recognized her.

They had been neighbours for eight years before she married Stephen. Sometimes, in the days when Friedrich was still touring with his trio, she had taken care of Mendelssohn, which was a ridiculously long name, she had always thought, for such a small and silly dog.

She smiled at him, then leapt up the steps, two by two, and kissed him on both cheeks.

'Everything is all right?' he asked, frowning suddenly, 'you're not moving back, I hope . . . At least, I would love . . . but . . .'

'Everything's fine! And thank you so much for the gift you sent!'

A miniature xylophone had arrived in a brown paper parcel tied with hairy string shortly after Ben was born.

'He likes it?' Friedrich asked, delighted.

'Well, he's a bit too small right now, but he loves it when Stephen plays him a tune!'

'And Stephen?'

'He's very well, thank you.'

'Good!' Friedrich had been overjoyed when she had told him that the man she was to marry played the piano.

Suddenly she realized the reason for the inquisitive frown that kept playing over his wizened old features. Friedrich was the area's own Neighbourhood Watch scheme. A stranger sitting on his stoop would not have gone unobserved.

'Sarah-Jane has moved out,' Alison improvized, 'and I'm going to have a bit of work done.'

'So, you had a man to give you — how do you say it?' he searched for the word.

'An estimate,' Alison filled in for him.

'Yes, an estimate,' he agreed.

Was his English really still so bad, after living here for fifty years, she wondered, or was it his way of trying to tell her that sound travelled both ways? Was she glowing with such radiance that anyone who saw her would know what she had been doing? Normally, such thoughts would have preoccupied her, but she was feeling so happy, surreally happy, she felt she could deal with anything.

'Yes,' she said blithely, daring herself to add, 'he may be around quite a lot. It was lovely to see you again,' she added as they parted, and she walked off with a spring in her step, feeling as if she were playing a part in a film. The script was written: she had not read it, but she seemed to know the lines; the cameras were rolling, and she did not know when the director would shout, 'Cut.'

'That was delicious,' Neil said, eating the last of the lasagne straight from the Pyrex dish and scraping at the crusty, burnt bits on the sides. 'Here, I'll do that,' he added, seeing that Lia was starting the washing-up. 'Really, you sit down, you must be tired.'

She was too exhausted to protest.

'It was a long day,' she admitted, pouring out a cup of tea and sitting down with it at the kitchen table.

The tomato sauce turned to acid in his stomach, sending the taste of old garlic back to his mouth. Was this the prelude to her asking why he had been late home? Did she know? He felt guilt exuding from every pore in a cold, sticky sweat. He plunged both hands into the hot washing-up water, scalding himself, trying to wash away the stain of sin.

'But then it was a long day for Ginger too . . .' she went on, 'you know how it is, your first day back? She thinks she will usually be able to be back here by five-thirty, six at the latest. She's going to ask whether she could start earlier and finish earlier, which would mean she had more time with Guy in the evening . . . and it would be better for me too, because I'm always up so early . . .' Lia chattered on, clearly unaware of his anguish.

'Really?' he tried to encourage her to talk, not trusting himself to.

'Poor Ginger, her boss sounds so horrible, although apparently she was a bit nicer to her because she had heard how good she was on telly, and apparently there's a possibility that Ginger could get a better job, but it involved meeting the man, you know . . .'

'Who?' he asked, distractedly, not really listening, but sensing a pause.

'The man she had the affair with,' Lia said.

Again, he began to tremble inside. 'What do you think of her doing that?' he asked abruptly.

'I think it would be a good idea to see him again, get it sorted out once and for all,' she said.

'No, I meant, what did you think of her screwing someone who was married?'

'Oh, he's not married.'

Was she being deliberately evasive, attempting to catch him out?

'Well, attached, then?' he said, bracing himself for a sudden explosion of anger.

'What do you mean, do I think it was right?' she asked, pleasantly surprised at his sudden interest, adding, after some thought, 'I don't really think it's her problem, morally, after all, he's the one with the girlfriend.'

Had he really hoped that she was going to give him a kind of indirect absolution, he wondered, trying to get a grip on himself, scouring the Pyrex dish vigorously with wire wool.

'It's OK,' Lia said, unable to bear the grating sound of metal on glass, 'leave it to soak. I'll do it later.'

'No, you relax. Turn on some music or something, I'll be with you in a minute.'

She began to protest, then stopped herself. It was no

261

good complaining that he didn't help enough if she wouldn't let him. Anyway, they were both working now, she reminded herself, and, boy, could she tell. Her whole body felt tired, worn down by the responsibility of two small lives. She slumped into the sofa and was asleep by the time he joined her there.

Later, as he lay in the bath, his feet stretched out beside the taps, his whole body submerged, the water like a warm blanket drawn right up to the lobes of his ears, he could hear Lia singing to Anouska as she fed her before putting her down for the night. He had not been able to look at them tonight. He could not face that picture of sweetness, mother and child together communing with an intensity that made it seem as if they were surrounded by a magnetic field – soft, golden and impenetrable. He thought he knew now why artists had drawn haloes round the figures of the nativity. He found he could no longer envisage Lia's breasts without a tiny mouth puckered around them, Anouska only releasing her suck to look up at her mother occasionally and smile.

Alison's breasts were small and firm, the skin white and smooth as marble, the nipples dark pink. They tasted of perfume, and the bedding smelt unused, just slightly damp and dusty, with no sickly, pervasive taint of human milk that smelt of overripe melons and Dairylea cheese.

He closed his eyes and remembered her face lit by joy, her conker-coloured hair swinging, the proud way she walked. She looked so strong and determined, and yet underneath she was as soft as clay. It was a devastatingly attractive combination. He wondered if others saw the vulnerability beneath the hostile expression she had when she was frightened, the arrogant toss of her head when she was nervous. Did anyone else dare to ruffle her sleek hair, and smudge her thick red lipstick all over her face? Suddenly he was wrenched by jealousy for every man who had ever touched her, and he opened his eyes to see his erection standing out of the water, like a lighthouse.

Alison was lying in the conservatory listening to her LP of *Hotel California* knowing that any minute the euphoria must come to an end and the guilt take hold. She tried to think of Lia. She was a lovely person, and a friend, and she could not do this to her. But she was not able to associate Lia with anything that had happened. It felt as if she had reclaimed something that was hers, something that had nothing to do with anyone else.

The sound of Stephen's key in the lock made her jump up and switch off the turntable. By the time he had hung up his coat she was filling a kettle at the sink.

'You look well,' Stephen said as she turned to greet him.

'Do I?' she frowned.

'Positively glowing,' he said, 'you look as if you've been for a long country walk in the cold! Making some tea?'

She looked at the kettle in her hand, as if surprised by its presence. She had grabbed the nearest thing as a prop, something to hold onto so that he wouldn't see how her hands were shaking.

'Would you like some?' she asked.

'I think I'd prefer a gin and tonic,' he said, wandering through into the sitting area to the cupboard where they kept bottles of spirits.

'I'll make you one. You sit down. Bad day?' She busied herself slicing a lemon, grabbing a handful of ice from the dispenser in the fridge, clinking it into long straight glasses.

'The usual,' he said.

It was as much as she ever heard about his day to day work. In the beginning, she had hated the simplicity of his response, taking it almost as an insult to her intelligence, but she had come to realize that he needed his own mechanisms to get over the stress of his job, and talking only made it worse for him.

She sat down opposite him and, looking into her glass as if she could see many fascinating things there, said breezily, 'I decided to go to the flat. I'll think I'll have some work done on it.'

'Right . . .' He paused, then added, encouragingly, 'Good!'

She smiled at him.

'We could always move back into London, you know,' he said, seeing how her excursion had invigorated her.

He had seen that she had never been entirely happy since their move to Kew, but had not understood it as a problem of geography before. Maybe it would be better for them to be nearer to old friends. In his mind, he began to calculate how much money they would need to buy an equivalent house in Islington, or somewhere slightly cheaper, like Kentish Town. If Alison were to sell her flat, there would be plenty of money.

'After all the work I've done to get this house in order?' The sharpness of her tone sliced into his thoughts.

'Well, only if you wanted to . . .' he said.

'I don't think so. Not now,' she said, returning to the examination of her drink.

'I've been wondering,' he went on, 'how you would feel about a much bigger move, actually.'

She looked up, startled. He somehow knew that it was not the right time to discuss it, but now he had started, he went on, 'In New York the other day, I was offered a visiting chair, with a view to tenure, I think.'

'When was this?' she asked, playing for time, barely able to contain her surprise at his news.

'I think it was on New Year's Day, actually,' he said, absent-mindedly.

264

'So you've let a week go by without bothering to tell me?' Alison fired back at him.

'We haven't really seen much of each other . . .' he offered in explanation.

'And whose fault is that?'

'I know, I know. I am sorry. Look, we'll discuss it another time.'

'I'm not a computer, you know, you can't just diarize me so that I pop up in a couple of weeks when it may or may not be convenient for you to have a conversation,' she said angrily.

'OK, OK.' He was furious with himself for handling things so badly. He had not understood the extent of the resentment that had been building up inside her, festering like an abscess, ready to discharge its poison when touched.

It had been an indulgence to go to the seminar, he realized, and he should not have succumbed to it. She had needed his support and he had let her down by overloading her, just when she had begun to cope so well with everything. Now, his suggestion that they move back into town, which had been offered with her interests at heart, appeared like a palliative designed to soften her up for the free-ranging discussion he had wanted to have about his career, her career, America, the future. Inwardly, he kicked himself for his insensitivity.

'Are you hungry?' she asked him sullenly.

'No, I ate late,' he said.

'Well, I've got some things to do,' she said, getting up and leaving the room, despising herself for her tantrum with Stephen, unable to comprehend the easy way she had manipulated the argument in order to make him the guilty party. Already a traitor, now doubly treacherous. It was the kind of cowardly performance she abhorred in men who had affairs.

Later, she lay in bed, her back to Stephen, pretending to sleep. A dry whiff of irritation still hung in the room. Her body was so tense, she felt it would snap if he touched her, but he seemed to know that, and didn't. She closed her eyes, trying to wipe out the memory, the memory she had suppressed for twenty years.

'We're going to move,' her mother had told her, the morning after she had returned from the clinic, handing her a cup of tea and sitting down on her bed, as she did when she wanted a confidential chat. 'Daddy wants to retire early and we've bought a house near Littlehampton.'

'When?' Alison had asked, feeling as if all her blood had drained away.

'As soon as possible,' her mother replied, staring out of the window.

'But . . .'

'You'll be away at college during the term, after all, and it will be nice for you to have holidays by the sea.'

'I don't want to,' Alison had said, like a spoilt ten-year-old.

'Yes, but it's not really up to you, is it?' There was a threatening edge to her mother's voice.

'No, I suppose not,' she admitted, defeated. Her mother always got her own way. There didn't seem to be any point in protesting any more.

She knew why they were leaving; her mother knew why. She wondered if her father knew too. It didn't seem very important any more whether he did or not. It would only mean that her mother had told him, and she hated her mother so vehemently that even if she had betrayed their secret, it couldn't make things much worse now.

Ever since she had started going out with Neil, her mother had made her disapproval transparently clear. As she had witnessed her daughter falling in love, she had wheedled, manipulated and undermined for two years, and in the end she finally had the reason to insist that she no longer see him. Margaret was so determined to make their separation stick, she was

266

even prepared to move far away, and Alison was so weakened by the sustained onslaught, she could no longer find the strength to resist. She turned over in bed, towards the wall, and stared at the flowery lemon wallpaper, until she heard her mother leave the room. Then tears began to fall, making the pillow hot and wet beneath her cheek.

Now, she stared through the gap in the curtains to a cold, starry sky. She would not let anyone take Neil away from her. Not now that she had found him again.

Through the plate-glass window, Charlie Prince watched his lunch-date arrive.

'It's lovely to see you,' he said, kissing the air near each cheek, and showing her where to check in her luminous yellow jacket.

The girl on the desk held the coat a long way from her slim, black-clad body, as if it were contaminated, and handed Ginger a ticket.

'Did you cycle here?' Charlie asked unnecessarily, as Ginger also handed her back bike wheel over the counter.

'Yeah, sorry about that, but I've had two nicked before, and it's really not difficult to take it off – as I worked out when I realized the bloke who stole my last one can't have taken more than five minutes.'

'Right,' Charlie said uncertainly, adding, to return to territory he was more used to discussing, 'Have you been here before?'

'No,' she said, grabbing a handful of the very tasteful black-and-white promotional postcards from the reception desk. He watched, amazed, as she stuffed them into her black shiny rucksack.

'So why did you want to come here?' he asked lightly.

'I've read about it. It's had good write-ups, and I fancied the idea of eating my lunch in a bank, although it doesn't look much like one now, does it?'

Ginger's eyes wandered to the spiky modern chand-elier that covered the huge expanse of ceiling.

Everyone was opening restaurants in premises formerly used for completely disparate purposes. Buildings that had once been courts, warehouses, factories, even the casualty ward of a hospital, were now the foodie palaces. After the long, hungry gloom of the early nineties, people in London were eating again. Ginger had been expecting more of a themed décor, with old-fashioned wooden panelling, tellers to place your order with, and a dining room at the back in the manager's office, but the light interior of this restaurant no longer bore any resemblance to a bank. It was modish and fun, and it was the most expensive place that had sprung to mind when Charlie had surprised her by calling on her first day back in the office.

They sat down and listened patiently as the wait-ress told them about the specials.

'I never remember a word they've said after, although I do try really hard to concentrate, and I usually nod and smile and say that it all sounds delicious,' Ginger admitted, picking up the menu as soon as the woman had gone.

She had it in mind to choose the most expensive dish, whatever that was, reasoning – unfairly, she knew – that she was saving Charlie hundreds of pounds each month by not giving his name to the Child Support Agency.

She was finding it very difficult to look at his face; because there were so many similarities with Guy's, she kept having to stop herself reaching forward to plant a kiss on his cheek. Anyway, she thought, he had invited her, so he could bloody well make the small talk.

'So how's the Beeb?' he said eventually, after giving the waitress their order.

'OK,' she said, non-committally, 'I've only been back a week.'

She had promised herself she would not talk about work, or Guy, but now she wondered how on earth she was going to get through the next hour, because there was absolutely nothing else in her life, she realized, apart from the very occasional visit from a friend. She had not been to the theatre, a film, or even hired a video, for months. She had not had the energy or concentration to read a book, a magazine or a newspaper, except to consult the TV listings, and often, when she turned on the television after bathing and putting Guy to bed, she fell fast asleep on the sofa, waking up to see minor politicians chewing the fat, uncertain whether she had seen the news or dreamt it. Her idea of a rewarding weekend had become one where she managed to do all the washing and get it dry by Sunday night. She liked her new life, but, God, was it boring for anyone else to hear about. She belatedly realized why it was that the only real friends she saw these days were Alison and Lia who were in much the same position.

She looked up from under her brows and saw Charlie expectantly waiting for her to continue. She shrugged her shoulders.

'That good, eh?' he said.

'Well, it pays the bills,' Ginger replied.

'Why won't you come and work for me?' Charlie asked, almost plaintively, as if it was something they had been talking about for ages.

'Well, you haven't asked,' Ginger replied cautiously, sensing a trick somewhere.

'I'm sure I have,' he said breezily, spearing a circle of shiny, claret-coloured bresaola on his fork, 'I've certainly wanted to, but I have had the strangest sense that you've been avoiding me.'

'Really?'

She wished she had not ordered oysters. It was going to be impossible to maintain some level of dignity and eat them at the same time. She squeezed the half-lemon over them carefully, playing for time.

A sharp squirt of stray juice hit the corner of her eye. She wiped the involuntary tear away with the heavy cotton napkin, trying to remember whether she was wearing mascara.

'Can I try one?' Charlie asked, as if sensing her distress. His hand hovered over the half-dozen rocky shells.

'Go ahead,' she said, taking one after him, and tipping it down her throat at the same time as he did.

It was a sweet gesture he had made, almost like holding her hand to negotiate a tricky step. She smiled gratefully, feeling a little confidence return.

'Why would you want me to work for you, anyway?' she asked, trying to pick up the conversation. 'In what capacity?'

Another oyster went down successfully.

It was odd, she thought, how polysyllabic words could often sound inadvertently sexual.

'In what *capacity*?' Charlie repeated, clearly hearing the same potential for innuendo as she had.

'Isn't it funny how long words embarrass the English?' Ginger said, elaborating on her thought. 'In a sitcom, you've got a woman applying for a job, the male boss says, "Let me take down your *credentials*," and there's a laugh . . . why is that?'

'Perhaps we're all frightened of using language wrongly. It becomes a kind of taboo, and somehow sex creeps in.'

'Hmm,' Ginger said, suddenly not wanting to pursue the subject further, 'anyway, to put it another way – what have I got that you want? God, that sounds even worse!'

'Listen, Ginger,' Charlie said, his face suddenly serious, 'this really isn't an elaborate kind of pick-up. We had sex once. I enjoyed myself. I hope you did, too' – he left no time for her even to nod – 'but I'm not interested in your body, I'm interested in what's in your head. You have great ideas, and anyone who can stand up to a professional Tory bitch like you did on television should not be stuck in a rut at White City—'

'Oh well, that was just because I'm a loud-mouth,' Ginger interrupted, trying to get some space to understand everything he was saying, but it was rather like the waitress and the day's specials: they sounded great, but then you immediately forgot every dish. And, she couldn't stop herself thinking, what's wrong with my body, anyway?

'No, you really have a gift for simple, commercial ideas,' Charlie went on, 'a kind of common touch, if you like, that is very rare. I remember you telling me about a game show you had come up with, and I thought then, no, it'll never work, but we've worked it up, developed it, you know, and we've just had the OK for a pilot. That's a real talent you have, and I wanted to thank you.'

'My idea?' Ginger said, putting down her last oyster, fearing she would choke on it.

'Yeah, that food-quiz game-show thing, *One Man's Meat*, I think was your name for it. We've gone for *If You Can't Stand the Heat*, which sounds hipper, less carnivorous, but the idea was all yours and the broadcasters love it. You can't go wrong with a spin on cookery these days. It's our bread and butter—' he said, smiling at his pun.

'Hang on – you've used my idea, and you've got a pilot?' Ginger interrupted.

'Yup!' he looked triumphant.

'And what do I get out of it?'

'Well, no copyright on ideas, darling, but I'd love to pay you to come up with more.'

'You really are an arrogant shit, you know,' Ginger told him.

'Fish and chips,' said the waitress, lowering a large white plate, 'and the lobster. Is there anything else you need?'

'I beg your pardon?' Charlie said.

'Is there anything else you need?' she repeated.

271

'No, not you, we're fine.' He dismissed the waitress.

'You're an arrogant shit,' Ginger repeated. 'Did you really think that I would be so flattered by your stealing my ideas that I would come and work for you? I'm sorry, but I've made that mistake before, and I'm possibly not quite as naïve and stupid as I look . . . and,' she said, standing up and throwing her napkin down on the table, 'you can stuff your lobster.'

She turned and walked towards the door. The passageway past the open kitchen seemed endlessly long and, half-way down it, she began to feel as if she was walking in slow-motion, like a dream where your legs let you down. Finally, she reached the check-in desk and retrieved her jacket and bike wheel with as much insouciance as she could muster, and turned, with relief, to the revolving door, but somehow, at the last hurdle, she was defeated. The bloody door was stuck. As she swung her hand back to hit it in frustration, she felt him catch her arm.

'I'm prepared to pay for an uneaten lobster,' he said, 'but not for a glass door smashed by a bike wheel. You're pushing the wrong bit,' he added.

Instantly, she saw her mistake. 'Oh, thanks.' Her anger evaporated.

'You are wonderfully primitive,' he told her on the street outside.

'Oh, that must be where I get my "common touch",' she said, looking over his shoulder at the menu written in white paint on the window of a sandwich shop.

'Look, I seem to have made a complete hash of this,' Charlie admitted, 'could we start again?'

She thought of the lobster sitting on her plate, and the metal crackers beside it, and she could not face wrestling with it, and having her hands stink of seafood for the rest of the afternoon. What she would really like, she decided, was avocado, bacon and mayonnaise on a granary bap. She had won some kind of battle with Charlie. To re-enter the restaurant with him now would make her completely justified anger look like a tantrum.

'I don't want to work for you, Charlie,' she said, 'so I don't think there's much point.'

'But why?' he said, having to shout above the traffic as several red buses roared past at once.

'There's no point in discussing it. It just wouldn't work. I'm sorry,' she added, slightly gratuitously, rather liking the sense of power his mortified look was giving her, but wishing he would just go, so that she could get her sandwich.

'Well, call me if you change your mind,' he said, holding out his hand. She shook it.

'Well,' said Robert later that afternoon when she phoned him to tell him how lunch had gone, 'just don't ever moan to me again about your job.'

Unusually, Ginger thought before replying.

'Actually,' she said, the confrontation with Charlie having given her a strange kind of confidence, 'I can't remember ever complaining to you about my job, it's you that is always complaining to me about my lack of ambition, how I've ruined my life, thrown away chances ... Honestly, you're as bad as my head-mistress at school.'

'Don't be ridiculous. I'm only interested in your well-being.'

'She used to say that as well. Listen, I've got to go,' Ginger said, putting down the phone as her boss emerged frowning from the smoke-filled office that adjoined the narrow space where Ginger sat. She noticed her boss's face suddenly light up as someone entered their office suite, so she swivelled round on her chair to see the woman from the reception desk in the main lobby downstairs holding an enormous bunch of multicoloured balloons. Red, blue, green, purple, gold and silver, shiny round cushions of helium, they drifted and bobbed about in the warm wafts of air that blew up from the heater. Their long narrow gold ribbons were attached to a miniature straw basket out of which peeped the corner of a small white envelope.

'They were just delivered. We've got the PM coming in, and I didn't think it created the right impression, so I brought them up,' the receptionist explained, smiling.

'Oh, they're lovely!' Ginger's boss held out her hand to take them, 'so much wackier than a bouquet. Shall I tie them to my sofa, Ginger?'

'Just make sure that your window's closed,' Ginger said, wondering who on earth could possibly like her boss enough to send such a wonderful gift. 'I sometimes buy one for Guy, but you have to be really careful not to let go . . . Whoosh!'

'Of course! Don't let me take them home without giving you one for him,' her boss offered, with her customary generosity, Ginger thought, since there were at least twenty in the bunch.

'But they're *for* Ginger,' the receptionist said bluntly, holding tightly on to the strings, backing away from her boss's outstretched hand.

'Oh, lucky you, how lovely!' her boss said, trying to keep a forced smile on her disappointed face as she retreated back into her office.

'Don't let me go without giving you one!' Ginger mimicked softly, sticking her tongue out at the door as it closed and making the receptionist giggle.

The envelope contained a cheque for five hundred pounds and a small white card. *This is an ex-gratia payment for your help with the programme*, Ginger read. *I was hoping to make it part of your salary package. Take care, Charlie.*

'Why balloons?' Pic asked later that evening, when Ginger phoned excitedly to tell her the day's events.

'I don't know,' Ginger replied impatiently. She had been expecting a less pedantic response. 'Perhaps he

274

thought I was more of a balloons kind of person than a flowers kind of person. He's right as a matter of fact. You can say a lot more with balloons than you can say with flowers. I like getting flowers, but then they fade and die, and I can't bear to throw them out and then the water has that horrible smell . . .'

'If you trimmed the stems and arranged them, rather than dumping the whole bouquet, cellophane and all, into the first vase you could lay your hands on, that might not happen.'

Ginger wondered why it was that everyone today seemed to be scolding her. Everyone except Charlie, she thought, allowing herself a quick memory of his astonished face as she had taken a spanner out of her rucksack and reattached the back wheel of her bike.

'How on earth did you get them home?' Pic asked her, ever concerned about the practicalities.

'I tied them under the saddle. I think people thought I was advertising a circus or something,' Ginger replied.

There was a pause as her sister tried to imagine Ginger's progress through Shepherd's Bush in the rush hour.

'You can't possibly accept the money, of course,' Pic went on.

'I've already banked it.'

'Ginger!'

'I shall spend it exclusively on Guy. I thought about it and I realized it would be quite wrong of me, as a mother, to send the money back,' she added firmly, and was surprised when Pic did not pursue it.

'Have you thanked him?' Pic asked.

'No, not yet. I wanted to calm down a bit. I want to sound pleased, but not too pleased, you know.'

'Honestly . . .'

She couldn't help thinking that behind Pic's exasperated tone there lurked a tiny shred of jealousy. It was impossible to imagine Ed ever sending a bouquet of balloons.

'Anyway,' Ginger said, wanting to change the subject – Pic's criticism was slightly spoiling her exhilaration – 'have you thought about our birthday yet?'

'It's not for ages.'

'No, but we ought to organize something special.'

The balloons had put her in the mood for more celebrations.

'Do we have one this year?' Pic asked.

It was particularly unfair, Ginger had always thought, that they only got a proper birthday once every four years, especially since they had to share that day with each other as well. They had been born at one o'clock in the morning on 29 February.

'Yes, we're going to be seven.'

'Shall I have a dinner party?' Pic volunteered.

'No, no, it shouldn't be you doing all the work,' Ginger said quickly. She didn't feel she could stand another dinner party like the one Pic and Ed had hosted at New Year.

Why was it that convention demanded there be equal numbers of men and women sitting down to eat? Ginger would have far preferred talking to another woman than the person Pic and Ed had invited to be her partner for the evening. He was someone who worked with them, and she assumed that they had felt sorry for him because it was New Year and he was a long way from home. The thought that he had been asked as a potential date for her was too awful even to contemplate. He was one of those people who, when you ask them what their job involves, tells you in considerable detail. He was one of those men who takes the time and trouble to explain, in full, the rules of ice hockey when you say, lightly, that it is a sport you have never understood.

'I really don't mind,' Pic was saying, 'we could invite Doug again. He really liked you.'

'No,' Ginger said immediately.

'Didn't you like him? He's very good-looking.'

276

'Pic, he's Canadian . . .'

'You say that as if it's a code word for something. I know loads of nice Canadians.'

'That's the point. I don't like nice. They're too bloody nice . . .'

'You can't write off a whole nation—'

'All right, name me one interesting Canadian.'

'I thought people said that about Belgium?'

'At least Belgium has twenty different ways of cooking mussels and they serve mayo with chips – and you don't see Belgian backpackers with their national flag carefully stitched to their rucksack.'

'Oh, for heaven's sake!'

'I'm sorry,' Ginger apologized, pleased to have diverted Pic from the dinner-party idea, 'I kind of fancy doing something special. Why don't we go out, just the two of us? It's a Thursday, we could go to the ballet, and have supper after. I'll book it.'

'OK. Let's do that. It would be lovely to have an evening, just us, together.'

Pic missed her, Ginger realized as she put down the phone. These days they hardly ever seemed to talk about her. It was always Guy, or Ginger's problems with work, or men, and when Ginger remembered to ask how she was getting on, Guy would often start demanding her attention, and between exclamations of, 'Good boy, clever boy,' she wouldn't be able to concentrate on what Pic was saying. Next time, she promised herself, she would make sure she gave her sister time to talk.

She lay back on the sofa, looking at all the balloons floating round the ceiling, then closed her eyes, picturing Guy's face when Lia had brought him home that evening, the way his eyes had sparkled with happiness and disbelief.

'I have discovered the reason diets never work.' Ramona leaned across the desk, as if she were about to reveal a secret of international importance.

277

'Oh?' Alison asked, with little interest. She was trying to think of a headline for the article about bathrooms and the copy had to be ready before she left the office. *April Showers*, she typed, but the piece was for March. She deleted the words.

'Yes, I was looking at Jonty's Physics homework. Apparently, mass always remains constant, so I've worked out that the logic is this: if someone loses two pounds, it has to go somewhere, and usually it decides to go to my thighs.'

Alison laughed a little, unwilling to encourage Ramona, who had obviously finished for the day and was in a chatty mood.

'You've lost weight recently,' Ramona observed.

'Have I?' Alison continued to look at her screen.

'I don't know, but I seem heavier than ever.'

'Oh . . .'

Ramona tried another tactic. 'Are you coming to Bill's leaving party?'

'No, look, I've got to finish this, and then I've got to run. I'm having some work done on the flat. I'm meeting someone there.' She had said the words several times now and they didn't sound like a lie any more.

Alison looked up and caught a retreating expression of surprise on Ramona's face. For just a moment too long, she held Ramona's eyes, challenging her to believe her, then looked away quickly. Ramona had no reason not to believe her, she realized, checking herself. Her over-detailed excuse might only have given her away.

'Look,' she added, more softly, 'will you say I'm really sorry? I did sign the card . . .'

She was late, but he had waited in the pub at the corner of the street, checking the basement windows of her apartment for a light on every ten minutes. She had only just taken her grey winter coat off when he knocked softly at the door.

His eyes travelled up and down the plain black DKNY suit she was wearing, the simple shell-pink silk blouse, the Chanel pearl earrings. He offered no greeting as he stepped forward and pulled her against him. She drank the taste of beer and cigarettes from his mouth.

He pushed her against the dining table, tipping her back from the waist. She lay perfectly still, her head in the middle of the table, feet on the floor, as he looked at her. Then he dropped slowly to his knees, pushed up her short skirt and nudged his head between her legs, tracing the tops of her stockings with his tongue, his nose grazing the loose silk of the French knickers she was wearing. Her feet came off the floor the moment he began to suck her. She began to climax almost immediately, her legs locking themselves around his neck holding his mouth onto her. His hands prised her thighs away from his ears, pushing them so far apart she felt the skin at the top of her legs stretching. Then he stopped sucking, leaving her raw, exposed. She could feel the cold air on her clitoris like an open wound.

She watched him unpeeling the stocking from her left leg, pulling the fine denier nylon taut, then he picked up her left arm, holding it limp on the flat of his hand as if testing its weight. She felt as if the limb did not belong to her, until he wound the stocking around her wrist and pulled tight. She was shuddering in the knowledge he was going to tie her to the table and her exposed skin prickled with goose-bumps. He looked directly at her, silently asking for her permission. From somewhere deep in her chest she heard a tiny strangled voice whispering, 'Please.' She had never been tied before and yet, at that moment, she wanted it more than anything in the world. His face was frowning in concentration, the tip of his tongue covering his bottom lip, as he knotted the other end of the stocking around the far table leg, and pulled. Then he came back to take off the other stocking, slowly, his eyes constantly watching her face, getting her consent. This time, she stretched her arm above her head to make his job easier. She closed her eyes, spread-eagled, totally vulnerable, giving herself up to trust. She sensed him walking beside her and kneeling again, between her legs, flickering his tongue over her, his hands gently holding her pelvic bones down as her body jerked in involuntary spasms from the acute pleasure of his touch. She heard the rip of his zipper, then the iron-hard mass of his penis splitting her in two, and she could not believe she could bear so much pleasure, and still live.

Afterwards, he lay on top of her, inside her, for a long time, until her arms had pins and needles and she asked him softly to untie her. She shook her wrists, stood up, pulled down her skirt. He handed her stockings back, looking at her with pale, soulful eyes.

'What the hell are we going to do?' he asked, eventually.

She rolled a stocking in her fingers and unfurled it onto an outstretched leg, fastening her suspenders with practised efficiency.

'I don't know,' she said, standing up and smoothing her skirt over her thighs, becoming instantly the cool, well-groomed woman again.

'We can't go on, but every time I want to tell you that, we end up . . .' He gestured defeatedly at the table.

'I keep thinking that it will become clear,' she said, retrieving her shoes from opposite sides of the room, 'but it becomes more complicated.'

'I love you,' he said, so quietly she didn't know whether she had heard him.

'I've always loved you,' she told him, holding out her arms. 'Always . . .'

They held on to each other, both terrified of being the first to let go.

Chapter 8

FEBRUARY

'Look, snowdrops!' Lia exclaimed, pushing the double buggy to the very edge of the path so that the babies could see the tiny white flowers peeping through the undergrowth around the bottom of a tree. 'A bit later, this whole forest will be covered with bluebells,' she told them, 'you'll see. It'll be like a carpet of blue. You'll love it.'

'Bababababa . . .' Guy replied.

He had begun to babble a couple of weeks before. Sometimes she thought he was imitating her, making fun of the way she kept up a constant commentary on what they were seeing. Anouska had not attempted to speak yet. She seemed to be a naturally retiring child – like her father, Lia thought – who watched everything, and only occasionally smiled. It was good for her to have a laughing extrovert like Guy around. She wondered if they would grow up to be friends. Perhaps these earliest encounters with the opposite sex would fix the pattern for later attractions. She smiled at the thought of her daughter grown up, bringing home a jolly public-school aristocrat, as Guy was bound to become. How Neil would hate it!

Lia caught herself wondering whether she had been quiet as a child, or boisterous, or whingey or happy. Had she been born with curly hair? When had she

281

said her first word? What was it? They were not things you considered until you had a child yourself, but now she found herself thinking about them often.

When Ginger returned from the country after Christmas, she had brought back a big mulberry-leather album of photographs of herself and her twin sister Patricia as children. She and Lia had sat next to each other on the huge, uncomfortable old sofa in Ginger's dark living room, poring over the stiff parchment pages. For the first few months, it was impossible to tell which sister was which, but by the time they were a year old, it had become quite easy, as their individual expressions and body language emerged to differentiate them from one another. Lia had been curious about whether Ginger and her sister had enjoyed looking into mirrors, as most babies seemed to do.

'I suppose so. What do you mean?' Ginger had asked.

'Well, you would have seen yourself before – when you looked at Pic.'

'Of course! I hadn't thought of that,' said Ginger. 'When Guy first started getting fascinated with his reflection, I tried to work out what he must be thinking. How could you understand your reflection when you have no sense of self? But for us it must have been twice as weird – or maybe, it wasn't so weird at all.'

She looked up from the album staring blankly at nothing, reminiscing.

'It was great when we were first experimenting with make-up. We would sit opposite each other and do each other's eye-shadow and mascara, except that Pic used to get fed up because I always put too much on her,' she laughed.

It must be wonderful to have someone there all the time, just for you, Lia thought, feeling a sudden enormous weight of sadness, someone who had known you from the day you were born. Nobody knew her like that.

'Come on,' she said to the babies, turning the buggy in the direction of home, 'home for lunch, and this afternoon, we're going to have an adventure.'

Taking two babies to the West End was not as easy as she had imagined. They both fell asleep in their seats in the back of the car, but the traffic was moving so slowly, she began to wonder whether she would make it up to town and back by the end of the afternoon. She had never parked in central London before. Eventually, she found herself being whirled into a subterranean spiral beneath Cavendish Square, and as she manoeuvred the double buggy up the steps to daylight again, trying to hang on to her handbag, the bottles and wipes, and all the other paraphernalia, it crossed her mind that she hadn't really registered where she had parked the car. In the shop, other mothers sympathized, and helped, pointing her in the direction of the lifts and looking with interest at the two very different babies, one chubby boy with masses of dark curly hair and a cheeky smile, the other a delicate solemn little girl in a bonnet. When she finally reached the cafeteria on the top floor of John Lewis, exhausted, she did not dare leave the babies for a minute to get herself a drink from the counter, so she sat down on a stool, and waited. Trace did not appear. After half an hour, Lia asked the woman who was clearing away the cold dregs of tea and half-eaten Danish pastries from the tables whether Trace was on, but she said she did not know her. Perhaps Trace too had changed her name, Lia thought, disappointed, not really understanding why she had come. Trace would not have been able to tell her anything about her mother, after all. She might only have known how to start looking. Trace always knew how things operated. Trace's absence, and the great struggle she had had to get there, were signs, Lia decided. There were things she was not meant to know.

The car park fee was unbelievable. Lia only just had enough money in her wallet. She returned to Richmond, chattering brightly all the way home to her two small companions, pointing at buses, traffic lights, a policeman on a horsey, but after she dropped Guy off at Ginger's flat, and put the key in the ignition to drive home, she was choked by a sudden flood of tears. It was stupid to feel lonely, she told herself, holding her breath to stop the sobs. She had good friends, the sweetest baby, a man so gorgeous that women in the street stared at him. She was lucky, very lucky. Brushing the tears from her face with the sleeve of her coat, she turned and smiled reassuringly at Anouska, then started the car, and drove home.

'No, watch Daddy,' Neil told his daughter, trying to demonstrate the mechanics of crawling. In slow motion he lifted one hand, then a knee, making gradual progress across the carpet. Anouska lay on her stomach watching him with an amazed look on her face.

'Come on, push up with your hands, like this,' he said, as if he was teaching an eleven-year-old pupil to use the gym.

Anouska giggled.

'I thought they were supposed to imitate,' he said to Lia, who was watching, unable to keep her eyes off their game.

It was as if he had finally understood that the more you put into Anouska the more rewarding she became. Maybe his New Year's resolution had been to make more of an effort. She could see that he was beginning to enjoy the time he spent with the baby, and he had started to refer to himself as Daddy. When Lia first overheard him saying it, quietly, as if trying it out to see how it sounded, she had to gulp very hard to keep back tears. She wondered if the change she perceived in him had anything to do with selling his motorbike. It was as if he had also finally relinquished the part of him that hankered for the days of freedom before they had the baby, and accepted that his life was different. It was only when you stopped railing against something that you could start to appreciate it. Only rarely now did she catch him looking at her with that odd lost look she had first noticed around the time that the baby was born.

It was nice playing happy families, but they didn't get enough time together, she thought, wondering what they could do about that. His school was due for an Ofsted inspection and all the additional work of preparing for that meant that he often came home very late. Now that she was working too, they were usually both too tired to talk much or relax together on their own. She hadn't told him about her excursion to John Lewis, she realized, because she didn't know his mood at the moment well enough to predict how he would react, and she couldn't face another explosion like the last time.

'Can we afford a holiday this year?' she suddenly asked him.

He looked up from the baby, smiling at her. 'I wondered why there suddenly seemed to be brochures everywhere.'

'Well, they're free, and they've got lovely pictures, so I thought they'd be good for her to tear to shreds . . .' she began to explain why she had picked up the brochures from the travel agency earlier in the week.

It made him feel terrible when she tried to excuse her housekeeping expenses. Was he really such a mean bastard that he had made her afraid to spend money?

'You don't have to justify every pound you spend,' he told her gently, 'I know I was worried at Christmas, but we're doing OK now. Thank God for Ginger Prospect!'

Lia beamed. It was the first time he had acknowledged that her job had been a good idea. Perhaps things were also getting better now because she was contributing to the housekeeping. It must have been a strain for him. It was easy to assume that his life had not changed much, that when he left each morning for work, he closed the door on all the responsibility. She hadn't really considered the extra pressure he was under, having to provide for all three of them. Neil was a worrier. He never spoke about the things that were bothering him, but silently churned them over inside. She glanced at his hands, usually a barometer of his anxiety, and saw that the nails were chewed to the quick.

'So can we?' she asked him, excitedly.

'Go on holiday? Why not?' he said, feeling even more guilty as he saw how happy the simplest of sentences could make her. 'At half-term maybe? For a week?'

'Shall we go to Portugal? We could get a self-catering package, and if we went back to the village, they'd be so happy to see us with a baby, we could probably eat free!'

'Yeah, all right,' he said, not certain that he wanted to return to the place they had met, but not sure why not.

'I'll make some enquiries then.'

'Go ahead and book it if you find what you want,' he told her.

'I noticed that they've got an offer of a discount if we book now,' she said, wondering whether her own motives for picking up the brochures had been as innocent as she had just made out.

He smiled at her. 'Even better, then,' he said, getting up from the floor. 'Look, do you mind if I pop up to the club? There's a bloke there on club night who says he'll restring my tennis racket.'

'Of course,' Lia replied, 'have a drink while you're there. Do you think you'll want supper?'

'How about if I bring us back some fish and chips?' he offered.

'Great!' she said.

He walked towards the door.

'Neil?' she said, just as he was about to open it.

He turned round quickly. 'Yes?'

'Your racket.' She pointed at his sports bag that lay under the stairs.

'Right,' he said, snatching it up.

He could not understand how some people could lie all the time about lots of different things and still carry on as normal. How did they keep track? One lie led so easily to another, and before you knew where you were you had created another world, like one of those virtual worlds the kids at school were always talking about the morning after *Tomorrow's World*. All he wanted to do was make a phone call, but now he had said he was going to the club he thought he'd better go, because she might ask whom he had seen, and even though his racket didn't need stringing, he thought he'd better get it done, because he had almost slipped up back there, and Lia was sometimes almost uncannily perceptive about what was going on in people's heads. He was dicing with danger and it was ironic, he thought, because the phone call he was going out to make would end it. It had to stop. Now. His place was with Lia and their baby. He was not a liar.

The phone was situated in the passage to the toilets, next to the cigarette machine. He stood staring at the gold tower of Benson and Hedges, trying to work out what to say. He was just about to pick up the receiver when the captain of the first cricket team walked past.

'Thought you'd given up, mate,' he said, pausing to share a word.

'I have, mostly,' Neil said, putting three pound coins into the slot and pulling the drawer hard at the bottom of the Marlboro tower.

Another lie to support another lie. He didn't want to make it obvious that he was about to make a phone call, so he felt compelled to buy the cigarettes, and he hadn't given up, just discovered an even more expensive way of smoking: he'd lost count of the number of full packets he had bought in order to smoke just one before giving up for good. One usually became two or three, and then he would throw the rest away in disgust. Shaking, he took out a Marlboro and put it in his mouth, cadging a light from the captain on his way back to the bar. He took a long drag, then picked up the phone.

'She's not here at the moment,' a young female voice told him, 'she's gone to a party. Can I give her a message?'

'No,' he said, quickly, 'no thanks,' and put down the phone.

What party? She hadn't told him about a party. He pictured Alison standing, laughing, holding a glass of wine in her hand, in a room full of men who were staring at her, all visualizing what she was wearing under that smart, buttoned-up black suit. Neil stared at the phone, raging with jealousy, then he hit the shabby gloss-painted wall of the passageway hard with the flat of his hand.

The next time they met was a Saturday afternoon. She had put a cover on the duvet, a new cover, the folds from the wrapping were still stiff. It looked like a great big yellow and white checked tablecloth.

'I feel like we should be having a picnic,' he said, sitting up.

'Do you like it?' she asked him, tucking herself under the hook of his elbow.

'It's OK,' he said bluntly, an alarm ringing in his head.

There could be no building of nests. That was forbidden. There could be no relationship, affair, whatever it was, he reminded himself. There could be

288

no love. But when he looked down at her face and saw that he had hurt her by his abrupt dismissal of the new duvet cover, he knew that it wasn't possible. He could not stop loving her. It was in his genes. He was blood group A, he had blue eyes, and he loved Ally. Nothing could change that.

'It's light,' he said, his eyes drifting away from her face to the window, 'it's never been light before.'

It was something to say. He had to say something.

'No,' she agreed.

'How did you get away?' he asked.

'I offered Justine Valentine's Night in exchange for this afternoon. She's got a new boyfriend – it was an irresistible deal.'

He wished he had not asked. Now he wanted to know what she would be doing on Valentine's Night. Staying in, obviously. With her husband. Or would he be working? He seemed to work very long hours. Perhaps he was having an affair. Doctors were renowned for it. Perhaps Ally's reason for being there was purely revenge. No. No. No. He tried to get a grip on his tumbling thoughts.

'What about you?' she was asking.

'They're out with Ginger ... at the zoo,' he stuttered, unable to say Lia's name. 'I wasn't invited. She knows I can't stand Ginger.'

'Can't you?' She turned over onto her front, as if about to enjoy a good gossip. 'I like her.'

'Why's that, then?' He pushed his fingers through her shiny hair. The ends fell back into place heavily, like a silk tassle.

'She's open, direct, really honest ...' She stopped as she realized what she was saying.

'Qualities you admire?' he asked, bitter sarcasm in his voice.

'Don't ...'

'We can't do this, you know,' he told her, turning away from her onto his side. It was easier to say what he had to say if he couldn't see her.

'Talk about them?' she asked.

'Yes. It's wrong.'

'So is ringing me at home,' she said.

'How did you know?'

'Justine just said someone had called. I don't think she'd put two and two together, but . . .'

He had meant that they could not go on seeing each other, but she had twisted the conversation and suddenly they were writing a set of rules for themselves.

'Alison.' He turned back over, and gazed at her face. He placed a fingertip gently against her mouth so that she could not interrupt when he said what he had to say.

Alison. He never called her Alison. The word sounded strange on his lips. She knew what was coming.

'We can't do this,' he said quietly.

'I know,' she said, her eyes filling with tears.

'Do you believe me?' he asked, taking her by the shoulders.

She shook her head, her face scrunched up in an effort not to cry. He wrapped his arms around her, and she sobbed against his shoulder, his face in her silky, fresh-smelling hair.

They made love again, slowly, with exquisite tenderness, as if they were bruised and trying not to cause each other further pain.

Later, when it grew dark, Alison lay dazed, with no idea whether they had slept, or what the time was. All she was sure about was that she did not want to go home.

'Do you remember the youth club?' she said suddenly.

'Which one?' he asked.

'The Catholic one . . . I'd forgotten the others. There was one in practically every church hall, wasn't there? Do you think they were trying to convert us?'

She leant right out of bed to pull her handbag alongside, then extracted a packet of ten Marlboro.

'Didn't work,' he said with a grim chuckle, 'I'd only just gone to the trouble of lapsing. Here, give us one of those . . .'

She looked at him questioningly, and handed one over, lighting it for him with a match from a slim shiny white box she had picked up in a restaurant. She loved the paraphernalia of smoking, she realized, almost as much as the cigarettes themselves.

When they first smoked, she remembered, he would always light hers from his, inhaling in small puffs as the clean ochre tobacco caught and glowed. He always left the filter-tip dry, not wet with saliva, as some boys did. It was one of those teenage rituals that had been *de rigueur* when you were going out with someone. A public staking of territory. Now it seemed such an obvious sexual symbol, but she didn't think they had known that then.

'All we seemed to do was take it in turns to snog in that big dilapidated armchair,' she mused, lying back and blowing a funnel of smoke straight up into the air.

'We played a bit of pool too, while we were queueing for the chair,' he laughed.

'You were good at pool.'

'I still am.'

A flicker of worry crossed her forehead. It was only safe to talk about then, he realized, not now.

'I remember you beating that bloke with the moustache,' she went on, 'what was his name? The one who just appeared in town on his motorbike and nobody knew where he came from . . .'

'Tim?'

'Yeah, that's it,' she said, delighted.

'He came from Watford, I think,' Neil said.

She burst into giggles.

'What's so funny?'

'Well, Watford . . . it's hardly the place of legends,

291

is it? He was this tremendously romantic and glamorous figure at school – his name must have been the second-most-scrawled on desks.'

'Yeah? Who was the first then?' he asked, flicking ash into the empty coffee mug she offered him.

'You *are* kidding?' She rolled over onto her tummy again, her knees bent, feet in the air and looked at him, searching his face for signs of false modesty.

'No.' Clearly, he didn't know.

'You, of course,' she told him.

'Me?'

'You were probably responsible for a record number of compass points broken. The technique was to gouge out the wood with your compass and fill in with felt tip – like a tattoo, I suppose. Actually, some of them were like tattoos, hearts with blood dripping and your initials. Don't worry, I never did that. The compass always slipped and I could never get both halves of the heart symmetrical.'

'You carved my name on a desk?' he asked, astonished.

'Yes sir,' she said, remembering that he was now a teacher, and amused by his shocked intolerance of minor vandalism. 'It was one of the things you did. There were loads of things like that. Totems, I suppose . . .' She tried to think of an example. 'Like, you used to write the boy's name above your name—'

'On the desk?'

'No, this is a different one, on your exercise book. Then you used to cross out the letters that matched and count off the rest in a sort of chant: "Like, love, hate, adore, like, love, hate, adore . . ." and then when you had established which one it was, you did: "Silk, satin, cotton, rags . . ."' She jabbed her finger against his chest to illustrate. 'I was mortified when ours came out that I loved you and you hated me, but then I discovered you had a middle name, so then it worked, and you adored me . . .' She saw that she had completely lost him. 'I was the envy of the entire school because I was with you,' she added.

He smiled to himself. 'I expect I was too, but we didn't talk about that sort of thing. Definitely didn't write it on the desks. Football teams, maybe, but girls!' He raised his eyes to the ceiling.

'No, you don't understand. Nobody at school could understand how *I* had got *you* . . . I couldn't either,' she admitted.

'But you were lovely—'

'Were?' she said instantly.

The insecurity was so close to the smooth surface, you could practically touch it, he thought.

'Yes. Now, you are' – he searched for the right word – 'Beautiful.'

'So, I've improved with age? Like a cheese?'

'No . . . yes . . .' He was confused by the quickness of her retort. He hated it when she turned things round like that.

'I wish you wouldn't . . .' he began to say, but thought better of it, letting his voice trail away like smoke.

They both finished their cigarettes in silence. The room was very dark now, and the air was chill, but she had no desire to get up to switch on a light.

She spoke into the darkness. 'Do you remember how we all used to dance in a row with our hands on our hips and twisting from the waist?'

'Yeah – the greaser dance. Skins did a kind of reggae thing . . .'

'Do you remember what album was playing the first time we danced?' she asked him softly, snuggling down beside him, shifting one of her legs between his legs, and feeling his instant arousal.

'Bryan Ferry. *These Foolish Things,*' he murmured distractedly, lifting her hips as if she weighed nothing and sliding her vagina over his erection as effortlessly as putting on a glove.

'You remembered!' she said, gasping with delight.

'Well, you told me enough times,' he said, the glitter of mockery in his eyes.

She tapped his face gently, playfully, then closed her eyes, trying to commit to her memory all the sensations of this moment now, joined to him, filled with him, completed by him.

'What are we going to do?' he whispered to her after as she slumped down onto him, satiated, exhausted, her damp flesh meeting his with a loud smack.

'Pray?' she suggested, trembling.

'I'm lapsed, remember?' he said.

She nodded mutely, but inside she was saying the last-hope prayer of the desperate.

Dear God, if you can find a way to make it all right, I promise I will truly believe in you and I will never do anything bad again.

It was Valentine's Day and there were two envelopes on the coconut doormat. One was yellow. The address was written in spindly capital letters in an unsuccessful attempt to disguise Pic's handwriting. The other was a small white Jiffy bag which had a printed address label. She thought it was probably a free sample of something. Once you had a child, you kept getting free things through the post, nappies and creams and tiny packets of breakfast cereal. Ginger opened the yellow envelope first.

There was a picture of a bear floating in the sky, his paw grasping at the string of a heart-shaped balloon. Inside the message was 'I love you' and there was a G underneath.

'Thank you, my sweetie-pie,' Ginger said, planting a kiss on top of Guy's head. He looked up at her. 'Look, it's the Valentine you asked your aunty to send me,' she said, giving him the card, which he opened and shut a couple of times, as if checking the message, then discarded.

She tore open the white parcel and withdrew, to her surprise, a handmade card, with a red velvet heart

294

and various bits of wire and dried flowers and lace and stuff stuck on in a kind of collage. A few of the elements were badly glued and fell on to the carpet. It was the kind of card that cost you a fortune in an expensive boutique in Covent Garden market, wrapped in eco-friendly cellophane, with a handwritten label claiming that it was a limited edition of a unique design by an artist. What they didn't tell you was that the artist employed a whole sweatshop of piece-workers to churn out replicas of the unique design and pedalled them to trendy little shops in renovated arcades all over the country. Still, it was pretty, Ginger thought, opening it to find that the inside was blank. She couldn't imagine who might have sent it, but guessed it was probably Robert, since he had been known to make the occasional thoughtful gesture, he worked in Covent Garden, and he no doubt assumed that she wouldn't be getting any Valentines this year.

'But he didn't realize that you had already sent me one, did he?' Ginger said, kissing Guy's head again.

Guy was fascinated by the Jiffy bag, so she tipped it up to make sure there were no more bits for him to put in his mouth, then handed it to him and placed the card on the mantelpiece in the living room, where it fitted in with the general bric-à-brac that included a Lalique glass candlestick, an ebony cased clock that stood on four gold Ionic columns, Robert's Christmas party invitation, a dummy, three mismatched ear-rings, a bottle of perfume, an empty can of Diet Coke, a framed photo of herself and Pic taken on their eighteenth birthday, and a half-chewed quarter of a peeled apple.

A car horn beeped twice outside.

'Come on, mister,' Ginger said, forcing Guy's reluctant arms into his jacket and pulling his hat down hard over his ears, 'Mummy is going to work and Guy is going to play with Lia and Anouska.'

The bit of the day she found hardest was when Lia waved and pulled away, and she went back inside to get her bike. The flat seemed completely empty without Guy there.

The front wheel crunched on something as she pushed the bike to the door. She looked down to see that one of the little bits that had fallen out of the Jiffy bag had been crushed under it. It looked like a piece of painted shell. Why couldn't Robert have just sent a card with a crude joke like everyone else, instead of being so damn tasteful, she thought, meanly. She pushed the smithereens around with the toe of her boot so that they blended in with the general fluff and debris on the carpet, and promised herself that she would hoover that weekend.

Neil managed to find a seat upstairs on the bus. He opened his newspaper, holding it like a shield around his face. The thing he most disliked about having sold his motorbike was the journey to work. It wasn't the bus so much as the schoolchildren on it, with their constant questions.

'Sir, can't you afford a car, sir?'

'Sir, what happened to your Kawasaki, sir?'

'Sir, do you like my new skirt, sir? My mum says it's too short, what do you think, sir?'

He didn't mind dealing with it within the school grounds. It was what they paid him for. But at eight o'clock in the morning, he just wanted a bit of peace.

He began to read an eye-witness account of genocide in Africa, but his eyes kept travelling to the top of the page, to the incongruity of a cartoon cupid pointing his bow towards the centre of the paper where there was a pull-out section of Valentine messages. He couldn't remember Valentine's Day being such a big thing in the past. Now, everywhere he looked, there were hearts: shop windows, newspapers, even the supermarket was advertising heart-shaped cakes and every one of them seemed to be accusing him, reminding him of his duplicity. The flower stall by the station was crammed with red roses at three times the normal price, and there was no refuge even in the newspaper, which he normally used to block out the world in the morning.

Distractedly, he flipped to the Valentine supplement. They were usually good for a laugh.

Flopsy Bunny, be my ball of fluff for ever, Peter Rabbit.

Shameless Blonde, you make an old bear happy.

He couldn't imagine how people had the guts to ring these messages in. Bad enough that some folk called each other pet names in privacy. Even printing them for the whole world to see had a kind of anonymity about it, but picking up the phone and telling an operator, giving your credit card number . . . he couldn't make sense of it. He took a pen out of his top pocket and drew circles around some of the more ridiculous ones, intending to read them out after the morning staff meeting. It would be something to brighten up the staff common room, before the inevitable onslaught of the day.

His eyes travelled down the page.

Noodles loves Peaches.

How on earth had they arrived at that? he wondered.

Then his eyes stuck on one message. It seemed familiar. He read it again and again, trying to work out where he might have heard the words, then he remembered.

N – *You came, you saw, you conquered me,*
When you did that to me, I somehow knew that this had to be – A

His first thought was that it was weird that two people with the same initials had the same theme song as they did. He decided to cut it out and present it to her the next time they met.

Then he remembered that she had asked him what paper he read, last time as they were leaving the flat. He had told her, wondering whether it was the right

297

thing to say, adding, 'We sometimes get yours on Sundays,' in case she was offended that he wasn't a regular reader of the paper she worked for.

He found himself chuckling out loud, then quickly checked that no-one was watching. Most of the other passengers looked as if they were not quite awake. There were no small people in uniform. He breathed a sigh of relief. He should be feeling annoyed with her for risking such a public declaration, he thought, but it was clever, coded, a message just for him. It was special. Now he knew what it felt like to be Noodles, or Flopsy Bunny. Blushing, he pulled the paper closer in around his face.

Lia had been into several kitchen departments, but nobody had what she was looking for. Eventually she found one, in a packet of Christmas shapes reduced to half price in a basket outside a hardware store. She had to buy the whole set, but it was worth it. She walked all the way home smiling. She wanted to do something special. She had given him a card, but it didn't seem enough after the enormous bunch of long-stemmed roses he had hidden in the shed overnight. She had wondered why he was up so early, and why her breakfast was made for her on the kitchen table. She had wandered around eating a piece of toast until he had told her, with barely concealed impatience, 'Please sit down to eat!'

She had pulled out her chair, and there they were, a dozen, tightly-furled velvety red blooms, with beads of dew. Neil certainly knew how to choose flowers. They didn't really have a tall enough vase, and she had had to trim the stems down, but they looked luscious as they opened slightly in the steamy warmth of the kitchen, the most beautiful flowers she had ever been given. And it was odd, because she had been so sure she would only get a card. Neil had been complaining about the commercialization of Valentine's Day ever since the first heart motifs appeared in the shops soon after Christmas. It was a con, he had said, just a licence to print money, and he wished it would stop.

Alison knew that she shouldn't be disappointed, but she couldn't help it. Throughout the day flowers had been arriving, and each time the boy from the postroom walked into the open-plan office with another basket or bouquet, her heart had stopped, wondering whether this might be it. Invariably he had walked in the opposite direction, or past her to the Arts desk, and she had received nothing. She tried to keep her eyes from glancing up at the door whenever the rustle of cellophane announced another entrance, but it was impossible.

'Are you celebrating tonight?' Ramona asked her, taking a slurp of coffee.

'Well, our nanny's out, so we're in. I think I'll pick up something nice to eat on the way home,' Alison told her.

'What's Stephen's favourite food?' Ramona asked.

'He's equally happy with foie gras on toasted brioche, or McDonald's. In fact, I'm not sure he could tell the difference,' Alison said fondly, looking up to see a hand-tied bunch of red roses and gypsophila walking towards her, then past.

'Perhaps he's bought you something,' Ramona said, seeing the disappointment on her colleague's face.

'Oh, probably, if he's remembered. He usually does, because I give him a card in the morning,' Alison replied, flicking her eyes back to the computer, then glancing back at Ramona.

So why are you so disappointed he hasn't sent you flowers, she could see Ramona wanting to ask, but stopping herself, knowing, somehow, that such a question would touch a very raw nerve.

Alison left the office at five o'clock and stood on the pavement outside the building. It was very cold. She stepped up and down on the spot, trying to decide which direction to walk in. The alternatives were to take the tube home and hope that the local shops would have something nice left to eat, or to hop on a bus to Soho and go to Camisa's for fresh pasta, Provolone cheese and basil growing in a pot. Or, she thought, she could just pop to the flat, just to see . . . No. She would only be disappointed.

She walked towards the bus stop, hoping a bus would come along straightaway and whisk her in the opposite direction. It didn't. Two free taxis went past, before her will let her down. Then, having decided that she would take the next one, there were none. If there isn't one within five minutes, it is not meant to be, she told herself, checking her watch. As she looked up again, a black cab with its orange light glowing pulled into view and her arm shot in the air. It was a sign, she thought, jumping in and turning on the heater. But there was no post in the flat. Not even a leaflet offering discount pizza to make her heart stop momentarily mistaking it for a card. She even picked up a corner of the mat to check that nothing was hidden under it. Nothing but dust.

Serves me right, she thought, making a quick check of the rooms, her eyes lingering wistfully on the bed, the lemon-and-white checked duvet cover thrown back as they had left it. She leapt onto it, kneeling, and bent her head to the white fitted undersheet, burying her nose in it, breathing in the faint scent of their sex over the slight mustiness of the little-used mattress. She was going to be late, she realized, pulling herself together, standing up and switching off the light. In the darkness, she noticed for the first time that the answerphone was blinking. She had bought it a couple of weeks before so that they would both be able to leave last-minute messages if they couldn't get there. She watched it for a few seconds, her hand still on the light switch. There was one message. It was probably one of those cold callers offering a free quotation for double glazing, she told herself, trying to resist the pull of the tiny red light, pulsing in the darkness.

The loud electronic beep in the stillness of the room made her jump. For the first few seconds, there was nothing except the distant sound of traffic, then a deep breath, an embarrassed throat clearance, and then his voice whispering, 'Well, here goes,' and he began to sing, very softly, as though he might be overheard. *Oh, will you never let me be?* A pause, then his voice again, becoming stronger and more confident:

> *'Oh, will you never set me free?*
> *The ties that bound us are still around us,*
> *There's no escape that I can see . . .'*

He sang the whole of the song and then stopped abruptly. 'That's your lot. Bye, now.'

The answerphone clicked and whirred and beeped. Unable to believe what she had heard, she pressed *play* again. Again the muffled traffic noise . . . and then his voice. She closed her eyes and imagined that he was there in the room with her, and he began to sing . . .

'. . . That's your lot. Bye, now.'

He must have been in a phone box, she guessed, picking up the phone to dial 1471. The message confirmed that the caller had used a payphone, at one-seventeen. In his lunch hour. She began to speculate whether he had forgotten what day it was, or whether he had tried to resist doing anything, lasting out the morning but finally caving in, or whether he could possibly have seen her message in the paper. He had sung their song and she had completely forgotten that he could sing.

How curiously memory operated, she thought, lying back on the bed, playing the message again. Before he had walked back into her life, if she had ever thought about him, her mind had pictured him standing at the bottom of the hill, waiting for her.

301

That had been the predominant image retained: his slightly awkward stance, white shirt, arms folded, and his face breaking into a smile as she approached him. She had not been able to hear him, or smell him, or remember what his skin felt like to the touch. It was as if each sense had been restored to her in turn: his soft, Northern voice, the recognition of which had made her pass out that first day; the scent of him during their first kiss at New Year; his skin . . .

She grabbed a pillow and hugged it hard. How could she have forgotten his singing and his amazing memory for lyrics? Strumming a borrowed guitar, he used to play 'Where Do You Go To, My Lovely?' on the concrete steps outside the youth club, remembering all the words (no-one else got past Marlene Dietrich) looking up at her every now and then, when he wasn't watching his fingers as they hesitantly picked out the tune. He wasn't much good at the guitar, but when he got over the first few hoarse, nervous notes, he could really sing, and his voice was pure, like Paul McCartney's. His brother and his greaser friends hovering around menacingly on their revving motorbikes would chime in, 'Dee Da Da Dee Da Da Dum, Der Der Dum Dum Dum Dum Dum Dee Der, Derdy Der, Derdy Der . . .' their heads nodding in gentle mocking imitation of the accordion accompaniment.

Eventually, she let the message end. The tape rewound and clicked off. Silence reinhabited the room. She got up, smoothed down her suit, shook the duvet out, and switched off the light. Then she changed her mind, switched it on again, and walking across the room to the answer-machine, she removed the tape and placed it in the zipped inside pocket of her handbag.

'This looks too good to eat,' Neil told Lia, admiring the food on his plate – heart-shaped pieces of smoked salmon resting on heart-shaped buttered brown bread.

The only thing that wasn't heart-shaped was a crescent of lemon on the side.

Lia smiled. 'I got the idea from one of the recipes in that paper Alison works for, last Sunday,' she explained, pleased that he liked it. 'I hoped you hadn't noticed.'

'Noticed what?' he responded, as calmly as he could.

'The recipe . . . I thought, well, he doesn't usually look at the cookery section.'

'Right,' he said, putting a salmon heart in his mouth. He could barely swallow, and yet it was his favourite food, and he would have to eat every morsel because he had told her the moment before she put the plate in front of him that he was starving.

It served him right for allowing himself to believe even for a second that it became easier to lie once you had got away with it a couple of times. He chewed, knowing she was watching his jaw make heavy work of the light food, unable to look back at her.

'This is great,' he said, his mouth still full, wanting to break the silence that seemed to be ticking on for ever. He searched for a relevant comment, staring at his plate. Two hearts eaten, three to go, he picked up his third, looking at it admiringly,

'Hey!' he said, suddenly, 'you managed to make both halves symmetrical!'

He looked up at her, pleased with the remembered phrase, but his eyes met blank incomprehension in hers.

'I used a biscuit cutter,' she said with a slight frown, inferring criticism from his comment.

Then he remembered that they had not been Lia's words.

Ally, Lia, Ally, Lia, their names were shouting in his head, running into one another so that he could not tell which was which. He put down the heart.

'I'm sorry,' he said, 'I think I've got a migraine coming on.'

And he bolted from the room, racing upstairs to the bathroom, where he was violently sick.

Justine was telling her about their day.

'We had a lovely time, didn't we?' she asked Ben, who was sitting in his high chair, elbow deep in puréed apricot and custard.

He banged his spoon on the tray, spattering the floor with orange pulp.

'Really?' Alison wasn't really listening.

'We saw Guy and Anouska, didn't we, and we're getting really good at swimming, and Aunty Lia said—'

'No, don't call her that,' Alison interrupted, abruptly, adding more soothingly, 'she's not his aunty. When I was little my mother made me call all her friends "Aunty", and, well, I don't want him to, that's all . . . listen,' she said, looking at her watch, 'you must go and get yourself ready. I've already made you late . . .'

Justine's face smiled with relief. 'Well, if you're sure . . .' she said, not waiting for her to change her mind.

Alison unpacked the food she had grabbed from the delicatessen in Islington round the corner from her flat. Fresh pasta, black olives, a tin of anchovies, a jar of sun-dried tomatoes, panettone in a pale blue box and a packet of glacé fruit left over from Christmas. Ben watched fascinated as she named each item as she withdrew it from the tall brown paper bag. It was funny, she thought, how having a child makes you see the world differently. She wasn't sure that she always noticed colours and shapes before she had started pointing them out to Ben. She unwrapped the panettone, and handed Ben the box to examine in that serious, curious way he had. She arranged slices of panettone in the bottom of a glass bowl, then chopped the glacé fruit and scattered it on top, finally adding a good drizzle of Cointreau. She whisked eggs, milk and sugar together and poured the mixture over, then made a bain-marie with water in a baking tray and left it ready to put in the oven. The pasta could wait until after Ben's bath, she decided.

Now that Ben looked so much like a baby and could sit up, holding his limbs firmly, she wasn't so frightened of touching him. It was like dealing with another human being now, not a tiny dependent little new-born creature who oppressively needed her all the time. She knelt by the side of the bath, one hand supporting his back, the other lathering his chubby, cherubic body with soap. Her favourite bits were his wrists, she decided, taking each in turn, holding it in the palm of her hand and marvelling at the simplicity of the design – just a little fold in the flesh where the arm joined onto the hand, no knobbly bones and protruding veins, like adult wrists had. They were so perfect. And so were the elbows, she thought, soaping his arms, with their soft dimples, and the shoulders. She paused, and looked into her baby's face. He was watching her appreciation of him very seriously, but suddenly he smiled at her, and she had the strangest feeling that she was meeting him for the first time.

'What's this? It's delicious,' Stephen asked.
'*Spaghetti alla puttanesca*,' she told him.
Whore's spaghetti. She looked at the blood-red sauce and wondered if a kind of subliminal guilt had made her choose to cook that particular dish for this evening. She had added sun-dried tomatoes to the recipe, which made the flavour even more pungently strong. Perhaps she should rename her variation adulteress's spaghetti, she thought, pushing her plate aside and helping herself to green salad.

It was the first evening they had spent together for a long time. She had been surprised by the absence of guilt, until now. Most evenings, Stephen was not home from work until late in the evening, and it was easy to lie in bed reassuring herself that he was clearly having an affair too. It wasn't as if he was a house doctor any more, she would rationalize, and consultants surely didn't have to work such long hours. Even if he wasn't actually screwing someone else, he was obviously more enamoured of his job than of her, and so . . . and so, she would fall asleep, exhausted by the demands of her job, her lover and her son, and her husband would come home and slide in next to her without her even noticing.

'The flowers are gorgeous,' he commented, 'thank you.'

She had bought him an armful of star-gazer lilies which filled the room with their intoxicating perfume.

'And this is for you.' He pushed a slim narrow box across the table.

It was the moment she had been dreading. It would have been so much easier if he had picked up some wilted roses from a bucket outside a garage, or even just forgotten it was Valentine's Day. It was the first time in her life she had not been thrilled to receive something wrapped in a distinctive blue Tiffany box. She pulled off the white ribbon, opened the box and gasped, her eyes filling with tears. It was the diamond necklace she had always coveted: a single diamond, not too large, but not small either, set in a plain gold chain just long enough to let the diamond rest in that hollow of bone at the base of the neck. What she liked so much about it was its lack of ostentation. The diamond wasn't a pendant, it was just part of the chain. It was the ultimate in understated elegance.

'I bought it in New York – I don't know why I haven't given it to you before, actually,' he explained, embarrassed by her reaction, 'it's just, well, we don't seem to have seen much of each other.'

'It is absolutely beautiful,' she told him, forcing herself to look at his eyes, 'how did you know?'

'You once said,' he answered, 'that time we went to dinner with Sir Giles.'

She recalled the evening with the man who was technically Stephen's boss but who behaved more like a benevolent uncle, clearly proud of his protégé and warmly welcoming to his fiancée, as she then was. She could remember that they had talked a great deal about music, arguing vehemently over Wagner's place in the pantheon of composers (Sir Giles for, Stephen against), but she could not remember any talk of diamonds.

'Lady Cressida,' Stephen explained, 'she was wearing a diamond necklace which you considered vulgar. We talked about it in the car on the way home. You said you thought diamond solitaires were fine, which was just as well, considering the ring I'd just given you, but no diamonds anywhere else, except – and then you described it. I drew a sketch as soon as I got in that night so that I wouldn't forget. I've been into jewellers all over London but they've never known what I was talking about. But in New York, they did.'

'New York's like that,' she said, turning the chain over and over in her hands so that the candlelight caught all the brilliant's facets, 'you can get whatever you want there.'

'Do you need some help?' Stephen asked her as she fumbled with the safety clasp.

'Please.'

He rose from his chair and walked round to her side of the table. She handed him the necklace and he fastened it quickly and efficiently, then stooped to plant a delicate, dry kiss on the back of her neck.

'You have a most beautiful nape,' he told her.

She shrugged her shoulders up and giggled at the tickle of his touch and the precision of his vocabulary. It reminded her of the afternoon they had once spent in bed when he had touched every visible part of her body giving its proper Latin name. She had found it intensely erotic at the time, and now the memory was making her wet.

'Shall we go to bed?' she asked him, almost shyly.

'Mmm, yes please,' he said, taking her hand and pulling her to her feet, 'I shall have to bring home diamonds more often.'

The remark jarred. Normally, she would have taken exception to such a comment, and Stephen would have apologized, mortified by his unintentional thoughtlessness. She tensed, then let it go, realizing she felt wounded only because the implications were true. The gift *had* turned her on, and they had not made love since Christmas. Did that mean that her husband now had to buy her sexual favours? She tried to halt the train of thought, to think of Stephen, only Stephen, and the wonderful sex they had always shared, but the moment had passed. The fine gold chain around her neck felt like a garotte tightening as she followed him out of the kitchen and up the stairs, leaving the dining table with its guttering candles, the heady-smelling lilies and the unfinished plate of whore's spaghetti.

On their birthday, Ginger was the first to arrive.

'He's not here yet,' she said, as Pic waved, and approached the banquette at the side of the Palm Lounge she had bagged.

'Happy Birthday, twin!' Pic said, bending to kiss her.

'Happy Birthday,' Ginger replied, somewhat grudgingly, adding, 'although it would be a lot happier if you hadn't invited Daddy. Honestly, Pic, I thought the whole idea of this was that we spent some time alone together for a change.'

'Oh, I'm sorry,' Pic said, smoothing her skirt as she sat down, 'but he seemed so eager to see us, and he never usually remembers. I just felt sorry for him, I suppose.'

'His secretary probably reminded him,' Ginger said, 'it's hardly a difficult date, is it? Especially since it's only once every four years . . . and the bloody Savoy, for heaven's sake. He only likes it here because people recognize him. Why didn't you insist on a loud, smoky bar?'

'Well, it is near to Covent Garden, and it's better than putting up with him all evening. He was threatening to get a box. Thank God we chose ballet and not opera,' Pic defended herself, gently as ever, always the conciliator, never rising to Ginger's temper.

It was futile to go on complaining.

'You look nice,' Ginger told her, changing the subject. Pic was wearing the plain navy suit she had worn to work, but she had tied a very pretty Liberty silk scarf at the neck and, unusually, she was wearing make-up. 'Very grown-up,' Ginger added, thinking how unfair it was that Pic had inherited all their mother's taste and grooming and not even a chromosome of it had been allocated to her.

'So do you,' Pic told her, 'I'm so pleased you wore that.'

Ginger was feeling rather over-dressed in her red velvet frock, and wishing that she had brought something to cover her shoulders. She summoned a passing waiter and ordered a Stolichnaya on the rocks for herself and a glass of white wine for Pic.

'Shall we do presents now?' Pic said.

'What makes you think I've bought you one?' Ginger asked her.

'Oh, that's fine,' Pic began to say, 'I've just got you a couple of very little things . . .' Embarrassed, she handed over one parcel wrapped in pretty floral paper, another with poster-coloured jungle animals marching across it, and a label in the shape of an elephant, which read, 'To Mummy, love from Guy.'

Ginger ripped off the paper. Inside was a black twinset in pure cashmere.

'I never know what clothes you'll like, but I thought I couldn't go wrong with black,' Pic said, almost apologetically, 'although it's a bit of a sombre gift from a seven-month-old.'

'What extraordinary good taste my son has,' Ginger remarked, immediately putting the cardigan around her shoulders, 'must get it from his aunt. It's lovely and just what I needed.' She bent forwards and kissed Pic on the cheek, and then opened her rucksack and began to delve.

'Open the other one, open the other one,' Pic urged her, eager to see her sister's reaction to her other gift.

'OK.' Ginger weighed the parcel in her hands trying to guess what it was. It was surprisingly heavy. She had no idea. She ripped off the paper.

Inside was an antique evening bag made from fringes of jet beads and lined with black watered silk.

'You said you didn't have a handbag to go with . . .' Pic said, pointing at the dress and nervously looking for Ginger's reaction.

'It's just beautiful,' Ginger told her, her face breaking into the broadest smile.

Pic smiled back, thrilled that her special gift had found favour.

Ginger started rummaging in her rucksack again and finally produced two parcels with a flourish, as if she was drawing from a tombola.

'I thought . . . oh, you were joking,' Pic said, blushing, as her sister placed them on the table in front of her. She opened Guy's present first. It was a gold charm in the shape of a teddy bear. The other gift was also a charm, a large cut-topaz in a Victorian setting.

'Oh, they're beautiful,' Pic exclaimed.

Hermione had given them both heavy gold charm bracelets when they were born. Ginger had lost hers when she was ten, but Pic had sensibly kept hers in the bank as Daddy had advised, going with him each year after their birthday to add the latest Victorian charm Hermione donated to the collection. When she was twenty-one, she had decided she was responsible enough to look after it herself, and she had worn the

310

unique bracelet on her wedding day as the something-old element.

She looked at Ginger and saw that there were tears in her eyes.

'I can't take too much credit,' Ginger admitted, 'I found the topaz in her desk. She obviously meant it for you, so I thought I would give it to you on your birthday, as she would have done. I did buy the one from Guy, though!'

'They're both beautiful,' Pic said, reaching out to hold Ginger's hand.

And then their father made his entrance, flanked by two obsequious waiters, whom he was addressing in the over-loud, jocular voice he employed when he wanted people to notice that he had arrived.

'My daughters are seven today!' he told the older waiter with a familiar wink, 'work it out . . . Ah, I see you got it straightaway, leap year, you see. Do you serve champagne to under-age drinkers, ha, ha?'

'Oh, I think we can manage that for you, sir,' the waiter responded, with a kind of servile mateyness. 'And three glasses?'

'Two,' Ginger interrupted, unable to bear the embarrassment any longer. 'I'm drinking vodka.'

'Three,' her father overruled, rewarding her with an indulgent smile, which she found hideously patronizing. She bit her lip.

Pic stood up to kiss him, so she felt obliged to follow suit. She noticed that there were beads of sweat on his forehead, and when he sat down in an armchair he took some time to get his breath back.

Serves you right for all that showing off, she thought, wondering whether he realized how very unattractive the bright navy double-buttoned pin-striped suit made him look. In the muted colours of his country clothes, he sometimes managed to appear rather dashing, in a middle-aged, slightly overweight kind of way, but the City suits that always seemed to exude the odour of stale cigars did nothing for him.

She accepted the glass of champagne with good grace, sensing Pic stiffen on the sofa next to her as it was offered, and not wanting to spoil her sister's evening.

'Where's Edward tonight?' their father asked, picking up his glass with one hand and loosening his tie with the other.

'He's playing squash,' Pic replied.

'Good man,' her father replied automatically.

It was his stock response to any information about his son-in-law. Ginger wondered idly whether he would say just the same thing if Pic had replied that Ed was screwing the arse off a night-club hostess. He probably would, she thought, given that his party colleagues seemed to consider that perfectly acceptable behaviour for married men with family values.

He raised his glass for a toast.

Meekly, both sisters raised theirs too.

'To my heavenly twins,' he pronounced. 'Many happy returns.'

'Thank you,' they both said, wondering about the etiquette of drinking to themselves, but relieved that he had not tried to include the other drinkers in the room in some ghastly tribute.

'Now, I didn't get a chance to buy you anything, but I thought you would rather do it yourselves,' he said, producing two House of Commons envelopes from his pocket. 'Go on, open them.'

There was a piece of writing paper with the House of Commons crest inside, on which he had scribbled, almost illegibly, 'Happy Birthday, love from Daddy', and a cheque, written on his personal account at Coutts for five thousand five hundred pounds.

'Thank you very much,' Ginger said, surprised, unable to resist a peek at Pic's cheque. 'Why do I get more than Pic?' she asked immediately, seeing that her sister's was for only three thousand pounds, and suspecting a trick.

'Tax. I can give you three thousand pounds each tax

free if I backdate it. But I also wanted to give Ginger something for my grandson,' their father explained, looking at Pic and adding, 'Of course, my darling, if you need it, you can have whatever you want too . . . Never be afraid to ask.'

'Daddy, you're too generous!' Pic told him.

'Will you be able to get something you want?' he asked, twinkling at her.

'Oh yes.'

'I shall open an account for Guy with his bit,' Ginger found herself saying, still staring at the cheque in amazement. It wasn't that it was particularly generous. Her father had so much money, he really didn't need to worry about gift-tax allowances, but his financial recognition of Guy was enormously symbolic. She couldn't help being moved.

'Good plan,' her father said.

'And the rest will pay my child-minder for the next six months,' she worked out. 'That is absolutely fantastic . . .' she added, beaming at him.

'Hmm.' Her father did a quick calculation. 'You pay your childminder six thousand pounds a year, and you complain about our party's policies on wages . . . you wouldn't be able to get away with it if we set a minimum wage, you know.'

'If I got tax relief on child care I would be able to pay her more,' Ginger protested, but her heart wasn't really in it. She didn't want to get into a situation where she would be morally obliged to return the cheque to him. Just once, she decided, she would allow him to buy her acquiescence. Because it was her birthday. Because he was trying, she realized, and that was a very difficult thing for him to do.

'I thought you handled that very well,' Pic said to her, as they waved their father's car down the Strand, and hurried towards the Opera House.

'It's the new, mature me,' Ginger said, self-mockingly, 'actually, I think I'll blow the lot on drugs.'

313

'Ginger!'

'Not really! Thanks for arranging that, by the way. Very worth while. I think we should definitely see our father for a birthday celebration every year from now on ... in fact, I'm trying to work out how much it's cost me *not* seeing him before. I don't mean it!' Ginger said, seeing her sister's crestfallen face. 'Actually, he's not such a bad old thing, is he? God, I must have had a lot of champagne!'

They ordered two more glasses for the interval by which time the quantity of alcohol and lack of food had made them both rather giggly.

'I must have a wee,' Ginger said, peering round the Crush Bar, trying to see a sign that said 'Ladies'. She handed Pic her almost empty glass. 'Get us another one.'

'No. We're both pissed,' Pic whispered.

'Oh for fuck's sake, if you can't be pissed on your birthday ...'

'OK, OK,' Pic said hastily, just to shut her up. There was a good deal of chatter in the high-ceilinged room, but Ginger's expletives seemed to be bouncing off the chandeliers.

The five-minute bell rang.

'Oh do hurry,' Pic told her.

When she returned the lights were going down and they had to climb over people's legs to get to their seats. Ginger couldn't stop herself giggling. There were several shushes and hisses around them.

'Have you got a pen?' Pic whispered.

'What?'

'Shush.'

'Never mind.'

'What?'

'SHUSH!'

Terrified of being thrown out, they huddled down in their seats and watched the second half of the ballet in silence.

'What did you say?' Ginger asked her when the

lights came up and they had applauded enthusiastically.

'I wanted to write you a message,' Pic said, putting on her coat.

'Why?'

'So we wouldn't have to whisper.'

'I know *why*, I meant what message . . .' said Ginger, following her up the steps to the exit.

'Because somebody I didn't know came up to me while you were in the loo and said, "Hello, Ginger!" and I think it was—' She turned round and stopped talking mid-sentence as she saw who was on the steps behind her sister.

There was a tap on her shoulder. 'Hello, Ginger.'

Ginger turned round.

'Hello, Charlie,' she said, and then, thinking on her feet, 'I gather you've already met my sister?'

'I thought it was bad enough that there was one of you in the world, let alone two,' Charlie said teasingly.

'Oh, don't worry, Pic's not at all like me,' Ginger told him.

It seemed such a contrary thing for her to say, standing as she was, next to someone with an identical face and shape, that he laughed loudly.

'Pic?' he said.

'Short for Patricia,' Ginger informed him, 'my father was raised on Beatrix Potter and he thought it would be amusing to nickname us Ginger and Pickles, you see.'

'How charmingly English of him,' said Charlie's companion, a rather handsome middle-aged man with an American accent.

Ginger smiled at him. 'You didn't have to grow up with it,' she said.

'Well, I suppose it's better than Tabitha Twitchit . . . or Jemima Puddle-duck,' Charlie interjected, thinking of other Beatrix Potter names, 'or Flopsy and Mopsy . . .' he added as they walked down the stairs together to the foyer.

Pic laughed politely, as if it was the first time she had heard someone say that.

Ginger asked the American which part of the States he was from.

'What are you up to now?' Charlie said, as they stepped out into the street, the wintry chill of the evening hitting their faces like a slap.

'We're going to eat,' Ginger told him shortly.

'Have you booked somewhere?' Charlie asked.

'No,' said Pic straightaway, then seeing Ginger's expression, added quickly, 'unless you did, Ginger . . . ?'

Ginger couldn't think quickly enough.

'Come and have supper with us at my club,' Charlie suggested immediately.

'It's our birthday . . .' Ginger protested.

'Well, I'm sure they'll have some sort of cake, if that's what you're worried about.'

Pic laughed again. Ginger wished she would stop encouraging him. Charlie Prince had a big enough idea of his own wit, without Pic's support. She glowered at her. Pic held her look, defiantly making it clear that she wanted to accept Charlie's invitation. Perhaps she fancied an evening with two rather delectable-looking men, Ginger thought, softening a little. After all, Pic didn't get out much, and the kind of media chat that Ginger found tedious was probably quite exciting for her.

'All right then,' she caved in, hissing as the men strolled off ahead of them down Floral Street, 'You owe me one for this.'

'Oh don't be such an idiot,' Pic replied, uncharacteristically sharply.

They went to the club where Robert had held his Christmas party and the meal was more fun than she had expected. The American was an independent financier whom Charlie was trying to entice into backing one of his movie projects. Ginger intuited quite soon after they sat down that the meeting was very important for Charlie. Having made the extravagant gesture of inviting the twins to join them, he was now slightly anxious in case they began to rock the boat on the deal he was on the point of clinching. It gave Ginger a tremendous sense of power, but one that she resisted exploiting, because she found Charlie's vulnerability in the situation amusingly touching.

As they left the club, Charlie flagged down a cab and gave the driver his firm's account number. 'Charge it to me,' he ordered, kissing Pic on the cheek, and then turning to say goodbye to Ginger. 'I can't believe you didn't tell me you had a twin,' he scolded her, 'especially such a beautiful one.'

What difference would it have made, she wanted to ask. Or maybe he was one of those men who got turned on at the idea of going to bed with both of them. They had encountered quite a few of them. No, she decided, he was only trying to be charming, and it was late, so she would let him have the last word. They both looked at each other for a second, then she turned to get into the cab, and he grabbed her hand and kissed it. She closed the door, then she and Pic twisted round and waved as the cab roared off down Old Compton Street.

'He's nice,' Pic said, facing frontwards again.

'Well, only if you fed him the right line so that he could recount one of his many "amusing" anecdotes ... I thought he was pathetic actually, and I didn't believe for a second that he had met Jackie O,' she said, bitchily.

'Not Aaron, Charlie,' Pic replied.

'Very charming, yes,' Ginger said, pretending to stare at something very interesting just outside her window. 'I couldn't believe the way you were flirting with him, as a matter of fact, and all his comments about how beautiful you were, wasn't that a bit over the top?'

'Honestly,' Pic said impatiently, 'you are unbelievably thick at times! He was only using me as a kind of conduit. He was really flirting with you, trying to tell you that you were beautiful without actually saying it. I mean, for God's sake, we look just the same!'

'You seemed to be enjoying it,' Ginger remarked rather sourly.

'I was basking in your reflected glory,' Pic said, 'and he is rather a dish, so why shouldn't I? Anyway, I think he's completely smitten.'

'Oh don't be ridiculous,' Ginger said, hoping that her sister couldn't see in the darkness of the cab how red she had gone.

'I'm not being ridiculous. I don't see why you have such a problem. He seems perfect for you. He's sparkling and clever and almost as opinionated as you are—'

'Yes, but you're forgetting one thing,' Ginger interrupted, 'Lucretia.'

'But do you *really* know that they're together? She wasn't there tonight. He didn't mention her once. If they're so close, then why wasn't she roped in to charm the pants off Aaron?'

Ginger had a reason instantly. 'Well, Aaron was gay for a start.'

'Yes, but gay men like dining with beautiful women, don't they?'

'Oh God, you don't think Charlie's gay, do you?' Ginger suddenly asked.

'For heaven's sake,' said Pic, 'one minute you can't have anything to do with him because he's got another woman, not that that has ever stopped you before, the next, he's out of the question because he's gay. Of course he's not gay. You should see the way he looks at you.'

'He was only grateful that we were entertaining Aaron. I should have known there was no such thing as a free birthday supper.'

'Don't be such a grouch,' Pic said as the cab pulled

318

up outside her house. 'I bet you a pound he'll call you tomorrow.'

'A pound – you must be very confident! I don't care if he does,' Ginger said, wishing that Pic would just shut up and get out of the cab.

'I think you do!' Pic replied in a sing-song voice, kissing her.

'I must remember never to let you drink champagne again,' Ginger told her affectionately, 'it makes you turn into a kind of posh version of Cilla Black. Now go and have a wonderful birthday fuck with your husband and leave me alone!'

Chapter 9

MARCH

Ginger's phone buzzed. She jumped, as she had each time it had rung, silently swearing at Pic for implanting in her head the idea that Charlie might ring. She said, 'Hello?' out loud a couple of times, practising a bored, slightly indifferent voice, before picking up the receiver. It wouldn't do to have him think she was waiting for his call.

'Hello?' Breezy, busy, I'm-in-the-middle-of-something-actually. She congratulated herself on the perfectly pitched tone of her answer.

'Ginger? It's Alison. How are you?'

'Oh, fine,' Ginger replied, disappointed, 'you?'

'Fine, listen, I was really calling about work . . .' In the background, keyboards rattled and phones rang as if to confirm her point. '. . . I've had this idea for a regular feature – well, I say idea, more a shameless rip-off of a couple of our competitors' columns that I've kind of combined. I'm calling it "Home Cooking".' Alison spoke much more rapidly than she usually did, utterly confident in the role of magazine editor. 'Here's the pitch: two relatives, preferably the provider and the consumer, talk about a favourite family dish and then we have the recipe. I was wondering . . . ?' She let Ginger's imagination finish the rest of the sentence.

'Me and Pic? Oh, you mean me and my father,' Ginger said, 'Umm, I don't think it would work, actually. Cook always did the cooking, you see. Anyway he'd have to make it into a photo-opportunity: Sir James Prospect triumphantly holding up a great bloody slice of British beef, dripping with as much BSE and E-coli as possible, challenging those impertinent little micro-organisms to be brave enough to hurt him.'

Alison laughed.

'The real reason is, I don't really want to ask him any favours right now. There's a delicate kind of cease-fire in operation at the moment,' Ginger explained, 'I do think it's a good idea, though,' she added, trying to be helpful, 'except I would call it "Like Momma Used to Make".'

'That's good,' Alison said, thinking how quick Ginger was with words, and scribbling down her suggestion, 'that *is* good. Listen, you don't have any other suggestions for famous parents and children?'

'I suppose you could ask Carol Thatcher what Maggie used to make – gruel, I should think, whatever gruel is. They were always eating it in Dickens and I never knew, did you? I thought it was a kind of cross between vegetable scrapings and washing-up water . . .' she mused. 'Then there's all the usual suspects . . .' She trotted out the names of famous acting and writing dynasties.

'Hey, slow down . . . that's great,' Alison said, 'listen, if you ever fancy a job as a researcher . . .'

'Watch it, I might take you up on that,' Ginger said with a laugh, trying to suppress an incipient fantasy about what it would be like to work for a newspaper, and wondering why it was that everyone else's job seemed more attractive than her own. 'How are you, anyway?' she asked.

'I'm fine, thanks,' Alison said.

'And Ben?'

'He's fine too. What about Guy? How is the

321

arrangement working?' Alison found she couldn't bring herself to say Lia's name.

'Very well. Of course, I miss him, but he's in very good hands. Lia is fantastic with children, isn't she? I can see her with a great brood, can't you, like the woman who lived in a shoe?'

'I suppose so,' Alison replied, unable to resist asking, 'Is she thinking of having more, then?'

As soon as she had said it, she realized she did not want to know the answer.

'Oh, I expect so, don't you?' Ginger replied, 'I really envy her being able to have them all at once. I mean, I know it's hard to have lots of young ones together, but then you've got that bit over with and you can enjoy them growing up. The way my life is going, Guy'll be twenty before he gets a brother or sister. What about you?'

There was a pause, then Alison replied, as if she had only just heard her question, 'Me? Oh God, no, never again . . . Listen, I must run, but let's catch up soon.'

Ginger had to race to get 'Bye!' in before she hung up.

'You're not getting a coke habit, are you?' Ramona asked when Alison returned from the Ladies.

Alison stared at her, bewildered.

'It's just that you've been to the loo at least six times this morning, and whenever you come back to your desk, you've got red eyes and you're sniffing.'

'No,' Alison said, 'I'm just a bit under the weather.'

'Is there anything I can do?' Ramona said kindly. She obviously knew that Alison had been crying. 'Do you think you're depressed again?'

'No,' Alison said, 'thanks, but I don't want to talk about it.'

'OK,' Ramona agreed, 'but you know where I am, if you need me.'

'Thanks,' Alison repeated and, seeing Ramona's face fall, she added, 'You're a good friend . . . I'm sorry, but this is something I kind of have to work out by myself.'

'OK, OK,' Ramona smiled and went back to her work.

'Hey!' she said, after a few minutes' silence, 'would a weekend in Paris help?'

Alison laughed. 'What do you mean?' she asked, seeing that Ramona was about to make a proposal.

'I want a piece about the young British designers and how they're taking over the trad old fashion houses. We've had all the stuff about Britain leading the world in fashion, London being the new Paris, and all that, but we get that every year around London Fashion Week. I want something about Paris being the new London, and I want something that goes beyond the clichés, maybe as much as three thousand words . . . what do you say?'

'It's a good idea,' Alison said.

'But would you like to do it? You're always saying you'd like to write again. I know it's fashion, but I'm throwing in expenses for a spring break in the world's most romantic city. When's Stephen's next weekend off?'

'I'll think about it,' Alison replied. Ramona loved to solve people's problems so much that it was often difficult to resist getting swept along in her generosity.

'Well, not too long,' Ramona warned.

'No, I'll think about it at lunch,' Alison assured her.

Spring had arrived, suddenly, and it was as if someone had switched on the light after the long, gloomy winter. There was real warmth in the sun, and trees that she had not even noticed existed were sprouting lime-green leaves, a colour so bright against the clear blue sky it almost looked artificial, like the fluorescent citrus colours that were beginning to appear in the shops for the summer's beach gear.

It was on such a day as this, she thought, that she had married Stephen in St Bride's Church off Fleet Street. The austere church with its tall plain glass windows had been radiant with sunlight, and in their wedding photograph they were smiling at the camera with a passing red double-decker bus and the old *Daily Telegraph* clock in the background. It was a very urban setting. A journalist's wedding in the journalists' church. She was proud of the triumph it represented over her mother, who would have done anything, even hired a pastel-painted backdrop, she thought, to have had her daughter pictured in a white candy-floss dress under the lych-gate of a country church.

Alison had worn a floor-length gown of ivory silk with no decoration except a length of soft chiffon that made a gauzy stole about her bare shoulders and was held in place by a cluster of five pale gold rosebuds. She had carried a small, tight bunch of similar roses as she strode down the aisle with the confidence of a woman who knows she looks the best she has ever done. Stephen's eyes had sparkled with appreciation as she drew near.

Alison crossed the road to the sunny side of the street, and started walking briskly in the direction of the Thames, stopping at the French pâtisserie opposite the tube station to buy a hot, delicious-smelling croissant, filled with smoked ham and gruyère, and a polystyrene tumbler of *cappuccino*.

The wedding had been perfect, she remembered, and the honeymoon heavenly. She had left it up to Stephen to choose, partly because she had organized every other bit of the ceremony and was fed up with deposits, decisions, fittings and confirmations, partly because the small, bourgeois part of her that had wanted a traditional wedding, also wanted to be surprised by her new husband's choice. But when the day drew near, she had not been able to resist guessing where they were going. Stephen had played his role perfectly, she recalled, shrugging when she asked him what she should take to wear, and throwing her completely off the scent by leaving a pocket Italian dictionary next to his bed one evening when she was staying at his flat.

When they arrived in their suite at the Hilton Heathrow after the reception, there was a brand new suitcase sitting in the centre of the room, tied with a broad white ribbon, her name carefully printed on the address label. Even then, he had refused to let her open it, or to reveal their destination. It was only as they walked through the miles of passageway towards the departure gate that she discovered that they were heading for a tiny privately owned island in the Caribbean. And he only told her then, because he realized that Florida, the destination on the flight announcement board, where they would be making the connection, would be a slight anticlimax for her after all the mystery.

It does not get better than this, she had thought, completely at peace with the regular rhythm of her own breathing, as they were snorkelling one afternoon in crystal-clear water that shimmered with the movement of a million jewelled fish. But as they surfaced and waded out of the water, the sounds of the terrestrial world suddenly loud around them, she had shivered with a kind of sinking premonition that if life could not be better, it could only be worse. She had reached for Stephen's hand to pull her through the shallows.

In a couple of months, it would be their anniversary. Five years. She wished she could truly think, five happy years, the best five years of her life. But they had not been. After the honeymoon, there had been the excitement of buying a house together and decorating it, and after that, everything merged into a blur of attempts to get pregnant.

At first, making love without contraception had been gloriously exhilarating. It had made sex more emotional. They were doing something profound together, and the depth of trust it required seemed to take her to the very edge of her being, a place where there were no words.

There was only the slightest catch of disappointment in her chest when she bled the first month. The second, a little irritation. She realized she was spoilt, unused to not getting exactly what she wanted, when she wanted it. The third time, she bought an ovulation prediction kit. The fourth, she began to worry. After that, every month rolled into the next. Sex became something they had to do, whether they felt like it or not, on the right days. If Stephen was working, she went to the hospital in her lunch-hour hoping to catch him between operations so they could fuck quickly on his consulting-room floor, the door locked, the blind on the door pulled down, but everyone outside knowing exactly what they were doing. Before they were married, it might have been a turn-on. Now it was perfunctory and humiliating. But not as humiliating as the injections administered each morning during the *in vitro* cycle, the operation to extract her eggs, his masturbation to fertilize them. The meeting of their genes, that extraordinary explosion of life that she had imagined in the beginning with such erotic effect, would now take place under a microscope, with someone else looking.

Conception had become a goal in itself. Swept along by her determination to succeed, she had long ceased to think of the bigger goal, the child they would produce. They had never really talked about it, frightened to discuss what might elude them. Talking about sex became a no-go area, so did sex for the sake of sex.

Perhaps, she thought as she reached the riverbank, attempting to make sense of her treachery, that was why she had started an affair. No, she thought, sitting on some steps that led down to the river, hearing the wash of a passing pleasure boat lap against the ancient stone, and the faint drone of the captain's commentary wafting across on the fluctuating breeze. There was no point in trying to excuse it like that. Sex had been fine with Stephen since the baby was born. Infrequent, maybe, but not mechanical and passionless as it had become before. So, it wasn't that. She was having an affair because she loved Neil. She had always loved Neil. And he loved her. When he had not called for several weeks, she had almost been glad that he had been brave enough to take responsibility for finishing it. But now he had called again, wanting to see her and she had agreed, and she didn't know what she was going to do.

Opening her paper carrier bag, she pulled out a flake of croissant between forefinger and thumb. They never tasted as wonderful as they smelt. She popped the top off the cup and sipped the *cappuccino* hesitantly, wondering how it could be that the chocolate-flecked froth was always cold, whilst the liquid underneath remained scalding.

The sound of lapping water brought back a memory of the afternoon she had sat drinking lemonade beside the same river, in Richmond, with Lia. She was sure there was an ancient Greek saying that you never sat beside the same river twice, and that afternoon seemed so long ago, it was almost like another life. A life where things were uncomplicated. From what Ginger had said this morning, at least Lia sounded happy. The affair wasn't affecting her. Stop it. Alison told herself. Just stop it.

She glanced at her watch. In five minutes she would have to head back to the office again, into the noise. There was never any time, never a quiet moment for herself. If she only had time for her brain to rest, it might have a chance of attaining once again the purity of thought, the simplicity of truth that she had felt in the silence under the Caribbean Sea. And if she achieved that then she would know what to do.

'I will do that piece for you,' she told Ramona when she returned to the office, 'but I'll go alone. I need to spend some time on my own.'

'Fine,' Ramona said. 'Great. You're right, men always get in the way when you're shopping.'

'Did you manage to find somewhere to put your bike?' Charlie asked, greeting Ginger with a kiss on each cheek at the bottom of the stairs.

The screening theatre was situated in a basement on a street that led from Soho to Oxford Street. Ginger was surprised by how shabby the entrance looked. She had stood outside for several seconds wondering whether this could really be the right address, or whether the invitation had, after all, been just an elaborate joke.

By the time Charlie finally rang, not the next day, as Pic had predicted, nor even the day after, Ginger had long since abandoned her pause-and-answer strategy, finding that all the throat clearance was giving her mild laryngitis. Her boss had just asked her to make coffee for three and she had her hands full of cups, so she wasn't in the best mood, and had simply grabbed the receiver and shouted, 'Yes?'

'Er, Ginger?' Charlie had asked.

'Yes?' still impatient.

'Bad moment?'

'Yes,' slightly mollified.

'Shall I ring back?'

She didn't want to hang around waiting another week wondering whether he would call. 'No, *dígame*,' she said.

'I was wondering whether you'd like to come to a screening?' he had asked.

'Sure, when?'

'Next Tuesday?'

'No can do,' Ginger said, hating herself for using

idiotic hip phrases that people like Charlie always used. 'Pic only does baby-sitting on Fridays.'

'Well, there's one on Friday too,' Charlie said.

'OK, then,' she had said, holding the receiver between her shoulder and chin, and reaching for a biro to note down the address. She hadn't even asked what was going to be screened.

'I didn't bring my bike, actually,' Ginger now explained as he indicated the way downstairs, 'I thought there might be alcohol. There often is at screenings,' she told him knowledgeably, 'and I don't drink and drive.'

'Very sensible,' Charlie said, ushering her into the room.

It was cold, dark and dank, and it smelt of damp, and ash trodden into the carpet from a previous press screening. There was no-one else in the room, only a projectionist in a box behind the back row.

'Oh, am I early?' Ginger asked.

'No,' Charlie said, waving at a trestle table that had been set up with a white cloth, a silver bucket containing ice and a bottle of Bollinger, and two champagne flutes. He opened the bottle with just the right amount of a pop, and poured her a glass. Then he waved at the rows of seats, indicating that she could sit anywhere she liked. She sat down in the front row. Charlie stood in front of the screen and began to make a speech.

'Ladies and gentlemen, before we begin tonight's screening, I'd like to say a word or two about its origins,' he began, as if he were the master of ceremonies at the Oscars. 'We're very happy to have here tonight the person without whom I can truly say that this show would never have happened. She's a talented little lady, and I'd like you to give a huge round of applause to Miss Ginger Prospect.' He waved his hand at the projectionist.

From the speakers came a huge blast of pre-recorded applause.

Ginger couldn't help smiling,

'And now, I hope you'll sit back and enjoy *If You Can't Stand the Heat . . .*'

The lights went down, Charlie grabbed the bottle of champagne and came to sit next to her, ducking his head down to avoid his shadow falling on the screen.

There was a catchy theme tune and bright, jazzy graphics, more applause, which died down as the recording opened in a studio built to look like two kitchens, with oversized illuminated plastic onions, chillies, and fruit dangling from the ceiling.

Ginger's concept had been a hands-on food quiz, with some quiz-type questions as well as blindfolded tastings and practical tasks for the celebrity contestants, like making mayonnaise in two minutes, or poaching an egg. She had to admit that Charlie's production company had really brought her idea to life. The show was fun and informative without being patronizing, and, the essential ingredient, it gave people ample opportunity to make fools of themselves. She could see it would be a big ratings success, and she felt peculiarly proud of herself and, even more oddly, grateful to Charlie for realizing her idea.

In the darkness, she could feel his eyes watching the side of her face for her reaction, and she could sense him relax in the seat beside her as she smiled, even laughed once or twice, at the jokes. As the host signed off at the end of the show, she turned to congratulate Charlie, but he nudged her arm, hard.

'No, look, this is the best bit coming up,' he said, as the credits began to roll, and after the cameramen, designers, production assistants, came the phrase: *Based on an idea by Ginger Prospect.*

It was the first time she had ever seen her name as it were in lights and she was thrilled. 'Now you'll have to pay me a format fee,' she whispered.

'I think we might find a way of giving you a percentage of the format fee,' Charlie replied, ever a businessman.

Afterwards, he took her to his club, and the maître d' greeted her as if they were old friends, even though it was only the third time she had been there. They drank more champagne and she began to feel almost euphoric. As they sat down to eat, she told Charlie how much she had enjoyed the screening. He smiled indulgently at her. It was at least the sixth time she had said it.

'And I still can't persuade you to work for me?' he said.

'No,' she said, hoping that he wouldn't ask her why, since she had temporarily forgotten what her objection was.

'Well, if I can't see more of you during the week, how about one weekend?' Charlie asked.

Perhaps Pic was right, she thought, and he wanted a relationship. The champagne whirred her brain round at top speed, like a waltzer in a fairground.

'Oh no, weekends are for Guy,' she said, adding quickly, 'my son.'

'Well, I could come and take you out for the day . . . I love children,' he suggested.

'Do you?' She couldn't disguise the surprise in her voice.

'Yes. I was the oldest of five boys, so I've had a lot of experience with little fellas.'

Guy has five uncles, Ginger calculated, and she had been feeling guilty for denying him the presence of a man in his life!

'Oh hello!' Ginger greeted the waiter as he came to take their order, knowing that she knew him, even though his dour face showed not the slightest sign of recognition. Then a hideous memory of drunken flirting passed through her mind. Mickey something, she thought he was called.

'Now, have you decided?' Charlie was asking her.

'Hamburger, I think,' she replied, without raising her eyes from the menu.

'Good choice,' Charlie said, ordering two, rare.

He clinked his glass against hers.

The champagne roller-coaster tipped over its summit and was plummeting downwards. Whatever Charlie wanted, and she couldn't work out what it was right now, it certainly wasn't commitment. He wouldn't like children nearly so much if he were to discover that he had a son. Even if they were to start a relationship, and she couldn't think how that could happen with the Lucretia question still out there somewhere, like a sleeping scorpion, then, with her track record, it was bound to last only a few weeks, or months at the most, and she had to protect Guy from disappointment.

The roller-coaster reached the bottom and rattled along the ground for a while as she munched her chips.

'Can I ask what the problem is?' Charlie said, bewildered by her sudden change of mood, leaning forward so that he could not be overheard.

'There's no problem,' she lied, not very convincingly.

'Why won't you go out with me then?' he demanded.

Her heart jumped. Go out with me. Do you mean just for the day, or for a while longer, she wanted to ask him.

'Because of Lucretia,' she said, on the spur of the moment.

'What the hell has she got to do with it?' he asked, throwing himself back in his chair, exasperated by her excuses.

'You tell me,' Ginger replied, levelly.

'Well, it's true that Lucretia and I had a brief relationship at Oxford, if that's what you're referring to,' Charlie said, 'but that was before she discovered that she preferred women, and before I discovered that I preferred women who didn't smoke cigars in bed. We could never be business partners and sleep together . . . or is it the business partner bit that you're objecting to?'

'No, no, not at all,' Ginger said, wanting to ask all sorts of questions. Was it public knowledge that Lucretia was a lesbian? If so, why hadn't Robert told her? Why did she believe him? Surely Charlie wasn't such a rogue that he would lie about something like that?

The roller-coaster was cranking upwards again. Charlie was so very handsome, sitting there staring at her with great brown eager eyes like one of Mummy's spaniels. What could be the harm in spending an afternoon with him? Chances were he'd pay for a smashing lunch. Guy was far too young at the moment to form an attachment to him, so what was holding her back? Suddenly she thought of the perfect, neutral venue.

'Why don't you come and watch the boat race with us? I need someone who can hoist Guy on his shoulders so that he can see above the crowds,' she said.

Charlie laughed loudly. 'OK,' he said, 'it's a date . . .'

It was almost time.

Neil took a long draught of his lager. He was going to meet her and finish it once and for all. It sounded simple enough in the abstract, but as the hour drew nearer, and nervous adrenalin was churning in his stomach, he could feel himself growing weaker.

I gave up for a month, he thought, grimly, shaking a cigarette out of the packet he had just bought. He wasn't even pretending to have stopped smoking now, telling anyone who asked that it was the pressure of the imminent Ofsted inspection getting to him, but knowing that he was not strong enough to give up two things at once. Alison and Marlboro. The addiction to Alison manipulated his brain even more furtively and ingeniously than the nicotine.

He had decided on Valentine's Day that he could not go on. The deceit was making him ill and it had been easy enough not to pick up the phone for the first few days, especially since he was sure that she would not ring him. Even if she knew which school he worked at, and he wasn't sure that she had ever asked, she wouldn't risk ringing there. It wasn't her style. So, all he had to do was hold out. Just say no. This was the cold turkey bit. Soon, it would get better.

He was right about her not calling, but not about it getting better. It didn't. He had nightmares about running in to her in Waitrose. A clash of shopping trolleys, an exchange of guilty looks, their partners standing beside them, and knowing. Then, walking along the tow-path beside the river with Lia one Sunday afternoon, he thought he saw her up in front of them, her husband pushing the pram. He slowed their pace, pretending to be interested in the boats, squatting beside Anouska's buggy, pointing at the swans. Straightening up, he saw to his horror that the family ahead had sat down on a bench. He would have to pass them. His legs turned to jelly. It was only when they drew nearer that he saw it wasn't her. The woman was shorter, much shorter. He must have been hallucinating.

He began to stay in at weekends. Lia went out by herself, looking at him anxiously, not quite daring to ask what was wrong, but knowing that there was something. He was still lying to her, the treacherous addiction whispered inside him, there was only a difference of degree. It was sophistry to think that this way was less dishonest. And the phone was like a magnet, drawing him across the room.

He tried diversionary tactics. Gardening. It had always absorbed him in times of crisis. Like the autumn after Alison went to college, when he had hacked all the roses in the park to the ground, swept up the leaves, paper-dry after the hottest summer on

334

record, daily, hourly even, and planted hundreds of bulbs in the well-turned borders, bulbs that hid all winter, then sprang to life in bursts of gold and white the next spring.

He put himself to work on their long narrow back garden, weeding and clearing away the debris of winter. The bedding plants he bought and planted optimistically early died in a sharp frost, but the spring bulbs appeared, and flowered as usual, but even they reminded him of missing her.

The words of 'These Foolish Things', recalled after twenty years by their exchange of Valentine messages, now refused to be forgotten again. They reverberated in his head, taunting him.

First daffodils and long excited cables . . .

Yes, he remembered, with a flood of bitterness, after she left, the daffodils had arrived as usual, but not the cables. She had not phoned, nor sent a letter, not even a postcard with a red double-decker bus on it saying she was doing OK in the Smoke, but that they were finished. He could almost have understood it if she had told him she had found another boy, a student with a scarf, who would talk about plays and books and things she liked. It would have been hard, but fair enough, at least he would have known. But it was as if he had ceased to exist. He had written to her at college, persuading himself when he received no reply that the letters were going astray. It was a big place, after all. When he had finally tracked down her parents' phone number, at their new home by the sea, her mother had spoken to him as if he were a pariah, and ordered him never to call there again.

Now Alison claimed that she had always loved him, and spoke of their separation as if it had been just as painful for her. And the strange thing was, he believed her. So what had happened, then? He had to know why he had spent twenty years feeling as if some part of his capacity to love had been amputated.

335

He only wanted it resolved, he told himself, stubbing out his cigarette. Finished. So that he could start afresh and get on with his life.

It was almost time.

He let himself into the flat. She had cut a key for him, but he still preferred to wait for her in the pub. It didn't feel right being there on his own. He sat down on the sofa and opened his *Evening Standard*. It was like being in a dentist's waiting room, only minutes away from the drill. Then, before he had time to rehearse the speech in his head again, he saw, through the front window, her legs stepping down the cast-iron steps from the street, and her face changing suddenly when she caught sight of him from an austere frown to a smile of such innocent joy, it took twenty years off her age, and made him want to hug and kiss and protect her.

He forced himself to remain seated.

'I'm sorry . . . it's ridiculous when I only have to come a mile or two, and you travel all the way across town . . .' she apologized for her late arrival, throwing her handbag onto the table, kicking off her smart black shoes and jumping onto his lap, facing him.

She smoothed his hair back from his face, belatedly noticing his stiff, ungiving posture. 'What's up?'

'Nothing,' he said.

She bent her head and kissed him. He tried not to respond, but it was impossible, with her legs straddling him, her bottom on his thighs.

'We have to talk,' he mumbled between kisses.

'Later. I've missed you,' she said firmly, taking his hand, pulling him to his feet, leading him to the bedroom.

Afterwards, they lay beside each other, smoking.

'When I'm here with you, I feel as if I've come home. I've never felt that before. I always hated home . . .' She laughed. 'Do you know what I mean?'

336

She had put into words exactly what he had been feeling. The flat was a safe place when she was here with him. However much he had prepared himself beforehand, he found that here, lying beside her, all the guilt and anxiety he felt in the outside world simply evaporated, and he had to struggle to pinpoint exactly why he had been worried. It was the most natural thing in the world to make love to her, and to be together in bed, chatting. It felt as if this was what they had been created to do. He tried to remind himself of Lia and Anouska, but they were distant figures and he was numb to their pain.

'How do you deal with the guilt?' he asked her, quietly.

She turned to look at him, unsure that she had heard what he said. They did not discuss their partners. They were crossing into new territory.

'I tell myself that I'm not hurting anyone if they don't know,' she said finally.

It was pretty weak, she already knew that, but it sounded so much weaker out loud.

'But Stephen,' he said hesitantly, 'wouldn't he be angry, if he knew?'

'Angry?' She considered her answer. 'No, I think he would be sad.'

Hearing the words made her feel sad too. She thought of Stephen's face when he saw her walking towards him between the choirs of St Bride's. He had been so sure of her. She had not lived up to his devotion.

'Sometimes, I watch them,' she went on softly, her head on the same pillow as his, speaking against his neck, 'playing together, perfectly happy together . . . Stephen is brilliant at making up games out of the simplest things, he can do all that Peepo stuff. I never knew that,' she sighed, pulling back her head to look closely at Neil, and taking a deep breath, 'and I wonder what would happen if I had to choose . . .'

She was brave, he realized, braver than he was, and

cleverer. She was daring to pose the ultimate question, straightaway, up front, and yet to phrase it so that he could veer away if he wanted to. He didn't want to. The conversation had begun. He could not stop it now.

'Lia wants another child,' he said after a pause, 'and I'm not sure I do. It doesn't seem fair to let her go on hoping—'

'Stop,' she interrupted him, quietly, 'you're doing what I did at first. You're trying to find a way of blaming them for something that is just to do with us.'

Her eyes were fiery with honesty, and he felt humbled by her perceptiveness.

They both fell silent for several minutes.

'Were you happy until you met me again?' Alison asked him finally.

He didn't need to think about it.

'Yes, very,' he said, and saw her face fall.

She had wanted him to say no, he realized.

'Not as happy as I am here with you,' he added quickly. 'How about you?'

'I wasn't,' she admitted. 'It wasn't anything to do with Stephen. Stephen alleviated the problem, he didn't cause it.'

'What caused it, then?' he asked.

'I don't know,' she said, drumming her fingers on the mattress, looking at the ceiling, 'perhaps just the process of ageing. That awful point when you realize that this is it. All that time you spent dreaming about the life you would have, and then you have it, and it doesn't seem so wonderful . . .'

She looked at him again and saw he was listening, trying to understand what she was saying, but finding the concepts alien. He didn't talk in the language of therapy, as she and all her friends did. He wasn't used to discussing his feelings.

'Did you get the life you wanted, then?' he asked simply.

'Well, that's what I'm saying,' she explained

338

elliptically. 'I gave up everything I had for a dream of something else, and then I got the something else and I think I would have preferred what I had . . .'

Finally he understood.

'Me?' he asked, his eyebrows raised, pointing at himself like a child.

'Yes, you,' she said fondly, running her forefinger over his sternum.

'Is that why you left me?' He sat up in bed, as if he had just seen something in the shadows on the other side of the room. It was all becoming clear.

'I needed space . . . I needed to see what there was for me,' she said, hurrying after the easy opportunity he had given her to justify herself. All of it was true, she told herself. 'I didn't want to settle so young . . .'

'But why didn't you tell me?' he asked her.

Deftly, she turned the question back to him. 'Would you have understood?'

'Maybe not,' he said resignedly, looking down at the checks on the duvet cover, 'but you never even gave me a chance, did you?'

'I don't know why I didn't,' she said, putting her arm around his back, knowing he would not ask her again, and hating herself for lying to him.

He sat for a long time with his back to her. Then he shook his head, as if shaking off a bad dream, and leant forward, picking up a discarded stocking from the end of the bed.

'*Silk stockings thrown aside . . .*' he said.

'Oh, sing it, please sing it . . .' she pleaded.

'That bloody song,' he chuckled, 'you know how once you remember something, you can't think of anything else? I just can't get rid of it . . .'

He sang it to her, the whole way through, and she lay back in the pillows, treasuring the moment.

'It's all about a dirty weekend in Paris, I realized,' he said when he came to the end of the last verse. 'They're having an affair . . . I never thought about the words before.'

'I'm going to Paris for a long weekend, the first one in April,' she said.

'Lucky you!' He sounded unimpressed.

'D'you want to come?' she asked him, a solution to everything suddenly occurring to her.

'What do you mean?' he asked suspiciously.

'Come with me,' she said, sitting up cross-legged on the bed. 'Look, we can't keep meeting in this place, trying to give each other up. It's just a waste of time and it's never going to work, until the day that one of us gets found out, and that'll be ugly. That's not the right way to do it, is it?' She leaned forward, eager for his support.

'No,' he agreed, still cautious.

'Look, this way we're not giving it a chance.' The echo of his earlier words hung uncomfortably in the air.

He said nothing.

'We never spend any time together. Don't you see? Either we're going to be together, or we're not. If we are, then we're going to have to make some horrible decisions about Stephen and Lia and our children, but we're never going to know if we meet for the occasional hour just to fuck, are we?'

She saw him wince at the word fuck. He was such a traditional old romantic.

'Anyway, I can't say I'm decorating this place forever,' she added, as if that sealed the matter.

'And I can't go on giving the Ofsted inspection as my excuse for working late. It happens after Easter,' he pitched in.

'Well, then,' she said, clapping her hands together, as if it were a *fait accompli.*

'Hang on — did you plan this?'

She realized that he hated being manipulated. She was overwhelming him, expecting him to read her mind, to grab her half-baked ideas and run with them. She slowed down.

'No,' she said, 'actually, I've got to do an article. I

planned to go by myself, to sort everything out in my head, but now it seems so obvious . . . it seems almost as if it was planned for us . . .'

'Hey, before we get totally carried away, haven't you forgotten something?' He tried to interject some sense into the conversation, but he was as excited as he could see she was. The fact that he had said 'we' gave it away. He wanted to go.

She looked at him quizzically. How dare you challenge the wisdom of my idea, her expression seemed to say. It made him laugh.

'What?' she asked.

'You have the demeanour of a duchess,' he told her, 'when you're after your own way.'

She blushed, embarrassed.

'I'm a teacher, remember? I can't just go off to Paris to "do an article",' he mocked the casualness of her remark.

'Well, couldn't you say there was a school trip? They do still have school trips these days, don't they?' She was thinking on her feet. There must be a way.

'I don't like lying,' he protested, ineffectually.

'Oh God, I'll book us somewhere lovely, and we can make love all day and eat wonderful food and talk and walk by the Seine at twilight . . .' she said, throwing her arms around his neck.

'I've never been to Paris . . . oh, maybe once on my Interrail, but only to change trains,' he said.

'You'll love it,' she told him, suddenly turned on by the thought of a whole weekend together. She locked her wrists behind his neck and dragged him down on top of her, wriggling underneath him, her legs wide apart, her hips wantonly thrusting at his groin.

He kissed her, drew his face away to look at her, then kissed her again, mumbling into her ear, 'You have the demeanour of a duchess . . . and the sensibilities of a barmaid.'

'And that's the nicest compliment you've ever paid me,' she squealed with delight.

* * *

'What's sex like?' Ginger asked Lia, the Friday evening before the day of the boat race. She had persuaded Lia to stay for a drink when she dropped Guy back at the flat. It seemed ages since they had enjoyed a proper chat. 'I mean what's it like when you've had a baby?' she qualified her original question.

'Don't ask me,' Lia replied, sipping her coffee, 'we never seem to do it these days. Either I'm tired, or Neil's tired . . .' She smiled, but couldn't quite manage to mask the discomfort she felt about the subject. 'Why, are you thinking of having some?' she asked, over-brightly.

'No,' said Ginger, 'well, I suppose there might be a possibility, but, well, I don't know . . .'

She told Lia about her date the next day with Charlie.

'Are you planning on Guy being around?' Lia asked.

'Of course,' Ginger said.

'Well, if you want a piece of advice, don't,' Lia told her, 'there's nothing more of a turn-off than the baby waking up just as you're getting in the mood, and if he's anything like Anouska, he will. It's as if they know,' she laughed, 'anyway, I find that I just can't relax and enjoy it properly even if she's asleep, because you've always got a little bit of you that's thinking about them, haven't you?'

'So, what do you do?' Ginger asked, mystified. She knew that Lia had not spent a night away from Anouska since she was born.

'We put her in the shed, of course,' Lia said, deadpan, then burst out laughing. 'What we don't do is have a lot of sex,' she admitted.

'God, how awful,' Ginger said, 'to have someone who looks like Neil lying next to you and not . . .'

'Hmm, looks aren't everything, you know,' Lia said, feeling as she said it rather like an older, more experienced woman giving advice, 'after a while, you don't really notice. Anyway, it's different from sex

342

before, because it's all wrapped up in having a baby, isn't it? You don't quite think of it in the same way. I find, anyway.'

'God, the way you're going on, I don't think I'll bother,' Ginger exclaimed. 'It's probably not on the menu anyway. I haven't really worked out what Charlie wants. I just know he must want something . . .'

'Well, listen, if you want me to look after Guy, I'd be more than happy. I'm not doing anything special. I suppose we might go down to the river, but we could always take you too, couldn't we, darling?' She tickled Guy under his chin.

'Da da da da da!' Guy said.

'Oh dear,' Lia said, 'you'd better tell Charlie straightaway that he says that to everyone.'

'God, I hadn't even thought of that,' said Ginger, adding quickly, 'thanks a lot for the offer, but you already do more than enough for me enabling me to have a job. You don't have to enable me to have a sex life too!'

'Well, I don't mind at all, I love looking after Guy. We quite miss him at weekends, don't we, Annie?'

Her delicate little girl smiled on hearing her name. She was so quiet and sweet-natured that it was quite easy to forget she was present, Ginger thought, especially since Guy was so boisterous and vocal. She hoped that he wasn't overwhelming Anouska, but Lia insisted that his vigour only helped Anouska along. Ginger looked at her, seeing her properly for the first time in weeks. She was beginning to look like a really pretty little girl with a head of soft little curls, the same colour as her mother's, and an expression of total concentration as she tried to imitate Guy's crawling, but collapsed on her tummy.

'Oh dear, and I want her to be a ballet dancer!' Lia said, watching her child.

'Do you?' Ginger said.

'Well, I thought that's what she looked like when

she was born. A little ballerina. That's why I wanted to call her something Russian.'

'Do you like ballet, then?' Ginger asked, surprised there were so many things about Lia that she didn't know.

'I love it. One Christmas, when I was little, all us girls got taken to see *The Nutcracker* at the Festival Hall. I don't think I ever got over it!'

'Have you been to Covent Garden?'

'No. It's very expensive, isn't it?'

'Well, I'll take you, one day,' Ginger said.

'Oh no, I couldn't let you do that. Come along, love,' Lia said, scooping Anouska up, 'kiss your boyfriend goodbye and wave.'

Both babies' mothers obediently flopped their babies' hands up and down.

'Bye then, see you Monday. Thank you,' Lia said, taking the envelope Ginger gave her containing her week's wages in cash, and walking towards the door. She was never quite sure how she should behave when taking the money. It was the one point of her working week she did not like, when the boundary between friend and employee became clear. She was almost at the door, when she turned back and gave Ginger a spontaneous hug, and said, 'Best of luck tomorrow!'

Ginger stood at the window with Guy in her arms waving at the red Peugeot as it pulled away. She hoped Lia was all right. She very rarely spoke about her life, apart from what she had done with the children. She kept a diary for Guy, as well as one for Anouska, detailing what he had eaten, what he had said and what they had done. She was an extraordinarily dedicated carer, who seemed to think that she had failed in some way if the weather had been too bad to take the children out for a walk each day, or if, by the end of the week, they had not gained a new skill. It was as if she had no confidence in herself, which was ridiculous because anyone could see that she was bright and kind and beautiful – the embodiment of practically everything worthwhile.

Even though they were friends and she was eternally grateful to her for minding Guy, Ginger never felt she was getting any closer to her, and that was why. It wasn't a class thing, as she had first thought, but a matter of confidence, although the difference in their upbringing must have had something to do with it. Lia always tried to say something nice about everything, and sometimes Ginger felt like telling her she would like her much more if she would just occasionally be a bitch.

Ginger was sure that her relationship with Neil didn't help. Lia never said anything disloyal, but he never seemed to be around, and from what she had said this evening, their sex life sounded pretty dismal. In Ginger's experience, men as good-looking as Neil were usually arrogant and always unreliable, and even if he was the exception, he had enough chips on his shoulder to supply McDonald's for a week.

Still, Ginger thought, giving Guy a squeeze as the car disappeared from their sight, there was nothing she could do about it. In the end, Lia had to find the confidence herself. It wasn't something that could be bought, or given, and even when she had tried to treat her to the ballet, the offer had been politely, but proudly, rebuffed. You had to be careful about these things, Ginger could almost hear Pic's voice warning her.

'What are we going to do this evening?' she asked Guy, putting him down on the floor beside the sofa. He immediately started trying to pull himself up to standing.

'Da da da da da,' he replied, triumphantly wobbling beside her knee before sitting down abruptly on his bottom.

'Hmm, I think you're right. We'll watch a bit of television, have a bite to eat and a bath, then bed, shall we?' Ginger interpreted.

Guy smiled and pulled himself up again.

The phone rang. Ginger picked it up, laughing. 'Hello? Oh hello, Daddy.' She looked at Guy and raised her eyebrows to the heavens.

'Are you well?' her father asked.

'Yes, thank you. Tired, as usual, but fine.'

'And that little chap?'

Ginger found great pleasure in the affectionate way her father now referred to Guy.

'He's fine. He is standing right beside me.'

As if to disprove her words, Guy lost his balance and sat down again with a thump.

'Standing? At his age? My goodness, he is coming along,' her father said.

She could almost hear his pen jotting down the information so that he could boast about Guy's latest achievement to his friends who had young grandchildren. Her father believed in competition in every aspect of his life. Ginger wondered vaguely how he would have been if Guy had been a frail little girl like Anouska, rather than the robust bruiser he was turning into.

'Now, I hope I'm going to see you both at Ian's tomorrow to watch the boats,' her father said.

His closest friend had a house backing on to the river in Hammersmith where he hosted an annual boat-race party. Ginger and Pic had been every year since they were old enough to carry a bowl of peanuts around the grown-up guests who congregated in the garden and cheered the rival boats past as loudly as football hooligans. Every year, except the previous year, when she was pregnant and in disgrace, she remembered. That fact alone gave her father's offer added significance. She and her son were being welcomed back into polite society and it was a command rather than an invitation.

'Oh, I'm sorry, Daddy, but we've already arranged to meet a friend,' she said.

'Well, bring her along too,' her father ordered.

'No, I'm sorry, we can't,' Ginger told him, firmly, resisting the temptation to overturn his assumption that her friend was a woman.

'Patricia and Edward will be there.'

Bully for them, she wanted to say, but she struggled to be diplomatic. 'We still can't,' she said.

'Why ever not?' her father persisted, unwilling to be disobeyed.

'I'm sorry, but that's none of your business,' Ginger told him, bristling at his tone. This was one battle she had to win. There was no way she was going to have her father interrogating Charlie, as he had every other man she had ever been foolish enough to introduce to him. 'I don't mean to be unkind,' she added, thinking that she had sounded rather rude.

'Unkind?' he echoed, haughtily, 'I just thought my grandson would have a better chance of seeing all the razzmatazz, but if you have other plans, as you say . . .'

'Well, I think he's a bit young to know what's going on anyway,' Ginger tried to humour her father. There was nothing worse than his self-pitying phase. 'Maybe next year,' she said, so that he would know that she wasn't refusing his invitation on principle, 'when he can really appreciate it?'

'We may not all be here next year,' her father said.

Oh God, emotional blackmail now. It was all Ginger could do to keep her temper in check.

'Don't be ridiculous, Daddy,' she said briskly.

'Very well,' he capitulated.

It was the first time she had ever heard him sounding old. The sad resignation in his voice was the only thing that came close to making her change her mind. No, she decided, if he thought that tactic would be a winner, there would be years of hell to pay for everyone around him.

'Thanks so much for the offer,' she said.

'Goodbye, darling,' he dismissed her, banging down the phone.

'I've brought a podium and a couple of periscopes,' Charlie said the next day as he fixed Guy's car seat in the back of his car. It was one of those ridiculous jeep-type things, with four-wheel drive and a rhino bar, more a fashion statement than a means of transport. Ginger had never been able to understand who would be stupid enough to drive one in London. And now she knew.

'You've what?' Ginger asked, trying to think whether she had remembered everything they would need. Bottles, a jar of baby food, a bib, his buggy, a cellular blanket to cover him if he wanted to sleep, changing bag. How could such a small individual require so much stuff just for a couple of hours?

'I thought about what you said, about not being able to see over the crowds, and I had one of the carpenters we've got on the set knock me up a podium. He got slightly the wrong idea and covered it in red velvet, but I think it'll solve our problem.' Charlie waved at the back of the car, and Ginger stood on tiptoes to peer in. There was indeed a red velvet podium with a step, looking like the kind of thing the Queen Mother would stand on to present a racing cup.

'How very practical,' she said, giggling.

Charlie turned round, his face pink with the exertion of fitting the car seat, and smiled at her. 'Let's go and pick our spot,' he said, taking Guy from her outstretched arms and swinging him into the seat. 'Come on, little fella,' he said.

'Da da da da da,' Guy replied.

'He says that to everyone, by the way,' Ginger remarked as nonchalantly as she could, climbing into the front seat, so that Charlie would not be able to see her face.

'So, is his father around much?' Charlie asked, pulling a seat-belt across his chest and starting the engine.

'Not much, no,' Ginger replied, truthfully.

'Do you mind that?' Charlie dared to probe a little further. He didn't sense that there was anyone else in the frame, but somehow it was easier to ask things like that when driving. You didn't have to look at the other person's face.

'I'm used to it,' Ginger said, 'I decided to have the baby without consulting him, so I didn't expect anything.'

'Right,' Charlie said, realizing that Ginger didn't want to discuss the matter any further. 'He's a great little fella,' he added.

'Well, I think so,' Ginger said, swelling with pride. 'I know that most people think I'm stupid,' she added, wondering as she did why it was that she always felt she had to justify herself, 'you know, to wreck my career and all that, but I look at him and I think, well, what more creative thing in the world could I have done than bring this little being into the world?'

Charlie took his eyes off the road for a second and smiled at her.

'What I didn't realize was how completely like himself he would be. He was, right from the moment he was born,' Ginger went on, encouraged by Charlie's reaction and unable to stop herself telling him more. It was a wonderful feeling to be able to reveal these things about his son, without exactly telling him. She hadn't realized how nice it must be to have another parent around, to share all the excitement, as well as the work.

'So it's nature, not nurture, is it?' Charlie asked.

'Definitely, I mean, sure, you *can* help them develop, and I'm sure if you damage them emotionally you leave scars, but they are absolutely born with characters and anyone who says they aren't hasn't had a baby,' she told him categorically, as if he were about to put up an argument. Seeing that he was only listening with interest, she added, more gently, 'I think of him as a gift, and all I can do is take as good care of him as I can, and hope he turns out OK . . .'

Charlie let her chatter on, unable to resist the occasional glance at her face, which, when animated by delight in her baby, was quite sensationally pretty. Zest and enthusiasm for life seemed to hum around her and, when she was speaking of her son, you could almost see the aura glowing golden. She had to be the most vivacious, truly vital person he had ever met, and he suddenly realized, as they stopped in traffic on Kew Bridge, that he was in love with her. It was a strange, almost humbling, sensation, that made him feel simultaneously weaker and stronger than he ever had been before. It surprised him so much that all the words he wanted to say to her seemed to blow away through the open window of the car, over the Thames, fluttering out of reach, like the bunting on the pleasure boats.

At that moment a police siren started wailing behind them, and he had to manoeuvre his vehicle to allow it to pass.

'I thought we'd go to a pub,' he said prosaically, as the traffic began to move again.

'Which pub?' she asked.

'I think it's called The Dove, do you know it?'

She knew it very well. It was not more than a hundred yards from the house where the rest of her family would be watching.

'Oh no,' Ginger told him, 'sorry, I hate that pub,' she explained.

'Do you have any other ideas?' Charlie asked, alarmed by her stark refusal.

'Er ...' She couldn't help being slightly disappointed. She had allowed herself to entertain a wild fantasy that Charlie, with his trendy media connections, might have wangled a table at the River Café.

'Look, tell me if this is really stupid,' Charlie suddenly said, as they crawled towards the Chiswick roundabout, 'we're right on the M4 here. It's a lovely day. Why don't we dare to break with tradition and get out of London?'

Ginger thought about it for all of two seconds. Actually, she hated the boat race. She had never been tall enough to see the boats go past, and she associated the tribal cheering with public schools, Oxbridge rivalry and the Conservative Party at play, three of her least favourite things.

'Fine,' she said, 'where to?'

'It's a secret,' he said, and was delighted to see her impish smile as she wriggled down in her seat, trying to resist the temptation of spoiling the surprise.

He would take her for a balloon ride, he decided, temporarily forgetting that they had a baby with them. There was a place near Bath. But in the car park of the Membury service station, his plans were foiled. The turning to Bath was further than he remembered, and the baby, who had slept for over an hour, woke up demanding to be fed. There was also a distinctly unpleasant smell wafting over from his region of the car. So they piled into the Little Chef to drink coffee and give Guy a bottle and change him, and then they all got back into the jeep.

He turned the key in the ignition, but nothing happened. He tried again.

'What's wrong?' Ginger asked.

'It won't start,' he replied, turning the ignition again.

He got out and looked at the engine, twiddled with a couple of things, and got back in. Nothing.

Eventually, he called the AA on his mobile phone and they all went back into the restaurant for lunch. By the time the AA arrived, Ginger had eaten fish and chips, fed Guy a jarful of mush, carried him three times around the video games lounge in the main building and changed his nappy again, using the last one in the changing bag.

The AA man could not start the car either, but offered to tow it to a garage. Charlie was clearly mortified but Ginger was secretly finding the whole adventure rather amusing. Charlie deserved the

351

embarrassment for driving such a ridiculous, fashion-victim car. She was almost disappointed when he insisted on calling a local minicab to take her and Guy and all their paraphernalia back to London. Charlie carefully transferred Guy's seat from his car to the minicab, negotiated the fee with the driver and handed him notes in cash, then he turned to Ginger, who was holding the baby on one hip.

'I am so sorry,' he said, for the umpteenth time.

'No, it's fine. Guy's enjoyed it. Really,' Ginger assured him, adding jokily, 'Can I have my surprise some other time?'

Charlie's face lifted for a second or two. 'Of course . . . if you'll ever trust me again,' he said.

She had been tremendously impressed throughout the proceedings that Charlie had not once lost his temper, but when she turned to wave at him as the cab drew away from the service-station car park, she was amused to see him kicking his safari vehicle very hard, as if to hurt it.

The flat felt strangely empty when she got in. She gave Guy another bottle, then turned on the television to see who had won the boat race. Cambridge. As usual. The day seemed unfinished. It was too early to start going through all the bedtime routine, and too late and chilly now to go out for a walk. She picked up the phone and dialled Pic's number. Still out. Knowing Pic, probably still at Ian's riverside house, clearing glasses from the garden and tipping the platters of half-eaten vol-au-vents and cigar droppings into the dustbin; then offering their father a lift back to his Dolphin Square apartment, his nose crimson, his speech slurred and mawkishly sentimental as he held forth in the passenger seat about the glorious day he became a Blue.

Ginger dialled Lia's number and amused her for half an hour with a description of their unsuccessful trip to the country.

'So, no sex, then?' Lia asked finally.

'Well, I've done it on the back seat, but even *I* draw the line at a busy car park,' Ginger replied, 'but I did actually have a very nice time.'

'Two hours down the motorway and two more in the Granada, and you still get on?' Lia said, 'it must be love!'

Ginger smiled, thinking of Charlie kicking his rhino bar as soon as he thought he was out of view. 'I don't think so,' she said, quickly, 'but maybe we can be friends. He's very considerate, oddly enough' – she told Lia about the podium – 'and personally,' she concluded, 'give me DIY before sex any day! So what have you been up to?'

'We went for a walk,' Lia said, 'while Neil creosoted all the fences. I can't stand the smell. To tell you the truth, I didn't feel very well. I think I may be getting flu, my legs ache and I've got a headache.'

'Sorry, I haven't helped by wittering on in your ear . . .'

'No, it was lovely to hear about it,' Lia said, 'it really cheered me up.'

'Do you have everything you need?' Ginger asked her.

'Yes. I'll be fine. Really. I'll see you Monday.'

Ginger rang off, and jumped up from the sofa, with a sudden determination to tackle the week's washing-up. She scraped the remains of several Marks & Spencer ready meals into the bin, and threw plates and mugs into a sinkful of hot foamy water, trying to avoid stepping on Guy, who seemed intent on crawling about the dirtiest parts of the floor.

Later, she decided it was a kind of prescience that had driven her to clean up the flat and get Guy bathed and into his cot early, because the minute his eyes had closed, the doorbell rang, and when she went to open it, Charlie was there, with a bottle of champagne in one hand and a takeaway meal in the other.

'How did you know?' Ginger asked him, 'I was about to order something in.'

353

'Well, order me in, instead,' he said.

'Get in here!' she shouted at him, forgetting her sleeping son for an instant, then remembering and freezing, mid-gesture, holding her breath. Miraculously, the baby did not stir.

She stood back to let Charlie in and pointed to the door of the living room. He walked straight over to the mantelpiece.

'So you did get it?' he said, picking up the Valentine card, that had found its natural place amongst the bric-à-brac.

'What? Oh, that! Did you send it?' she asked, amazed.

'Yes . . . didn't you see?' he said, exasperated, 'I had it made specially with all the things I associated with you . . . look, there's a bike wheel, and a piece of red velvet, a bit of champagne cork and there was something else – lobster shell . . .'

'Oh that's what it was!' Ginger said, understanding. 'It fell off. Goodness' – she took the card from him and looked at it in a new light – 'how extraordinary! Why did you do that?'

'Because I wanted you to be my Valentine, I suppose,' Charlie admitted tentatively.

'But what does that mean, exactly?' Ginger asked, suddenly very nervous, and playing for time. 'I've never known. I mean who was Saint Valentine anyway, and what do we know about him, or her, for that matter?'

They were standing next to each other, very deliberately not touching, looking at each other's faces in the mantel mirror.

'I think it means . . . well, what I was trying to say was, well, I'd like to see more of you . . . I don't know. What do you think?' Charlie said, suddenly bashful.

'I think,' Ginger said, turning towards him, 'I think you'd have been very good at courtly love. You offer lovely presents: balloons, cards and now an Indian takeaway—' she said.

'It's Thai,' he said.

She giggled.

Charlie looked into her eyes. 'Then will my lady favour me with a kiss?' he asked her softly.

'Oh all right,' she said, throwing herself into his arms with such unladylike enthusiasm that they both collapsed onto the floor, laughing. Then he drew back, and looked at her for a moment before bending his head to kiss her with mind-blowing fervour.

The tin trays of food remained uneaten in the carrier bag until the early hours of the morning, when the two of them surfaced, starving hungry, and stuffed each other's mouths with cold spoonfuls of chilli-hot green curry and white rice fragrant with coconut.

Lia was quite wrong, Ginger thought, as they both jumped back into bed to get warm again, pulling the duvet right up to their noses. Sex was no different after you'd had a baby. It was fantastically, wonderfully, brilliant, and she wondered how she could have lived for so many months without it.

Chapter 10

APRIL

'Are you sure you'll be all right?' Neil asked as he hoisted his kitbag on to his shoulder.

'We'll be fine,' Lia assured him.

'You've got the number of the hotel, in case you need it?'

'Yes, but I won't ring. If there's an emergency, I'll be surrounded by people, won't I? Anyway,' she added, 'there won't be.'

'Do you think you ought to be taking Annie when she's got a temperature?'

'Well, I can hardly leave her, can I?' Lia joked, 'she's only got a virus. A change of scene and a bit of country air will probably do her the world of good . . . and if Guy was going to catch it, he's had ample opportunity in the last week.'

Anouska had been running a fever for a couple of days. As Lia had begun to recover from her bout of flu, Anouska had developed similar symptoms. There was nothing visibly wrong with her except that she was grisly and out of sorts, which Lia could understand only too well if the child was feeling as headachy and generally low as she had done. She had taken her to the doctor, who had told her how to keep her temperature down, but said that there wasn't much else he could do. There was a lot of it about. Lia had

356

worried about the risk of passing the infection on to Guy, but so far, he seemed to have escaped it.

When Ginger had discovered that Lia and Anouska would be spending Easter on their own, she had invited them to the country for the whole weekend.

'Mummy and Pic and I will look after Anouska, and you can get some rest for a change,' she had volunteered, 'you both need to convalesce and we won't have to worry about shopping, or food, or cleaning, because all that's taken care of. The only minus is Daddy, but it's a big house and it's quite easy to avoid him. Mummy says that there are two families of ducklings on the lake already,' she added, as if Lia needed further incentive.

'We're going to a stately home, for heaven's sake, not some damp hovel,' Lia reminded Neil.

'Well, those places are sometimes very draughty,' he said, as if he had long experience of the dwellings of the aristocracy.

She was touched by his concern for their child's health, but thought he was worrying unnecessarily, and she wished he would just go. It was six-thirty in the morning and she was freezing cold standing in the doorway.

'You have a lovely time,' she told him, wondering why he seemed so reluctant to leave. She knew it wasn't really a holiday, because he would be chaperoning a bunch of schoolkids around, but he was going to Paris, after all. She wished he would be a bit more cheerful about it.

'Right, then,' he said, making a move again.

He put his arms round her, and held her very tight, then he broke away and walked smartly down the street, turning around to wave only when he was right at the end, and she could no longer see the expression on his face.

Closing the door, Lia took a deep breath. Four whole days! They had not been parted from each other for more than a night since the day they met, and that was only when she had stayed in hospital after giving birth. The night she and Ginger had drunk champagne perched at the end of Alison's bed, she remembered. She smiled, realizing how much she had been looking forward to a weekend of girls' talk and conversation that flowed easily and was interspersed with laughter.

Recently, Neil had become increasingly introverted and quiet. The Ofsted inspection was hanging over his school like a raincloud, the teachers spending most of the longer evenings preparing progress reports and work schedules for each pupil, and getting increasingly nervous about their performance. Every time she bumped into someone she knew from the school, they talked about the inspection in the same way she had overheard schoolchildren talking about their imminent GCSE exams. It occurred to her that in the decade she had spent out of the country, a climate of fear had developed that had made everyone insecure about jobs and forced them to live their lives in a kind of low-level panic. It seemed weird to her that teachers, whom she had previously considered figures of authority, could have been reduced to such paranoid wrecks. Or maybe, she thought, it was just that she had not lived with one before.

When Neil was home early enough for them to have supper together, he was often so tired that it was difficult to have a conversation with him. As she sat jabbering on, telling him about Anouska, or Guy, and the things they had done together, he seemed so preoccupied that she had wondered, on occasion, whether he would even notice if she casually inserted a sentence like 'and then I bonked the milkman' into her account of the day.

When he had tentatively informed her that one of the staff on the Easter trip to Paris had dropped out, and he had been asked to fill in, she had greeted the idea with such immediate, unchecked, enthusiasm, that he had looked hurt. It was just what he needed, she told him, urging him to accept when he appeared undecided. A change of scene. Of course she would be fine on her own with the baby. When am I not? she had felt like asking.

Even if Ginger had not asked her home for the weekend, she would have been happy to see him go. She knew it would be good for him, but she hadn't realized, until he disappeared at the end of the road, and she sighed with relief, how much she had been longing for a break too.

Anouska's forehead seemed hotter when she checked it, but she was breathing nice and evenly. Lia decided to let her sleep a little longer while she packed a case for them both. It was only when she woke her up and started to dress her, that she found that her neck was swollen on one side, and her temperature had risen. She gave her a spoonful of Calpol and rang the doctor, who was at the very end of a night on call. He popped by on his way home, examined Anouska thoroughly and assured Lia that it was still the nasty flu. The glands often swelled with this type of infection. There wasn't much point in prescribing antibiotics since he was sure it was some kind of virus. Anouska had quite a bad case of it, but she would soon be better. Lia showed him out, feeling guilty for bothering him, but when she went back to check Anouska in her cot, there was something about the way she looked that made her want to run into the street after him and ask him to look at her again. She went to the window, but his car was pulling away. Don't be so silly, she told herself.

Ginger was lying awake in bed, staring at the ceiling, enjoying a moment of perfectly contented consciousness. She had no idea what the time was, but since there was no sound from Guy's room, she imagined it must be early. He usually woke up just before seven.

Beside her, Charlie slept, blowing gentle rhythmic blasts of breath into her ear, his dark curls fanned out on the pillow, his features innocent in sleep. She did not know whether she liked the going-to-bed-with-him bit or the waking-up-with-him bit best. The waking-up-with-him bit was almost more special, because it was always a surprise to her that he was still there.

Don't start liking it too much, a tiny voice inside her warned, because one of these days he will be gone, leaving you with a heart drawn in lipstick on the mirror, and a few nice memories. Men like Charlie don't hang around for long. The only reason he is still here, the voice said, is that you are managing to stay cool and relaxed about it. At the moment, he is fascinated because he is not quite sure how much you like him, but once you let him know, you can forget it.

Over the last year, she had forgotten about relationship angst, the awful insecurity of the first few weeks and the great dilemma – whether to be yourself, or to try to be the woman you think he would like you to be. In Ginger's experience, it didn't really matter which choice you made because after two or three weeks, the real you would always surface, but that had never stopped her trying. Now she didn't have that worry, because when you had a child, you couldn't pretend to be aloof and mysterious. Guy would just be frightened. So it was just a matter of enjoying it until Charlie got bored and decided to split. They had fantastic sex together and lots of fun, and there was no point in stopping doing something just because you knew it couldn't last, was there?

The sun was coming up. Bright white light seeped round the dusty tassles at the edges of the heavy olive-green velvet curtains. Charlie turned over, taking the whole duvet with him.

'Hey.' Ginger tried to grab some of it back.

She snuggled in closer to him, fitting her body to his back, her knees tucked under his bottom. And then she just couldn't resist feeling to see whether he had an early morning erection. She loved the warmth of his skin in the morning, the way his arms flopped around her sleepily, his whimpering little groans, and his eyes scrunched up closed against the unwelcome glare of daylight. Finally, he opened his eyes and smiled. 'Hello!'

'Hello,' she said, trying to remember all her resolutions. God, he was handsome in the morning, with his hair muzzy, his breath tasting stale and human, his dark eyes glittering with the prospect of naughtiness.

He kissed her lazily, then pulled away, looked at her for a moment, and came back harder, with real urgency. It got her every time, that pulling away, as if checking to see whether she was real. The idea that you were being kissed more passionately just because you were you was so deliciously, hornily, flattering. He does it with everybody, the voice inside her warned, he saw it in a movie once, and it works every time.

'Mmm, do you have to go away this weekend?' he asked her.

'Yes, 'fraid so,' Ginger told him.

'But I only ever see you at weekends, and the first time we get a four-day stretch, you decide to go home . . .' he moaned plaintively.

She rationed him to weekends. On weekday mornings, it was too much hassle to get him woken, washed, dressed and fed, as well as doing all that for Guy, and making herself presentable for work. She had to be careful not to let him become a habit, or a regular presence in their lives.

'I've promised Lia, and anyway, I want to go,' she told him.

'Why can't I come too?'

'Why can't I come too?' she mimicked his little-boy voice. 'Because I haven't invited you, that's why,' she told him.

'But why not?'

'Because I want to spend some time with my friend,' and I don't want Mummy interviewing you

361

and Daddy trying to score points off you for four days, she thought.

'All right,' he agreed, reluctantly, as if he had a choice, 'when are you back?'

'About six o'clock on Monday, I should think.'

'Can I come round?'

'Well, as long as you bring something to eat,' she told him.

'So what else is new?' he teased her, ducking out of the way of a friendly swat with the pillow. He picked up a pillow himself and retaliated, she scampered up onto her knees and whacked him hard with hers, and they bashed each other long and hard, screaming with laughter, until they were both out of breath and the thin beams of sunlight now streaming into the room danced with dust motes.

Then, simultaneously, Guy woke up, and the phone rang.

Ginger pointed at the phone, indicating that he should pick it up, and went to be with Guy.

When she came back into the room with the baby smiling in her arms, Charlie was saying, 'She's right here, hang on one minute, Pic.'

And she knew instantly that something was wrong.

She grabbed the phone.

'What is it? . . . Oh no! What do you mean, serious? . . . Oh . . .. No, I'll come as soon as I can. I'll be there, well, as soon as I can. I'll try to leave him with Lia. I'll be there.'

She put down the phone then picked it up, instantly, and dialled, with Charlie hovering around her, trying to be helpful, but getting in the way.

'Go and make some coffee,' she told him. 'Oh Lia, hi, listen, bad news, my father's had a stroke. Pic's just rung. I've got to go to the hospital . . . Yes . . . He's in intensive care. Sounds bad . . . I'm so sorry.'

At the other end of the phone, Lia said, 'Don't worry. I was just about to ring you and cancel anyway. Anouska's not very well at all. I think I

362

would be mad to move her. I was thinking, well, it would be fine if everything went OK, but what if the car broke down, you know, like it did with you and Charlie, and we had her there with a temperature? It would be madness . . . but I was so looking forward to it . . .'

'Right,' Ginger said, wishing she would shut up, and wondering how she could ask her to look after Guy in the circumstances.

'Do you want me to have Guy for the day?' Lia volunteered, as if she had heard her thoughts.

She is an angel, Ginger thought. 'Could you? I'm so sorry to ask, but . . .'

'No, I'd be glad of the company. But I can't pick him up. I just don't want to take Annie out in the cold.'

'No, it's OK,' Ginger said, thinking lucidly, 'Charlie's here. He'll bring us.'

Charlie called from the kitchen, 'Where do you keep the milk?'

'Sod the bloody milk. Bring it black and put some cold water in it! Sorry, Lia, I'm panicking here.' She suddenly burst into tears. 'Pic sounded so frightened,' she said between sobs.

'No, it's OK,' Lia soothed her, 'just get Guy dressed. I've got everything here. I'll give him his breakfast too. Be strong.'

'OK, sorry.' Ginger put down the phone, not quite knowing what she was doing. Panic had made her forget the order of things. Dress Guy, dress herself, go to Lia's, then to the hospital. She took a deep breath. Soon. Pic had said. Please wait for me, Daddy.

'We have to be strong,' she told Guy, hugging his sturdy little body hard, bringing herself back to reality.

It was very different from London. They were stepping off the same train they had stepped onto just over three hours before, into a station that had signs

363

in both languages, newsstands with English newspapers, and cash machines where you could withdraw money from your English account, but it felt very different. Waterloo smelt of rain and metal, the Gare du Nord smelt of hot toasted sandwiches and disinfectant. In London, men wore suits or sports jackets, in Paris, they wore navy blue overcoats, or beige macs, and they looked, well, French.

As their taxi raced over squares that were bumpy with cobblestones, past art deco signs for the Métro, and cafés where no-one was idiot enough to be sitting outside in the cold wind, he began to relax. Every time the door to their compartment in the train had opened with a sigh, he had jumped, expecting to see someone he knew, not a waiter bearing breakfast, in a miniature tray, like an airline. In the taxi, that reeked pleasantly of French tobacco, he was safe. Even if someone did by chance recognize him, they were travelling too fast for them to be sure.

Alison had asked him whether he wanted to go for lunch, or to the hotel first, and he had said the hotel. The Eurostar omelette was still sitting, undigested, blocking the opening to his stomach, and he wanted to be a long way away from the station, from any link with England, in a room with a lock on the door.

The hotel was off a narrow street; in front of it there was a courtyard with a fountain and stone urns spilling over with flowers. It was an old building, and the long windows had shutters with peeling paint. Alison checked them in, in French, and signed the registration book as if she did this all the time. He picked up her suitcase and his kitbag and attempted to follow her to the lift, but a boy in uniform stood in front of him.

'*Monsieur?*' He was pointing at the bags.

'No, it's fine, really,' Neil told him, not wanting anyone to accompany them, and anticipating with dread the moment when he would pause for a tip. He had no French change, and even if he had, he would not have known how much to give.

The boy shrugged and moved out of the way.

'We're here,' Alison said, excitedly, as the lift creaked up to the third floor, 'I can't believe we're really here!'

'Nor can I,' he replied, trying to smile back.

He hadn't been able to believe the ease with which he had got away. When he had first invented the school trip, he had mentioned it very quietly and cautiously, almost just to test out how it would sound, but Lia had jumped at it, filling in the details for him, almost grateful for the excuse to spend some time away from him, he thought.

The room was small and almost entirely filled with bed. Unless you were squeezed up against the window, looking out at the courtyard, there was no way of avoiding its accusation.

'It's very comfy,' Alison said, sitting down on one side, kicking off her shoes.

He sat down too, bouncing up and down as if trying it out in a department store.

'Yes,' he said.

'You're nervous, aren't you?' she asked him, stroking his arm.

'I suppose so.'

'I am too.'

'Are you?' He turned to her, and saw there was fear in her eyes.

'Yes,' she said, 'I'm afraid that we won't like each other . . .'

'No,' he said, putting his arms around her and rocking her from side to side, 'there's no chance of that.'

'What are you afraid of?' she asked him, throwing her head back from his chest to look at him.

'That we'll like each other too much maybe, I don't know,' he said, not able to describe the confusion he was feeling, not sure he even wanted to.

She reached out both hands and held his face between her palms. 'Whatever happens, you do know that I love you?' she said.

'I've always loved you,' he told her.

'Sing the song?' she asked him.

'No,' he said, 'not any more. We're here now. We're doing it. It's not a dream any more.'

'Well, let's have lunch then,' she said, laughing.

'And a lot to drink,' he suggested, feeling a little better.

He rose, walked round to her side, and pulled her to her feet, and they left the room, arm in arm, like old friends.

'Isn't it amazing,' Alison said, spearing a forkful of frisée lettuce, and letting the vinaigrette drip on to the white plate before putting it into her mouth, 'how the French can make steak and chips and salad taste absolutely delicious, but you wouldn't dream of ordering it in England?'

'Wouldn't you?' he asked, thinking how much he always liked steak and chips, especially a really thick slab, not a thin slice like the one on his plate. He poured them both more wine.

He was beginning to feel pleasantly, warmly, drunk. They had had glasses of kir while they waited for their meal, and now they were almost at the bottom of a bottle of red. All the crystals of anxiety that seemed to be stiffening his limbs had melted away. On the second glass, he had decided that there was no point in worrying. They were here all weekend, and there was nothing he could do about it, so he might as well enjoy himself and start worrying hard again on the train home. He was in Paris, in a café so perfectly as he had imagined a Parisian café might be that it felt like a film set, and he was with the woman he had always imagined being here with.

Alison was wearing black. Slim black trousers and a

fine black jumper under a short black jacket with a
black velvet collar. She had tied a brightly-coloured
silk scarf around her neck and clipped hemispheres
of pearl to her ears which made her look as chic as
any of the smartly dressed French women taking tea
at nearby tables. She always looked so expensive,
he thought, suddenly turned on by the sheer quality
of her. Her skin was smooth, clear and cream, she
never left lipstick on her glass, and she knew exactly
the right outfit to wear for lunch in Paris. Unbelievable!

'Come on,' he said, glancing at the tab, and throwing a couple of notes on to the table. He stood up and
took her hand.

'I wanted coffee . . .' she said.

'You can have coffee later,' he told her, wanting to
rip her clothes off right there.

Underneath the different layers and textures of black
was soft silk underwear. The shine of the fabric
caught just slightly against the pads of his fingertips
as he ran splayed hands from the jutting bones of her
pelvis up over the rack of her ribs and on to her
breasts, covering them, feeling her nipples harden
against the lifelines on his palm.

His mouth tasted of red wine and the saltiness of
her juices. He ran his tongue up the centre of her
body, under the vulnerable arch of her chin, on to her
mouth. Then, crouched over her like an animal, he
looked down at her lying beneath him half-clad, red
lipstick smudged, hair fanned out, staring at him with
eyes lazy in submission. He thought, she is my
mistress. We are acting out a fantasy. This is not real.
Then he pulled aside her panties and plunged himself
into her, and the suction of her flesh tight around his
felt a hundred times more real than he had ever felt.
Indescribably real. It was that moment he kept coming
back for, that momentary clasping of her flesh around
his.

367

Afterwards, they slept with their heads on the hard, narrow bolster, and when they woke, they were cold and grumpy with muzzy heads and the dry, stale taste of wine in their mouths. They showered together, standing under a meagre jet of lukewarm water, soaping each other's bodies, slightly embarrassed, as if this act were more intimate than anything else they had ever done together.

When he brushed his teeth, he made a horrible throat-clearing sound as he spat out the water, she noticed.

When she brushed hers, she squeezed the toothpaste from the middle of the tube, and failed to rinse out the bowl, he saw.

He threw his wet towel onto the bed and left it there.

She walked around the room still dripping wet, leaving damp patches on the carpet.

He took the only chair for his awful nylon kitbag, leaving its contents spilling out on to the floor.

She used every hanger there was for her clothes without even asking him if he needed one.

These were the tiny irritations of sharing an environment, she thought.

'Let's go out and do some sightseeing,' he suggested.

'Good idea!' she agreed hastily.

They sat by his bedside holding each other's hand. He seemed to be wired up to a dozen different pieces of apparatus. He looked grey and expressionless, as if all the lines and switches and screens were making him work, rather than just registering some kind of activity inside him. When their mother arrived they left her with him and went to the hospital canteen together.

'What happened?' Ginger asked her sister, carrying their tray to a clean table.

'I'm not really sure. Mummy was in such a state

when she rang me. His housekeeper called an ambulance and said she'd found him unconscious, thought he was dead; she was completely hysterical, apparently, I don't know . . . the hospital called Mummy and she called me,' Pic replied, pulling the tea-bag out of the cup and putting it carefully on her saucer.

'He was at Dolphin Square?'

'Yes.'

'I didn't know he had a housekeeper there,' Ginger said.

'Well, the woman who cleans . . . I don't know,' Pic said, going rather red.

'Well, what was she doing there at six o'clock in the morning?' Ginger asked, perplexed.

'Well, quite, my thoughts exactly,' Pic replied. 'For God's sake don't say that to Mummy, though.'

'Course not!' Ginger replied. 'Have you talked to any of the doctors?'

'Well, yes, but they're not really saying anything. They may have been waiting for Mummy, or perhaps they just don't know. They can't tell until he regains consciousness what damage there has been, they say, if any . . .'

'*If* he regains consciousness,' Ginger said, sipping her tea, remembering why she never drank it. She hated tea. But Pic had bought her one nevertheless. It was what you drank in a crisis.

'Yes, if,' Pic said.

'I think he will, don't you?' Ginger said, brightly, trying to suppress the overwhelming sense gathering inside her that he would not.

'I don't know,' Pic said, 'he looks awfully grey and old lying there, doesn't he?'

Ginger stirred her tea. 'Is there a tall, good-looking consultant on?' she asked suddenly.

Pic looked horrified.

'No, I don't mean . . . Honestly, am I that bad? No, I just remembered that I know one of the doctors who works in the cardiac bit. He's married to one of the people from the ante-natal group ... he's bald,' she added.

'Oh, I know the one you mean.' Pic was smiling as she suddenly remembered Stephen. 'He looks strange but rather beautiful; violet eyes, really long black lashes, doesn't smile much, but when he does, wow!'

'Yes, I think we're talking about the same one,' Ginger said, bursting to laugh. Pic could be so prudish, but she had just rather given herself away with the detail of her description of a fanciable man.

'No, I haven't seen him,' Pic said, abruptly.

'Let's go back to Mummy,' Ginger said, abandoning her drink.

When they heard their mother's shrill voice talking as they went into his room, they both thought that he had woken up, but he had not. They went and stood on either side of her.

'One of the nurses said it might help if I talked to him,' she told them, 'but I didn't know what to say, so I've been telling him about the garden, which is probably very silly, because he's never been the slightest bit interested ...' She turned to Pic, her lip quivering uncontrollably.

Ginger looked away, knowing that her mother would be embarrassed later. She came from the class that thought it impolite to express emotion, especially in front of the children. The only time she could remember her crying before was when one of the dogs got run over by a combine harvester. Ginger realized that she had been fooled by that for all these years into thinking that she didn't feel very much for Daddy. She was a good Tory wife for whom loyalty was the overriding concern. Loyalty meant putting up with his capricious behaviour, encouraging his pomposity, and smiling nicely for the photo on his election address. In return, he left her in peace during the week, free to potter in her garden with her spaniels, invite her female friends to lunch or, occasionally, to travel to London to attend a private view in one of the little galleries off Bond Street that dealt in unadventurous paintings of vases of flowers. She loves him, Ginger thought, shocked.

Every time she glanced at her father, she expected him to open one eye and shout, 'Boo!' at her as he used to sometimes in the summer, when she had chased him round the croquet lawn until he pretended to drop down dead with exhaustion.

She wandered out into the busy corridor, not really knowing what to do. How long should she wait? What was going to happen? The hospital was like a parallel world with rules of its own. It was difficult to imagine that outside the traffic was still moving, and people were going places on the tube, and life was just going on. Here, she felt they were all in a state of suspended animation, waiting for him to wake up, or to die. She did not know which to expect.

Outside the stroke unit, by the lifts, she found a payphone and rang Lia, who sounded very anxious. She had just changed Anouska and she couldn't decide whether she had a rash, or whether she was just pink because she was so hot.

'Why don't you get the doctor to come again?' Ginger suggested.

'It's Good Friday . . .' Lia said.

'Don't worry about that,' Ginger said, wondering how doctors had managed to build themselves up into such figures of respect. They were public servants after all, not the selfless charity workers they sometimes made themselves out to be. 'You pay his wages, don't forget.'

'I suppose so,' Lia said. 'I wish Neil was here.'

'Why don't you ring him and get him to come home?'

'Well, I don't think he'd be able to leave. They have to have a certain ratio of teachers to pupils, and I don't want to worry him . . .'

'Why not? You're worried. Why shouldn't he be

worried too?' Ginger asked impatiently, not understanding why Lia always seemed to want to shield
him.

'What good would it do?' Lia asked.

'Well, it might make you feel better,' Ginger told
her.

Lia giggled.

'That's better,' Ginger smiled, 'Look, are you OK
with Guy?'

'He's fine. He's keeping me sane.'

'I don't know how long I'm going to be here, but I'll
keep calling.'

'OK,' Lia said, 'good luck!'

'Thanks,' Ginger said, replacing the receiver.

She tried to think of other people to ring, but all the
numbers she knew off by heart had answerphones on.
It was Easter weekend. Nobody was in London. She
hung up, not wanting her friends' return from holiday
to be greeted by the message: 'Hi, Ginger here, my
father's in a coma and I just wanted a chat . . .'

Charlie had told her to call, but she resisted,
thinking that his friendly voice might make her cry.
And that wouldn't do any good. He would think she
was getting clingy.

The doctor told Lia that babies often had rashes for no
reason at all. He prodded Anouska's skin a couple of
times and said it was possible that it was a mild case
of measles. He suggested she sponge her down with
lukewarm water and give her plenty of fluids. Her
temperature was high, and they didn't want her
getting convulsions, he said casually. Convulsions!
Lots of children had them, and they were rather
frightening, but usually nothing to worry about. Don't
anticipate the worst, he told her with a smile, and
asked if her husband would be home soon. She
explained that Neil was away. Well, that's a shame,
he said, gently, because when you've not had a lot of
sleep, it's easy to start imagining terrible things.

'What a patronizing bastard!' Ginger said, when she heard all this.

'I'm sort of glad to know it's something, though,' Lia said, 'we've all had measles, haven't we? I'm sorry if Guy gets it . . .' she added quickly.

'Don't be ridiculous,' Ginger told her.

She looked in the cot at Anouska. The rash was barely visible on her face but her lips seemed unnaturally red. She didn't want to worry Lia more, but she thought that if it had been Guy, she would have wanted a second opinion.

'I tell you what, I'll stay the night,' Ginger said, 'then you can get some sleep.'

Lia was so exhausted by worry, she did not automatically object, as she usually would have done.

'I'll get a cab home, get a change of clothes for me and Guy, and pick up a Chinese on the way back. OK?'

'That would be fantastic,' Lia told her, truly grateful for the practical support. 'Are you sure?'

'Course I'm sure,' Ginger said, 'I didn't want to be on my own tonight, anyway. I'd only lie awake and worry about Daddy, and it's ridiculous for me to be doing that two miles down the road, when I could be here!'

She returned with two carrier bags of Chinese food. As she stood at the counter with the taxi waiting outside, she had simply not been capable of choosing. She had struggled all day to keep the rising tide of panic at bay for her mother's sake, but it was beginning to burst through the barriers she had put up when she least expected it to. As she stared at the hand-painted sign that usually made her laugh with its odd spellings and lack of plurals, the letters and numbers merged into one another illegibly and she could not remember what she usually liked. She asked for the first dish in each category and dashed to the off-licence next door for a bottle of wine. The face of the Chinese woman serving registered no trace of surprise as she pushed the order through the hatch to the kitchen at the back.

Lia laid the table in the kitchen and started taking the lids off the foil trays: sweet and sour prawns, sweet and sour chicken, sweet and sour pork, sweet and sour duck, plain boiled rice and lychees.

'I hope you like sweet and sour,' Ginger said, looking despondently at the containers brimming with lurid orange sauce. How could she have done that?

It didn't really matter because neither of them had an appetite.

'Let's get drunk, anyway,' Ginger said, pouring them both a glass of white wine.

'I don't think I'd better,' Lia said, taking a spoonful of rice, 'I want to have good judgement in case Anouska gets worse . . .'

'Yes, you're right,' Ginger said, sombrely, corking up the bottle.

It was going to be a long night.

At two-thirty in the morning, Ginger looked at her watch and wondered how she was going to make it through. She was twitching with tiredness, but the sofa, which she had truthfully assured Lia was really comfortable when she first lay down, seemed to have shrunk in length and now sloped so that she constantly felt she was rolling down a hill.

When she looked at her watch about five minutes later, she saw that it was six o'clock, and she had been woken up by the sound of Lia crossing the room upstairs. She went into the kitchen, tiptoeing past Guy who had slumbered peacefully the whole night in the travel cot where he normally took his afternoon nap.

When Lia came down, Ginger handed her a steaming mug of tea.

'I put sugar in,' she said to her, 'I don't usually take it, but these are exceptional circumstances . . . Is she all right?'

'Yes, she's sleeping peacefully, and I think she looks a bit better,' Lia said.

They both blew long sighs of relief.

'I feel as if we're in the war. We've survived a long night during the Blitz or something,' Ginger remarked.

Lia thought how apt that comparison was. During the night, she had found herself saying a sort of prayer to keep going. If I can just get through tonight, it will be better in the morning. And, somehow, it was. The sun was coming up on a new day.

The clothes were even more stunning up close, when you could see the quality of the material and the detail of the decoration, and feel the sensuous texture of the fabric. Back in London, when she had watched the video of his first collection for the great Parisian couturier, there had been one dress that she had fallen in love with for the sheer simplicity of its drape and the shimmering rainbow beauty of its fabric, and now it hung in front of her. She wondered if she dared ask.

'Do you want to try it on?' John-Fabrizio Jones asked her, recognizing the desire in her eyes.

'No . . . really?' Alison said, knowing she shouldn't. Her objectivity as a journalist would be totally compromised, but then, she reasoned, it was only a fashion piece. Ramona had told her that she wanted a celebration of Englishness in Paris. Her genuine enthusiasm for his work was one of the reasons the designer had granted her an exclusive interview on Easter Saturday morning.

He waved in the direction of a kind of medieval tent that rose out of the thickly carpeted floor of the salon. She took the dress, on its padded hanger, and slipped inside. There was a gold-framed cheval mirror, an antique armchair with gold curlicues and brocade, and a small table for her briefcase. Which rich and famous women had undressed on this spot, she wondered excitedly as she stripped to her pants and stockings and slipped the dress over her head. It slid on like a glove.

She admired herself for a few seconds, wishing that someone she knew were here to witness the moment and make it more real. She imagined Stephen sitting in the armchair, smiling at her as she twirled around in front of him. And then she stopped. Not Stephen, Neil, she remembered. But she could not imagine him sitting there. He would either be standing, awkward in these surroundings, or else fucking her over the table. She smiled naughtily at herself in the mirror, then pulled back the heavy curtain to show John-Fabrizio how she looked.

'Yes,' he said, making a circle in the air with his finger.

She twirled round obediently.

'You have the height for it,' he said, 'but if I were making it for you, I would choose the gold.' He hung a swatch of another fabric next to her face. 'You can't get away with silver with your colouring at your age . . .' he said, his casual assessment sending her high spirits crashing.

She understood now why they called him the wide boy of the fashion world. He was supremely talented, very attractive in a rough kind of way, but there were as few frills on him as there were on the clothes he created. He said exactly what he thought.

As she took the beautiful dress off, she consoled herself with the thought that the whole episode would make good copy.

'We sometimes have a kind of ex-pats brunch on Sundays,' John-Fabrizio told her when she emerged again from the tent. 'If you're still around tomorrow, would you like to come along?'

'I'd love to,' she said automatically, flattered to be asked.

He gave her his address. 'It might give you some insights, but we would be off the record . . .' he warned her.

'Of course. What sort of time?'

He told her not to arrive before twelve, and then they parted, shaking hands, and as soon as she was safely out in the street, she did a little jump for joy, before running all the way to her rendezvous with Neil.

'Actually we got on quite well, he's asked me for lunch, well, brunch, tomorrow,' she told him breathlessly, waving a waiter over and ordering coffee. 'You don't mind, do you? I mean, it's quite a coup. I'd forgotten the buzz it gives you . . .' she said, thanking the waiter as he put a cup and saucer in front of her.

'What does?' he asked.

There were bright spots of colour on her cheeks, and her eyes sparkled with a look of triumph he had not seen before.

'Writing about something you're interested in,' she explained, adding, 'He let me try on a dress!'

He did not understand how unusual that was.

'It was probably worth about ten grand!' she told him proudly.

'People pay ten thousand pounds for a dress? That's disgusting,' Neil said.

She felt as if he had stuck a pin in her bubble of elation. 'You're right, I suppose,' she said. The rush of phrases that had filled her head in her dash to the café came to an abrupt standstill. She wished she had just stopped in the street and written them down.

'So, you're going to have *brunch* with him, tomorrow?' He said the word 'brunch' with sneering heavy emphasis, as if it were a terribly pretentious way of describing a bowl of cornflakes.

'Yes,' she said, irked now by his refusal to share in her excitement. Surely he didn't think that he had any say in whether she went?

'Right,' Neil said.

'Hey, you're not jealous, are you?' she asked, trying to make light of the mood that seemed to have settled around him. 'He's gay, you know.'

'No, I'm not jealous,' Neil said evenly.

'Good,' she said.

'You didn't mention that you were here *with* somebody, then?' Neil asked her.

'No, of course not.' She was beginning to understand why he was looking so sulky. 'It's work,' she said, more gently, 'you just can't say, "Oh by the way, can I bring a friend?" It wouldn't be professional . . .'

'But it's perfectly OK to try on a dress in front of him?' Neil said.

She had underestimated him, she realized, flushing with embarrassment. He had spotted the discrepancy in her behaviour and zoomed in immediately on something she already felt uncomfortable about.

Why was it that she hadn't asked John-Fabrizio if she could bring a friend? She was trying to get away with not asking herself that question, but she would have to face it. It was a matter of difference, she told herself. Over the last twenty-four hours, she had discovered how different she and Neil were. There wasn't anything wrong with that, she kept assuring herself. Right and wrong didn't come into it. She just wasn't used to being with people whose idea of enjoying a weekend in Paris was to visit Montmartre, the Champs Elysées, and the Eiffel Tower, for heaven's sake. She had never been up the Eiffel Tower before, and the view was fantastic, but it was just so *naff* to be herded along with coachloads of Americans like a tourist.

So, they had different tastes. What was wrong with that? You didn't fall out of love with someone because they asked for steak well done rather than rare, or because they queued for hours to see the Mona Lisa only to pass the artistic judgement that it was very small. Did you? She had managed to stop herself wincing at some of the other comments he made about things, but, she now admitted to herself, the idea of introducing him to a group of the coolest people in Europe was unthinkable.

'Anyway, you'd hate it,' she told him, brightly.

'I'm sure I would,' he said, seeing how tense she had become, and not wanting to argue with her. It was only a short time they had together. They might as well enjoy it.

Both children were asleep. Anouska did not seem to be any better, but she didn't seem any worse either, Lia thought, peering into her cot. When she was sleeping, she looked more or less the same as she usually did. It was only when she was awake that she grew concerned, because she was so miserable, not at all the baby she knew. But she had had so little sleep herself over the last couple of days, she was beginning to wonder whether she could judge any more.

She went downstairs and made herself a cup of tea, spooning sugar in, as Ginger had done, to give herself energy. This kind of tiredness was like a massive hangover, she thought, sipping the hot, sweet liquid, as she slumped down on the sofa in the living room, that shivery but flushed, febrile state after the worst of the headache has disappeared and it feels as if you're half a second behind the rhythm of the world.

Only two more days, she told herself, trying to keep her eyes open. Forty-eight hours. If she could just last as long as she had lasted so far, then Neil would be home, and everything would be easier. The stretch of time since he left, not even forty hours, seemed much longer, and she had been so preoccupied with Anouska's health, she found she almost couldn't remember what it had been like not to be constantly teetering on the edge of worry. The flash of freedom she had experienced as he turned and waved at her before disappearing round the corner now made her feel guilty, as if she deserved to be missing his presence so much.

What would he say if he were here? Would he tell her she was being silly, or would he take one look at Anouska and drive her to hospital? Probably the former, she reasoned, since he hated hospitals. On the other hand, he had never had much respect for their doctor. What if there was something terribly wrong with the baby and Lia had just accepted the doctor's word that she would be OK? Neil would go mad. Anouska was his child too, and yet she was assuming sole responsibility for medical decisions about her. Perhaps she was being too feeble. Or was she just completely neurotic? Panicking, she went into the kitchen and picked up the phone. Then put it down. What would she say to the doctor? That Anouska seemed the same, but she was still worried? He would become impatient with her. All she wanted was for someone to tell her that she was worrying unnecessarily. All she wanted was for someone to tell her that her baby would be all right. She picked up the phone again, her eyes scanning the fridge door for the piece of paper where Neil had left the name and number of his hotel in Paris.

It was such a relief to hear the connection had been made, it didn't occur to Lia, until the receptionist answered, that she did not speak French. She said Neil's name a couple of times.

Silence.

'He is staying with you,' she said, speaking very slowly, 'he is a guest at your hotel.'

She didn't understand the response, but it sounded negative.

'Does anyone there speak English?'

The reply was frosty and negative.

'¿Habla español?' desperate now, she tried another language.

'Si, poco.'

Encouraged by the sound of a smile in the woman's voice, she asked her questions in the little Spanish she could remember.

No, there was no-one of that name staying at the hotel, the woman responded.

He's a teacher, with students. From London. Surely she would now recognize him?

No, came the reply, this is a small hotel, only twelve rooms, we do not take schools here.

'So sorry,' Lia said, apologizing automatically, and putting down the phone as if she had dialled a wrong number. She checked the piece of paper again. No, it was the right hotel. The name was the same as the receptionist had said on answering. There had to be some mistake. She picked up the phone again, then put it down. There was no point in going through the same routine again. She must work out what to say.

Then the doorbell rang and Ginger was standing there looking very pale.

'How is he?' Lia asked, worried.

'No change,' Ginger said, despondently, 'the longer he doesn't wake up, the worse it is, apparently. How's Anouska?'

'Asleep, and no real change, I think,' Lia said.

'Do you want me to stay again?' Ginger asked her, sagging into a chair.

'Would you mind?' Lia asked, too tired to start protesting.

'As long as we don't have to eat last night's leftovers,' Ginger said, sitting up, animated all of a sudden. 'I think I'll always associate sweet and sour sauce with hospitals. Have you noticed that when you don't sleep much, your mouth can't get rid of the taste of the last meal you ate? I've tried everything, apples, breath mints, I even bought a toothbrush from the hospital shop, but it's still there . . . How's my son?'

'He's just fine. He had a nice bath and went off beautifully,' Lia said, giggling with relief that someone else was there.

Now that Ginger was back, it didn't seem to matter nearly so much that she had not been able to speak to Neil. She considered asking Ginger whether she spoke French, but decided not to. There was only a day and a bit to go, and then he would be home, and everything would be all right.

Alison was right. The Place des Vosges was the perfect place to be on a sunny Sunday morning. He had bought the *Observer* from an international newsstand near Notre Dame, and he was sitting on a stone bench in the middle of the square reading the sports pages, relieved to be by himself, with only a few mangy pigeons for company. The square was oddly quiet, as if the whole of Paris was still in bed and had not yet opened the curtains to see what a glorious spring day it was. The sun's warmth fell kindly on his face. He looked up between articles, and stretched his arms, still waking himself up properly from the best sleep he had enjoyed in months.

It was over, and he could almost relax.

He had never imagined how it would finish. If he had, he would have pictured a lot of shouting, and fucking, and tears. But there had been none of that. Perhaps that was still to come. It's all over bar the shouting, he thought, wondering idly where the phrase had originated.

An inquisitive pigeon picked a tentative path towards his feet. He scuffed at the gravel, shooing it away, and returned to the newspaper. One of the Premier division's managers had been sacked as his team faced relegation. The sports editor speculated about who would replace him. Neil read the words but did not take in anything the piece said.

He wasn't yet sure whether Alison knew too. The evening before, they had barely exchanged a word over supper, as if they had run out of things to say to each other. Afterwards, as they were walking along the riverbank, she suggested going to see an American movie that had not yet opened in England. He had not objected, although he thought it was an odd way to spend an evening in Paris, because it would put off the moment when they talked for another couple of hours.

Later, there had been an almost viscous air of tension in the room as they lay side by side in bed, not touching, as if the slightest contact would produce an electric shock. He knew that she wanted to ask him what the problem was, but she didn't quite dare. He knew that it would be kinder to tell her, but she would react in one of two ways – either arguing with him in that way she had, using language to trick him, and make him say things he didn't mean, or crying – and he hadn't the strength to deal with either. Eventually, he said good night and turned away, and the next thing he knew, he was awake, refreshed, surprised by the light from the window and the chill in the air that told him it was just after dawn.

She had clearly not slept well, and she had spent a long time trying to make herself look fresh and groomed for her brunch party, vacillating between a navy jacket over blue jeans, and the black outfit she had worn to travel in. He lay in bed, behind her, dozing. On one occasion, when he opened an eye, he caught her watching him in the mirror, as if she could read his mind if she stared at him long enough. When she saw that he was awake, she looked away quickly, pretending to investigate a non-existent blemish at the corner of her mouth.

He had taken a deep breath, about to explain, but she had risen, quickly, brushed down her navy jacket, looked at herself once again in the mirror, practising a smile, and squirted herself with perfume. She had asked him, in the clipped cold way she had when she was nervous, what he was planning to do and he had told her. She had suggested going to the Marais, showing him quickly on the map, and then she had gone, clearly as eager as he was to spend some time alone.

He could pinpoint the exact moment he had known that their relationship could not last.

It was in the Musée d'Orsay the previous afternoon. They had been standing in front of one of Monet's lily pictures.

'We've got that one at home,' he had remarked.

'Really?'

The cool aloofness of her tone was beginning to irritate him. He could tell that she wasn't happy traipsing round galleries or doing the sights, but he could hardly go home and say that he'd spent the whole weekend hanging about in carpeted boutiques with snooty assistants, while she fingered handbags or tried on shoes, or sitting in cafés drinking tiny bottles of beer that cost two quid a throw, could he? He thought she would see that.

'Yeah,' he told her, scrutinizing the picture closely, 'I think the colours are better in the poster.'

She hadn't been able to stop a grimace of contempt flashing across her face, and he had seen it, and that was the moment he had known for sure.

It hadn't even crossed her mind that he might be joking.

They spoke a different language, nowadays, Ally and he. She knew all about fashion and style, not just what clothes to wear, but what books you were supposed to have read, what films you were supposed to like, even what food you were supposed to eat. He knew nothing about all that, and cared less. For her, Sunday lunch was going with a few friends to a new place that combined the best elements of Japanese and Middle-Eastern cuisine and writing a restaurant column about it. For him, it was a pub with Lia and a crowd from the club. Fine, if the roast was still available, but he'd have been just as happy with a ploughman's. He doubted whether he would recognize a field of lemon grass if he drove past one, let alone the hint of saffron or cumin or coriander that she could detect at twenty paces, and then wax lyrical about.

Back in London, insulated in her Islington flat, she

had thought it amusing when he asked her what she was talking about. Out in the real world, it wasn't a joke. It mattered to her. He had wanted to tell her that he didn't really want to have brunch with a bunch of pansies who spent their lives designing unwearable dresses for the world's richest women, but it would only have sounded defensive.

But it wasn't just that, he thought. That was just the symptom of their problem. They had grown up in the same place, but now they lived in different worlds. Perhaps they always had.

He put down his newspaper and stared at the arcade of antique shops in front of him, not focusing, just thinking, recalling her hiss of impatience as a teenager when he had told her his ambition was to play cricket for England. She had wanted him to go to a 'proper' university rather than a sports college, he now remembered. And when they had imagined their future together, her dreams were always of money, and nice clothes, and one of those great big white stucco-fronted houses in Kensington, where she had taken him on one of their day trips to London together.

She had all that now, or the equivalent. She had done well, and he was proud of her, but she wouldn't give it up for him. Why should she? He wouldn't even want her to. He liked the life he had too, he realized, for the first time in months. He wouldn't want to give it up for her, either.

Monet's lilies. He smiled. He had always liked the picture that hung on his bedroom wall facing their bed, but he would have to find some excuse to take it down when he got back. Or maybe he could leave it there as a kind of trophy to remind him always of his mistake and his reprieve.

He would make it up to Lia, he promised himself, as a sudden sharp pang of guilt attacked him like a stitch. Bent double, his arms crossed over his belly, he stared at the gravel beneath his feet, seeing only her face, her soft, small, kind, dreamily beautiful face puckered, her dark eyes wide with anxiety.

He had betrayed her in the worst possible way, because she had known almost from the first moment he set eyes on Alison again that something was wrong with him. Yet she had not asked, because, like all good people, she had assumed it must be something she had done wrong. He had gone ahead exploiting her insecurity, even adding to it, because it suited him that way. She had borne his child and he had failed her. At the one moment she was relying on him to be strong, he had been weak. He had lied to her, and he had lied to himself, pretending to be carried away by the power of something greater than he was, when it had all been a ridiculous fantasy.

Now it was over. He could not be with Alison for ever. He did not even want to spend another night with her. He wanted to go home, now, to take the first train, or plane, or even hitch a lift. But stranded in Paris by his own lies, he would have to wait. If he went home now he would only have to make up more lies about why he had come back early, or tell Lia the truth.

She did not deserve that.

'Hello!' Ginger called to Stephen as he walked past the room where her father lay.

He looked at her, perplexed. His expression said that he recognized her, but he could not think where from.

'It's Ginger,' she helped him, 'I'm a friend of your wife. I've got a little boy the same age as Ben.'

'Ginger, of course, mother of Guy ... sorry, you look rather different out of your red dress!' His face was transformed by a smile of such brilliance, she felt herself begin to blush. The nurses must love him, she thought.

'How is he?' he asked her, pointing at her father.

'I thought you might be able to tell *me* that,' she replied, jokily.

'Oh, I'm sorry,' he said, approaching the bed, 'we have this sing-song way of talking to relatives, it's the only way you can do it, over and over, I'm afraid. Forgive me?' Automatically, he picked up the notes at the end of the bed.

'Of course,' she said, 'but I would like to know what you think. Seriously. I mean, is he going to die?' Her voice deteriorated to a whisper as she said the last word in case her father might hear her.

Stephen's face wrinkled with compassion for a fraction of a second, and then the doctor's impersonal, professional mask returned. 'We're all going to die,' he said.

'Yes, I know that,' Ginger said crossly, thinking how much more she hated being patronized than she would the truth.

Stephen looked at her steadily for what seemed like a long time, checking, she thought, for indications of mental instability. He began to walk out of the room.

'Sometimes miracles do happen,' he said finally, 'but not very often.'

'Oh,' she said, realizing then that the truth was indeed worse than the usual equivocating nonsense they threw at you.

She stared at her father, then looked out of the window at the rooftops and the sky. It was quiet outside. Easter Sunday in the city. It was impossible to imagine the world without her father's presence. Even lying here silently, he was the focus of everyone's attention.

When she eventually looked back into the corridor, Stephen had gone, and she wondered whether she had really seen him at all.

A couple of minutes later, his head appeared around the door again.

'Come on,' he beckoned to her, 'I'm on a break, and you look as if you could do with a cup of tea.'

'I hate tea,' Ginger said grumpily, 'why does everyone think that tea can solve things?'

'Coffee?' Stephen suggested.

'Yes, coffee,' Ginger said, following him out of the room.

Pic was just returning from the cafeteria with their mother. They walked past each other silently like the changing of the guard, but Pic's eyebrows rose when she saw that her sister was leaving the ward with the handsome professor.

Noticing the equally surprised looks of the nurses, Ginger hurried after him and asked, 'Isn't it a bit unethical to socialize with the relatives?'

Stephen chuckled. 'Technically, yes, I suppose it is, but as I don't intend to make love to you in the laundry cupboard, or, worse, talk about the patient, I expect I'll get away with it . . .' He turned and smiled at her, his violet eyes sparkling with good humour.

'Shame!' she said, under her breath.

When they reached the canteen, he showed her to a table, calmly removed a tray of empty crisp packets and dirty crockery, handing it politely to a woman who was wiping down the tables, then walked over to the counter and bought Ginger coffee and a piece of chocolate cake.

'Yummy! What a gentleman!' Ginger said, gleefully.

He laughed and sat down opposite her with his tea.

Since he had just informed her that he wasn't allowed to talk about her father, and he didn't seem particularly eager to take the lead in the conversation, she felt it incumbent on her to start chatting.

'How's Alison?' she asked, scooping a fingerful of the gooey chocolate icing into her mouth, tasting the rough sugary sweetness, delighted that the hospital served such unhealthy food.

'Fine. Or at least I assume she is,' he replied, 'she's away this weekend, working. I've had the last two days off, just Ben and I together, which I must say I've enjoyed, and today Justine is looking after him. I don't know what we'd do without Justine. It seems like very bad luck that we all have to work on Easter weekend, or bad planning, but this rather special interview came up and Alison so wanted to do it. We've promised Justine a week off in lieu,' he added, smiling.

'They're great fun at the moment, aren't they?' Ginger said, referring to the children.

'They certainly are. Where's your little boy today?' he asked, sipping his tea.

Ginger began to explain.

'. . . poor Lia. I feel terrible about it, really. Her man's away, and her little girl is very poorly. They were meant to be coming down to the country with me for the weekend. Then Daddy happened . . . Lia says she wouldn't have come anyway because of Anouska, but I think she's only trying to make me feel better . . .'

'What's wrong with her little girl?' Stephen asked, more from genuine concern than professional interest, Ginger thought. It was funny how a special bond had developed between the three families, just because the babies had all been born at the same time.

'She's got a temperature . . .' Ginger began to list Anouska's symptoms, ending with, 'and this morning, her hands and feet were really red, as if she was sunburnt and beginning to peel. I said to Lia that I thought it might be eczema . . . What do you think?' she couldn't resist asking him, noticing alarm in his eyes.

She had urged Lia to call the GP again this morning, or get a second opinion. Now, there was one sitting in front of her. She knew that doctors hated being asked about illness at dinner parties. Well, this was hardly a dinner party, she reasoned. Damn the ethics of it. It was too good an opportunity to miss.

'Well, it's impossible to diagnose *in absentia*,' Stephen began to excuse himself, 'and I'm not a paediatrician . . .' He paused, as if deliberating whether to go on, then finally he added, 'But it does sound as if someone should have a proper look at Anouska . . .'

'Oh, could you come on your way home tonight?' Ginger leapt at the opening she thought he had given her.

'No. No, I really wouldn't be the right person,' he said, apologetically.

Ginger sighed and explained how unsympathetic Lia's GP had been.

'Look, I think this is what you should do,' Stephen said. 'Ring Lia and tell her to take the little girl to the nearest hospital. What'll that be? I should know. I live just down the road . . . Does she drive?'

'Well, yes, but she's got Guy too. Maybe I should go home and get a taxi with her?' Ginger asked, hoping that he would tell her to stop being so ridiculous. Something about his tone had made her very frightened.

'Yes, good idea,' Stephen said, standing up, even though he had hardly started his drink, 'as soon as possible, I think. She should tell whoever's on duty she'd like to speak to the Paediatric Registrar and tell him, or her, that you've spoken to someone who thought it sounded potentially like a case of Kawasaki syndrome. Now, it probably won't be, so don't alarm Lia unduly, but if it is, it is essential she get treatment quickly.'

'What's Kawasaki syndrome?' Ginger asked, horrified, quickening her step to keep up with him as they approached the ward again.

'Mucocutaneous lymph-node syndrome,' Stephen said, as if that would help her, then seeing her face, he added, 'It's a childhood illness and most children make a complete recovery, but for a few it's not very nice. I probably know a little more about it than most doctors because it can affect the coronary arteries, you see . . .'

'Is it catching?' Ginger said, hating herself for

390

immediately thinking of her own child, who had shown none of the symptoms.

'Not that I'm aware. Now, look, keep calm.' He saw her looking at the door of her father's room. 'There's nothing you can do for him at the moment,' he said gently.

'But what if he dies while I'm gone?' Ginger asked, tears catching in her throat.

'There'll be nothing you can do about it,' Stephen repeated.

In the taxi, she thought about that phrase. Stephen must have thought that her father was about to die, otherwise he would have said something like, it's unlikely, or, he won't. 'There'll be nothing you can do about it' sounded very final. She made herself imagine how she would feel if he were to die. Relieved, she thought. Relieved that he had gone quickly and without suffering too much. Relieved that he hadn't woken up a vegetable. She hadn't talked about that eventuality with Pic but she knew that's what they had both been thinking.

There's nothing you can do about him, but there was something she could do about Anouska. That had been Stephen's implication. She had called Lia from the hospital before she left, and told her to get the children ready. She tried to sound calm, but Lia had started panicking none the less. Fortunately, the traffic was extremely light and she arrived within half an hour of her call.

Anouska looked so tiny lying in the hospital bed. They had put up cot sides so she wouldn't fall out but the expanse of white sheet between her and the bars looked too far for such a frail little thing to roll. And the tubes, drips and wires would surely hold her in place. They had given her intravenous immunoglobulin. When they finally got a cannula into her tiny ankle and the fluid went into her, Lia had felt an enormous sense of expectation that as soon as the

391

medication reached its target, Anouska would suddenly throw off the illness that had made her so listless and be transformed back into the placid and smiling child she usually was. But there was no sudden change, no change at all.

After many hours of questions and many different people examining her, from the house doctor to the most senior consultant, the hospital had agreed on the diagnosis. Kawasaki syndrome, as Stephen had suspected. It was an inflammatory process, the consultant explained to her, that had no cure, but possible complications might be prevented if medication was administered early enough. They had asked her over and over again when the first symptoms had appeared. She tried to remember, but the days blurred into each other and she couldn't be sure. It was important, they told her. A few days ago, she thought. Or perhaps longer. Depends what you mean by first symptoms. They went over it again. It was like being interrogated. Please tell me what you want to hear and I'll say it, she had wanted to cry, understanding suddenly how it could be that people under stress made false confessions to figures of authority.

'Possible complications', 'early enough', these were such vague terms, and when she tried to ask what they meant, she was rebuffed with kindness. Eventually, a female doctor in a white coat sat down with her and explained that it was too early to tell what Anouska might have suffered. They were arranging for her to have further tests at Great Ormond Street.

They gave Lia a bed in the little room where Anouska was lying, and she sat on it staring at her child, with no idea what to do, paralysed by a depth of fear she had never experienced before. It glued her to the bed, rendering her incapable of moving, even of lying down. She was terrified of falling asleep, in case something, she didn't dare to think what, happened and no-one was watching over her daughter. In any case, it was only late afternoon, not bedtime, she saw as she looked at her watch. It could have been any time at all. The window was frosted glass, and the hospital had a routine of its own that bore no relation to the outside world. The nurses were very busy. From time to time, one popped her head round the door and asked if she was all right. They told her there was a parents' room at the end of the ward with tea- and coffee-making facilities. She smiled at them, dazed, trying to make the appropriate grateful responses. She found herself praying to a God she did not believe in. Please let her survive. Please let there be no damage. Please don't let it be my fault.

As the ward outside filled with evening visitors, grandmothers bearing Easter eggs, aunts and uncles with fluffy pink and yellow rabbits, daddies arriving with grim, worried faces, being nudged into smiles by their wives, Lia began to feel desperately lonely. She could not allow herself to leave the ward to find the payphone, and even if she did, there was no-one she could ring. This was a time for family, she realized. Friends paid visits to hospital when the worst was over, and they could sit and chat and steal grapes from the basket of fruit on the bedside table. Family dropped everything for you and arrived wearing jeans spattered with cake mixture from the baking they were in the middle of doing when you called.

Lia longed for someone she could trust with Anouska's life just long enough for her to go to the loo, or get a Coke from the machine in the lobby, or step outside the hot fug of the hospital and fill her lungs with cold air. For the first time in her adult life, she wanted a mum. A tear dribbled down her cheek. She wiped it away with the back of her hand, refusing to allow herself to cry. She must be strong for her daughter. She could not desert her as her own mother had done. Here, in the hospital, sitting waiting at the edge of life or death, she could almost understand how her mother could have done that. It was awful being a mother when your child was suffering. It took away your sense of self, making you completely responsible, and totally useless at the same time. In life, there was always an exit route, you could get away from things you did not like, but, in mother-hood, you could not. You were trapped and no amount of railing and screaming could get you out, unless you just walked away. No. She clenched her fists, trying to control physically the train of thought that was beginning to gather momentum in her troubled brain. Freedom was a tiny price to pay for the life of your child.

At that moment, she became aware that someone was standing in the doorway waiting for her to look up, not wanting to make her jump.

'I brought you a mobile phone,' Ginger said, 'I'm sorry, I didn't have a chance to get anything else. Actually, this is Pic's, but the battery's charged, and I thought you might want to have a line of communi-cation with the outside world. We've found it very useful with Daddy. We've even taught Mummy how to use it. See, it's easy . . .' She came and sat down next to her.

Lia could hold herself together no longer. She put her face against Ginger's shoulder and cried and cried and cried.

'Where's Guy?' she asked, when the sobs finally subsided.

'Don't worry about him. Pic's at my place with him. I think he's the only one of us who just loves hospitals. He's been flirting with the nurses at Daddy's all afternoon. What a shame we're not all in the same one. It would make life a lot easier . . .'

'Sorry,' said Lia.

Ginger looked at her, exasperated by her continual apologies. 'Now, I can't be long, so you'd better tell me what you want . . .' she ordered.

'Nothing really,' Lia said automatically, 'except company,' she added, smiling weakly.

'Don't be silly. I'm going to get you a meal and some

drink for the night. I've brought you a pair of knickers and a long T-shirt I use as a night-dress. They're a bit crumpled, but clean,' Ginger insisted, 'and you can ring Neil now . . .' she said, handing over the phone.

'I don't know his number.' Lia told her about ringing the hotel earlier that day, or had it been the day before? She could not remember.

'Damn . . . but he's on a school trip, isn't he?' Ginger said, thinking quickly. 'Ring one of his colleagues and ask them to find out and call him.'

'Oh!' Lia exclaimed, 'what a good idea . . . I hadn't even thought of that.'

'Well, you've had other things on your mind,' Ginger consoled her. She went over and looked into the cot. 'She looks a little better, I think,' she said.

'Do you think so?' Lia said, finally getting up from the bed.

'I think our little friend is going to be just fine,' Ginger said, putting her arm around Lia and giving her a squeeze as they stood side by side looking over the metal bars at the sleeping infant.

'There may be damage to her heart,' Lia whispered.

'Well, we'll think about that if and when the time comes,' Ginger responded calmly.

'You sound just like the doctors . . .'

'Yes,' Ginger turned round, dropping her arm from Lia's waist, 'I'm getting a bit of a taste for it. I know all the right things to say. I think I've got the bedside manner down now, all I have to do is learn about anatomy and epidemiology and that kind of stuff.'

'Cinch!' said Lia.

'Quite,' said Ginger, glad that she had managed to get her friend to join in the weak joke.

After Ginger left, Lia ate the sandwich she had bought her from the canteen, solemnly munching the dry bread with its slime of margarine and watery ham, repeating to herself Ginger's instructions: You have to eat, you have to be strong for Anouska. She felt a little better swigging at the can of Coke, feeling the bubbles scour the grease in her mouth away, and the caffeine jolt her tired arms. Then she picked up the mobile phone and pressed the green button.

First she called directory enquiries, and then, jotting down the number with the biro Ginger had provided, she called Neil's junior in the sports department.

'It's Lia, Neil's—'

'Hello, Lia, how are you?' Bill said, very friendly.

'Fine,' she said, automatically, 'well, not fine, but anyway . . . um, this sounds silly, but I'm trying to get in touch with Neil.'

'He's not here,' he said.

'No, I know that, he's in Paris, and he gave me the number of the hotel, but I think there's been some mistake . . . I wondered if you knew where they were staying?' she asked.

'No.' He was clearly mystified by the question.

'Well, could you find out? It's just that I'm in hospital and I've only got this mobile phone and I don't want to use up the battery, calling directory enquiries trying to find out people's numbers and then if they're not in – you know . . . I'm so sorry to ask,' she added, sensing a reluctance in the silence at the other end of the phone.

'No, I'd love to help,' he said, 'but I don't see what I can do.'

'You could ring the school secretary, maybe, she must know where they're staying,' she suggested.

'Where who are staying?'

'The school party.'

'What school party? I didn't know there was one.'

'But you dropped out . . . Neil took your place . . . you broke your arm . . .'

'Er, no . . .' he said.

'Oh,' Lia said, feeling his embarrassment, 'it must have been someone else. I'm sorry.'

'I could ring the secretary if you want,' he suddenly volunteered, as if he had failed her.

'If you could, thanks so much.' She read out the number of the mobile phone that Ginger had written at the top of the piece of paper, then pressed the red button to end the call, and switched it off.

There was a simple explanation, Lia told herself. Of course there was. She thought Neil had said it was Bill who had dropped out, but it was a big school, there were probably several Bills, or maybe she had mistaken the name. That was probably it. Don't start imagining things, she told herself. Things are bad enough. Remember the last time you suspected him and all he was doing was keeping the car a surprise for Christmas. There was bound to be some perfectly simple explanation. She just had too much on her mind to think of it. She called Pete and Cheryl, remembering that she did have family, after all. When Cheryl heard what had happened, she immediately offered to drive up, but somehow, now that someone else in the world knew, Lia didn't feel quite so isolated and helpless.

'No, you don't have to do that,' she told her sister-in-law, 'it's just nice to know you're there.'

'Look, we'll come tomorrow,' Cheryl told her, 'first thing – if the baby doesn't come tonight.'

'No, you don't have to. Neil'll be home.'

'We'll come and be with you until he gets there.'

'But the baby—' Lia protested.

'Well, at least I'll be near a maternity ward,' Cheryl laughed.

'All right,' Lia agreed, pressing the red button and switching the phone off.

Then a nurse came in to take Anouska's temperature, and the tea trolley made its round, and by the time Lia realized that no-one could contact her if the phone was not switched on, it was past midnight, and there didn't seem any point in getting people out of bed.

* * *

Alison had already consumed quite a lot of champagne with John-Fabrizio and his friends, and it was such a glorious, warm sunny afternoon, the only way to spend it, she told Neil, was in the sun, drinking more.

They went on a leisurely café crawl of the Marais and then crossed onto the Île Saint-Louis, where the quiet shade of the ancient streets cooled their flushed faces. She took his hand and he put his arm around her, pulled her close into his side, and kissed the top of her head. They said very little to one another, but it felt as if that was because they were relaxed in one another's company, unlike the previous evening, when there had been a yawning gulf, filled with unspoken resentments.

They bought small sugar cones of sorbet from a *glacerie* near Notre Dame, apricot for him, cassis for her. The blackcurrant ice stained her lips purple. As they wandered on, she caught a glimpse of herself in a panel of stainless steel that shone like a mirror in the golden evening sunlight. She rubbed at her lips with a tissue.

'God! And to think that I used to buy lipstick that colour – do you remember?'

'Yes,' he said, 'you liked purple. You had purple loons.'

'No, I had dark green loons.'

'No, you had purple loons, and yellow ones.'

'You're right!' she said, skipping beside him, 'I'd forgotten the yellow ones ... You didn't wear loons ...'

'I never liked flared trousers,' he said, resting his elbows on the parapet of the bridge they were crossing, looking out over the river.

'That's right. You always wore straight jeans, and you were the first to have your hair cut when punk happened.'

'Trendsetter, me.' He turned and smiled at her, then looked straight ahead, his eyes watching the *bateau mouche* with its sloping bank of tourists, their faces hidden under sunhats, behind cameras. He wondered how many photographs he and Alison would appear in, standing on the bridge together, the moment fixed in celluloid and turning up in Japan and America and Australia, all over the world, evidence of their weekend in Paris together.

'Look, Ally,' he began to say, 'that was a long time ago—'

'God, you're telling me,' she interrupted him, 'you can tell when you're getting old when fashion that you wore comes around again. I even found myself toying with a pair of flared trousers the other day, except they call them bootleg trousers these days, and I can remember taking a solemn vow never, ever to wear flares again. By 1977 they just seemed the most hideous things, didn't they?'

'What shall we do now?' Neil asked her, defeated by her chatter. He understood what she was doing, and maybe she was right. Maybe now was not the right time to talk about it. Not when they had both had a lot to drink. She was drunk and happy, and he wished her no ill. Maybe they didn't have to talk about it at all. Perhaps that's what she was trying to say.

She had known that he had been going to say something, and she thought she knew what it was, but she didn't want to hear it, not here, not standing next to him in the sunlight on a bridge over the Seine.

In her head, she heard Bryan Ferry's plaintive voice:

The Île de France with all the gulls around it,
The beauty that is spring's,
These foolish things
Remind me of you . . .

'More drink,' she said, linking her arm through his, as they turned towards the Left Bank, 'lots more to drink . . .'

He died at nine o'clock in the morning, just after Mummy and Pic had arrived. It was as if he had waited for them.

Ginger and Guy got there a few minutes later. She knew that something was wrong because the door to his room was closed, and it had always previously been open.

She had thought that he looked dead when he was lying there in a coma, but now she saw that he had not. Living people who looked like death did not in fact. Dead people really looked dead. His body seemed already to have shrunk. The man he had been was not present any longer.

She was the only one of them crying, and it was strange to feel her mother's arms enfold her, as Pic took Guy out of the room, and to smell the curiously familiar powdery scent of her skin. It was an old lady's smell. It reminded her of Hermione.

'Could I have a moment by myself with him?' she asked, recovering herself slightly.

Her mother released her and left the room, leaving her in silence.

Ginger approached the bed and picked up his hand. It was still warm, but there was no tension in it, no muscle, just bone and skin. She recalled vividly the time she had come to see him before his surgery, how he had squeezed her hand quickly and tightly as she left, like a secret sign between them, a freemason's salute that meant that he loved her, but could not say it out loud. And she had been too proud to say she loved him too.

'I love you, Daddy,' she told him now, 'you did know that, didn't you?'

She could feel the warmth literally draining away from his hand. His face remained slack, his eyes closed. He was never going to open them again and say, 'Boo!'

How wrong she had been to think that she would

feel relief at his passing. Relief had no place in her mind. All she felt was total, overwhelming sadness, and her tears came thick and fast, dripping onto his dead, flaccid skin. She stood there for a long time, hearing only her own gasping breathing as she cried, and then a kind of heaving silence as the tears began to stop. Then the rest of the world came sharply back into aural focus as a familiar gurgle of delight cut through the air. Somebody was tickling Guy.

There seemed to be remarkably few formalities. Daddy's body was wheeled off to the morgue to await collection, and, after a suitably respectful few minutes which they all spent wondering what on earth they were meant to do now, Mummy suggested that they repair to the canteen.

After the sadness, a wave of euphoria seemed to settle on the three women. They began to chatter with each other, remembering good things about him in anecdotes filled with laughter. Every so often, one of them would stop, mid-giggle, and look sad and dignified, but the seriousness did not last for long as the memories came tumbling out, capping each other with their good humour.

At one point, Stephen came up to their table to offer his condolences.

'Thank you so much,' Mummy said, 'we were just talking about the time when . . .' She launched into a story about a punting prank of Daddy's when he was up at Cambridge.

Ginger saw Stephen's expression, struggling to be polite but not engaged, and was suddenly brought back to the real world with its smell of chips and its clatter of cutlery as the hospital prepared for lunch.

'Stephen . . . the professor doesn't want to know, Mummy,' she said gently.

With perfect manners, he made his excuses and turned away, but Ginger jumped up and followed him.

'Sorry . . .' she said.

'No, don't be,' he told her, 'she needs to talk, and we have to have time for that.'

But Ginger could see that he was grateful for her intervention.

'I just wanted to tell you about Anouska,' she said, realizing that now she was being as bad as her mother, holding him up when he wanted to get home, 'you were right about it. They're keeping her in. Nobody seems to be able to tell Lia anything for certain, but as soon as I can, I'm going to look it up on the Internet.'

'Be careful how you do that,' Stephen warned, his face full of concern, 'I know that you don't agree, but believe me, sometimes it is better for people not to know all the details . . . especially if they are in shock. Knowing everything about a disease doesn't mean you can cure it, unfortunately.'

She nodded, heeding what he said.

'And you must look after yourself too,' he told her, putting his finger under her chin and tilting her face upwards as if he were talking to a child. It was a gesture made with such delicacy that somehow she did not mind. 'You have had two big shocks this weekend, and you are coping very well, but there will come a time when you won't be so good at dealing with it, so take care . . .'

'I will,' she said obediently, 'two big shocks. Yes, I suppose I have. And they say that disasters come in threes.' She tried to sound light.

'I'm sure that no-one has ever proved that statistically,' Stephen assured her with a smile.

'You're probably right,' she acknowledged.

'Well, goodbye,' he said, offering her his hand.

She shook it. 'Goodbye, and thanks!' she said, watching him walk away down the corridor, suddenly overwhelmed by the strangest, sad feeling that she would never see him again.

Daddy's left and now I think that everyone is leaving me, she told herself, trying to rationalize the

402

sensation, as she went back to join her mother, her sister and her son.

'What do you want to do, Mummy?' Pic was asking their mother. 'You know you're very welcome to come back to Swiss Cottage with me.'

'No, I think I shall go home,' their mother replied.

'Home? To the country? Now?' Ginger asked, sitting down again.

'I think so,' their mother said, 'I shall need to make arrangements.'

She fumbled about in her handbag and finally withdrew her purse, before remembering that they were in a cafeteria, they had already paid, and there was no waiter to hail for the bill.

'Would you like me to come with you?' both daughters dutifully asked.

'No, I think I should like to remember him alone, if you don't mind,' their mother said, putting the purse back in the handbag and taking out a pair of glasses, which she put on for no apparent reason. 'I have the dogs . . . and there are plenty of people to look after my needs . . .'

Neither daughter knew what to say. It didn't seem right that she should be returning to the country alone, to find comfort in a spaniel rather than a daughter, but it was her home and if that was what she wanted, why should they stop her?

'Shall I get Tom to come for you with the car?' Pic asked, referring to the man who was Mummy's driver and butler and generally in charge of running the household.

'No, no, I shall take the train. You could call and tell him to meet me at the station.'

'Of course I will,' Pic agreed.

'I'll take Mummy to Waterloo, then,' Ginger told Pic, 'it's on my way home.'

Neil could remember standing on the bridge in the warm, golden glow of evening sunlight, and then the next bar, which they had left after one drink because it was packed with tourists, but after that, the evening merged into a vague bleary impression of street-lights and snatches of inane conversation about times and places of things that they had done twenty years before. She had been absolutely insistent that they had gone to Biba on the same day as they went to see Bryan Ferry, but he knew for sure that he had never been to Biba. She had gone with her mother, he told her. They had had a long, repetitive, pointless argument about it, and in the end, he had got up and walked out onto the street, not knowing where the hell he was going. He had been relieved to hear her footsteps running after him. After that, he thought he remembered being in McDonald's, but couldn't imagine that Alison would have consented to cross that threshold, even at her most inebriated.

It was very late when they had arrived back at the hotel. The night porter was asleep and not best pleased to see them as he unlocked the door. Neil couldn't remember whether they had taken the stairs or the lift, but he had woken up at dawn fully clothed with Alison snoring beside him. His headache had made speech virtually impossible. They had cleared the room and checked out without a word.

At the station, she had the presence of mind to buy a big bottle of mineral water, which they were taking it in turns to slurp. Now, she pushed a couple of white tablets across the table at him.

'Paracetamol,' she said.

'Thanks,' he replied, swallowing them.

The train was speeding through the fields of France.

'What are you thinking about?' Alison asked him, after a while.

The painkiller was beginning to work, flooding his skull with some chemical to neutralize the jets of boiling acid that seemed to be targeting and dissolving small pockets of his brain.

'I was trying to work out why French houses look

different from English ones,' he said, pointing at the window as a village flashed past, 'I think it's because the fronts and backs are flat so the roof's got two sides not four – like a triangle not a pyramid, if you see what I mean . . .'

She looked at him astonished. 'What a typically male thing to be thinking,' she exclaimed, laughing.

'Why?' he asked her, then, afraid to start another futile argument, agreed, 'I suppose it is. What were you thinking?'

She was thinking how little he had changed. The day before, she had thought that he had changed a lot, and that was why it would never work between them, but it wasn't that. She was the one who had changed, or even if she hadn't, fundamentally, then the standards against which she measured things had. At seventeen, he had everything that everyone considered most desirable – he was handsome, he had a motorbike, he was the captain of both the school football and cricket teams. And now he still had all these things, and yet they meant nothing to her. But these were thoughts she could not share with him.

'I was thinking about Ben,' she told him, snatching at a neutral subject. She paused as the waiter refilled their coffee cups. 'This is the first time I've been away, and I've missed him. I didn't think I would . . . apparently, he's missed me too. Apparently he said ball, so his vocabulary has increased by fifty per cent,' she added.

'How do you know?'

'Justine told me . . . I called yesterday morning.'

'Oh.'

Why hadn't he called home too? he asked himself, suddenly panicking, then remembering it was OK. They had agreed he wouldn't because they were at Ginger's house in the country. Lia would call him if there were any problems. He had given her the number of the hotel. Slowly, he calmed himself down.

'So, Ben says words, now, does he?' he asked Alison.

'Not really. He babbles. Da da da,' she imitated her baby, 'and Stephen gets awfully excited, but apparently they all start off with that!'

'Do they?' Neil said, 'Annie claps and she can wave bye bye,' he added proudly.

'Really? Ben doesn't wave yet.' Alison said, as the train rushed into the tunnel and they both fell silent.

And Neil thought how ironic it was that they should have ended their illicit weekend together talking about the only thing that they had left in common: their two small children.

At Waterloo, he carried her smart case to the end of the platform then put it down on the ground.

'I'm getting a taxi,' she said, 'I'd offer you a lift, but . . .'

'No, I'll take the tube,' he said.

They both stood looking at each other for a long time. Then, he stepped forward and took her in his arms, and kissed her. It was a kiss of regret and longing and nostalgia, and when they finally pulled apart, he could feel her arms trembling, and he knew that she was trying very hard not to cry.

'Bye now.' He picked up his bag and turned away.

Alison stood and watched him go, then she took a deep breath. Her eyes were so full of tears, she did not even notice an elderly lady holding a baby who was looking up at the departure board, and next to her, Ginger, whose eyes followed her disbelievingly, as she walked straight past them towards the sign that said 'Taxis'.

Stephen and Ben were sitting beside each other at the kitchen table having tea when Alison walked into the kitchen. She kissed them both on the top of the head, and sat down opposite. For a while she picked at the pasta that he had prepared, then she helped herself to a plateful and began to cram it into her mouth ravenously.

'I'm completely hungover, I have to admit, and utterly starving,' she said, 'this is delicious!'

Stephen smiled at her. He had always thought that hangovers rather suited her, giving her a slightly dishevelled look. She was clearly tired, but sparkling, as if she were still high on the champagne she was telling them she had consumed the day before at John-Fabrizio Jones's stylish party.

'What have you been up to?' she asked him, her mouth full.

'Well, let's just say you picked a good weekend to go away,' he replied, with a slight, dry chuckle.

It didn't even occur to him that the news about Ginger's father and Lia's child would change her mood so dramatically. Her fork dropped from her hand, and her face went white with shock. He thought for a moment that she was going to pass out.

'He almost reached his three score and ten, only a year off, and that's not bad for someone who drank and smoked—' he began to say.

'Oh, I don't care about him,' Alison interrupted, so angrily Stephen was taken aback.

'Of course not,' he said, 'well, I just don't know what to say about the baby. It's entirely possible that she will make a complete recovery,' he explained, as Alison sat staring at him, nodding, wanting to hear that it was going to be all right, 'but there is the chance of sudden death ...' He was attempting to make a balanced, but realistic, assessment of the dangers, but Alison was clearly not hearing anything he said.

She jumped up, rushed to the phone, picked up the receiver, dialled a number, then put it down, rushed back to the kitchen table, lifted Ben from his high chair, hugging him tight to her, stroking the back of his head, with his face to her shoulder. When she finally returned him to his chair, her smart black jacket was smeared with Baby Organix Vegetable Pasta.

She began to question Stephen, harshly, as if it was all his fault. Was there any way the illness could have been spotted earlier? How could he be so unsure about the prognosis? Was Anouska receiving the best possible care? Would money help get a more expert opinion?

They were the sort of questions that he was used to hearing from close relatives who wanted someone to blame for the tragedy and were desperate to hear the doctor say that it was not their fault. He wished he had found some gentler way of telling her the news. The shock of learning of two tragedies so close to home when she had been abroad and powerless to do anything had clearly shocked her deeply. He tried to understand the hostility of her behaviour towards him as transferred guilt because she was imagining subconsciously what would have happened if Ben had fallen ill and she had not been there.

'The chances are that the baby will be fine,' he told her, again, 'the real danger is when the disease is misdiagnosed. Anouska is one of the lucky ones,' he added, mentally crossing his fingers that the reassurances he was giving her would prove correct.

'No, she won't ... I know she won't,' Alison kept repeating.

He noticed Ben's face, bewildered by her behaviour.

'Why don't you go and have a lie down?' he suggested, anxious to minimize their son's distress.

She looked up, angrily, on the point of arguing, then saw that he was nodding at Ben's frowning face.

'I think I will,' she agreed, leaving the room, hunched and trembling.

Pete was waiting for Neil in the living room when he arrived home.

'Where the hell have you been?' he asked as he came through the door.

'Paris,' Neil said, dumping his kitbag by the door

and slumping into the armchair opposite his brother, 'school trip.'

'There wasn't a bloody school trip,' Pete sat forward, coldly spitting out the words, 'you stupid bastard!'

'Look,' said Neil, 'it's not what you think—' He stopped mid-sentence, realizing that it was exactly what his brother was thinking. 'Where is everyone?' he asked, trying to avoid Pete's gaze, and then, slightly frightened by the silence that followed, 'Why are you here, anyway?'

When Pete started talking about Kawasaki syndrome Neil thought, for a few bleary seconds, that it was all an elaborate joke that he did not quite understand, something to do with his motorbike. But then one glance at his brother's face told him that it was not.

In the moment's silence that followed his account of what had happened, the phone rang. Neil went to the kitchen and picked it up. Nothing. He knew who it was, but all he could think was that her taxi ride had taken just as long as his on the tube. He wished that they had never returned from Paris, and then, as the British Telecom message yelled in his head 'The other person has now cleared . . . the other person has now cleared . . .' he slammed down the receiver, furious that she had ever lured him away.

'Let's go,' he said to his brother, coming back into the room, looking for the car keys, before seeing that Pete was dangling them in front of him.

'No, you go and wash your face,' his brother ordered him contemptuously, 'you've got lipstick round your mouth. Lia's been through enough without that.'

Lia was surprised that the main emotion she felt when she saw him was relief, closely followed by sympathy. He looked so worn out, worried and repentant, she wanted to hug him and tell him it would be all right, but she could not. She did not know that it would. Instead she took his hand, and led him to the cot where Anouska lay sleeping. She could see that he was frightened by the heart monitor and the line going into her foot.

'It's just a drip, to give her the medication,' she explained.

'Is she going to die?' Neil whispered.

'I don't think so,' she told him, quietly.

There had been moments in the last twenty-four hours when she had caught herself on the point of wishing that she would. Death was almost easier to contemplate than the responsibility of living with the threat of a heart attack hanging over her all the time. A heart attack, for God's sake, and she was not even a year old. Then she would hate herself for even allowing the thought to cross her mind.

With her eyes fixed on Anouska, unable to look at Neil, Lia began to explain the little she knew, and by relating it to him, she realized that she had learnt much more than she thought. They were going to go by ambulance to Great Ormond Street the next day. Anouska was going to have something called an echo scan which would show up any damage to her arteries. After that she didn't know what was going to happen. She supposed they would come back in the ambulance. The doctors were all saying that Anouska had a good chance of survival, but nobody seemed to be able to promise more than that.

She felt Neil bristle with impatience by her side, and it made her recognize the cycle of emotions she had gone through the day before. Impatience, anger, impotence. It was a hospital. You expected them to *know*. You could deal with yes and no, live or die, but not with this terrible uncertainty.

'Is there a cure?' Neil asked.

Well, she began, knowing how frustrating he would find the answer, if medication was given early enough then complete recovery was possible, except that nobody even knew that for certain. The disease had only been discovered in recent years, although it was becoming increasingly common. The treatment was very simple. Either it would arrest the disease, or it would not. It was too early to say.

She felt Neil's arm around her shoulder and did not attempt to shrug it off. She did not know whether they were lovers, now, or even friends, but they were together as parents of a child. Nothing could alter that. It would bind them for ever. Or for as long as their baby lived.

Chapter 11

MAY

Pic and Ginger ambled slowly through the bluebell wood together, taking it in turns to push the buggy. The canopy of tall trees shaded the fierce sunshine of early summer, the flowers around their ankles were so blue that a blue haze seemed to colour the air above them. The rustle of leaves and the birdsong were like balm to tired spirits. If it hadn't been for the regular roar of planes above, on their noisy descent into Heathrow, it would have been easy to imagine that they were wandering through some enchanted forest in the country, and not the Royal Botanic Gardens only five miles from the heart of London.

'Have you seen Charlie much?' Pic asked her sister.

'No. He rings, but I don't want to see him. I don't see the point,' Ginger said grumpily.

'But why?' Pic asked.

'Oh, I don't know,' Ginger replied, clamming up and taking a few quick steps ahead so that Pic could not see her face.

Grief had affected them in different ways. At the funeral, Pic had tears in her eyes as Daddy's favourite piece of Bach spilled out of the organ and filled the church with its harmonies, and she had concentrated on how beautiful the music was, and how much Daddy would have liked it. She doubted whether Ginger even heard it as she stood next to her shaking with uncontrollable sobbing. Pic had noticed the concerned surprise on their relations' faces as the two of them faced the congregation and followed the coffin out of the church, Ginger hanging on to her arm for support. It was so unlike Ginger, they had been thinking. Ginger was the clown who would laugh through anything, Pic was meant to be the serious one.

As each week passed, Pic could feel her own sadness retreating. There were times when she would put down the phone after talking to Mummy, or Ginger, and think, I must ring Daddy now, then remember that she could not. If someone at work praised her, she found herself dialling his number before she realized that he was no longer there to tell. Now that the by-election in his consituency had been called, the press was full of speculation, and she often found herself wondering what he would have made of it all. It was as if he was still around, but just out of reach. Her overwhelming feeling about him was fondness.

Ginger's grief was darker. It hung around her like a mood, diminishing her, closing her to the world. Pic had visited her every weekend since his death. Each time she arrived at the flat, she expected Ginger to open the door recovered, joking, normal again, but it didn't happen. If she smiled, there was no light in her face. It was as if she was just going through the motions of living, but not really engaged.

Her relationship with Daddy had been difficult, and it had been left unresolved. It didn't seem to make any difference however much anyone tried to reassure her that he had loved her. She stubbornly refused to be consoled.

When the will was read and it emerged that Daddy had not only made generous provision for Ginger, but included Guy too, Pic had looked at Ginger, expecting to see her face lift, but it had only fallen aghast.

'There, you see, he did love you . . .' she had whispered, holding her sister's hand under the big mahogany table at the solicitor's office.

'I know that,' Ginger had hissed, 'but he didn't know that I loved him too.'

'I'm sure he did,' Pic insisted, but even as she said it, she wasn't quite convinced it was true.

Ginger had always done a pretty good job of disguising any affection she felt for her father. They had communicated by scoring points for several years, but that didn't mean that Daddy had loved her any less. Yes, she told Ginger, she had outraged, annoyed and offended him, but he had delighted in it. He loved a scrap.

'You both gave him enormous pleasure, in your different ways,' their mother had told them the day he died. Pic kept reminding Ginger of that. But it seemed to have no impact.

'Don't you think it might help if you saw a few people?' Pic tried again, as they came out of the wood and onto the sunny open lawns by the lake.

'No,' Ginger said sulkily.

'What about Robert? He usually cheers you up.'

'I don't need cheering up,' Ginger told her, 'I'm perfectly all right. I've got enough on my plate trying to work out what to do about work, and Lia and Guy.'

'How is Lia?' Pic asked, grateful for a change of subject. Perhaps if Ginger talked about her friend, she would realize how lucky she was in comparison.

'I think she's coping a bit better,' Ginger said. 'The first week Anouska came out of hospital she was very jittery, but she seems a bit calmer now. She says she's happy to start having Guy again, but I don't know what to do . . .'

Ginger hadn't been into work since their father's death. Ironically, she missed it, and would have welcomed any distraction from the constant pounding guilt, but she had not been able to bring herself to leave Guy with a stranger.

'You don't have to work now,' Pic suggested, making oblique reference to the fortunes they had both been left.

'Nor do you,' Ginger countered immediately.

'No, but I enjoy my career and you don't,' Pic reasoned.

'Yes,' Ginger conceded, adding, 'I just don't think I'm in a fit state to make any big decisions right now.'

Pic had to admit that was sensible. Ginger was not herself. She only wished she could find a way of making it better for her.

'I just think that if you allowed yourself to have some fun—' she began to say.

'Oh why don't you just leave me alone!' Ginger shouted at her, then, shocked by the sound of her own raised voice, she dissolved into tears. Pic put the brake on the buggy and walked forward with outstretched arms. She held Ginger tight for several minutes.

'I was screwing Charlie when I should have been seeing Daddy,' Ginger blurted into Pic's shoulder. 'Daddy asked me to that boat race party, he made a point of ringing and inviting me, and I just refused. I didn't even think . . . I was so keen to see Charlie, and there was Daddy trying to make a place for Guy in the family, and it was a really big deal for him to do that, and I couldn't even give him the time of the day . . .' All the sentences that had been whirring in her brain, punishing her, began to tumble out. 'I was just so selfish, and I never got a chance to tell him I was sorry . . . He waited for you to arrive before dying, but he didn't wait for me . . .'

'That's not true,' Pic told her, holding her sobbing body as it sagged against hers, 'it's just not true . . .'

'It is, it is,' Ginger insisted, 'I was horrible to him, and he died thinking that I hated him.'

'No he didn't,' Pic told her. 'We saw him on our birthday, didn't we, and you were really good. You didn't shout at him once.'

'Didn't I?' Ginger lifted her face from her sister's shoulder for a moment.

'No. You were really gracious.'

415

Seeing that this approach had a chance of working, Pic racked her brain to think of other examples.

'At Christmas you played charades together, don't you remember, and you won, of course, and Daddy fell in love with Guy . . .'

'He did, didn't he?' Ginger said, a glimmer of a smile breaking onto her wet face.

'He certainly did. He used to ring me up and tell *me* all the things that he had heard from Mummy that Guy had done.'

'Did he?' Ginger asked, surprised.

'Oh, he was always going on about him . . . he was really proud of him, and you. He thought you were doing a good job.'

'No, he didn't,' Ginger said modestly, blowing her nose and secretly wanting to hear more.

'He did, he told me that he didn't know how you were managing, but you seemed to be,' Pic told her.

'That's not quite the same as thinking I was doing a good job,' Ginger pointed out, wiping her face.

'Well, it was for him,' Pic said, adding, seeing that Ginger was calmer now, 'anyway, the boat race party wasn't such a big deal.'

'It was. That phone call, Daddy even said that he might not be here for the next boat race – and he was right . . .' She burst into tears again.

'I expect he meant that he wouldn't be an MP any more,' Pic said. 'He was convinced they were going to lose the next election, lose badly.'

'Do you think that was it?' Ginger said, replaying the phone call in her head for the millionth time. All her guilt seemed to have focused on those two minutes, when she had been offered the opportunity of a truce, and had refused to accept it.

'You mustn't blame Charlie, you know,' Pic was saying.

'I don't blame Charlie, I blame myself,' Ginger said.

'Well, you mustn't do that either,' Pic said, simply. Ginger looked at her sister and felt an enormous rush of affection. Pic was so clever intellectually, but she was such a simple soul when it came to psychology. She had almost exhausted her entire emotional vocabulary in her attempts to make things right for Ginger.

'Daddy would have been delighted, you know,' Pic said, making one last earnest effort to assuage her sister's guilt, 'about you and Charlie. He worried about you. He was old-fashioned. He thought you needed a man to look after you . . .'

She saw Ginger's face flash with anger and was relieved. That was much more like Ginger. Anger and defiance suited her. Depression and guilt did not.

'Charlie doesn't want to look after me,' Ginger said, resignedly, 'he wants to screw me. Anyway, I hate men. They're all bastards.'

'Except Daddy,' Pic chimed in automatically.

'No, Daddy was a bastard too,' Ginger said, giggling suddenly, 'there's no point in making him into a saint just because he's dead.'

'No,' said Pic uncertainly, caught between her desire to keep Ginger happy, and her discomfort about speaking ill of the dead. 'No, you're right,' she confirmed eventually, 'he was wonderful in lots of ways, but in lots of ways he was a bit of a pig. Forgive me, Daddy, wherever you are . . .' She looked up at the clear blue sky.

'Forgive me,' Ginger echoed, taking her sister's hand and walking down towards the lake to feed the ducks.

'I thought I might take a few days off, take Ben to the seaside. Seems such a shame to work in this lovely weather,' Alison suggested.

'I think that's a marvellous idea,' Stephen said encouragingly, 'will you go to your mother's?'

'I thought I might,' Alison replied.

They were kneeling on the bathroom floor beside one another bathing their child. Over the last few weeks, they had developed a habit of doing the whole bedtime ritual together, when they were both home. There was something very soothing about sponging his chubby little form with warm water and pushing his ducks up and down. Stephen found it a wonderful way to unwind, and he had noticed that since Easter, Alison had been getting home from work in time to join them. It was as if she had been so troubled by the news about Lia's child that she had started to value every precious moment with Ben.

She had been so very, very frightened when he told her what had happened to Anouska, and the fear seemed to have remained with her ever since. He could see the constant tension in her facial muscles, creating lines where her skin had been smooth. Any unexpected noise, from the doorbell to a clanking pipe in the attic now made her jump. He was aware that he was more than averagely inured to death and illness, that was the advantage, or disadvantage, of his profession, but he felt her reaction was too extreme and it troubled him.

He picked Ben out of the bath and Alison enfolded him in a large white towel, drying and tickling him at the same time. It was a beautiful sight, a mother's communication with a baby, it thrilled him to witness it.

'When were you thinking of going?' Stephen asked her, as they each took an arm and a leg and shoved them into Ben's Paddington Bear babygro.

'This weekend. I'll take the back half of the week off and stay till Sunday, if that's OK?'

'Fine.'

'You'll be working?' she asked him.

'I will,' he sighed. 'Will you take Justine with you?'

'No, I thought I'd ask her to go round and help Lia. The baby's out of hospital now,' she explained.

'Or we could just give her the time off?' Stephen suggested.

'No, she likes Lia. They see each other anyway.

It would be one way of me doing something to help.'

The idea of sending your nanny around to help someone else seemed curiously feudal to him. He saw the potential for offending Lia and the rather chippy man she lived with, but said nothing. He had been surprised that Alison had not wanted to go to the hospital herself. She had made work an excuse and sent flowers. It looked like denial, and was one of the many slight oddities in her behaviour that had concerned him.

'You won't let your mother get you down, will you?' he said gently, taking her hand as they switched off Ben's light and left the nursery.

'I don't intend to see much of her. She can play with Ben to her heart's content and cook me restorative meals, and I shall walk by the sea . . .'

'Good,' he said, 'I'm very glad to hear it.'

Lia lay under the apple tree in the garden on a reclining chair with Anouska asleep in the pram beside her. It was a beautiful warm day, their dinner was in the oven and clean clothes flapped on the line. If someone had told her a year before that there would come a time when the quality of the day was measured by the number of loads of washing completed and dry, or the quantity of baby food consumed and unregurgitated, she would have laughed at them. But that was what looking after a baby was all about, and, as long as Anouska continued to thrive, she was happy enough with it.

When they had finally brought Anouska home, Lia had assumed that she would relax back into the old routine, leaving the strain and worry behind her at the hospital, but the anxiety followed her home. The scan at Great Ormond Street had indicated that the disease had not damaged her arteries, but the doctors wanted to do another scan in a few weeks' time. The only medical aftercare they would have to administer was a small dose of aspirin each day, which seemed simple enough, but Lia found herself in the grip of almost paralysing panic the moment the red Peugeot had pulled out of the hospital car park. The hospital had staff and systems to protect Anouska. Outside, it was solely up to her.

The first day, she had not been able to see how they would survive. The stress was too much for anyone to bear. Every cough or moan or fidget that Anouska made sent her racing to her, and when there was no sound she panicked all the more, and ran to check that she was still breathing. At night, Lia would lie in bed, her head spinning with terrible scenarios, and when she finally drifted into sleep, she had dreadful nightmares that blended in with Anouska's waking, and she would dash to her, half-sleepwalking and shaking with fear. Eventually, she put a mattress on the floor beside the cot.

But each day got a little easier, Lia thought, staring through the pale pink blossom up to the sky. After one day had passed, you knew at least that you could survive one day, and after one week, you realized that it was possible to survive a week. After two weeks, you had changed your routine in little ways to help you cope, and after three, you could almost allow yourself the optimism that Anouska would live to see her first birthday. And if she could live to be one, there was a chance that she could live to be two, and so on. You built confidence day by day. It wasn't the life you had expected to live, but it was a kind of life. At least it meant you experienced it and found pleasure in little things. The luminously delicate pinkness of the apple-blossom against the blueness of the sky, the fragrance of newly cut grass, these were things you never really noticed before. Nothing slipped past as it had when you thought that life would go on for ever.

'I've made you a cup of tea.'

Neil's voice directly above her woke her suddenly.

She had fallen asleep. She sat up quickly, her eyes shooting to the empty pram.

'It's OK, I've got her here, look . . .'

She held her arm up, shielding her eyes from the sun, and saw that her baby was sitting on Neil's hip, a leg each side of his waist, waving at her.

'Hello, my darling,' Lia said to her, and then she picked up the mug of tea and said, 'Thank you,' to Neil.

They had found a way of existing together. Neil went to work and came home as soon as school ended. It took the pressure off when there was someone else in the house. She had to admit that he had become very good with Anouska, taking her for late-afternoon walks whenever it was warm enough, or just talking to her gently, and reading her books with flaps before bed.

The school's long-awaited, much-feared, Ofsted inspection finally happened, and the sports department had been singled out for praise, so it had been worth all the long evenings he had spent preparing for it. If that's what he had been doing. Lia didn't know, didn't ask, and was surprised how little she cared. Anouska's health seemed to have taken over every cell of her waking brain. Sometimes she forced herself to imagine Neil with another woman, or even a man, and she tried very hard to feel something. But she couldn't. An affair was nothing compared with Anouska's life.

Sex was not part of their relationship any longer. Even if he hadn't been having an affair, she didn't see how they could have found the peace of mind for it. The few times he had tried to embrace her, she had turned away from him, determined to avoid the complication of feelings getting in the way of her care of Anouska. Once or twice, she had noticed the pain in his eyes, and felt guilty. Perhaps he had done nothing. Perhaps there was after all a perfectly innocent explanation for his secret trip to Paris. But if there were, she would remind herself, then surely he would have told her. His silence only confirmed his guilt.

In her heart, she knew that it was impossible for two people to live together for any length of time with no real contact, but at the moment, it was enough just to get through each day.

'The tickets arrived this morning,' she informed Neil's back as she followed him into the house to prepare their supper.

'What tickets?'

'The tickets for our holiday,' she told him, 'the last week in May . . .'

'Are we still going?' he asked eagerly, sensing a glimmer of reprieve.

'I don't know if I dare,' she said, 'but she'll have had the second scan by then. If that's OK, I've been thinking, then she should be as safe there as she is here, shouldn't she, if we're careful about the heat. We can take her aspirin. The air might do her good. They have hospitals, don't they?'

It was as if she was trying to talk herself into it. He knew how much she had wanted to go back to Portugal.

He attempted to catch her eyes and smile. 'Well, let's go then, if the scan's OK.'

'Right then,' she said. There was no excitement in her voice. She opened the fridge door. 'We've got lasagne. D'you want salad with it?'

'Yes,' he said, sadly, 'salad would be great.'

The sea air had tired Ben out. He had been in the garden most of the day, looking rather colonial in his white sunhat with chinstrap, crawling all over the lawn and pulling the petals off Margaret's red dahlias. Now, he was so peacefully asleep, Alison had to lean right into the travel cot to hear he was breathing. She kissed her fingertips then touched them against his cheek.

'I love you, my angel, sleep tight,' she whispered, tiptoed out of the room and went downstairs.

'I thought I'd go for a walk,' she told her mother, who was loading the dishwasher in the kitchen, 'it's only just after six.'

'Is it really? It seems later.' Margaret straightened up slowly.

'Yes, it's exhausting looking after him all day, isn't it?' Alison said. 'It's a full time occupation for two people . . . I don't know how single mothers cope!'

She hadn't intended to imply any sub-text in the observation, but she saw that her mother glanced at her face before agreeing, 'Yes, it must be terribly difficult.'

Margaret had mellowed, Alison thought. When her father was alive she knew that her mother's knee-jerk reaction to such a statement would have been something like: 'Well, nobody makes them have babies on their own.'

And she would have felt obliged to remind her mother about divorced women, and widows, women who were single through no fault or desire of their own, and there would have been a long argument, which would achieve nothing at all, and would end with Margaret saying something like, 'You can twist words whatever way you like to try and catch me out, but you know exactly what I mean . . .'

And they would not have spoken to each other for the rest of the evening.

Perhaps they had both softened, she thought as she opened the gate that led onto the stretch of grass that separated the estate from the beach. Perhaps her mother had become as bored as she had with the old patterns of behaviour, or perhaps she had worked out that if she wanted to see her beloved grandson, she must not argue with her daughter. It occurred to her that it was a horrible kind of power to wield. Ben could not be made a pawn in the game of their relationship.

423

The shingle crunched under the soles of her deck shoes as she walked down the beach. She picked up a stone and threw it into the water with a satisfying plop. The sea was calm, milky turquoise in the evening light. There was no-one around, and no sound except the gentle turn of the waves. She decided to walk westwards, into the setting sun.

Over the past few days, she had seen her mother differently. In London, where she always looked smart and perfectly groomed, it was easy to forget that she was getting older. Here, she noticed her slowness in the mornings, the effort it was for her to walk upstairs, the almost obsessive way she planned the day at breakfast, telling Alison what they would eat for lunch and supper, running through the ingredients in case there was anything she had forgotten to buy. There never was. It was only her way of maintaining control of her environment, her way of warding off the two things that all old people feared most, memory loss and dependence.

There was a point in life when parents stopped being people who looked after you and began to need looking after themselves. Margaret wasn't there yet, and she was clearly determined to avoid it for as long as she could. Alison found she rather admired her for that. The death of Ginger's father had made her aware suddenly how little time she and her mother had left together. She wanted to be big enough to enjoy that time, and not to waste it in fruitless recrimination about the past.

The weekend before she had come down to the coast, she had run into Ginger in Waitrose. She had seen Guy first, sitting up like a toddler at the front of the trolley, and then she realized that she had walked right past Ginger because she looked so different. It wasn't so much her face, which was sad and pale, but her posture. Normally, you could identify Ginger a hundred yards away. There was a spring in her step, an open joyousness in deportment that marked her out, but now she seemed stooped, weighed down, physically gloomy.

'Thanks for your card,' she had said, acknowledging the few sympathetic sentences Alison had jotted down and sent to her.

'How are you?' Alison had asked.

'Oh, pretty bad,' Ginger told her, staring ahead, not really looking at her, 'the sadness I can see an end to, but not the guilt . . .'

Alison had nodded silently. She had never really known her own father, or liked him, and when he died, she found there were lots of questions she had not even been aware of wanting to ask him, that would now remain unanswered. She understood about the guilt. It never really left you. You learned to live with it, but it was always there.

'Shall we have a coffee?' Alison had suggested.

'No, thanks,' Ginger said, suddenly focusing on her with a scowl, 'no, I don't want one, thanks,' and she had turned away without saying goodbye.

Alison had not insisted. There was nothing worse than someone else telling you that they knew how you felt. Sometimes when you were unhappy you just wanted to be left alone.

In the distance, a single row of electric bulbs strung between lamp-posts along the seafront burst into tiny glowing stars of coloured light. The sun was slipping down through the soft high cloud turning the sky blue-pink. It was the time of evening when even happy people reflected for a moment on the transience of life, and sad people sighed at the passing of another day. Alison felt the warm, salty wind blowing the tears from her eyes.

For the thousandth time she asked herself how she could have been so destructive. What was it that had made her reject her own happiness, and ruin someone else's life? Destiny might have thrown her and Neil together again, but destiny had not cast her into his arms, and provided a flat for them to fuck in, or enticed him away when his child was in peril. She had. And now he hated her. But not as much as she hated herself.

She had spoken to him only once since they kissed each other goodbye at Waterloo. They had both known it was over, and they had both thought they could pick up their lives as if nothing had happened. How complacent they had been.

Late that night, when Stephen had fallen asleep, she had crept downstairs to the phone and dialled his number again. He had picked up the receiver immediately.

'Hello,' she said.

He did not answer for several seconds. Then he said, 'I thought it might be the hospital.'

'I just wanted you to know I was thinking of you . . .' she had faltered.

'I don't want you to think of me ever again.'

'I know, I know,' Alison began to sob into the phone, 'I feel so terrible.'

'You don't,' Neil told her coldly, 'you don't even begin to feel . . . I didn't even know what feeling was until this afternoon . . .'

And then he had put down the phone.

It was all her fault. If she had been strong enough to resist the pull of indulgence on New Year's Eve, if she had been strong enough to resist her mother that summer twenty years before. If she had been strong enough, just once, it would never have happened. But she had been weak. She had always been weak, and now she had ruined his life, not once, but twice over. And her own.

The tide was coming in, pushing her back up the beach. If she were brave, she thought, she would walk into the sea and keep walking, but she was not brave. The water would be cold, and she didn't want to die. She thought of Ben sleeping in his cot, and how much she loved him. He would miss her even if he did not know what he was missing, and she could not do that

426

to him. In the future, he would one day see how weak and selfish she was, and he would hate her, just as she had hated her mother for so many years, but until then, she had to keep herself alive for him.

She hadn't really known how much she loved her son until she heard about Anouska's illness. It was only then, feeling so awful on someone else's behalf, that she had begun to imagine how much worse it would feel if she were to lose him. She had never believed or even understood those people who claimed that terrible things happened for a reason, but now she could see why they said it. The simple truth was that Anouska's suffering had forced her to see how much she loved her son. That epiphany did not make her believe in God, because she thought it would be a strange, malignant deity that made an innocent person suffer in order to show an arrogant one how lucky they were, but she recognized, as she never had before, the meaning behind the symbol of the crucifixion. Ben, alive and well, was the greatest gift. She felt constantly grateful for his sturdy little form. He had kept her afloat, when she had felt she was sinking.

The sun glowed gold on the horizon. The pale flood of light would soon be gone. She sat on the cold stone wall across the road from the little row of seaside shops, eating chips out of paper. The smell of fish frying, the taste of vinegar, the chink, chink, chink of the boats in the harbour, all made her think of holidays long ago, and she was filled with longing for those innocent times when her most pressing concern had been the optimum time to eat her second ice-cream of the day. Life had been simple then.

For a moment, time stopped, and she felt at peace. She watched the swans, surreally white in the last light of the evening, floating silently on the gently undulating, dark water.

Playing with Ben in her mother's garden these last

few days, she had begun to experience a similar simplicity. You saw things differently when you were trying to explain them to a child. Flowers, ladybirds, a big bumble bee all seemed fantastically interesting and vivid. Perhaps that was what was meant by living through your children. Perhaps it was not such a bad way to live.

Maybe life could be simple again if she could only stop herself being dragged down by the undertow of the past. She remembered Mrs Goode, the therapist who had helped her twenty years before, saying that it was sometimes easier to let yourself sink into depression than to take the challenge of pulling yourself out. It was a way of avoiding the responsibility of living. Alison stood up and took a deep breath. They were all growing older, even Ben, and she had a choice to make: either ruin all their lives with her regrets, or throw the past away, grab what was left of life, try to do something with it. Scrunching the chip paper into a ball, Alison casually aimed at the litter bin, and as it left her hand, it suddenly became tremendously significant whether the paper ball reached its target or not. She froze, her eyes following its trajectory and, with a dull rustle, it fell in.

Margaret was sitting at the dining-room table when she arrived back. 'That walk did you good,' she said, smiling when she saw her daughter's flushed face.

'I had chips,' Alison told her.

'I thought you might. I kept something in the oven for you, but I was so hungry, I didn't wait, I'm afraid.'

It would be so easy to bristle with indignation at this point, to take her mother's statement as a criticism, but she was not going to do that. Forget the past, Alison told herself sitting down at the table.

'Do you fancy a drink?' she asked Margaret, determined to be positive.

'Ooh! What a good idea!' her mother exclaimed

enthusiastically. 'You have a look and see what there is. I'll get some glasses.'

'No, I'll get the glasses, you just sit down,' Alison said.

She poured herself a gin and tonic and a large glass of sweet white vermouth with ice and lemonade in it for Margaret.

'This is nice,' her mother said, tasting her drink and shuddering with pleasure, 'it's one of the things I miss about your father not being here – being able to have a drink.'

'Why ever not?' Alison asked, sitting down again opposite her.

'It's not good to drink alone,' Margaret said, and Alison remembered her sitting at their table at home, a glass of Cinzano Bianco in front of her, her eyes sparkling in anticipation of a gossip. Had she had a drink problem? It had never occurred to her before.

'Don't you have drinks with friends?' she asked her.

'Oh, not in the evenings. You don't get a lot of invitations for the evenings when you're my age,' her mother said, 'especially when you're a widow.' She winked at her daughter, and took another sip of her drink.

There was a cheekiness in the look that made Alison wonder whether her mother was considered a threat. She was still a handsome woman, who dressed well and looked after her figure. Maybe she was the *femme fatale* of the geriatric South Coast. There were some things she preferred not to know.

She found her handbag and took out a cigarette. 'Do you mind? I don't in front of Ben,' she said, excusing herself quickly, 'in fact I'm not allowed to smoke at all at home – which is probably a good thing,' she reminded herself.

'I don't mind, as long as I can have one,' her mother replied.

Astonished, Alison pulled one out of the packet and handed it over. It was clearly going to be a night

429

of revelations. 'I thought you had given up years ago,' she said.

'I never even knew you knew,' Margaret replied, surprised. 'I never smoked at home.'

'No, but I saw you from my bedroom window.'

Margaret's eyebrows rose. Then she lit up and blew out through her nostrils like a woman in a forties film.

'I was only able to give up because I promised myself that I could smoke again when I got to seventy,' she revealed, 'and I had forgotten that until a minute ago.'

'So you haven't had one for some time?' Alison asked.

'About twenty years,' Margaret replied.

Alison laughed. 'If I'd known that I would never have given you one . . .' she told her.

'I'd love to say that I wasn't enjoying it,' Margaret said, inhaling, 'but it's just as good as I remembered.'

They both giggled like naughty schoolgirls sharing an illicit midnight feast. Alison got up to shut the door so that the smoke would not waft up to Ben's room, and then she poured them more drinks, and brought a plate in from the kitchen for them to flick their ash onto.

'It's like old times,' her mother said, smiling at her.

Instinctively, Alison recoiled. This was not meant to happen. She was supposed to be forgetting the past, not reliving it, especially not in a companionable chat with her mother. But perhaps sometimes you needed to unwrap the past, give it a good shake, and look at it again. This was her opportunity, her last opportunity, before real life began again.

'I ran into Neil Gardner the other day.'

The words sounded odd. Locked away for so long, they were dusty, and they caught in her throat.

'Really? How is he?' her mother asked through pursed lips, keeping her voice determinedly neutral.

'Fine . . . He has a child the same age as Ben.'

'Does he? What a coincidence.' Margaret tried to

sound disinterested, but the air hummed with her agitation.

'Actually, you met his wife. Lia.'

Her mother thought for a moment. 'The very beautiful girl?'

A pulse of jealousy shot through Alison's body. It was pathetic to be thirty-eight and still jealous when your mother paid someone else a compliment.

'Yes, she is, quite beautiful,' she agreed briskly.

'She seemed very nice,' her mother said.

'Yes, she is . . .' Alison said, stubbing out her cigarette.

She decided not to say anything more.

'I expect he's a good-looking man. He was such a handsome boy . . .'

For a moment, she wasn't sure whether Margaret was aware who they were talking about. Handsome? Margaret had hated the ground he walked on. Handsome?

'Yes, I suppose he still is,' she said, pouring more gin into her drink. 'I wondered, actually, what it was about him that made you hate him so much?'

The 'actually' gave away the fact that the question was not as casual as she wanted it to seem.

Her mother gave her a long, hard look.

'Apart from the obvious, of course,' Alison added quickly. 'I meant before that. You were always against him . . .' She looked round the room, at the clock, the mantelpiece, the photos in their silver frames, anywhere, to keep her eyes from catching her mother's.

'I hated the effect he had on you,' Margaret finally replied, sighing. 'If you really want to know, you became very silly when you were with him, like one of those problem pages in those awful magazines that friend of yours, Sally, was so keen on. He wasn't as intelligent as you were, and you tried to make yourself stupid to make him feel better.'

'Oh, that's just not true,' Alison immediately protested.

431

'Oh, but it is,' Margaret told her, 'believe me, I could recognize the signs. I had done it all myself and I didn't want you wasting your life too.'

'It wasn't like that . . .' Alison said, but somewhere inside she knew that it was.

She didn't remember it like that, but over the last weeks she had realized that there were a number of things she hadn't remembered correctly. She had forgotten the way Neil retreated into threatening silence when something didn't suit him. Tell me what it is, she had wanted to shout at him in Paris, but she had not dared, because, as her mother so rightly said, when she was around him, she became a silly, nervous, twittering girl.

She thought of the time they had spent together. Neil felt more comfortable with her when she was in distress, or crying, than when she was on a high, saying clever things. He liked what she had been, not what she had become. She made him insecure and she tried to compensate for that, because part of her felt responsible for his insecurity. She had left him without an explanation when he was just a boy, and that must have had an effect on his life.

She thought of the way they had made love in the flat, and the overwhelming craving she had for him to dominate her. Spread-eagled, tied, submissive. It was as if she were offering herself up for sacrifice. It had been exciting to be at his mercy, shocking almost, but afterwards she had always felt weird, not like herself.

The two women each lit another cigarette. The room filled with smoke and unanswered questions and disturbed snatches of thought.

Finally, Alison heard herself asking, 'Mum, did we go to Biba together?'

Her mother's face lit up with relief that the strange, pregnant silence had come to an end.

'Of course we did! I bought you that purple dress, don't you remember? We had lunch in the Spaghetti House — cannelloni. It seemed so exotic in those

432

days,' she chattered on, not allowing any more pauses, 'but now I have a frozen one at least once a week. And for dessert we had profiteroles, a great pile of them with chocolate sauce and cream. Then, where did we go? Harrods, maybe, to Way In on the top floor. No wonder you have such expensive tastes – I'm afraid it was all my fault!'

She smiled across the table, proud of herself for rearing such a well-dressed daughter.

'Yes, it was, all your fault!' Alison echoed, smiling back at her.

In the early mornings, the sand was cool enough for them to play on. The first day, Anouska had been wary of the unfamiliar texture against her skin, so he had sat her on a beach towel and built a castle as tall as she was, decorating it with shells and she had watched fascinated as it grew, eventually getting up courage to reach out and prod it. The next day she had been braver, scooping up handfuls and watching the grains run through her fingers, and soon, she found she liked the sand so much, she wanted to eat it.

'Not in your mouth, Annie,' he told her gently, and she looked at him with a quivering lip, not liking to be told no, but understanding. Nine months old, and she understood what he was saying!

He found he could talk to her now. In the beginning, Lia had been able to, but he hadn't. He had found it embarrassing to chat away to a tiny being that showed no sign of hearing anything he said. It was like talking to yourself. But now he didn't care what anyone thought.

'Here, grab hold of this.' He handed her a miniature shovel, which she banged up and down like a drumstick.

'That's right, bang, bang!' He smiled at her and she smiled back.

'Baba!' she said.

'What? Say it again,' he encouraged her, unable to believe that he had heard her speak.

She looked at him, mouth firmly closed, with a look that said, well, you should have been listening.

'Say it again!' he urged.

She banged the spade again.

'Oh well, please yourself,' he said, smiling and glancing at his watch. Nine o'clock. The sun was already getting warm. He gathered the buckets and spades into the beach bag and swung it over his shoulder, then he bent and picked Anouska up, throwing her into the air above his head and catching her. She was as light as a feather, but she had the throaty, breathless, uncontrollable laugh that older children let out when they are being tickled. The sound of it sent pleasure bubbling through his veins.

He kissed her cheek.

'Now, cheeky, let's go and see if Mummy's up,' he said.

It wasn't much of a lie-in, he thought, but at least it was two hours more than she got at home.

Lia was watching them from the balcony. She waved at them. Neil pointed at her, telling Anouska to wave, and then, when she didn't, he picked up her arm and waved it for her. It had been a good idea to come to Portugal, she thought. Life was easier here. In the large, cool apartment Luis had given them for the week, with a warm breeze blowing in off the sea, she had been able to sleep. With rest, everything looked more manageable. She found she was thinking calmly for the first time in weeks and it dawned on her that she had never, even at the very beginning, been quite comfortable in Neil's house. Here, they took it in turns to cook, wash up, clean out the bath. In London, it all fell to her. It was fair, since he had his job, but she had never felt equal. She had become a lodger, dependent on his income and his goodwill. She had never had to depend on anyone before. If we are going to be together, she thought, it will have to change. If.

When they arrived in the village by the sea, it had felt like coming home. People were warm and physical here. They did not peer at Anouska through the window of the hired Seat, as English people would have done. Instead they threw open the car door, pinched her cheeks, lifted her out and threw her in the air. What a beautiful little girl! Just like her mum! When she explained that the baby had been very ill, and was still frail, they were concerned, but not frightened. She will grow strong here, they promised her. We will put the colour back in her cheeks with a little sunshine, some good food. It was a matter of pride for them that she recuperate in their village. In England, people looked at the baby anxiously, as if to say, for God's sake don't die in front of me.

Neil was happy here too. His skin tanned quickly and against it, his eyes shone bluer than ever. He loved the sea. Every day, when she was bathing Anouska and getting her ready for bed, Neil swam widths of the bay, backwards and forwards, serious laps in a giant swimming pool, and then came running back to the apartment, dripping, to shower off the salt. On the second evening, as he towelled himself down inside the room that led on to the balcony, where she was sitting drinking beer, she had caught herself staring at his lean, brown torso. An unexpected little twitch at the top of her legs had said, hello, I'm still alive down here, and she had wanted to go inside and touch him, but she had looked away pretending to watch the sun go down, embarrassed by the unwanted flicker of desire.

It was too hot for the beach during the day, so they wandered around the cool stone portals of the old fish market in Lagos where the fish the locals called swordfish lay across the stalls, long, flat and silver like blades, next to crabs clawing impotently at the air. Or they drove away from the coast towards Monchique, stopping to buy great dripping wedges of watermelon from little farmers' trucks parked in the dust on the side of the road.

They discovered a tiny spa village perched on the side of a wooded hill, its stone square, no bigger than a courtyard, offering permanent shade and the cool, trickling sound of running water.

'Life is very simple when you have a child, isn't it?' Neil remarked, when they found themselves there for the third day in a row. He took a corner from the loaf in the plastic basket and spread it with the sardine paste that appeared on every restaurant table of the Algarve.

'Yes,' Lia said, uncertainly, 'in some ways . . .'

She pulled the middle out of a piece of bread and handed it to Anouska who was sitting on her lap.

'I just mean the pace, I suppose,' Neil nervously qualified his generalization. 'You find a routine that suits and you slot into it. It's the slowness that takes getting used to.'

'Yes,' she agreed.

'I quite like it,' Neil said, putting down his knife and stretching back lazily on his chair.

'You sound as if it's the first time you've noticed,' Lia said, smiling.

'Well, maybe. It gives you a different perspective, being out here.'

'Yes.'

They were beginning to talk to each other again, she thought. Tentatively and very carefully, they were sounding each other out, gently testing for reactions. Their conversation had begun to have a little meaning again. At times like these, she thought it would be easy enough to slide back to how they had been, but she didn't know if that was what she wanted any more. She was too exhausted for confrontation, but she didn't think that they could just go on as if nothing had happened.

It felt peculiar to drive past places that triggered memories of how blissfully, besottedly in love they had been. It seemed so long ago, part of another life. It wasn't that she felt nothing for him now, but she did not feel anything strongly. Not passion, not even anger. It was as if the shock of life being turned upside down had anaesthetized her to pain and to pleasure.

That evening, when they returned to the village, Neil said, 'Why don't we go out to eat tonight? If we feed Annie first, we can walk her round the bay and when she falls asleep, we can let down the back of the buggy.'

'All right,' Lia agreed.

In Portugal, children were welcomed in restaurants, and she wondered why they had not thought of going out at night before now. Perhaps neither of them had dared suggest it, because it was more intimate to be locked opposite each other at a small table for the duration of a meal, than it was to graze on salad and beer, wandering from kitchen to living room to balcony. Checking that Anouska was sleeping in the bedroom provided a convenient escape route from any conversation that threatened to get too deep.

They sat drinking *vinho verde* under a trellis of rambling purple flowers.

'Is that bougainvillaea?' Neil asked, 'I never know. Guidebooks always talk about bougainvillaea, but I've never known what it is.'

'I think it's that pink stuff,' Lia replied, pointing at a different type of flower without looking at him.

He tried to initiate a conversation again. 'Are you able to relax a little here?'

'Here, as in the restaurant, or here, as in Portugal?' she asked, pushing a long ringlet of hair back from her face, inadvertently catching the expression on his face. He looked so sad, she felt a pang of guilt that she was making it so difficult for him.

'Yes, I am,' she conceded, 'I've always liked this village.' Then she couldn't resist adding, 'Sometimes I wish I'd never left.'

The statement hung between them for several minutes, then Luis's cousin, who was serving, came up and asked them what they would be eating.

'Well,' Neil said, 'what d'you fancy?'

'Grilled swordfish,' she said.

'You haven't even looked at the menu.'

'They always have grilled swordfish,' she told him, 'how about you?'

'Chicken *piri piri*,' he said.

'Yes, that's good, too.'

They gave their order smiling at the waiter as he poured more wine from the ceramic jug, then they sank into silence again, as their eyes followed him back to the kitchen.

There was no-one else in the restaurant. It was the beginning of the season, and even at its height, this village was one of the few left in peace by the hordes. The track that linked it to the main road was not yet wide enough for coaches.

Neil leaned over the table and looked into the buggy to check whether Anouska was sleeping. He adjusted the cellular blanket over her, unnecessarily making sure that it covered both her hands, then he said, 'She's a lovely little girl. You've done a fantastic job with her.'

She smiled weakly at him.

'No, I mean it, you're a really great mother. You're a real natural—'

'What? Letting her have a temperature for days and not taking her to hospital?' Lia blurted out, with a bitter, uncharacteristic edge to her voice.

Neil was startled by her reaction. He hadn't realized that she was angry with herself as well as with him.

'The doctor said—' he began.

'Yes, the doctor said, but I didn't believe him. I knew there was something wrong with her,' Lia interrupted, 'I should have just trusted my instincts. They tell you the mother's instinct is the most important thing but when you're telling them you're

worried they say you're worrying too much. If something's wrong it's your fault and if nothing's wrong
you're neurotic . . .'

The statements were gathering steam; they poured
from her mouth as if they had been stuck in her
throat, choking her.

'If I had taken her straightaway, they could have
given her the medication earlier . . .' She was becoming almost hysterical.

Neil tried to calm her down. 'But the scan said that
her heart wasn't damaged, so she did get it in time.
Anyway, if you had taken her to A and E they might
not have diagnosed it. They said it's very difficult to
diagnose. You can't feel guilty, you did everything
you could.'

'But I *do* feel guilty . . . No, not guilty,' she looked
heavenwards, despairing, 'it's just . . . it's just I did
everything I could, and it wasn't good enough . . .'
Finally she succumbed to tears.

'Lia, Lia, please . . .' He sat with his hands just off
the table, wanting to touch her, but terrified that if he
reached out, she would swipe him away. 'Lia,' he said
again, and then he could bear it no longer. He got up
and went round to her side of the table and bent and
held her shoulders, and she turned her face against
his jeans and wept and wept into his crotch.

Finally, she wiped her face with the paper napkin
he offered her.

'Sorry,' she said, sniffing.

'Don't be,' he said, sitting down again, touched that
she allowed him to take her hand across the table.

'It's the uncertainty I can't bear,' she sniffed, 'the
idea that I'll bring her up and then bang, one day . . .
Do you ever feel that?' she asked him.

'But the scan—'

'Yes, but the consultant said long-term follow up
after Kawasaki was essential. I wish they wouldn't say
things like that. What is long term? How long?' She
began to grow agitated again. 'He wouldn't have said

that if he was sure nothing was going to happen to her – there's no guarantee . . .'

'But no parent has a guarantee. I know it's worse for us at the moment, we've had a big shock, but she's OK. Our little girl is OK . . .' His words trailed away as she looked up sharply and slid her small hand out from under his.

'Maybe.' She didn't sound convinced.

'She's alive, she's well—'

'Yes, I know there are other people with far worse problems,' she butted in, 'I know we're lucky . . . just sometimes it doesn't feel like that.'

'You've been so brave, and Annie's been so brave too . . . she's a lovely little girl, a real fighter,' he said again, as if she didn't know that.

'Yes, she is, isn't she?' Lia smiled, gratified that he seemed to like his daughter so much these days.

'We just have to do everything we can to give her as good a life as possible,' he said gently.

'Yes.'

I know all this, she wanted to say to him, why are you telling me all this, talking to me like a social worker or a teacher or something? He was leading up to something, she could tell. His face was very grave and she could see he was making a big effort to keep the momentum of conversation going. She wondered if he was about to tell her that he was going to leave them.

'I want to be part of it, Lia,' he said quietly, 'I mean, really part of it, whatever you decide to do . . . if you'll let me. I know I did something terrible . . .' Then he was lost for words.

'What did you do?' she asked him.

He looked up at her, with an expression on his face that asked whether she really wanted to know. She continued to hold his eyes. He took a deep breath.

'I met someone I had been in love with a long time ago, and I thought I was in love with her again, but I wasn't,' he said, then, seeing that that wasn't enough, he went on, 'I didn't really expect it to be like this when you had a child. I'm not blaming you or Anouska,' he added quickly, as her eyes widened, 'I'm blaming me. I thought I would be such a good father, and then, well, I didn't like it much, if I'm honest, not at first. I like it now, now that she's a person, she's got hair and everything . . .'

'Hair?' Lia said disbelievingly.

'You know,' he said.

'So where were you when you said you were in Paris?' Lia asked, not letting him off the hook. She didn't want to hear about his difficulties as a father. As far as she was concerned that was immature indulgence. You did something, you took responsibility for it. You couldn't just back out.

'Paris. I was in Paris. I had given you the right number. It was just that I hadn't thought it was all in her name . . .'

'So if I'd asked for Mr Smith . . . ?' she said, trying to make a joke.

'Something like that,' he said, grimly.

'But it wasn't just Paris, was it?' Lia asked him, 'it had been going on for much longer than that.'

'Yes,' he admitted.

'But not any more?'

'No, not any more. It finished in Paris. Before I found out about . . .' He pointed at their sleeping baby.

'Yes, I thought so,' Lia said, looking at the sky. The light was always best at this time of night, the few moments after the sun had gone, before darkness took over and the crickets began to sing.

Their food arrived. It was cold. Lia guessed that the waiter hadn't wanted to barge into their conversation. The fish still tasted fresh and delicate. Either the wine or the crying, or something, had made her feel curiously light-headed and hungry.

'If you're wondering what I'm feeling, I'm actually feeling relieved,' she said, eventually. 'You've just confirmed what I thought all along. I knew that there was something going on, I knew all the time. I didn't know who, or why, or where, but I did know. The funny thing is that I don't really care that you fucked someone else, but I hate you for lying to me. It's the worst thing you can do to someone. You made me feel as if I was going paranoid, or something was up with my hormones, or I was just being stupid, but there wasn't anything wrong with me . . . except you.'

As she spoke to him, he found he was feeling more admiration for her than he had ever felt. She was so strong and brave and honest. When he first met her he had been attracted not just by her beauty, but by exactly that independence of spirit and self-reliance. She was so much younger than him and yet she had seemed to know about the world and how she fitted into it, and that had made him feel safe with her.

Over the last year, the aura of integrity she carried around her had faded and she had become more dependent and eager to please. The steel wire that seemed to hold her together, body and soul, had been replaced by cotton wool, and he had begun to despise her displays of weakness. Now, she was calmly telling him that he had been responsible for the change in her and he had fostered it because it had given him an additional excuse to abuse her trust, and he realized that what she was saying was true. After you had lied to someone a couple of times and got away with it, you could easily slip into convincing yourself that they were stupid for believing you. It was the loss of respect that was so insidious.

'I love you,' he told her, vehemently, 'I know I don't deserve to, but I want to be with you and our daughter more than anything else in the world. I'd do anything to have you forgive me . . .'

She looked at him coolly. 'I may be able to forgive you, but I don't know whether I can trust you again — and it's no good you telling me that I can,' she said, seeing him open his mouth, 'because it doesn't work

442

like that. I thought that I knew everything about you that I needed to know, and I found that I didn't. It's a shock. I don't know what happens now.'

'Marry me,' he begged her.

'Oh, for heaven's sake, Neil,' she said impatiently, 'we're not in a film. We can't just kiss and make up under a canopy of flowers and live happily ever after, you know.'

'I know, I know.' He held up his hands in defeat. Whoever was it who said that women were more romantic than men?

'Anouska comes first. We'll stay together for the time being, because of her, because she needs us both,' Lia told him, 'and then, well, we'll see. I won't punish you with it the whole time,' she added, seeing the dismay on his face, 'we'll just try to get back to normal. I can't promise anything else right now . . . Will that do?'

'No,' he said, smiling at her, admiring the honesty of her position. There was clearly no negotiation to be done. 'No, but I suppose I'll have to get used to it.'

Ginger had just reached the top of the hill when she spotted the unmistakable four-wheel-drive-with-rhino-bar safari vehicle that couldn't even make it the length of the M4, let alone overland to Africa. Briefly, she considered an about-turn back into town, but the thought of pushing the pushchair all the way up again later defeated her. Why had he come, she asked herself, just when she was beginning to get herself together?

Charlie was sitting on her doorstep. He jumped up when he saw them approaching, then sat down again in a failed attempt to disguise his eagerness to see her.

'If Mohammed won't come to the mountain . . .' he said sheepishly.

'I wish that Mohammed had spotted us at the bottom of the bloody mountain and given us a lift up,' Ginger told him, fumbling in her pocket for her key.

'Since you won't pick up the phone at home, I called you at work. They said that you'd left,' Charlie said, ignoring her crossness and following her into the flat.

'Yes. I haven't really been back since Daddy died. Lia couldn't look after Guy at first and now she's gone on holiday, and I couldn't be bothered to find anyone else, and in the end I just thought, what the hell, I hated that job, and it was never going to go anywhere. I'll start looking around when I feel a bit better . . .'

'You can always come to us,' he volunteered immediately.

'Jesus, Charlie, you're like a record that got stuck. How many times do I have to tell you no?' she said sharply.

She found she did that these days. Most of the time she felt so low she could hardly speak, then suddenly the smallest thing would goad her into temper.

'OK!' he said, taking a step back, 'I won't ask you again, all right?'

'All right,' she said, pulling Guy out of his push-chair. 'God, you are getting so heavy,' she told her child.

It was the first time he had ever heard her speak to Guy with anything other than sweetness in her voice.

'How is the little fella?' he asked.

'He's fine, thank you. He's about the only thing that keeps me going,' she said. 'Do you want coffee?'

'No thanks,' Charlie said, casually picking up a magazine that was lying on her table and flipping through it.

Make yourself at home, why don't you, she thought, wishing he would just go away.

'Actually, I wondered if you'd like to drive some-where nice for lunch?' he asked, looking up.

'Little Chef?' she said bitchily, 'or perhaps we could ring the changes and go for a Happy Eater?'

'I was thinking of somewhere nearer,' he bantered

444

back, 'I can never rely on my car over difficult terrain. How about Richmond Park? It's rhododendron time.'

'Rhododendron time?' Ginger repeated.

'Yes, you know, those great purple bushy flowery things . . .'

'I know what they are,' Ginger said, 'I just don't see what that has to do with lunch.'

'Guy will enjoy looking at them,' Charlie told her, 'you said that he likes flowers, you said that Lia takes him for a walk in Kew Gardens every morning. I thought he might like a change.'

'All right,' Ginger said, bewildered.

She couldn't remember telling him any such thing, but she did like the idea of the rhododendrons. There was a rhododendron plantation at home in the country, and somehow their arrival always seemed to herald the beginning of summer.

They got into the car and Charlie turned the key in the ignition. The engine coughed a little then died.

'Oh not again!' Ginger said, sighing heavily.

Charlie tried again and it purred into life. 'Just kidding,' he said, smiling wickedly at the road.

He had packed a hamper, or, more likely, Ginger thought, he had ordered his secretary to go out, buy a hamper, and fill it with everything she had ever resisted buying in the Camden branch of Marks & Spencer. There was poached salmon and smoked salmon and asparagus mousse and Parma ham and coronation chicken, two pork pies and a selection of cheeses. There was Californian salad and Italian salad, French bread and tiny little soft rolls encrusted with seeds. There were strawberries and clotted cream and *tarte au citron* and chocolate-dipped meringues. There were Belgian chocolates and Florentines, fresh peaches and cherries, champagne, freshly squeezed blood-orange juice and a bottle of still lemonade.

'Oh,' said Ginger, feigning disappointment as they

reached the packet of napkins stowed away at the bottom of the basket, 'no sandwiches, then?'

'So why have you been avoiding me?' Charlie asked her, lounging back in the long grass, after they had picked at the food for a while.

'Guy's favourite thing is the middle of the lemon tart . . .' Ginger observed.

'So you're not talking to me either?' Charlie asked.

'What makes you think that?' Ginger replied, looking at him directly.

'Oh, I think it was something to do with the fact that you haven't returned any of my calls for a while . . .'

'I suppose it never occurred to you that I might be sad and not wanting to talk to anyone?' she asked.

'Yes, it did, that's why I called, to see that you were all right,' he said patiently.

'You're very considerate all of a sudden.' Her tone was sing-song sarcastic.

'God, you're in a foul mood today,' he said, picking a piece of grass and chewing it.

'Well, fuck off then, I never asked you to come over.'

'What has got into you?' he sat up, suddenly.

'My father's died, my best friend's child nearly died . . .'

'I know, I know all that, but what's it got to do with me?'

'Some things don't have anything to do with you, Charlie, I know that will come as a shock to your ego, but—'

'That's not fair,' he said, exasperated.

'All right. It wasn't. I'm sorry.' She pretended to be playing with Guy.

'So what is the problem?' he asked her more gently.

'Look, relationships are risky things and I just can't take risks at the moment, OK? Ergo, I don't want a relationship. OK?' She was silent for a few minutes, and then she blurted out, 'I saw Lia's husband kissing another woman. I saw that bastard necking with

Alison who is supposed to be our friend. I saw it. I don't want that to happen to me—' She stopped, wondering why she had told him something she had told no-one else, not even Pic.

'But it won't happen to you. Not with me. I promise,' Charlie told her. He tried to put his arm around her shoulder, but she wouldn't let him.

'Oh, no, never with you, Charlie. Not with good old Charlie, Mr Reliability, the man who bonks you stupid then doesn't call for nine . . . nearly a year.'

He looked shocked that she had brought up the subject of the one-night stand. They had always avoided discussing it before.

'Is that what this has all been about?' he asked, incredulous. 'But I didn't even know you then! For God's sake, Ginger, you were after a job! Your foreplay consisted of whispering sweet programme ideas into my ears, and very nice it was, but I didn't exactly force you, did I?' he said, his eyes sparkling with innuendo.

'Piss off, Charlie,' Ginger told him, getting to her feet wearily, then bending to pick Guy up off the ground, 'I just don't need this at the moment.'

She began to walk away.

'I'll give you a lift,' he said, throwing packets into the hamper, then stopping and running after her.

She accepted, reluctantly, and they drove back to her home in silence. She didn't invite him in.

With Guy perched on her hip, she watched as he drove away in his ridiculous car, and then she sighed and said, 'Well, my darling, I'm afraid that's the last we're going to see of your daddy.'

'You're wearing my necklace!' Stephen observed, as Alison slipped her jacket over the back of her chair. The diamond added a discreet sparkle to the plain sleeveless black shift she had on. He noticed with concern how thin her arms were.

'Yes,' she said, fingering the diamond nervously

447

and picking up the handwritten menu. 'Well, we finally made it,' she remarked, 'this is the first time we've been here since Ben was born.'

'Is it really?' Stephen said. 'Seems like yesterday to me.'

'Does it? It seems like years to me.'

She wondered now whether the River Café had been the best choice of restaurant for this occasion. It was a fine evening, but there was still a chill in the air so they had opted to sit inside. It was noisy, open and informal, but that meant that nobody really took any notice of you, which is what she wanted. It would have been impossible to say the things she had to say in the sort of place that had pink cloth napkins folded into cones, waiters with a cloyingly intimate notion of service, and a sommelier who spoke in hushed and reverent tones about the choice of wine.

They gave their order, then smiled at each other, happily anticipating the simple, rustic food in this light and airy temple of style. At the next table, a film star Alison secretly rather fancied sat chatting with his actress wife. On any other occasion she would have been straining to hear what they were talking about so that she could report to Ramona the next day that yes, she thought the rumours about the marriage were clearly true, or no, there was no chance that he was gay, but as the waitress swept away their starters, she realized that she hadn't even had the presence of mind to spot what the famous couple were eating. She nodded her eyes in the direction of the neighbouring table in case Stephen had not seen.

'What?' he asked, looking at them immediately but showing no sign of recognition.

'Doesn't matter,' she said, trying to suppress a giggle. Many women would have given a week's salary to sit in the seat he was occupying, and he hadn't the slightest idea that he was in the company of celebrities. She felt a great wave of fondness for him wash through her body, and she tried to hold on to it, like a mental video, in case it was the last time she would be allowed to feel it. What she had to say could not wait any longer, but when she had said it, her life would be changed irrevocably.

'I think I need a break,' she began.

'Yes, shall we go somewhere nice?' Stephen jumped in, clearly eager to show that he had been thinking about holidays too. She often accused him of leaving everything like that up to her. 'I wondered if we might rent somewhere in Tuscany. Do you think you can ask a nanny to come on holiday with you, so that you actually get a break, or isn't that on? It wouldn't be her holiday entitlement, obviously . . .' Stephen was thinking out loud.

'I meant a bigger break than that,' Alison informed him, her nervousness making her brusque. 'I was wondering whether that chair in New York was still open to you . . . ?'

He couldn't disguise his surprise. 'Well, yes, I should think so,' he said uncertainly.

'Do you still want to go?' she asked, firing questions like an interviewer.

'Not without you,' he said.

It couldn't wait any longer, not even past the starter, and certainly not until they had finished eating. She had gone over it again and again in her head, but there never was going to be a right moment to say what she was going to say.

'Stephen, there's something I have to tell you. Please listen, and don't interrupt, otherwise I may not be able to say it . . .' She sounded like a school-mistress, she thought, despairing. This was not how she had wanted it to be.

He nodded, sensing something momentous. His violet eyes were pools of fear.

'When I was eighteen I had an abortion,' she said, quietly.

She looked up at him. He was just listening. There was neither approval nor disapproval in his look. Doctors were good at that.

'I think that's why I seemed to find it so difficult at first to bond with Ben,' she continued. 'You see, when I couldn't get pregnant naturally, a part of me thought it was a punishment for what I had done, and then when we did manage, with help, I thought it couldn't be right. I didn't deserve it, or something . . .'

She looked up again. She could see that he was struggling to resist the urge to comfort her, knowing that was not what she wanted.

'Then when I had Ben, he seemed so small and vulnerable and I kept thinking of my other baby, and how I wasn't a fit person to be a mother . . . I'm not trying to excuse how I behaved, but it may explain some of it to you . . .' She grabbed her tumbler of water and drank from it to slow herself down. She was going too fast.

'Poor Alison—' Stephen began, reaching across the table for her hand.

'No, I haven't finished,' she said, hastily, 'I haven't even started really . . . I never told anyone, except doctors. The only person who knew was my mother. I don't even know whether my father knew. I didn't tell my boyfriend. I left him without saying anything. It was just before university. I told myself we would have broken up anyway. I told myself it was better that he didn't know. I made myself forget about him . . .'

She wanted to be completely honest, but she realized she was using a kind of shorthand. To stop and go into the complexities of everything that she felt at the time would take hours. She had to compress it to keep the momentum going.

'At university, I had a kind of breakdown, I think, but I found someone to talk to, a kind of student therapist. I think she saved my sanity, really. She was kind. She told me that it would damage me to keep it secret, and she was right, but I didn't believe that then. I felt so much better, and I thought it was enough that I had told her. And it was. Until you and I decided to have a baby, and then it all started to come back . . .' She took another sip of water. 'No, there's more: everything went a bit peculiar. It was as if everything was coming full circle, the past was catching up with me, I couldn't get my head round the idea of having a baby, but I was about to give birth, and then out of the blue, my old boyfriend suddenly appeared . . . and . . . and . . . I had an affair with him,' she finally said.

They sat facing each other for several minutes. His face was grim, disbelieving, and then, as his brain processed what she had told him, so sad.

'Well, aren't you going to say anything?' she asked him, unable to bear the look of utter dejection. She wanted anger, tears, anything that would stop him looking quite so lost.

'You told me not to,' Stephen said, evenly.

'I've finished,' she told him.

'No, you haven't. You haven't told me what happens next.'

She took a deep breath. 'I don't know what happens next,' she said, 'I think that's up to you.'

Chapter 12

JUNE

When the girl finds out that the handsome prince is betrothed to another, she goes mad and dies of a broken heart.

Ginger's eyes flitted between the ballerina twirling manically on stage, and the profile of Lia's face, tears streaming down, just beside her. With one last plangent chord, the ballerina collapsed and the heavy red velvet curtains cascaded down in front of the tragic tableau. *Giselle*, she realized, had perhaps not been the most tactful choice of ballet.

Lia took out a tissue and wiped her eyes, and when the lights came up, her face was sparkling with pleasure. 'This is fantastic,' she told Ginger, 'so beautiful and moving. I never thought I would cry in a place like this,' she gestured round the red and gold auditorium, 'but it just got me.'

'I love classical ballet,' Ginger said, breathing a sigh of relief, 'it's a bit like listening to country and western music, it's so corny and manipulative, you know you shouldn't cry, but you can't help it.'

They climbed the stairs towards the bar and Ginger recalled the last time she had been there, when Charlie had appeared. She couldn't resist a quick glance behind her, but this time she was being followed by a man with a little girl in a smocked dress.

'Why did the lady go to sleep?' the little girl was asking.

'I expect she was tired after all that dancing,' her father told her, winking at Ginger.

It had never crossed her mind before that most of the major classical ballets were horrifically full of sublimated sex, violent death and unquiet souls exacting retribution. She looked around the Crush Bar at all the nice little girls in their Liberty dresses and black patent bar shoes, and thought how these same well-intentioned parents would probably complain if their children enjoyed *EastEnders*.

'It's all so spectacular,' Lia said, looking up at the crystal chandelier as they stood eating ice-creams out of paper tubs, 'not just the ballet itself, but the whole ambience. It's just like I imagined the Bolshoi to be, not somewhere in London.' She turned to Ginger. 'It's such a treat, just exactly what I needed, thank you.'

Lia had called Ginger during the week to ask her a favour.

'You know you said if there's anything you could do?' she had asked. 'Well, there is. If you still want to . . .'

'Of course,' Ginger had replied straightaway.

'I think I need to get away for an hour or two. I've just got into a kind of neurotic state where I don't feel I can leave Anouska, and it's silly. So Neil's going to look after her on Saturday afternoon, and I'm going to go out, except I know I'll find some excuse to stay in, unless I have a date – so, will you be my date? Maybe we could go to a movie, or shop, or we don't have to do anything, really, as long as I'm out of the house . . .'

Ginger thought it was a very sensible idea, and was flattered Lia was asking her to help. When she called Pic, who immediately agreed to come over and look after Guy, she had come up with the idea of the ballet.

'I'm just going to call Neil,' Lia said, taking a mobile phone out of her handbag.

'That's new, isn't it? Good idea,' Ginger said.

'Neil bought it for me. He thought I would feel better if I knew I could be in touch. I spent the first five minutes in there dreading it ringing, but then I got so caught up in the ballet, I completely forgot I had it,' she said, smiling, as she carefully keyed in her number.

'He's fine. They're both fine. He's going to take her out for a walk in the buggy now,' she informed Ginger, pushing in the aerial and disconnecting the call. 'It makes you feel funny when there's nothing you can do, doesn't it?' she added, 'as if you're superfluous.'

'Well,' said Ginger, 'that's the whole idea of getting you out for the afternoon, isn't it?'

'Yes,' Lia agreed, 'yes, I suppose it is.'

It felt funny coming out of the grandeur of the Opera House into the thronging streets of Covent Garden when it was still light.

'It's a bit like waking up after having a wonderful dream during your siesta,' Lia said.

'So what do we do now?' Ginger asked, fully expecting her companion to want to go home.

'Well, if we were abroad and it was a siesta, it's now that the fun starts,' Lia said with a kind of determination to try to relax. 'D'you fancy a drink?'

'Brilliant idea!' Ginger said.

They both called home. Pic was staying overnight with Ginger anyway. They were going down to the country together the next day. She was delighted to hear that Ginger was going for a drink.

'Have several,' she told her. 'Get drunk. It'll do you good!'

Neil was not in.

'He must be still out on his walk,' Lia said and, as she switched off the phone, Ginger saw that she was becoming nervous again. 'If there were anything wrong, then he would deal with it, wouldn't he?' Lia asked her anxiously.

'Of course he would,' Ginger confirmed.

'Probably better than I would,' Lia said, 'he's quite good in a crisis. He's done life-saving and first aid . . .' It was as if she were running through a mantra of positive thinking that she had taught herself, but hadn't quite learnt off by heart yet. 'Now, where shall we go?'

'What do you like to drink?' Ginger asked, surprised by the realization that they had been friends for almost a year and they had never been out together alone.

'Beer. I don't mean pints of warm ale, I mean cold bottles of pale fizzy stuff.'

They found an American Bar in one of the streets between the Piazza and the Strand. It was cool and dark inside and there were very few customers. Saturday evening had not yet begun. Ginger bought bottles of ice-cold Beck's, and chose Nancy Griffiths on the juke-box.

'It's quite feminist in a way, that ballet,' Lia said, thoughtfully, 'I mean those ghosts of women who have been betrayed punishing the men, making them dance themselves to death.'

'Hmm . . . yes, actually, but I don't know why Giselle bothers to save the prince,' Ginger added.

'Well, she still loves him,' Lia told her, 'you don't stop loving someone just because they do something terrible.'

'Don't you? I suppose not,' Ginger said, anxious to move the subject on, 'but I don't see why poor old Hilarion has to die. It's terribly class-ridden, isn't it? I mean, he never did anything but love Giselle, and yet because he's a nobody, he cops it, and the prince gets away with it . . . Or perhaps ballet doesn't lend itself to feminist or Marxist analysis,' she conceded, seeing Lia's expression.

Lia giggled and went to the bar for more beer.

'This is nice,' she said, sitting down a few moments later. 'It's like being single and free again.' She took a swig from the neck of her bottle.

'Do you sometimes wish you were?' Ginger asked her.

'Free in the sense of not having a child? No – well, never for very long, how about you?' Lia asked, deliberately avoiding the single part of the question, Ginger noticed.

'Having Guy is the best thing I've ever done,' Ginger said, 'and I've never regretted it for a second . . . but I've been lucky so far. He's so robust and cheerful. Maybe I won't be so keen on it when he turns into a monster at two . . . and I don't know how I'd deal with it if he were ill.' It was her way of saying that she admired the way Lia had coped.

'I don't know how I'd cope on my own,' Lia said, automatically reciprocating the compliment.

'Oh, in some ways, I think it's easier for me,' Ginger told her, 'I mean I just do what I want, and even though it's tiring, I don't have to bother about all that having-time-for-each-other crap. It's enough reading Guy a story and getting him to sleep without then having to soothe some bloody male ego sitting in my living room resenting the time I spend with my baby.'

Lia threw back her head and laughed.

Ginger was warming to her theme. 'Honestly, I think men are more trouble than they're worth at times.'

Lia thought Ginger was probably protesting too much. She had seen how happy she had been when she was spending time with Charlie, but she could understand why she didn't want to take the risk of a relationship with him.

They both drank some more beer. Ginger noticed that Lia was getting slightly fidgety.

'Ring again, if you want to,' she said.

'No, I don't want to, really,' Lia said, 'I just wish I

didn't feel in this constant state of alarm. This helps,' she said, picking up her empty bottle, 'but it's not exactly a clever way to suppress your feelings, is it? It helps to talk to you, too.'

Ginger smiled at her. The alcohol was taking the edge off her unaccustomed judiciousness. There were questions she wanted to ask Lia, and she was beginning to forget the reasons why she shouldn't. She went to the bar again, and returned with two more bottles and a bowl of tortilla chips.

'We should do this more often,' she said, crunching a chip, 'go out and have a laugh . . . if Neil wouldn't mind?' She was leading with the subtlety of a bulldozer, she thought, but Lia only responded with a wry snort of a laugh.

'No, at the moment, I don't think he would mind anything I did,' she said.

'Oh?' Ginger did her best to appear ingenuous.

'We've been through a bit of a difficult patch . . . not just Anouska, but our relationship too,' Lia admitted, 'but I think we're coming through that now, and he's very anxious for me to do whatever I want.'

'What sort of difficult patch?' Ginger was unable to stop herself asking. Lia was so infuriatingly loyal to the man.

Lia considered her reply for an agonizingly long time. Ginger was about to break the silence and change the subject, when Lia said, 'He had an affair. You might as well know, although he would hate it if you did. It doesn't seem such a big deal now. Honestly . . .'

'Do you know who with?' Ginger asked.

'No.' Lia looked up in surprise. 'I don't, does that sound peculiar? I didn't even ask. It didn't really matter who it was, because I could tell it was over, just as I could tell it was going on . . .'

'You knew it was going on?' Ginger almost shouted. Were there no limits to Lia's saintliness?

'I did, but I didn't, if you know what I mean. When

he finally told me, it explained everything that had been weird. So, in a way, it was quite a relief. I got my confidence back. It kind of empowered me . . .'

She looked up again. Now it was Ginger's turn to look surprised.

'I know you think I'm too nice sometimes,' Lia went on, 'but I'm not really. I'm not nearly as soft as I seem.'

For once in her life, Ginger was stumped for a response.

'It's really important to me that Anouska has a family. I can put up with a lot for that,' Lia said, 'and I suppose I love Neil,' she added, as an afterthought, 'whatever that means . . .'

Alison was sitting on the floor in the middle of the conservatory surrounded by bin-liners and the cardboard boxes Stephen had brought down from the loft. There was a bin-liner just for rubbish, one for Oxfam, and a large box set aside for storage. It was empty. Throwing things out was proving easier than she had thought it would be.

The boxes had travelled everywhere with her since she left home, and over the years, she had accumulated more. They were full of clothes and ornaments and bits and pieces, lovingly preserved junk that she hadn't been able to part with, talismans of her past. She wondered whether everyone had such a collection, or whether it was because she was an only child. Other people had brothers and sisters to remember special times in their family history. They told each other stories, layering their memories, putting different complexions on events as they grew older. Instead, she had her dolls, and a family of owls made out of shells brought back each year from lonely holidays in Cornwall.

It was like going through a huge photo album, each piece recalling a specific occasion: the little plastic basket with flowers on it she had saved her first pocket money to buy; a cracked cake of bright blue

Rimmel eye-shadow; an empty bottle of Badedas bath foam that had been Neil's first Christmas present to her. She remembered exactly the sense of anticlimax she had felt on opening it, sitting at home on Christmas morning, the smell of turkey permeating the house, and her mother's rather cruel, told-you-so expression, as she caught the moment her daughter's face betrayed her feelings.

Alison dropped the bottle into the rubbish, along with an empty green flask of Brut that still reeked with the smell that defined her adolescence. The clothes were harder to part with but they went into the Oxfam bag. The tank tops, the jeans with a V at the knee, the purple clinging dress from Biba. She knew she would not wear them again even though fashion had gone full circle. She now bought Nicole Farhi and Donna Karan versions of the Top Shop and Chelsea Girl designs she had modelled then.

At times, she felt almost unbearably sad that these cheap little things could have given her so much pleasure, but then she began to question whether they really had. If she had learnt anything from her recent experience, it was surely that her memory was unreliable. Her memories, she mused, were like the favourite childhood necklace she had discovered wrapped in pink tissue paper in the secret compartment of the jewellery box with the red velvet lining and the tiny ballerina that twirled when she opened the lid. She had unwrapped the carefully folded package with great excitement, only to discover that the beads were plastic, broken, and not at all what an adult would ever wear.

The house was on the market. Several people were interested, and she was expecting another couple to arrive at any moment. Stephen had taken Ben to Cambridge for the afternoon to visit his old tutor. It was hopeless showing potential buyers round when he was at home. He was either over-enthusiastic, which made people suspicious, or he started pointing out all the little repairs that needed to be done. The original idea had been for him to go on ahead to New York and find somewhere for them to live, while she worked out notice at the paper, but he was so unworldly, she feared some flashy realtor would talk him into a huge lease on somewhere completely inappropriate. So she changed her plans, and the tickets, and now they were all going to travel to the Big Apple together. It felt better that way.

They were still being as careful with each other as they had been on their very first couple of dates, both acknowledging that there was something very special at stake that must be allowed to happen, not forced along. Building a relationship took much time and patience; rebuilding it, even more. Sometimes she felt overwhelmed by the debt of gratitude for Stephen's continuing love. It had been the most difficult thing she had ever had to do to open her soul and let someone else peer into it, but making herself vulnerable seemed to have made them stronger.

They had sat at their table in the River Café, drinking litre after litre of spring water, oblivious to the boozing and schmoozing around them. The food, its aromatic perfume of mint and charcoal and olive oil wafting up from their plates, remained untouched. She had not even noticed the film star and his wife leave, and had performed a startled double-take, when, during one of the interminable pauses, when she felt her life was being weighed in the balance, her focus had come to rest on the far less glamorous couple who had taken their place at the next table.

When she thought she had told Stephen everything, she found she had only just started, and the intelligence of his questions brought answers that had lain hidden inside her, unexamined, unresolved, all her life. His reaction had been much more subtle than she had expected.

Initially, he was not angry, as she had almost hoped he would be, but sad.

'I thought it would be much worse,' he said.

'What could be worse?' she asked.

'That you were leaving me.'

That had made tears flow, but he had not moved to comfort her. Instead, he had become quietly reflective, as if he had been presented with a complex problem that required a great deal of careful thought. The silence was almost more difficult to bear than the agony of confession.

'It was Lia's husband, wasn't it?' he said, eventually.

'They're not married,' she replied immediately, then, knowing she owed him complete honesty, 'yes, it was Neil. How did you know?'

'I just worked it out. There was always a kind of tension between you. I felt it at Christmas . . . I didn't suspect anything, of course . . .'

'We weren't, then . . .' she faltered.

'And then, of course!' Stephen jumped in, as if he had just worked out the solution to a crossword clue, 'that terrible weekend you were away in Paris, and now I come to think about it, Ginger said he was away too . . . and your reaction when you heard about their little girl. No wonder you felt so terrible . . .'

The last item was stated as a fact, not as a goad to her guilt.

'Well,' he said, after digesting the information thoroughly, 'I suppose he does have a lot more hair than I do.'

She yelped with strangled laughter and pain.

'It never even crossed my mind to compare you, physically . . . in any way,' she told him truthfully, thinking how strange that was. Why had she not compared them? She decided it must have been because she had never really thought she would have to choose. It was as if Neil had been part of a different life, completely separate. She tried to explain. 'You know how I compartmentalize my life – work, home, friends, even – nothing crosses the boundaries I mark

461

out. You're like that too, you never talk to me about your work,' she added, getting side-tracked, then making herself return to the theme, 'well, I almost feel that this is what I was doing with him – the affair, kept in its box on the other side of town where it could not hurt anyone . . .'

'And Paris?' he asked, picking up immediately on the flaw in this analysis.

'Paris was because of a song, a ridiculous, romantic song. "These Foolish Things", Bryan Ferry. It was Our Song,' she said, and when she looked up, she saw that he had no idea what she was talking about. While they were mooning away their teens with pop, Stephen had been practising Mozart on the piano.

'Our song?' he repeated.

'Like whenever I hear that aria from *Così fan Tutte*, I think of going back to your place for the first time,' she explained euphemistically, feeling herself blush.

'*Soave sia il vento*?'

'Yes, you see, you *do* know what it means,' she said.

'Oh yes,' he said, smiling at her, 'I know what *that* means! Our song, eh?'

He looked pleased to have learnt a new fact, and that was the moment she had known that they were going to be all right.

Alison put the last of the clothes into the Oxfam bin-liner, and pulled up the drawstring, then she scribbled the word 'Clothes' on a sticky label and patted it onto the black shiny surface that gave off the faint smell of burning rubber. Clothes done, bric-à-brac done. Just the records left to do. She wrote another label 'LPs/Oxfam' and stuck it on the side of the box she had just emptied, then she opened the cupboard and started pulling out her albums.

Bridge over Troubled Water was the first to go. Which secret enemy of Paul Simon's, she wondered idly, had been the person who told him that that hair-style, that moustache and that hat looked just fine?

Next out was *Goodbye Yellow Brick Road*. She couldn't resist putting it on the turntable and singing along before parting with it. She had never had the slightest idea what the words meant, but they had sounded deep at the time, and now, shouting them out at top volume was wonderfully cathartic. The Beatles *Red* and *Blue* albums, *Hotel California*, *The Dark Side of the Moon*. It wasn't a record collection, she thought, more a catalogue of seventies clichés. All of them went into the box. She was getting quicker, almost reckless in her purge, she was about to decide to throw them all out, when the bell rang.

She caught sight of herself in the hall mirror as she went to open the front door. Her face was clean until she pushed back her hair leaving a dark smudge from the attic grime on her hands. Flustered, she wiped her brow with the back of her wrist, then smiled and threw open the door.

He was wearing a faded denim shirt, and he looked so tanned and relaxed that it took a split-second for her to recognize him. He had Anouska's buggy in front of him, like a buffer.

'I didn't think you were in,' Neil said, referring to the length of time it had taken her to open the door.

'I was in the conservatory,' she told him, 'I've got some people coming round to see the house.'

'Oh, well, I'll leave you then. We were just passing.'

'No, don't go,' she said, 'come in. It's OK, there's no-one else here,' she added.

He had not intended to go there, or maybe he had and he was kidding himself. Lia had told him they were going to America. She had heard the news through Justine. It's a shame, she had said, because Ben and Anouska get on so well together, although we never saw much of Alison after she went back to work.

He hadn't consciously decided to pass the big detached house, but it was on the route to the Gardens, and he had seen that the car was not there,

463

and something had drawn him up the garden path. He hadn't even considered the risk of finding her husband at home.

'We heard you were leaving.' He was talking to the back of her head as he followed her through the living room, kitchen and into the conservatory. 'Nice place,' he commented.

'I'm sorting some stuff out,' she told him, explaining away the general mess.

Her eyes scanned the room for anything he might recognize, and then she remembered with relief that she had thrown away the bottle of Brut.

'Is this really the first time you've been here?' she asked, formulaically, then, 'I suppose it is,' she answered for him, pointing at the chaise longue.

He sat down, pulling the buggy up next to him. Anouska was sleeping.

'How is she now?' Alison asked, leaning forward to look at her properly. 'She looks well. So do you.'

'We've been on holiday,' he told her.

'Oh, somewhere nice?'

'Portugal.'

'Lovely.'

They both fell silent, unwilling to participate any further in stilted small talk.

There was something different about the way she looked. He realized that it was that she was not wearing make-up. She looked younger, less intimidating, when her lips were pale browny-pink and not scarlet. Softer, less sure, more like she had looked when they had first met.

'I didn't want you to leave without saying goodbye,' he said.

He did not add 'again', but it was there, in both their minds.

'No,' she responded, 'I'm glad you came.'

Another silence.

Then they both said, simultaneously, 'Look, I'm sorry . . .' And they both laughed, embarrassed.

'You first,' she said, sitting down on the floor, pushing away the strewn albums to make space for herself.

He sighed, then said, 'I'm sorry I was angry with you on the phone that night. I needed someone to blame, but it wasn't your fault.'

'That's OK,' she said, waiting, then realizing that was all he wanted to say.

'Did you tell Lia?' she asked him nervously.

'I told her I had an affair. Not who with. She didn't ask,' he added quickly, lest she think he had been discreet on her behalf. 'And Stephen?'

'He knows. I didn't tell him, he worked it out. He's very sensitive . . .' Her voice trailed off.

Neil looked horrified. 'Well, I am glad you're off then,' he said, with a tight little smile. 'America, is it?'

'New York. Stephen's got a job . . .' she said.

She wanted to tell him that Stephen was not like ordinary men. He was not threatened by him. But she stopped herself. They had never discussed their partners before. Now was not the time to start.

'What are you going to do there?' Neil asked her.

'I want to spend some time with Ben. I haven't really done that since he was born and he's growing so quickly . . . I don't know, I'd like to do some writing, some journalism, or a book, possibly . . .'

'A book?' he repeated.

'I don't know . . .' She found herself back in the familiar pattern of stopping herself from saying things he might regard as showing off. She would have been grateful for any distraction from Neil's cool, disapproving appraisal of her home, her marriage, her future plans.

'Your turn.' Neil reminded her they had been swapping apologies.

'Yes,' she replied, uncertainly.

Her heart was racing as she tried to decide how much to tell him. Her eyes flicked from the stained glass of the high conservatory panels, to the shiny,

black piano, to the potted palms, seaching for anywhere to look except at him.

There was a choice. Either apologize blandly and
hope that the rest was understood, or go further.
Which? He looked as if he had regained a certain
equilibrium. What was the point of disturbing that
now? She stared at the polished wooden floor and the
scattering of albums she had been about to sort
through. Out of a sky-blue square, Bryan Ferry's
enigmatic, sceptical face stared back at her.

Unless she explained to Neil now what she should
have explained twenty years before, there would
always remain the chance that in a few years' time,
when resolutions made today had been weakened by
time, they would bump into each other again and . . .
Surely fate would not be so cruel? This way, she
thought, summoning her courage, if it ever were to
happen, he would simply look away and pass on by.
She had to tell him. It was the least she could do for
Lia. It was the least she owed her husband.

'There's something I should have told you a long
time ago . . . when I ended our relationship,' she
began.

The words sounded so matter of fact. Good. That
was the way she had wanted it to be. She tried to
engage him, but now he averted his eyes. The effort
that he was making to keep the forced look of
nonchalance on his face encouraged her to go on. He
was trying so hard to look as if he didn't care, it was
obvious he did. It was better that he knew. Better that
he hated her.

'I was pregnant and I had an abortion,' she told him,
'I'm very sorry . . .'

In the past, she had wondered whether the possibility had ever crossed his mind. Clearly it had not.
She did not know what he had been preparing
himself to hear, but not that.

'But you were on the Pill,' he said.

'Yes, but do you remember I had really bad

tonsilitis? The antibiotics affected it, or something . . . I don't know. Anyway I was.'

'But you told me you couldn't get pregnant.'

'Yes, well, maybe the abortion had something to do with that. I <u>was</u> pregnant,' she said again, annoyed by the implication that she had somehow mistaken the facts.

'Oh . . .' he said quietly, and then suddenly he shouted at her, 'Why the hell didn't you tell me?'

She had not expected him to raise his voice. The words were like blows. She shrank from them.

'Because you would have wanted to marry me, and I didn't want to.' Her voice began to wobble. 'I didn't want to live a life like your brother and his girlfriend, struggling to make ends meet in some awful caravan. I wanted a nice life. I wanted pretty things . . .' she said, finally dissolving into tears.

It sounded so pathetic, so materialistic. It wasn't just that, she wanted to defend herself, but held back.

He sat quite still, staring ahead, trying to take on board everything she had said, oblivious to her suffering. When her sobs began to subside, he said, 'Pete and Cheryl have the best marriage I know. They're still together. You can overcome anything if you love each other enough . . .' His voice was no longer angry, only sad now and resigned.

'I know . . . I'm sorry.' She could feel the emotion draining from her. Soon, it would be over.

'You didn't love me enough,' he stated bluntly.

'No,' she said, finally accepting responsibility, 'no, I suppose I didn't.'

He fell silent again for several minutes, and then he said, 'You did the right thing.' He rose from the chaise longue and turned the buggy towards the door. 'You were right. It never would have worked. We couldn't even last an afternoon in Paris without annoying the hell out of each other.' He smiled ruefully at her.

The blue of the faded denim shirt was the same as the blue of his eyes. Yes, Mum, she thought, he still is handsome. It would be the last time she saw him, she realized. He was almost at the door, and she suddenly didn't want it to end like this. She bent down, grabbing the pale-blue album from the floor.

'Here,' she said, holding it out to him, 'have this?'

He turned, saw what she was offering, and took it from her. He looked at the cover for a few seconds. '*These Foolish Things*,' he read out loud.

With a wry smile, he shook the black disc out of the cover and turned it over in his large, strong hands. For a moment, she thought he was going to put it on the turntable to listen to it together one last time; then, in one swift movement, he brought his knee to his chest and his hands down hard and snapped the black circle in half. The sound of a splinter of vinyl ricocheting off a window, skidding over the wooden floor, coming to rest against the skirting board, reverberated in the silent aftershock.

Then he handed her the broken pieces, and suddenly they were both laughing.

'Bye, Ally,' he said, furling and unfurling his fingers, the way you taught a baby to wave.

'Bye, bye,' she said.

'Shall we go up the drive?' Pic asked, as the road began to dip into the valley and the twin gatehouses appeared on the right.

'Yes, why not?' Ginger replied.

Pic braked gently, indicated and turned off. The gates were open. The car made stately progress down the avenue of oak trees, its wheels slowed by the depth of the crunchy gravel underneath the tyres. In the bright midday sun, the pale gold stone of the house shone almost white.

Pic drew up outside the Palladian portico and they both jumped out and ran up the steps to the front door. Inside the cool round hall, with its classical statues and marble staircase, they could hear the murmuring ebb and flow of distant conversation interspersed with peals of laughter. Exchanging bemused glances, they made their way to the dining room, where their mother rose to greet them. It had been Pic's idea to visit on their parents' wedding anniversary, but their mother had clearly forgotten both the day, and the fact that they were coming down, and had instead decided to host a lunch party.

'Darlings,' she greeted them, wafting them away into the drawing room, a pair of spaniels yapping around her feet, 'it is rather awkward since we're almost onto pudding, but, I'd love to have tea with you later . . .' she suggested vaguely.

'But—' Ginger began.

'I know!' exclaimed her mother, ignoring her, 'why don't you drive over to Bath? I believe there's some sort of festival in the gardens near the Royal Crescent. Bound to be fun for Guy. Where is he, by the way?' she said, as if she had only just noticed his absence.

'He's asleep in the car.'

'Well, then, that's perfect. I'll see you later. Shall we say about four?'

'But we've come all this way, couldn't we have lunch here?' Ginger asked. 'I'm starving and I know Guy—'

'I'm sure they'll have hot dogs or something there,' her mother replied, anxious to get back to her ladies.

'What a good idea,' Pic said, 'come on, Ginger.'

'But Bath's miles away,' Ginger protested, amazed that she should have agreed.

'Oh, it'll only take half an hour or so, come on, before Guy wakes up.'

'You're getting very bossy,' Ginger told her sister, hurrying to keep up with her as she marched back across the circular marble hall to the entrance.

'Makes a change,' Pic replied equably, taking the steps that led down from the row of Doric columns two by two.

'Do you think Mummy's losing it?' Ginger asked her as they drove round the back of the house and took the tarmac road lined with rhododendron bushes back to the main road.

'Well, she is getting a little forgetful,' Pic said, and Ginger could see that she was finding it difficult to keep a straight face. 'She seems perfectly well, though,' she added more soberly.

'It's not funny, Pic,' Ginger scolded her.

'Oh do lighten up,' Pic said, 'what could be nicer than a lovely drive on a day like this, and the prospect of an afternoon's shopping in Bath?'

'Well, I suppose if you put it like that . . .' Ginger said, settling down contentedly.

By the time they found somewhere to park the car, it was well past Guy's lunch-time and he was getting very irritable.

'We have to stop somewhere and get him something to eat,' Ginger told Pic as they hurried up Milsom Street.

'Oh, can't he wait until we get there?' Pic asked impatiently.

'What's the bloody hurry?' Ginger asked her. 'For heaven's sake, we don't even know there's anything on. If Mummy's memory is anything to go by, it will have happened last week or something.'

'Well, let's go to that café in Victoria Park, near the tennis courts, you know.'

Ginger looked at the places to eat around them: the choice was ice-cream, pizza or very expensive French cuisine. Guy had only four teeth. He found it difficult enough to get his mouth round the mashed up middle of a sandwich.

'All right,' she agreed reluctantly, 'but let's hurry up!'

'You're the one who slowed us down,' Pic reminded her.

'What has got into you today?' Ginger asked, bewildered by Pic's sudden stroppiness.

'Just come on,' Pic said, heaving a big, exasperated sigh and turning to lead the way again.

The cafeteria in the park was crowded and there were no spare tables, so they bought sandwiches and cans of drink and, with Pic taking her turn to push Guy's buggy, they went back outside to search for a vacant park bench. The flower-beds seemed to dance with colour and the path was thronging with people dressed in shorts and spangled bikini tops, their exposed flesh turning pink in the hot sun.

'It's like being at the seaside,' Ginger remarked, and then, as they approached the expanse of grass that ran down from the crescent, 'oh look! Guy! Balloons!'

She ran on ahead like an excited child to get a closer look at the hot-air balloons that were being inflated on the lawns, and then, as if suddenly remembering her responsibilities, she came back.

'It's OK,' Pic told her, 'you go and look. Guy and I are going to sit in the shade under one of these big trees and have our picnic. You go and look.'

'Are you sure?'

'Quite sure,' Pic said.

Ginger scampered up the slight incline, shielding her eyes from the sun as she looked skywards. There were plain balloons and striped balloons in bold poster colours, and all around the hiss of gas canisters. The first to take off was a balloon in the shape of a beer bottle, closely followed by one that looked like a very fat pig.

Pigs might fly, Ginger thought, smiling.

She loved hot-air balloons. They were so celebratory, so literally uplifting. Another one rose silently into the sky. It was covered in rainbows. She looked back to the tree where Pic and Guy were sitting. Pic was pointing at the balloons, but Guy was resolutely concentrating on tugging grass out of the turf. She was about to pull herself away and go back to them, when someone a few yards away said, 'Do you want a ride?'

She turned, startled by the sound of Charlie's voice. He was standing in a basket with another man who was concentrating on inflating the balloon.

'Hello!' she said, walking towards him, gesturing with her arms, 'isn't this lovely!'

'Yes,' he said, laughing at the expression of wonder on her face. 'Do you want a ride?'

'I'm with Pic,' she said, excusing herself, 'but I've always wanted to go in one,' she confessed, drawing nearer.

'We're ready to go,' the man next to Charlie said. 'Is she coming?'

'Are you coming?' Charlie asked again.

Ginger looked at her sister and saw that Pic was waving her arms, telling her to go.

'Yes!' she said, taking both his hands, allowing herself to be pulled up into the basket.

The ground dropped away beneath them, and she was suddenly terrified to see Pic and Guy becoming tiny blobs, and then dots, and then disappearing completely as Bath became toytown beneath them.

'It's OK,' Charlie said, putting his arm around her waist, 'Pic'll look after him.'

It only occurred to her then what an odd coincidence it was that Charlie just happened to be in Bath at the same time as them, and that her normally placid sister was behaving so oddly.

'You planned this, didn't you?' she said to Charlie as they soared out over the valley, 'you and Pic planned this. I don't believe it. My own sister. Get me down at once,' she ordered the pilot.

He looked at Charlie smiling.

'Charlie, get me down,' she pleaded.

'All right, all right,' he agreed, taking her hands, 'but I just want to ask you something first.'

'What?' she said crossly.

'Will you marry me?'

'Oh, for heaven's sake!' Ginger said, 'ha, ha, ha! I'll kill Pic when I get down. What's your name?' she turned to the pilot.

'Mike,' he said.

472

'Well, listen, Mike, could we go down, please? I'm worried about my son.'

He looked over to Charlie for guidance.

'No,' Charlie said, firmly.

'You're kidnapping me,' Ginger said, folding her arms and looking heavenwards. It was only then that she saw that the balloon they were hanging beneath was white and covered with red hearts.

'Oh my God, you mean it!' she cried, jumping in the air, shaking the basket as she landed.

'Will you marry me?' Charlie repeated, putting his arm round to stay her.

'I don't know!' Ginger shouted into the breeze. 'You can't expect me to make up my mind in a balloon!'

'Well, let's go down then,' Charlie indicated to Mike.

'No!' screamed Ginger. 'No, this is lovely! This is a wonderful dream ... I don't want to wake up just yet ...' She grabbed Charlie's hand and squeezed it very tight. 'Do you really mean it?' she asked quietly, wanting very much to be alone with him.

'Yes, I do,' he said.

'Guy is your son,' she told him, looking straight into his eyes, pleading with him not to reject them now.

He looked right back at her, his curls blowing in the wind. 'I've been wondering when you would tell me.'

'When did you know? Pic didn't ... ?'

'No, of course she didn't. Pic was just dragged in to get you down here, and I put her under the most unbelievable pressure, so you mustn't be cross with her.'

'When did you know?' Ginger asked him again.

'I think in an unconscious way I must have known when I met him, because that was the day I fell in love with you both,' he told her.

'Little Chef?' she asked.

'Before that. On Kew Bridge, actually.'

'Really?' she said, smiling when she thought of all the time in between she had wasted.

473

'But I only worked it out consciously after Richmond Park,' Charlie told her. 'I couldn't understand why you were so bothered about our one-night stand, and then I started to think back and calculate the dates and I felt such a fool . . . I want to thank you for looking after him so well,' he said, very seriously, 'he's a lovely little boy.'

'He is, isn't he?' Ginger said. 'I think so, but I find it hard to be objective.'

'Well, I'm hardly that!' Charlie said.

'Yes, but—'

'I know. You've done a really good job. I don't know how—'

'But you didn't ask me to marry you because you felt you ought to?' she asked, suddenly alarmed.

'I'm afraid I'm not that chivalrous,' he admitted.

'And you're not asking me because you know I'm rich? Although I don't suppose you'd tell me if you were . . .' she mused.

'I'm rich enough,' he said, 'and no, I fell in love with you because of your extraordinary brain . . . and your sensational body,' he added quickly, seeing her impishly pretty face fall.

'I suppose it's one way of getting me to work for you on the cheap,' she interjected.

'Yes, I thought you could feed me ideas for soap operas over breakfast.'

'Breakfast serials?'

Below them she could see farms and villages, and somewhere in the distance there was an avenue of oaks leading up to a Palladian house built of warm yellow stone where her mother was entertaining her friends. Had Mummy been dragged in to Charlie's plans as well, she wondered, or had Pic just rehearsed her in the lines she had played so well? Suddenly, she wanted very much to be with all her family, and then she remembered that Daddy was not there any more to tell. She looked at Charlie's proud profile, and wondered if her father would have approved.

'Shall we go back down now?' she asked him, feeling an urgent need to hug Guy.

'Can I take that as a yes? Because you're not getting out of this balloon until I've had an answer,' Charlie replied.

'Ask me again,' she said, looking down at the green and yellow patchwork of wheat and rape-seed, wanting to remember every detail to tell their children when they asked.

'Will you marry me?' he indulged her, dropping to one knee.

'Well, I suppose if you put it like that,' she said, 'yes, yes, YES!'

Epilogue

AUGUST

The four adults were sitting in a circle around the remains of a cake baked in the shape of a 1.

'It's a shame Alison and Stephen and Ben aren't here, really, isn't it?' Lia remarked, lying back in the grass, shielding her face from the sun with a slim brown arm. 'They went off so quickly I never got a chance to thank them.'

'Thank them?' Ginger said, astonished.

Neil saw the look Ginger shot at him, and knew instantly that she knew. She frowned at him. He stared back at her defiantly. They had never really overcome their initial hostility.

'For saving Anouska's life. If it hadn't been for Stephen . . .' Lia let the sentence finish itself.

'Yes,' said Ginger eventually, 'I suppose it is a shame.'

It was one of those hot summer afternoons where conversation is slow and relaxed, and Lia did not seem to notice the length of time it had taken her to reply. She glanced at Neil and saw him incline his head imperceptibly in gratitude for her restraint.

'Do you think Anouska will be able to walk by next month?' Ginger said to Lia, anxious to change the subject, as she watched the little girl in her pretty pink gingham shorts and hat, trying to push herself up to standing, 'I really want her to be a bridesmaid.'

'I don't know,' Lia said, sitting up again. 'You couldn't leave it a little longer, could you?' she joked, smiling at her child's efforts.

'Well, not really,' Ginger told her, 'if I want to fit into my dress . . .' She smiled wickedly, and took hold of Charlie's hand.

'Oh for heaven's sake,' Lia said, realizing immediately what she meant, 'you didn't hang about, did you? I always wondered which one of us would be the first.' She turned to Neil. 'We'll have to get on with it now. I want all my children to be the same age as Ginger's . . .'

'All?' he said, feigning terror as he turned to Ginger, 'how many are you going to have?'

'Just one more,' she announced, 'for the time being . . .'

'I think I can cope with that,' he said.

'Although of course there is a history of twins in my family,' Ginger teased, making a big effort to smile at him.

'I thought you were really good back there,' Charlie told her as they walked home along the tow-path, with Guy asleep in his pushchair in front of them.

'Well, if Lia likes him enough to have another child with him, then it doesn't really matter what I think,' Ginger said.

'That's a very mature way of looking at it,' Charlie said, mocking her.

'Actually, I hate the bastard. I cannot bear moody men. Don't ever get moody on me,' she warned him, 'or you,' she said, pointing at Guy's head, and then she laughed.

'What?' asked Charlie.

'Well, it's funny,' she said, 'Lia and Neil did everything the right way round. They met, fell in love, went to bed together and had a baby. We did it in reverse. We went to bed together, had a baby, then met and fell in love. I think it's a more sensible way of going about it. Love in reverse.'

'Sounds like a title for a romantic comedy,' Charlie said.

'Yes, well, before you go off and commission a script, just remember who thought of it,' Ginger told him, taking his hand as they walked together towards the fiery sunset.

At the same time, on the other side of the world, Alison was watching Ben stumbling about in a sandpit in the middle of Central Park.

'Is he yours?' A woman with a baby in a pram was sitting beside her on the bench.

'Yes,' Alison said, smiling proudly at her child, 'he's one today!'

'Happy Birthday!' the woman called to him. 'He's cute!' she told Alison.

She turned to acknowledge the compliment. 'Thank you.'

The woman was about her age, she judged, had long, dark curly hair, and was wearing genuine Gucci loafers.

'Is she your first?' she asked, pointing at the sleeping baby in the pram.

'Yes. He?'

'Yes.'

'We left it a bit late, but we made it,' the woman joked. 'There's a lot of stuff they don't tell you, isn't there?'

'Well, they do, but you don't believe them,' Alison agreed, responding enthusiastically to the overture of friendship.

'Lots of bad stuff, like the sagging plucked chicken skin that is now your stomach, and a lot of good stuff too . . .'

'Oh really, such as?' Alison asked, joking.

'Well, like you meet people. You start up conversations with people in parks. The only people who do that are crazy people, or people with children.' Her new friend was laughing. 'Children bring you together.'

'Yes,' Alison agreed. Scenes from Ben's first year flashed through her mind.

She shook herself back to the present and smiled at the new mother beside her.

'Yes,' she said, 'I suppose they do.'

THE END

PERFECT DAY
Imogen Parker

Can one day change your life?

If we were a song, what song do you think we would be?

On a perfect spring morning, Alexander catches an
early train into London, but he never reaches work.
Instead, he spends the day with Kate, a waitress he has
met the previous evening, a woman so unlike anyone
he has ever known, she makes the world shimmer with
possibility.

Such a perfect day, Nell takes her child Lucy to the
seaside, hoping that the sea air will blow away the
doubts she has about her life.

As Nell ponders why falling in love is so different from
loving someone, Alexander allows himself to imagine
leaving his old life behind and starting afresh. And by a
strange turn of fate, there's an opportunity to do just
that – if he chooses to take it . . .

0 552 99938 5

BLACK SWAN